THE RESCUE

Living on the Edge
Further Adventures of the Hollow Folks

PAUL H. JONES

© 2005 Paul H. Jones

Contact:
Paul H. Jones
1685 Oak Level Road
Bassett, Virginia 24055

phjones@sitstar.net

Printed in the United States of America by:
Video Publishing and Printing, Inc.
3102 Schaad Road
Knoxville, TN 37902

ISBN 0-89826-127-9

ACKNOWLEDGMENTS

The quiet environment for writing that continued for my fourth novel was no accident either as my wife, Margaret, provided time and space in our country home free of interruptions. Also, she again doubled as an encourager and sounding board while doing the job of chief editor and proofreader.

My daughter, Bonnie, as always, provided my computer wherewithal as she formatted the manuscript for printing. Her involvement went beyond on site to lengthy telephone calls to remove electronic snags.

Certainly, further adventures about the Hollow folks would not have been written, if it were not for the special encouragement by many of you who read my three other novels: The Hollow, Life in the Shadows, The Missions, Living by Faith *and* The Hijacking, Living Beyond Fear. *Your kind words added much to my enthusiasm to complete this fourth novel.*

Jokingly, my comment to you has been, "If I'm going to write these books, it's your responsibility to read them." Thank you for being faithful readers.

ABOUT THE AUTHOR

Born on September 20, 1933, in Henry County, Virginia, my youthful days were spent on Grassy Creek where home was a four room framed house nestled against a steep, wooded hill. The branch in front provided many experiences recounted over and over again during the later years.

School was very special at Spencer-Penn High School where I spent all my public school years with a dedicated, serious, caring and enthusiastic staff of teachers. Graduating in 1951, I entered Bluefield Junior College and later High Point College, receiving a bachelor's degree in business administration. A career in education began in 1955 with an outstanding large class of eager seventh grade students who provided enough successful days to plan a continuation of teaching. The assignment of principal came at age twenty-five, following a two-year stint in the military service. A career interrupted intermittently was enhanced by fulfilling requirements of a master's degree and later a doctor of education degree in the early seventies from the University of Virginia.

Genuine excitement ran through my family of wife and four children in 1973 when I was appointed superintendent of schools in my home community. This was followed by nineteen years as chief school officer in school districts in Virginia and Kentucky.

Writing The Hollow, Life in the Shadows, *during my initial fleeting retirement years was truly an exciting adventure and with the positive public response to my first novel, a second novel was printed.* The Missions, Living by Faith, *provides a further examination of the special group of people who so humbly undertook numerous acts of kindness in and beyond the remote area of southwest Virginia.*

Having served with my wife, Margaret, as International Service Corps volunteers in Costa Rica on two occasions for more than one and one-half years on two similar assignments and having completed a year of service in Mali in West Africa, I used these countries as settings for narrative generated in The Missions, Living by Faith. *The events by the characters in my novel in both countries were described in an environment in which I was familiar.*

During the past few years we have enjoyed our six grandchildren who live in Danville and Richmond, Virginia and Buford, Georgia. It has been a genuine joy to watch them grow and participate in all kinds of activities. Margaret and I are just like all the other parents as we are so very proud of our children, and now as grandparents, we are genuinely blessed to have the opportunity to watch their offspring as they develop.

FOREWORD

As more and more people become acquainted with the Hollow folks in my first novel, The Hollow, Living in the Shadows, *they probe their own existence to determine whether or not their relationship with others could match that of these special folks. With meager wherewithal the Hollow folks continued to present their armor of humility in such a way that it seemed so easy, yet, when we try to emulate their behavioral characteristics, most of us fall considerably short of the standard displayed by them.*

In my second book, The Missions, Living by Faith, *these same humble folks found themselves continuing to undertake a mercy mission activity much more difficult and complex than any of the other benevolent activities in which they were engaged in the past. With their selfless attitude they extraordinarily fulfilled a perilous mission in such a manner that it left all totally aghast.*

Also, a career missionary family emerges with a young daughter who delights soccer spectators in the jungle area of south Costa Rica, the home base of their mission activities. While following the Hollow parents and the exploits of this new mission family, the Hollow girls show the basketball world their playing ability on the college level.

Fulfilling all of the initial obligatory requirements stipulated when the first huge anonymous gift of money was received, the Bacon College president found himself faced with another similar challenge. This challenge was made even more difficult amidst the growing curiosity of the various media to discover the source of the benevolent money that so mysteriously was donated to the small college in southwest Virginia.

Playing basketball took on an entirely different meaning one morning in Roanoke, Virginia when three Mid-Easterners joined the team on a flight to the southwest. In The Hijacking, Living Beyond Fear, *the story of this situation involving Bacon College is written revealing how the team foiled the attempt of terrorists to do harm to those on their flight*

Having deep roots that were truly from the Hollow, they possessed an armor plate of protection from a secular world about which they knew but a little. Cohesive love was maintained all the while as they abundantly displayed the Hollow spirit in all aspects of their lives.

Loving their neighbor as they loved themselves took on an entirely different meaning when the Hollow girls discovered that three missionaries had been captured, held and possibly tortured by a terrorist group. In this book, my fourth novel, The Rescue, Living on the Edge, *they put themselves in harm's way to remove these young ladies from the grips of notorious terrorists bent on doing evil.*

INTRODUCTION

Following the demise of the coal mining industry, several of the children of the coal miners elected to remain in the area, really having no other place to live. One such group was from the Hollow, a remote community tucked away between two steep mountains that framed it in on both sides. Twenty-three strong and independent families lived in almost identical two-room wood frame houses stilted on the mountain without water, electricity or telephones.

Change came into their lives several years ago when a young pastor, his wife and daughter moved into the area, constructing a church at the end of the Hollow of lumber from two abandoned houses. Failing to cope with constant and continuous derision at school, no student from this remote area ever graduated from high school. Josh, the young pastor, and Charlene, his wife, attempted to correct the dismal situation, but wound up agreeing to teach the children instead of sending them to the public school in the area.

After school one day, Josh nailed an old bicycle rim to the wall of the church to be used as a makeshift basketball goal for the children to play. Play they did, as the girls were natural players, winning tournament after tournament over the next few years. Esther, whose mother died at childbirth, led this group on the basketball court as well as in daily activities. Coaxed, begged and cajoled, the parents finally agreed for the children again to enroll in the public school, entering the local high school. A delighted superintendent watched as the girls won all of their basketball games throughout their high school years, and enrolled in the small local college to the dismay of scores of recruiters from large and prestigious universities from all over the country.

They were known as the girls from the Hollow where their fathers extinguished a devastating fire that was burning out of control over numerous acres of pristine forest land in a nearby area, found a lost child when the professional personnel abandoned the search, and cleaned a small village that was inundated by water from a sudden flood. Although rumors precluded their plenary acceptance in the affluent society, the inhabitants of this remote area continued their gallant acts of servitude, being impervious to the demeaning comments being made about them.

Using food donated by two corporate food distribution centers in the area, Josh distributed the various food items to the families except for those that were utilized each Friday evening for dinner for the entire group. This was a special time each week.

The girls faced a different society from that experienced from their two-room houses constructed on the steep embankments up the Hollow when they entered college. At the small Christian college nestled in the mountains for many years, tranquility abounded, but with the emergence of the new basketball arrivals the other students knew that they were going to be part of something special. In the beautiful new athletic dormitory constructed from money given by an anonymous donor, the Hollow girls were greeted by Maudie Graves, the newly employed dorm maid, who immediately became a good friend and confidant of the girls' basketball team members.

Winning game after game, Bacon College swiftly fulfilled the stipulation included when they accepted the large donation of money, that of competing successfully on the Division I level in basketball. Being led by a young lady, Anna Bosley, who had never coached in college before, the team rose to the top of the basketball world immediately.

Far off on another continent it was discovered that following a second drought, the small West African country of Wasi was experiencing a devastating famine, causing many to die of starvation. Wanting to handle its serious plight of supplying food to its people, the government warned other countries that any unwanted assistance would not be welcomed. Wanting to help on the one hand and at the same time to adhere to the wishes of the country, our government decided to request for civilian volunteers to make food distribution to the people in a clandestine manner. The Hollow parents volunteered to conduct this mission project even though they had been warned adequately that it would be a dangerous assignment. The entire undertaking was skillfully handled although several, including Josh and Charlene, were physically abused.

Maudie's niece and her husband, Dan and Pat Travers, had a daughter named Mit who had built a strong reputation as being an extremely fast runner even at an early age by winning races with much older children. Saving a neighborhood child's life by pushing her from the path of an oncoming car, Mit nearly lost her own life, lying in a comatose state for several weeks. With Dan's losing his job and mounting medical expenses, they sold all of their belongings and moved into a low income housing project. Two communities raised thousands of dollars for them to use to pay off their huge debt. In the meantime Dan was completing seminary training through the local college. Following God's call, the family of three headed to Costa

Rica to become missionaries in the jungle area with Mit fully recovered.

While Dan and Pat studied their Spanish each day, Mit was enrolled in Challenge Academy where she led the very small Christian school to the country's Junior Olympics in soccer. This feat was duplicated after they moved to the jungle as Mit led the team of her Indian friends to the national championship, the first time a team from the jungle had ever competed.

With millions of dollars having been given to Bacon College again by the anonymous donor with the stipulation that it organize a soccer team and compete successfully on the Division I level, the president was again faced with an interesting challenge. Naming Anna Bosley to coach soccer in addition to basketball, her late arrival on the recruiting trail left few high school athletes to evaluate. A fax one day from a remote southwest area was the beginning of an unusual recruiting season, which ended in the South Zone of Costa Rica where the most outstanding young female soccer player in the world lived. Her name was Mit Travers

The world was changing around the girls as they entered the Roanoke airport one morning to go to Arizona to play a basketball game. Three Mid-Eastern men joined them on their flight not only to their first game but continued on the same schedule to Oregon, not before there was much concern expressed by Anna Bosley, the coach. The threat of a terrorist attack following credible evidence pronounced in newspapers and voice media throughout the country made the changing scene one of considerable anxiety. Without promised assistance by the FBI the Bacon College basketball team took matters in their own hands as the girls subdued the terrorists on their aircraft before they had an opportunity to fulfill their act of evil.

Following closely the precepts of God, the Hollow group just seemed to know how positively to fulfill their mission in life. All the while the world just watched from the sidelines wondering what they would do next in loving their neighbors.

Paul H. Jones

SECOND YEAR BEGINS

The Bacon College campus was teeming with activity as Mit and two of her friends from the jungle of Costa Rica arrived, and the staff was preparing to receive the other students. The rigid practice regimen of the girls' basketball and soccer teams was continued each day, and with the new arrivals from Central America to play soccer, Coach Anna was sporting a wide smile. In fact, Dr. John Damond, the president, was sharing in the pride because he knew that the major stipulation in the huge, anonymous and benevolent donation of money of providing a competitive soccer team partially had been fulfilled. In fact he was the first to greet the new soccer players when they arrived from the jungle with Mit's parents in Roanoke.

Esther was really carrying a heavy but secret burden now that she was to act on behalf of her special friend, Maudie, who still lay in the hospital recovering from a dreaded tropical disease she contracted when she and the basketball team of girls toured Costa Rica only a few short days ago. "No wonder anyone has ever discovered who the benevolent person is," Esther thought, as she headed again to Maudie's apartment. Sitting pensively each time at the antique desk in Maudie's quaint and extremely modest living quarters adjacent to the Bacon College campus, she would ruminate a long time trying to piece it all together.

"Why would Maudie want to live as she does when she has millions of dollars?" Esther continued to ask herself each time she visited her house. "Here she is working each day as an athletic dormitory maid in a building that was constructed with money she anonymously and generously donated to the college."

Reading again the special guidelines found in the black notebook on the shelf above Maudie's desk, Esther discovered no new revelations. It stated that the process would be simple with each gift being generated by a telephone call to an attorney who would expeditiously handle the rest. While she had not acted the part of the benevolent person so far, she knew the time would soon arrive. "What a frightening and humbling experience at the same time!" Esther thought, as she locked Maudie's apartment door and headed back to the dormitory, not wanting to be gone too long, thereby drawing suspicion from all those who so much wanted to discover who the mysterious benevolent person was.

It was Friday and the entire group of girls was preparing to go to the Hollow, participating in a regular practice, and following to eat in the small wood frame church that was constructed by Josh's family several years ago. Nothing had really changed over the years, but they could sense that the Hollow parents were close to making other decisions in addition to the home for orphans, which would change the whole physical landscape. The Hollow girls longed for this day to reunite with their parents who seemed to be living so comfortably in their two-room houses, precariously situated on the steep mountainside near the one lane dirt road meandering up the hill near the rapidly flowing stream.

Following basketball and soccer practices, Coach Anna loaded the athletic van to go to the hospital before they went to the Hollow. The parade of girls to Maudie's room took a while with each group returning with tearful eyes after having seen their beloved Maudie just lying there in the hospital bed connected with several tubes. She made no response even though they held her hand and talked to her.

Esther entered the room alone, squeezed Maudie's hand, and while weeping whispered to her that she was committed to acting on her behalf as the benevolent person. "Maudie, we all love you so much and eagerly await your healthy return to us," Esther said, as she departed her hospital room.

In the Hollow there was a festive mood, as usual. Mit and her Central American friends were really excited to meet the parents of the girls, and Marsha's group likewise showed much gaiety as they participated with the others. Josh and Charlene were their usual selves making everyone feel very much at home on this Friday evening in the Hollow.

Esther found herself overhearing a long conversation between Charlene and Marsha wherein Marsha was telling about her mother's serious back ailment that had caused her to be bedridden for several years. "Because my parents neither work in a business, industry nor in public work, they do not have insurance to cover any kind of corrective procedure for my mom," Marsha told her. "Several times we have been told that there is a hospital in the northwest near Seattle that has had much success in correcting back problems such as the one like my mom's, but we have not looked into it because of the huge expense of the procedure."

"I know that you are hopeful that one day your mom will have something done to remove the pain as well as the debilitating condition," Charlene stated.

"My mother never mentions her pain or her handicap at all," Marsha noted. "But I know she would dearly love to move about as the other women her age are doing."

"We can always keep her on our prayer list," Charlene indicated.

"I try to pray every day that something in God's will occurs that will improve the quality of her life," Marsha related, as a tear rolled down her cheek.

Hearing this, Esther knew she had discovered what she was going to do for her first benevolent act. "But suppose it will cost a lot of money, which it likely will," Esther thought. "What if the amount for the procedure is in the thousands of dollars? Would Maudie attempt to have this done as one of her benevolent acts?"

It was a huge question, but there was hope for a very wonderful lady, the mother of Esther's best friend. But would Maudie's lawyer feel the same way about it?

During the remainder of the evening, Esther was preoccupied with thoughts of her first B. P. (benevolent person) act to enjoy the merriment as the others. Being very quiet anyway, no one knew the burden Esther was carrying as the time for departure came only too soon for the entire group except one. "If only I could talk to my dad about this," Esther thought, as they loaded the athletic van to head back to college.

ANOTHER BENEVOLENT STRIKE

It was late when they arrived at the college, but
Esther told Coach Anna that she needed to go to
Maudie's apartment. So off she went on the short
trip down the street.

After dialing the number of Mr. Miller nervously, she
said, "Hello, this is Esther Minold at Bacon College."

"Hello, Esther. How are you?" Thomas Miller asked
immediately.

"I am fine," Esther replied.

"How is Maudie doing from your perspective?" he
asked.

"She is about the same as she just lies there in her
hospital bed not responding to anything," Esther told him.

"I have been checking up on her discreetly each day,"
he stated, "and your assessment matches mine because she
doesn't respond to anything around her yet."

"We all here at Bacon grieve each day and long for
her recovery so she can return to be with us," Esther
indicated.

"How may I help you?" he asked.

"I have a story to tell you and then I want to ask you
something," Esther said.

"Please tell me the story," he stated.

"Do you have time to talk to me?" Esther indicated. "I know you are so very busy so it took a lot of courage for me to call you tonight."

"Don't fret over ever worrying me, Esther," he responded. "I am truly your servant, and I want you always to understand that. I am honored that I have the privilege to have you to replace Maudie. We both hope and pray that Maudie will get well soon, but in the meantime, she appointed you to carry on with her benevolent activities. I am just your employee so don't ever feel embarrassed to call me about anything."

With this reassurance Esther began her story. "Several years ago when I participated in the National Foul Shooting Contest in Chicago, I met a young lady my age who befriended me. Her name was Marsha and for years I didn't know her full name. Recently our basketball and soccer coach was invited to go to New Mexico to attend the state finals in soccer. The invitation was sent by a young lady named Marsha Gavanto whose team won the state championship, and three of the players from her team were given full scholarships to come to Bacon College to play soccer. It is so good to have them with us, especially Marsha, whom I love so dearly.

"Marsha's mom has suffered for several years with a chronic back problem that some believe is correctable, if she could go to a unique back clinic in the northwest. But there is a serious problem. Having no medical insurance, they have not pursued this avenue, so Mrs. Gavanto continues to live with this agonizing pain and debilitating condition, which has stripped her of much of a good quality of life. My question to you is, do you think any kind of corrective procedures should be entertained using benevolent funds?"

"What a lovely and warm story!" Thomas stated. "I certainly do think so, if that is what you feel should be done. I tell you again. I am your employee. I will do whatever you ask, and for this, I think I can put this whole plan together for you. We shall have to stay in touch though."

"I will call you each evening when I slip away from the other girls," Esther indicated.

"I know it's hard on you to act on Maudie's behalf and not let others discover that you have the awesome responsibility to be the benevolent person," he stated. "Maudie has spent hours talking about you so I feel as though I know you. This year I am coming to some of your games so be prepared," he said with a laugh.

"I will contact you tomorrow evening about the same time, if that will be all right," Esther noted.

"That will be excellent," he responded, as they discontinued their conversation.

"Oh! I am so glad Mr. Miller thought it was a good idea," Esther thought, as she jogged back to the athletic dormitory to be with her special family of basketball and soccer players.

Esther had a lot on her mind the next day, but as usual, when soccer practice started, she was fully engrossed in her new sport trying to learn from her special friend, Marsha. Although college was not formally in session, there were many spectators waiting on the girls when they arrived at their new field, which was almost completed. "Maudie would be very proud to know where her money has gone," Esther thought, as she looked around at the most impressive outdoor soccer arena in this part of the country.

Mit's parents had returned to their jungle village in the southern portion of Costa Rica, and were continuing their ministry among the various Indian tribes that dwelled in that part of Central America. They too were suffering because Mit was their only child on the one hand, and secondly, she had been the backbone of their several years of missionary work with the native people.

Fighting off homesickness, Mit each day was adapting more and more to her new culture in the United

States after living with the beloved jungle people for more than ten years. Having two of her dear Indian friends with her, she was strengthened, and Mit had become wonderful support for them.

Following an early morning telephone call from Jonah in San Jose, Coach Anna was really a happy camper, having landed her seventh soccer recruit. The young lady was Nonita, a superb soccer player and a very close friend of Mit from Costa Rica.

With all gathered around, Coach Anna teased Mit just a little by saying, "Guess who called today and guess who is going to come to play soccer with us?"

With the double-barrel question directed to Mit, all the others watched her quizzical look only to be told shortly by Coach Anna about Nonita's coming.

"You mean Nonita is coming to Bacon College," Mit excitedly responded.

"That's right," Coach Anna stated. "Pastor Jonah called earlier today, and Bacon offered her an athletic scholarship. I am told that she is a very good soccer player."

"I can't believe Nonita is coming to college here. She really is a good player," Mit quickly indicated. "We have played a lot together in the jungle and around San Jose."

"Marsha, Mit, and the rest of you, we now have a seventh scholarship player to add to our team," Coach Anna happily announced.

"I am so glad that you provided my friends and me the opportunity to play for Bacon during the next several years, Coach Anna," Mit stated, as she hugged her congenial coach ever so warmly.

The numerous spectators in the area were very passionate about the Hollow girls and basketball, and they were now in a position to learn about the sport of soccer and many new girls who had come to participate. Mit and

Marsha were truly genuine leaders on the field as they practiced on this day, but Coach Anna could see that the Hollow girls were gaining skills all the while to help the team. With Esther learning so swiftly, Coach Anna knew she was going to have the strongest three soccer leaders ever assembled on the field. "I know the benevolent person would really be happy to see this unusual group of athletes from different parts of the country and world playing so skillfully together," Coach Anna thought, as she sat with the students and town folks in the bleachers.

Following dinner and basketball practice, Esther slipped out of the athletic dorm to go to Maudie's apartment to call Mr. Miller. "This is Thomas Miller's residence," he stated after the first ring, as though he was waiting for her call.

"This is Esther," she said somewhat nervously.

"I have some good news for you," he quickly indicated. "I talked to the directors of four clinics in the northwest today to see how well equipped they are to correct the problem of Mrs. Gavanto, Marsha's mother. Not really knowing fully at this time about her ailment, I just spoke to them generally about the situation. One of the directors assured me that his clinic had the finest facility, equipment and general wherewithal to correct her problem. He said that they had never run into a problem that at least could not be helped."

"That really sounds good," Esther said. "What do you think our next step should be?"

"I think that the rest should be left up to Marsha to guide her mother to this clinic," he stated. "The name and address of the clinic is as follows: Sarver Medical Clinic, 703 Motann Street, Tacoma, Washington. The telephone number is (231) 002 5116. Not knowing the exact expense, you may want to place fifty thousand dollars in a bank account for Marsha to handle. Marsha can be advised to request more, if needed."

"You have worked things out splendidly," Esther happily reacted. "Do you think Maudie would be pleased with this benevolent act?"

"Knowing Maudie and her love for you, she would be extremely happy and proud of you," he stated.

"As the benevolent person, I will write Marsha a long letter explaining everything," Esther noted.

"I will have the money in Community National Bank of Bacon early tomorrow morning," he stated. "Remember, I am your employee so call me whenever you want to perform a benevolent act of any kind."

"You make me feel very comfortable and I thank you for that," Esther said.

"Maudie has told me what an outstanding young lady you are," he stated. "I will be meeting you soon at a basketball game."

Using Maudie's typewriter, Esther typed Marsha a long letter to explain all the details of the plan, and upon completion put it into a brown envelope. Locking the door behind her, she briskly walked back to the dormitory, hiding the envelope under her books. As she entered the dormitory, she discreetly pinned the envelope to the bulletin board and joined the other girls in the commons area.

Esther was awake early the next morning as the sun rose over the mountains, but she just lay in bed anticipating the joy the brown envelope was going bring to the Gavanto family. "I just hope that my first secret benevolent act will be acceptable by Maudie," Esther thought.

Following the girls' devotional program in the commons area led by Mit, they all headed toward the dining hall, but suddenly, all stopped when Diane yelled, "There is a brown enveloped pinned on the bulletin board."

"It is addressed to whom?" Coach Anna asked, as they all hovered around the bulletin board.

16

"It says to Esther and the teams, as usual," Diane replied excitedly, as she removed it and handed it to Esther.

Opening it hurriedly, Esther began to read.

Dear Girls,

We all are so very excited about the upcoming basketball and soccer seasons. We can't wait to see you representing Bacon College around the country.

Congratulations on getting the new girls to play soccer this year. They are truly a special group that will genuinely uphold the Bacon tradition. As we all get older, there appears to be more and more physical ailments which reduce our quality of life. One of your girls, Marsha Gavanto, has a mother who has suffered quietly over the years with a serious back problem. This letter to you hopefully will be the beginning of the end to this pain that she struggles with each day.

In recent days I have received information about an excellent medical clinic in the northwest that I believe can correct the back problem of Mrs. Gavanto. The name of the clinic is Sarver Medical Service, 703 Motann Street, Tacoma, Washington 21112. The telephone number is (231) 002 5116. At this time the hospital and doctors' fees and travel costs are unknown, but an account is now available at the local Community National Bank in the amount of fifty thousand dollars. When more is needed, leave a note on the athletic dormitory bulletin board.

Thank all of you for being such special and loving students. Please advise Dr. Damond that he has masterfully fulfilled all the requirements of the previous donations to the college.

I love you all very much!

Sincerely,

An Admirer

With Marsha now crying uncontrollably, they all returned to the dormitory as one big and very happy family. Others soon joined Marsha as they cried together while sitting, holding hands and joyfully relishing this moment together. Marsha was so excited, but as soon as she was more composed immediately called her mother.

Mr. Gavanto answered the telephone and hardly before he said hello, Marsha blurted out, "I have such good news to tell you but because it involves Mom mostly, let me speak to her."

Getting Mom on the line, Marsha excitedly told her about the letter. "Mom, this morning when we started out the dormitory, there was a brown envelope pinned to the bulletin board. Guess what it said? Well, someone is giving you enough money to have your back problems corrected," Marsha told her while crying at the same time.

"What did you say?" her mother asked even though she heard what was said, but it was the believing what was said that was causing the biggest problem.

"Someone has given enough money to you and Dad to get your back well," Marsha repeated.

With the information sinking in now, Mrs. Gavanto joined her lovely daughter as they both were now crying. Filling her in on all the details regarding the money that was so generously donated by the secret benevolent person, Marsha then told her mother that she would work out all of the details and call her later.

Walking joyfully to breakfast in the college cafeteria, they sang almost all the way. Each knew that when the media discovered this large gift of money to an individual, they would pounce on the campus like they had never done before. Privately, they wondered who the wealthy B. P. could be who was so very generous with his or her money.

Following breakfast, the girls went to Dr. Damond's office to show him the letter. He was ecstatic when he read the part that the benevolent person was pleased with the recruiting efforts of the team. That afternoon before the basketball practice, he assembled all the students who were present to apprise them of the letter that had been received advising of the money to pay medical costs for Marsha's mother. He was always happy to keep the students informed about events and happenings on campus, and because of this the students loved him dearly.

Before Marsha had a chance to work out the details for her mother's visit to the clinic to receive medical attention, the media did pounce on Bacon College as it had never done before. Although Coach Anna was adamant with the media that they not speak with the girls, some discovered who the recipient of the money was and made pictures of Marsha as she walked on campus. One television station manager was so obsessed by it all that he stationed a cameraman on campus near the entrance of the athletic dormitory to watch to see all of the people who came to the building. While Dr. Damond was concerned about this undertaking, he decided not to preclude the station's action, thinking that the best decision regarding the matter was no action at all. He was sure the benevolent person who had remained anonymous for all these months would not let an overzealous cameraman stand in the way of further acts of kindness.

The real test for the quaint little campus came when a most popular talk show team arrived to develop its story for public consumption. They were more aggressive and seemed immediately to stake out their mission with much wider parameters of behavior. As soon as they arrived, Dr. Damond summoned Coach Anna for a conference regarding their new visitors who seemed to show up everywhere on campus.

"Thank you for dropping everything and coming to talk with me," Dr. Damond stated with what Coach Anna perceived as more than a tinge of anxiety. "Please be seated."

"Thank you for inviting me to your office," Coach Anna replied. "I always feel so honored to be in your presence."

"Thank you," he responded. "The media are really perplexed over the secrecy of the benevolent person and seem to have removed all stops to discover who the individual is. As you know, all of our correspondence indicates that the benevolent person wants to remain anonymous, and we never discuss it. I think about it from time to time, but I neither dwell on the subject nor do I try to figure out who it is except for a fleeting thought from time to time."

"Well, I could really say that I do likewise," Coach Anna said. "Ever since the girls arrived on campus, they have been the conduit for these benevolent acts such that the benevolent person must really respect them highly. But you know, they seldom talk about it at all. The subject rarely comes up with them, and they understand the importance of not talking to the media. In fact, they are really thankful that I do all the interviews."

"Now that the pressure on us is mounting, particularly as it relates to the new group who came on campus this morning, I thought it would be good for you and me to establish some guidelines as we deal with the current campus environment," he related, while looking at Coach Anna. "First, I think it's important that we provide information for their telecast on the one hand, but not to speculate on who we believe might be a benevolent person on the other. The fact that you have shielded the girls all the while makes it much easier as you and I will be the only spokespersons on campus."

"I know they will try to talk to the girls so I'll meet with them as soon as I get back to the dormitory," Coach Anna said.

"Because there have been so many different groups expressing a desire for information, I'm going to conduct a press conference," Dr. Damond indicated.

"That will be a splendid idea," Coach Anna quickly reacted.

As Coach Anna walked hurriedly back to the athletic dormitory, she was very sensitive about the various video cameras that were following every move she made on campus. In the dormitory she called a meeting of all the girls and apprised them of the present situation that had been precipitated by the anonymous gift of money to correct the back problem of Marsha's mother. "The media are in a state of frenzy so I want to caution you about talking with any of them or even strangers on campus," she stated. "It appears that they are now coming on campus in full force with the determination of not leaving until they have discovered who it is that is giving all the money to the college and to others in the area."

"How should we move about on campus?" Maggie asked, wanting to be sure they did the right thing.

"Our best mode of behavior is not to change what we have been doing but to be more cautious as we move about," Coach Anna responded.

"We don't move about too much anyway," Esther said, "because we only go to classes, the cafeteria, gymnasium and soccer field each day."

"As you know, each time you leave the building a camera will be making a video of you," Coach Anna told the group.

It was a good meeting that was put in perspective when Diane stated, "They don't really think that we have a fortune to give away, do they?"

Following much laughter after Diane's comments, they headed for the press conference being conducted by Dr. Damond.

With a capacity crowd in the gymnasium and a string of microphones in the center, Dr. Damond walked in to face the media with all the students in the audience. Standing before the group, he said, "During the past two days, several media personnel have come to our quiet campus asking about the benevolent person who has been giving money to the college and to various individuals related to the institution. In order to tell you all that I know about the situation, I thought it would be prudent to speak to all of you at the same time instead of answering the same question many times over. This way all of you will be hearing the same information.

"About two years ago Bacon College received its first gift of money with one stipulation that we begin a competitive Division I basketball program for girls. As you all know, this benevolent act stirred the community and caused the media to raise an eyebrow when you all discovered the amount. But that curiosity subsided soon, and we at Bacon began to attempt to fulfill the requirement of fielding a good basketball team. The Board of Directors really had a difficult time determining how best to proceed, but after much dialogue inundated with patience, they made their decision.

"Instead of reviewing the credentials of several outstanding Division I coaches, we decided that it would be best to employ a beginning coach who would grow and develop with the team. Of course, you all know we hired Anna Bosley from the high school ranks, and she has done a most outstanding job. Let me hasten to add though that when she recruited and signed the group of girls from the Hollow, I was very concerned about her leadership skills. During this time, I thought we would have to forfeit the gift

22

of money because we would never have a team to compete nationally. So much for my assessment as you all know what she has done with this team already.

"Recently, we received an anonymous note indicating that we had fulfilled the stipulation included in our first huge gift of money. In a sense this brought closure to the anxiety that I had to be sure we had done what was expected of us by the benevolent person or B. P. as the individual is now affectionately called. But there came another large donation of money with the only stipulation that we provide a soccer team that can compete on the Division I level.

"We have been very successful in basketball, although the pundits really didn't think it could be done so soon, if at all, by such a small institution playing among the giants, as they called them. But of course, we did under the leadership of Coach Bosley and her excellent group of girls from a remote area called the Hollow. Now we have the challenge to field a soccer team of equal stature. To fulfill this specific stipulation, we have asked Miss Anna Bosley to coach the soccer team in addition to the basketball team.

"Based on what she tells me and from what I've observed in practice, they are a fine group of young ladies. By the way, I notice that the Hollow girls are learning about soccer as they join players from New Mexico and from Costa Rica. What I most appreciate about Coach Bosley's girls is that they are very mannerly, humble and excellent students.

"In addition to the large donations of money to our institution, on other occasions gifts of money have been received by various ones on campus and others in some way associated with the college. Each time some gift is received, there is a flurry of activity to discover the source of the mystery, but each time all avenues are barren of any clues. Again, because so many are so enamored over the source of our benevolent gifts, I decided to hold this press conference to answer questions which will preclude having to answer them individually for all of you.

"If you have questions, I'll try to answer them at this time."

One young man sitting on the floor with his shirt tail out stood up and asked, "Why do you think the benevolent person only gives money to Bacon College?"

"We really don't know that money is only given to Bacon because this benevolent person may be giving money to several institutions and to other people," Dr. Damond responded.

"How do you know the person is pleased with the way you are using the money?" another reporter asked.

"From all we can determine to this point, we have fulfilled the stipulation included with the gift of money for the basketball program," he stated. "We are not really sure about the soccer money stipulation yet."

"Do you have any idea who this philanthropist is?" a young lady inquired.

"I have no idea at all," he responded.

"You must have thought about it just a little," she continued.

"From time to time there is a fleeting thought, but I really don't dwell on it," he indicated.

"Many people come on campus each day, especially since the Hollow girls started playing basketball. How many B. P. candidates could you pick from this group?" an older writer asked eliciting some laughter.

"Oh, I would say about fifty," Dr. Damond jokingly responded. "Whoever it is has some special love for Bacon College."

"How long do you expect these kinds of monetary gifts to continue?" a young man asked.

"It all began more than two years ago and has continued ever since," the president responded. "How long they will continue, I am not sure, but as for any recipient of gifts, we hope they will continue indefinitely."

"Do you ever wonder what prompted this person to start giving money to the college in the first place?" a young lady asked.

"I have thought about that many times," he said, "but I have not come up with a satisfactory answer to the question. Bacon College is more than one hundred years old, and until a couple of years ago it had not heard from the anonymous person. All the gifts to the college prior to that time had been given by someone who identified himself or herself. In the past we have not had people who gave large sums of money such as you hear and read about from the larger institutions, but we are so appreciative for what we have received over the years."

"If you were trying to discover who is donating all this money, how would you go about it?" another young writer asked, as he chuckled a little.

Grinning somewhat, the president said, "I really hope I never discover who it is, because the individual has advised us all along that if we found out who he or she is, the benevolent gift would be withdrawn, so we certainly would not want this to happen."

"If you are so concerned about the benevolent person being discovered, why do you let all of us come on campus to pry and probe to try to find out who the mysterious person is?" a national television reporter asked.

"Well, I thought about it a lot and decided that the best way to deal with the situation was to be as open as possible and not hide anything from our students and our beloved guests who visit with us from time to time," he responded. "You are considered our beloved guests, and we want you to feel that you are always welcome on our campus."

The students were really proud of Dr. Damond as he was questioned by the various reporters, while they all sat in the gymnasium. They were part of something that had whetted the appetites of the various news media throughout the land, and as far as they could tell, this was just the beginning of a massive process to attempt to identify the anonymous donor so that all the world would know the name of the person. They were surprised at the large number of reporters on hand in the first place, and secondly, the large contingent from the national television networks.

NETWORK'S PLOY

Meanwhile, one of the networks that had dubbed itself as the leading news carrier in the country became creative in its handling of these acts of kindness in this remote area of southwest Virginia. In the main studio the president conducted a meeting of his staff to delve into the matter further.

"We have a story here about an anonymous person that has attracted national attention beyond what any of us ever dreamed with the interest continuing to grow," the president of the Liberty Broadcasting Company stated. "It's not often that a story of such national interest emerges that captures the hearts of our audience as this one regarding the benevolent person back at the Bacon College community. I have asked you to be present at this meeting to determine what we could do to keep this story alive and at a high interest level for all our viewers."

Immediately, one bright young executive indicated that he had been thinking about an idea for several days now and wanted to see what his colleagues thought about it. "All of the activity of the benevolent person centers around the Bacon College campus, and it's not very large," he excitedly began to relate his thoughts to the group. "There are only three hundred fifty students on campus each day, a staff of

about fifty to seventy-five people who work on campus some
during each day, and a few visitors most days and a large
number only on a few days during the month. You already
know all of this, but I just wanted to remind you of the
setting.

"Suppose we place two or three cameras on campus
around the clock for a period of a month and let our audience
on a prime time television program review our tape to
attempt to name the benevolent person or B. P., as the person
is called locally. It could be a call in show or with a panel of
ordinary people who are selected from the audience in the
studio. Following the first show in which the possible
candidates are reduced, there would be a second show
wherein the group of possible candidates is reduced even
further to only four or five people. On the final show the
viewing audience would vote on their choice via internet,
and a person would be judged as the most likely candidate to
be the benevolent person."

After the young executive completed his rather
lengthy oral dissertation, his co-workers seated around the
oval shaped table thought it was an ingenious idea and began
to work out the details for the program.

"What would we do for the first show besides
showing the video of the various people on campus?" one
asked. "In other words how could this arrangement be made
interesting to the viewing audience?"

"Suppose we do a brief biographical sketch on
several of those shown on the video, including where they
live and what kind of car they drive," another added.

"That's a good idea," a young lady reacted.

"What could we include in the biographical sketch?"
another young executive asked.

"I believe it would be interesting to indicate
information about their family, their work experience and
certainly their connection with small Bacon College," an

animated young lady noted. "In addition we could show how they are involved in various civic functions in the area."

"But if we have hundreds of people on the video who have been seen on the campus, which ones will be included and which ones will be excluded?" an older executive asked who still seemed to be concerned that it would not be of sufficient intrigue to attract a large viewing audience.

"We could develop a very interesting internet web site where we could place the biographical sketches of all of those observed on campus," the initial young executive stated. "We could highlight a few on our one-hour live program, and then advise our audience that the remainder of those observed could be found on the internet."

"How would we go about selecting those who would be considered viable candidates and would continue on our second telecast a week later?" an astute older employee asked.

"It would be my thinking that the one hundred who received the most votes on the first round would be the survivors for the second program," the young executive indicated, enthusiastically taking the lead now. "The top ten selected could be a part of our next program, wherein these ten finalists could be introduced to our viewing audience and those in the studio. Each week one of our ten could be voted out of our group until only one remains. Each of these selected contestants or candidates could be paid well to be on the show and the longer each candidate remained the more money would be paid to him or her."

Speaking directly to the young man, the president praised him by saying, "You have done such a good job in your initial outline for such a weekly show, I want you to head a committee to work out all of the details. Let me say up front that I think it's important to move ahead as soon as possible so assignments should be made and approval be obtained from the president of the college immediately."

Impervious to all the activity by the media regarding the benevolent person, the Bacon girls continued to practice basketball twice daily and would participate in soccer once each day. It was really fun but provided a full plate for them as they participated in two major sports. Marsha and Mit were beginning to reveal their leadership skills as they lived in the athletic dormitory, and shared experiences with the basketball players.

Meanwhile their trips to the hospital to see Maudie were very frequent. She just lay on her bed not realizing that the girls were so very faithful to visit all the while. One evening the head nurse indicated that they were going to give her a stronger medication, hoping that it would bring her out of the coma and on a better road to recovery.

Dr. Damond was not usually one to be at a loss for words, but when the television executive met with him about the proposed program, he was dumfounded. "I have never been one to hedge on an answer to a direct question, but this one catches me coldly and without sufficient background to respond."

"I know that this is asking a lot from you without giving you sufficient time to think about it," the young man stated, realizing that the amiable, humble and helpful president had always bent over backward to assist others regardless of the cause.

"It's just a different kind of activity from what we are used to here in the mountains," he said. "We like to live quietly and peacefully here at our special institution of higher learning, so to answer your question positively would place us in a position of considerable notoriety."

"Not wanting to pressure you in any way, I would say to you that the program could be developed without your consent, but the president of our television station felt that it was very important to touch base with you before we continued our planning," the young man indicated.

"I am very pleased that you would request our approval before doing such a show," the president stated, "but my initial reaction is that I need to discuss this issue with the Bacon Board of Directors before giving you an answer."

"That will be excellent," the station representative stated while preparing to leave.

The called meeting of the Board of Directors didn't last long as they seemed to concur that the college only had one answer for the television program. Dr. Damond was instructed to advise the network that it had approval to develop the television program.

During the next several days on campus and in the community, there were about a dozen representatives of the powerful and popular LBC television network canvassing the whole neighborhood with their clipboards and video cameras. Every person on campus, including students who would talk to the media, were interviewed with the hope that someone would reveal some secret to identify the mysterious and very secretive benevolent person. Knowing that they had only thirty days to collect all of their information, the various personnel utilized extended hours to fulfill their mission.

Soon different media were presenting their thoughts on the subject with some including lengthy articles on the acts of benevolence at Bacon College. Realizing that the LBC television network was going to receive many plaudits for its coverage of the benevolent person, many in the same profession wanted to get its story out first to an already massaged audience just waiting for any kind of information on the subject of Bacon College benevolence. The craziness of the whole thing caused the Bacon campus to be in a state of turmoil such that Dr. Damond several times had entertained second thoughts, such that he wondered whether or not his generosity of permitting the television and other media on campus had compromised his basic principles of leadership. "After seeing the less than gregarious conduct and behavior of the various people trying to obtain a story, I wonder whether or not it would have been better to have denied the media such privileges on campus," he thought, as he observed the unusually large number of television cameras around the area.

WRITER'S TRICK

On the third day of the "media invasion" a young female reporter fainted and lay unconscious very near the entrance of the athletic dormitory. The Hollow girls saw her lying on the ground and went to her aid. As she regained consciousness, it was decided that they would take her into the dormitory to assist in restoring her to good health.

In the dormitory they put her on a couch, gave her some water and placed a damp rag on her forehead. It seemed obvious that she was one of the numerous media on site because she had in her possession a clipboard and camera.

"What are you doing on campus?" Coach Anna asked, already realizing that she was part of the media, as she held her head in position to get water.

"I work for a magazine," the young lady answered.

"What kind of story are you trying to write?" Coach Anna asked.

"I am trying to write a story about the benevolent person," she responded.

"Is that what everyone is trying to write about?" Coach Anna inquired.

"I guess so," the young lady stated. "But mine needs to be different because my manager is only going to give me this one last chance to write something interesting for the readers of their magazine."

"What do you mean?" Coach Anna probed.

"I have not written anything satisfactorily for several weeks so they were going to dismiss me, but I convinced them to give me another chance," she noted. "You see, I am the sole supporter for my very sick mother so I really need the job."

"How is your mother now?" Coach Anna asked.

"She is not doing well," the young reporter promptly replied. "We live in a house that has handicap barriers so my mother has to stay inside each day until I get home to move her about in her wheelchair. Her arthritis is causing her to deteriorate ever so swiftly now."

"Could your mother go outside in her wheelchair, if there were no barriers?" Coach Anna asked.

"This is what she longs to do again," the young lady said. "She lives for the day when she can be independent again and not depend on others and me to assist her."

"How long have you worked for this magazine?" Coach Anna asked, as the other girls listened.

"I got my job right after I received my college degree in journalism so this is the only place I have worked," she said, now lying more comfortably on the couch.

"I imagine your job has been very interesting, hasn't it?" Coach Anna inquired.

"I have really enjoyed it very much all the while, and even now I wouldn't get to know you all if it were not for my job," she related. "However, recently I have not been able to do a story that has been acceptable for the magazine so the editor has warned me to produce or else look for another job."

"This worries you very much, doesn't it?" Coach Anna responded.

"It really does mainly because of two reasons," she stated. "First, I like my job very much and secondly, I need the job to earn money for my mother and me to live."

"Have you thought about what you might do if you do lose your job?" Coach Anna asked.

"I really don't know because I need a job with only minimal regional travel," she answered.

"By the way my name is Anna Bosley, and these girls are my basketball and soccer teams for Bacon College," Coach Anna said, as she turned with her hand pointed toward the girls who were sitting attentively listening to the conversation.

"I am Jewel Throneberry," she stated. "I am sorry that I didn't introduce myself earlier."

"By the way, have you discovered anything to write about so far?" Coach Anna asked.

"I really have not to this point," she said, "but I hope to attempt a different angle from the large number of other writers. It seems that everybody is trying to get a story on this subject of the benevolent person, so to get one that would be unique would almost be impossible."

"No doubt it would be," Coach Anna responded. "While you are thinking about it, why don't you go to lunch with the girls and me?"

"I would love to do that, if it would not impose on you too much," she quickly stated.

"We would love to have you," Coach Anna indicated which was echoed by the girls as they got up to leave.

With television and other media dotting the landscape, the group made their way to the dining hall located several hundred feet from the athletic dormitory. "Who is that with you?" one of the reporters asked, as they group walked nearby.

"This is Jewel Throneberry," Coach Anna answered.

"Why is she with you?" he excitedly asked. "I didn't think you permitted the girls to talk to reporters."

"I don't, but this young lady became ill while doing a job similar to yours so we let her recuperate in the athletic dormitory," Coach Anna noted.

"I wish I had thought about that," he stated in a somewhat jealous tone. "I have always wanted to look inside the dormitory beyond the vestibule where the now famous bulletin board is located."

The meal was delicious that the sick reporter liked very much, having eaten a full meal. "You really were hungry, weren't you?" Coach Anna noted.

"I really was," she responded, "and maybe that was what was wrong with me after all."

"How could we help you not to lose your job?" Coach Anna asked, as she looked her in the eye.

"If I'm to write on the conduct of the benevolent person or something about the person, I'm still at square one," she said in somewhat of a hopeless tone.

Thinking that the young lady needed a good story badly to salvage her job, Coach Anna stated, "We don't really know anything about the benevolent person beyond what has already been written and broadcast publicly. Announcing each time that the act of benevolence is handled through us here in the athletic dormitory, we reveal all that we know, so for this story we have nothing to add. The benevolent person has really been discreet such that none of us to my knowledge knows who the person is, and as you know, the main stipulation regarding any anonymous gift from the mysterious person has been that his or her identify must remain anonymous."

"Do you think that you have any clues regarding this person?" Jewel asked.

"None whatsoever," Coach Anna said emphatically. "There are so many people who come on campus each week that it would be impossible to determine who it might be."

Following lunch, the reporter departed, and the girls headed to their afternoon basketball practice. Marsha and Mit had become active participants on the team to be available when needed and the soccer girls became spectators at each practice. The entire group of girls participated in soccer practice, and as each day passed, Coach Anna presented a wider and wider grin because she was so pleased with their progress as a team. The Hollow girls really were displaying their versatility, and Esther was playing at a skill level right along with Mit and Marsha. Of course, Mit was something special to watch such that the usual spectators returned each day to see what she was going to do differently that would elicit strong applause from those in the stands.

At the hospital Maudie was beginning to make some progress as she not only squeezed Ether's hand, but would open her eyes from time to time although not seeming to focus on anything in particular. Their visit each evening to see the progress Maudie was making was the highlight of the day for the girls. Each time the girls would bring her handwritten notes and place them on a snap hanger near the bulletin board in the room. "I hope she enjoys these when she is able to read," Dorothy indicated. "Some are really funny so I believe she will get some enjoyment from them."

"She seems more sensitive about our presence today," Coach Anna stated.

"It's as though she is trying to speak to us," Esther said excitedly.

In addition to the notes from the girls there were numerous flower arrangements, potted plants and an assortment of other items sent to Maudie during her illness since the Costa Rican trip. "Soon she will be alert enough to enjoy these things," Esther thought, as they said good-bye to their very special friend.

Back in her apartment Jewel Throneberry sat down at her word processor to write her story. It was difficult to get started because she had misrepresented herself to the Bacon coach and the girls. On the one hand her mother was neither ill nor handicapped, and on the other she was not under any kind of pressure to write a good story on her assignment or else lose her job. "Sometimes reporters have to resort to this kind of tactic to get information, so I was doing what any good reporter would do," she thought, as the computer was coming on.

The Margone Magazine had really been good to Jewel as she had been with the organization for nearly ten years and had moved up through the ranks to become assistant editor, moving ahead of many others who had been on staff much longer. Her aggressive and fearless style had made her a well known writer in the print media arena so her action at Bacon College was very mild compared to other charades she had conducted to get ahead in her business. Having a magazine that was the leading seller and carried the highest rate for advertising, the business was going extremely well such that large salaries were being paid to the executive staff which certainly included Jewel.

Because it was time to present a new and exciting story, she knew that the public was having an insatiable appetite for anything written about the benevolent person so she would use her information gleaned from the Bacon College trip to generate that story. It didn't take long for her to begin what would be a lengthy dissertation about her experience at the college with extremely elastic embellishments that even caused her to blink just a little. "These are not my facts but are my opinions which could be stretched to fit the occasion," she rationalized, as she moved ahead with her story.

"While all the powerful television media were clamoring for a story or were making pictures or taking video shots of the campus personnel, I had deviously worked myself into the inner sanctum beyond the line in the sand that had been drawn by college officials," she wrote. "Sitting there in the athletic dormitory where no other reporter had tread, I carefully examined my surroundings asking these questions all the while: 'Why am I here, and why would a philanthropic person pick this setting to deliver any kind of gift to anyone?'

"Feigning illness was the easiest of my actions on this day. If I had known the gullibility and the naiveté of the residents in the athletic dormitory, I would have just verbally gotten a pass to enter the quarters of those who had so many times before been the recipients of gifts of money from the benevolent person. They were so very backward that after a short while in my visit I began to accept their nescience as coming with the environment in which I found myself. The coach, bless her heart, was not originally from this hick area, but she had truly been living in the area too long because she was really very slow in making decisions. How she and the group ever overwhelmed the terrorists on the hijacked plane a few months ago, I'll never know, because she certainly didn't seem to me to be one who had sufficient wisdom to concoct any kind of viable plan to be victorious in any situation.

"As you all know, one of the trademarks of the basketball team has been the poor dress of the team. In fact when they play their games everyone usually makes a comment about their shoes being so worn out, having holes in the upper and lower portion. During my visit, I was privy to something that the public does not know. The girls have beautiful clothes as many paraded about while I was on the couch asking the others how they looked in their new dresses, blouses and shoes. They even talked about wearing their new basketball shoes, but delayed that notion because it would detract from their 'poor old' image that people had become to know.

"Why was it that the benevolent person used this group of country louts as a conduit for the many benevolent acts was a question that I asked myself over and over again, but nothing at first came to my attention. It was later in my visit that my first significant theory was generated. Was it because that the benevolent person wanted to remain anonymous never to be discovered; therefore, it was important to mislead those bent on finding out the philanthropist by letting the Hollow girls be the announcers of the gift? A better group could not be found because those attempting to use all means available to discover the benevolent person were spending all of their time and energy thinking about the couriers of the gift and less on the actual benefactor. What a brilliant scheme!

"As I sat on the couch for my final minutes, I suddenly realized that the team of girls included several Indians from Central America and three or four from the southwest. I wondered whether or not they really understand what a serious handicap they are faced as they attempt to learn a new culture from the uncouth group of girls that call the Hollow their home. Maybe there is still hope of hope that these Hollow buffoons will become the learners, and the new girls on the team from Indian descent will assume the role of teachers. Let's hope so."

The lengthy article was fraught with condescending statements that painted the Hollow girls in such an ugly manner. Little derogation was left unsaid, as it seemed that all disparaging avenues were well traveled by the word processor. Soon the scathing article would be included in this very popular monthly magazine.

INTERESTING CALL

A couple of days later Coach Anna received a telephone call from a colonel at Fort Torman in eastern North Carolina who wanted to meet with her the next day to discuss a situation with him. The rendezvous was to take place at Rocky Knob overlook just off the interstate highway on the Blue Ridge Parkway.

Following the mysterious call, Coach Anna went to see Dr. Damond to advise him of the request and to get his permission to go. "I have never received a call from my old green beret base before so I don't really know why I would get one now," she said to the amiable president.

"They really think highly of you so it must be very important," he stated, trying to render some comfort to her as she sat in his office.

"I would like to meet with you when I return if that would be satisfactory," Coach Anna said.

"Thank you for wanting to share it with me," he graciously said, as Coach Anna departed his office.

Telling the girls that she had been beckoned for a meeting with a military person on this day and would return later helped her somewhat because now her immediate family knew of her plans. Realizing that she and her girls were inseparable, the various television personnel who were still on campus thought it was strange that she suddenly left campus heading for an unknown destination. "What could this mean?" they mused.

Riding alone on the thirty-mile trip to the Parkway, her thoughts returned to her training at Fort Torman where she learned many combat skills with some that really she had never used. The serious conditioning was always fun as they ran many times in the dark with full combat gear for long distances only to have to run back. "It was work and it was fun," she thought with the pursuit in clandestine activities bringing the most rewarding memories on this day. She wondered what this meeting was all about as she traversed the serpentine road leading to the crest of the mountain where the scenic Blue Ridge Parkway was constructed years ago by the Civilian Conservation Corps during the depression years.

Up ahead she saw an olive colored vehicle with a man standing in front looking at the beauty of God's creation. "Was this the colonel she was supposed to meet?" she thought, as she pulled the van several parking spaces from his.

Without hesitation he walked directly and briskly to Coach Anna and said, "I am so pleased that you could meet with me this morning, Major Bosley. Let's sit at the picnic table at the end of the parking lot down there."

"That will be fine," Coach Anna responded.

"My name is Bill Carlton, and I would like to talk to you about your college team and much else, but there is a sense of urgency in my being here today," he pointed out.

"Before we get started, may I ask you one question?" Coach Anna said.

"Surely," he quickly stated.

"How do know who I am?" Coach Anna asked.

Chuckling somewhat, he said, "You know, I have to look at your picture every day hanging in the administrative office so I knew who you were the minute you drove in the parking lot."

"Now, why did you want to meet with me?" she asked, as she rested her elbows on the table looking directly at him.

Two days ago in the remote Muslim country of Abedistan three young missionary ladies disappeared from their living quarters. A few hours later a terrorist group announced that they were holding them, and following that they began to relate their demands to secure their release. Huge sums of money were being requested, several prisoners were demanded to be released and many weapons were requested."

"Why would they demand so much?" Coach Anna asked.

"They realize that they have valuable commodities," he noted. "One of the girls is a niece of our president and realizing this, they have elevated the stakes."

"Has our government decided how to proceed on this matter?" Coach Anna asked.

"Yes, they have," he responded quickly. "They are not going to give in to the demands and are developing a plan of rescue that will be carried out soon."

"Why are you talking to me about this kidnapping?" Coach Anna asked, now suspecting that she is more than just a sounding board.

"I want to talk to you about this rescue team," he said directly.

"What a shock!" she related in a high pitched voice. "I thought my days of rescue were over."

"I think they are just beginning," Colonel Carlton indicated with a shallow grin. "Let me tell you what we know at this point. We have not made contact with the young ladies since they suddenly disappeared, but we have heard from the terrorists several times as they freely relate their demands. At this time all seems to be tranquil and safe for the captives, but this is a wanton group of evil men holding these women so they will increase their challenge. As you know, we have committed ourselves to destroy all terrorists and their wherewithal so Abedistan will be invaded in the near future. In recent months they have congregated in this country, but because the ladies are being held there, our government is withholding any attack until a rescue can be undertaken successfully. The grace time has been set at forty days, enough time for us to rescue the young ladies, if it's possible to do so."

"How do I fit into this problem?" Coach Anna asked.

"We have had several meetings during the last forty-eight hours, and each time your name is the one most often mentioned to lead a team of rescuers," Colonel Carlton stated. "Obviously, we believe that if it can be done, you can do it."

"You know I have a full time job as coach of Bacon College," she indicated.

"We all took that into consideration, but because of the seriousness of this assignment, we wanted to send our best because in the end the whole world will be looking at us," he noted. "Our citizens expect us to do our best to rescue these girls, and you are our best so everyone on the committee voted for you to take charge. Although you have not been directly involved in the program in recent months, your handling of the hijacking convinced everyone that you could handle unique situations by making good decisions on the field."

"I am overwhelmed by all that you say, and as you speak, I am trying to juggle in my mind all the responsibility I have in my coaching job," she told the colonel. "I realize that some things are more important than others, and in this case the most important thing at present is to remove the young ladies from harm's way."

"There is so much at stake in this rescue," he pointed out.

"What do you want me to do?" Coach Anna abruptly asked, indicating her willingness to lead the rescue team.

"With your affirming assent, let me discuss with you another part of this mission," he stated, as he leaned toward her while looking from side to side to be sure no one was listening. "This truly is going to be a very secret mission such that we plan to handle it differently from any of the others in the past. Our model in developing our plans came from your dealing with the terrorists on the airplane in Portland. You used your own people to subdue the culprits. For this rescue unit we do not want to use any active military personnel, but people we can train in a short period. We want you to utilize six of your Bacon athletes to join you to make a team of seven to carry out this rescue."

"You mean you want me to use my girls in this activity?" Coach Anna emotionally asked.

"That's right," he indicated emphatically.

"But they are not trained and are so very young," Coach Anna responded.

"They are well equipped to do the job," he countered. "They are obedient, strong and committed to you so you would have a tightly knit unit of rescuers on this assignment."

"I spent many months in training to gain my skills," Coach Anna noted. "My girls are untrained and are truly neophytes when it comes to being involved in rescue missions."

"We have a crash training program waiting for them as soon as they agree to volunteer," the colonel stated. "All of you will be civilian volunteers with military savvy to overcome the enemy with force, if necessary."

"Did you say the mission will not last more than forty days?" Coach Anna asked.

"The count started as soon as you agreed so forty days from now you will be coaching again," he noted.

"Where do we go from here?" Coach Anna asked, now ready to begin to make plans.

"I want you to send me the names and other demographic information on the girls you choose for your team," he answered. "Tomorrow morning at ten o'clock, I want you to be at the Charlotte airport ready to travel to the Sacramento, California where you will rent a car to take you to Fort Santida in the Mohave Desert for a twenty-one day training session. The car will be returned for you upon your arrival. You will report to Lieutenant Colonel Edward Stokes who will advise you from that point, and the additional itinerary will be revealed to you at that time. All you need to have with you is one change of clothes. Do not wear any kind of clothing that might indicate that you are part of the Bacon College team because we want you all to get there unnoticed, so do whatever you need to do to maintain your surreptitious movement.

"At the airport tomorrow morning you will be handed a briefcase of documents for you to examine on the way to California. Keep the briefcase with you all the while you are training, but destroy it before you leave to head out on your mission."

The rendezvous ended about as abruptly as it began as Colonel Carlton got in his military vehicle, and Coach Anna got under the steering wheel of the college van to return to the campus with a very crowded mind. "How can I introduce this request to the girls, and how should their precious parents be advised?" she thought, as the engine fired up.

She had remembered her training at Fort Santida in the sand and hot days and cool nights, which included clandestine operations in a desert setting. Listening to the final talk to the group following the training, she recalled that the leader told them that the principal goal of the desert exercise was to get them comfortable in conducting operations in a sandy environment. Grinning just a little, she thought, "I am not really sure that I totally fulfilled the objective of working comfortably in the sand."

Paul H. Jones

SELECTING THE TEAM

A rriving back on campus in the early afternoon, Coach Anna assembled all of the girls in the commons area for a meeting, which would shock them as much as it did her earlier when she met with Colonel Carlton. "I know all of you have been very patient with all of our visitors on campus to try to discover the benevolent person, and I am very proud of you," she stated. "We have all been very discreet regarding matters of all kinds so what I am going to tell you will also need to be retained by you with supreme discreetness."

With all the girls now hovered around her, Coach Anna told them that she had been requested to lead a mission in the southern Asian part of the world to attempt to rescue three young ladies about their age who had been abducted by terrorists and held for considerable ransom. "I have been trained to do this kind of operation," Coach Anna stated, "and the military personnel have selected me to carry out this secret mission. As part of the operation, I have been asked to select six of you to volunteer to participate with me."

"You mean we are going to be asked to rescue these three people," Dorothy excitedly stated.

Without acknowledging any more questions, Coach Anna asked, "I know you all have many questions, but at this point, how many of you would agree to go with me on this mission?"

Without hesitation all hands were quickly raised.

"After practice I will select the six of you, and following that, we shall go to the Hollow to talk to your parents," Coach Anna indicated. "We want to get back in time to go to see Maudie tonight."

Remaining in the coliseum for just a while, Coach Anna departed and went to talk to Dr. Damond. "I want to report to you concerning my meeting this morning with Colonel Bill Carlton from Fort Torman," she stated to the kind president. "I have been asked to lead a team of seven to rescue three young ladies who were abducted by terrorists in Abedistan and now are being held for a huge ransom."

"Oh! That really sounds dangerous!" he responded, while sitting heavily in his high back executive chair. "I have heard about this abduction several times in the last forty-eight hours on newscasts, and you have agreed to lead this rescue group."

"That's correct," she replied. "I have been trained to do these kinds of things, and I am in the marine reserves so I felt obligated to save these young ladies from any harm. But there is another part of this mission about which you need to know. The military wants to train six of our Bacon College athletes to make up the team to perform the rescue."

"You mean they want our girls on this group," he blurted out excitedly, as he raised up from his chair.

"That's correct," she quickly responded.

"Our girls have not got training to do this kind of thing," he immediately stated, trying to defend the notion not to use his outstanding girls in any kind of dangerous activity.

"All of the girls have agreed to go so it's up to me to select the ones I want to take," she told the president who was still trying to catch his breath. "I am going to select Esther, Dorothy, Marsha, Mit, Hanna and Maggie for my team so all of us will need your approval to be absent from the college during this period."

"The college will be very supportive of you all as you undertake this rescue effort and will continue a prayer vigil until you all return," he said to his outstanding coach, as she rose to return to the dormitory to meet with the girls in a short period.

Following practice, the girls hurriedly went back to the athletic dormitory where Coach Anna was waiting. After the girls had gotten situated, Coach Anna immediately indicated that Esther, Dorothy, Marsha, Mit, Hanna and Maggie had been selected to participate on the rescue team. "As we continue in this endeavor, we shall keep all of you apprised of our efforts," she pointed out to the others who themselves wanted actively to be involved but knew only six could go.

Those chosen were warmly and lovingly hugged by the others as tears began to roll down their cheeks. "If we leave now, we can make it to the Hollow and back to get a late dinner in the dining hall," Coach Anna indicated. "Marsha and Hanna need to get in touch with their parents tonight, and Mit, you will need to call the mission business manager in Costa Rica for him to contact your parents so they will know about this rescue endeavor."

It was a quiet group as they rode along the crooked road with steep banks toward the Hollow. The beautiful day with the bright fall sunshine helped soften the emotions of the group as they peered out the window to see their "old stomping grounds."

"What are you all doing here at this hour?" Josh yelled, as he came out of the little church and saw the Hollow girls.

All jumped out and hugged Josh and Charlene, and in a short while would be doing likewise to the other parents who were making their way toward the church on the hill.

Coach Anna and Josh had gone into the church for a brief preliminary meeting before the others arrived.

Telling Josh the plans for the rescue in just a brief time, he was shocked to hear that our military was going to use Coach Anna and the Bacon athletes to attempt to pull off such an undertaking. "I wonder why they are not using the military," Josh pointed out.

"It was my understanding that our government wants to remove the terrorists from Abedistan soon, but because the ladies are being held captive, they will have to withhold any immediate intervention " Coach Anna related. "Any military involvement might cause the two powerful controlling groups to do even more harm to their hostages at this time."

"How would this action impact on our objectives?" Josh continued to pursue meaning to the shocking news he had received.

"The divisiveness inside the country causes it to be tranquil now so our strategies can be aimed at larger and more important areas in the region," Coach Anna explained. "Military strategists want this country to be last on the list and not the first, which might really cause our weaker allies to defect."

"But why do they want to use female volunteers on this mission?" Josh asked, still not fully satisfied with the information.

"Obviously, they want to have success so they believe women can handle the chore of the rescue much more skillfully than the males," Coach Anna responded. "Females can move around more easily in the street wearing their full covering, thereby not being recognized. Once the victims have been located, a surprise rescue might be more successful than one wherein males would undertake, having to wait for a more favorable environment."

"I really respect your skills and know that the girls you select will obediently follow your lead," Josh stated.

In the church with all of the Hollow folks present, Josh told the group the reason for the meeting, and then he turned the meeting over to Coach Anna. "It's so good to see all of you again," Coach Anna said to begin her remarks. "As you know, I am in the marine reserves and a member of the green beret group. I received a call yesterday from Colonel Bill Carlton to set a meeting with me on the Blue Ridge Parkway this morning to discuss a civilian voluntary mission to rescue three young missionaries who have been abducted by a terrorist group in Abedistan. This is a small Muslim country in southern Asia that is teeming with activity as two strong groups jockey for power. At the present time it's tranquil, but our governmental personnel don't believe it will remain that way too long. One of the young ladies is the niece of our president so the captors are using these young ladies, especially her, as leverage to attempt to get us to meet their demand of a huge ransom.

"Our military strategists believe that this rescue attempt should be handled with females, if at all possible, so that is the reason I was contacted because I have extensive training in search and rescue type missions. I have been a member of a few and have led some on the field. Agreeing to lead, it was suggested that my team be made up of civilians so that is the reason I am here to get your approval to use Esther, Dorothy and Maggie from the Hollow on this group. Others on the team will be Marsha, Mit and Hanna, completing the team of seven, including myself. I thought it would be best to talk to all of you and not just the families involved because you are such a closely knit group."

All realized that it was going to be a dangerous mission as they sat quietly, and with their silence Coach Anna interpreted this to mean that there was no overt objection to her using their girls, so she continued. "The details as I know them at this juncture are that we shall go to the Charlotte airport tomorrow morning to fly to California where we rent a car to travel to Fort Santida in the Mohave Desert for a twenty-one-day training session. Upon completion of this training, we shall be able to visit Bacon College for a brief period before we move to our objective."

Remaining long enough to answer several questions with most dealing with the danger of the mission, they soon were headed back to the dormitory so that Mit, Marsha and Hanna could call their parents about the situation.

Marsha's mother, who was feeling so much better after her special treatments, was really upset, and when she began to cry, Marsha followed as tears rolled down both their cheeks. The whole scene was duplicated when Hanna advised her mother of what was being planned about the rescue. Sobbing all the while, Hanna's mom said, "I have kept up with the events on television and realize the seriousness of the terrorists' demands such that I know it will be extremely dangerous anywhere in the country much less trying to rescue the young ladies. The main good that I see is that you are going to attempt the rescue following the best strategists we have, and if you were one of the hostages, I would want our best to try to rescue you."

Mit was the last to call. The business manager was very responsive to her request, and told her that he would contact her mom and dad immediately, even if he had to take the message himself to them in the jungle of southern Costa Rica.

As they headed for dinner in the cafeteria, Esther broke away saying, "I need to make one final check of Maudie's apartment before we leave."

Inside she walked directly to her desk where she got the notebook before she called Mr. Miller.

"Hello. This is Thomas Miller. How may I help you?" he stated.

"This is Esther at Bacon College," she said.

"How are you, Esther?" he excitedly responded. "It's so good to hear from you."

"I want quickly to tell you something," Esther noted. "I am going on a mission with Coach Anna to attempt to rescue the three ladies who are being held by terrorists in Abedistan. It's a long story that I will relate to you later, but now I need to hurry so the others won't come looking for me."

"That really sounds dangerous," he stated in a shocked tone. "May I help you in this perilous venture?"

"Would you mind putting enough money in the bank in seven days for Jewel Throneberry who works for Margone Magazine? Her mother has arthritis and can't maneuver well because her house is not free of obstructions for her to move about in a wheelchair," Esther told him.

"I'll see that it's done in a timely fashion," he promptly stated.

"Thank you so much," Esther so graciously said. "Maudie is getting some better now."

"I just checked on her condition this morning, and I was told that she is making remarkable strides toward normal health," he indicated. "May God be with you on this very dangerous mission activity."

"Thank you again and may God bless you and your family," Esther stated, as they terminated their conversation.

Esther quickly typed a note to put in a brown envelope that she carried under her sweater to join the others in the dining hall for a very delicious meal, as always, prepared by the very competent cafeteria staff. Late that evening, she put the envelope on the bulletin board under a couple of administrative announcements so it would not be discovered immediately.

ARTICLE

Early the next morning the rescue training team left at five o'clock to get to Charlotte to meet their flight to Sacramento. Others throughout the country would be faced with a story in the monthly issue of the Margone Magazine written by Jewel Throneberry that would take everybody by surprise. What a demeaning article about the very wholesome group of Hollow girls! Bob and Susan recognized the article for what it was which reminded them of other past articles and statements of others about the special Hollow people. "I don't really understand why anyone would want to write any kind of article that would not be complimentary of the Hollow folks," he stated with grief to Susan, who cried when she read the story in this very popular magazine.

Sales for the Margone Magazine really soared to great numbers as the oral advertisement invited nonsubscribers to read the piece. President Damond received numerous calls with many of the people behaving very much less than cordial to the affable college leader. Also, Jewel Throneberry was receiving hundreds of telephone calls from colleagues who were applauding her for masterminding single handedly the illness charade to enter the athletic dormitory and gain the confidence of the girls. No one seemed to question the veracity of the story because her counterparts were too enamored over the ingenuity of their colleague to pull such a stunt.

Many echoed a couple of her comments in the article that, "Over the last several months all we heard about was the basketball team from the uncouth Hollow that has been so loving, caring and so humble. If we had not been taken in by the aura of it all, we could have observed much earlier a veneer that underneath harbored bitterness of the affluent society by the 'have nots' as they enjoy being dubbed. The 'poor old' syndrome lasted a long time, but now that the cat's out of the bag, one wonders what will be their next move to maintain their popular relationship with the public."

Dr. Damond was heartbroken when he read the terrible story about his basketball team, but what could he do? The students were so upset that the president held an assembly in the gymnasium that afternoon without the media. "I realize that many of you have not read the terrible article found in the Margone Magazine that was on sale today," he began his statements. "During the last several days you all have witnessed many media on campus to attempt to discover the benevolent person, and I am so proud of the way you have gone about your work by just ignoring the group. The Board of Directors gave them permission to be on campus, thinking that they would somehow find their way on site anyway so they believed that a set period would be least of the evils.

"This article was written by the assistant editor of the popular magazine allegedly composed from notes gathered when she visited the athletic dormitory. I would like to ask you. Have you all ever been in the athletic dormitory?" Following this question, every hand was raised indicating that all of them had been in the dorm at one time or the other.

"You get to see the Hollow girls each day so you should know all about them. Is this a true article about our girls?"

"Absolutely not," they screamed out.

"Do any of you know anything that would be detrimental about the Hollow girls?" he continued.

No one said a word. "The girls you know and the girls written about by Jewel Throneberry are not the same group then." he stated. "We can just cower from the terrible article and know that it will just go away, or we can stand up for our special group of girls who have done so much for all of us during the last several months."

It was a good meeting, but as Dr. Damond walked back to his office, he wondered what would possess one to write such an ugly and false story. In his office he kneeled and prayed to God to forgive the writer and to care for the girls as they continued to be derided and demeaned.

Jewel Throneberry's telephone continued to ring through the evening in her plush northern Virginia apartment. "It's so gratifying to receive encouragement from your colleagues and to be congratulated by them," she thought, as she went to sleep that night. Sales continued to be brisk and other writers and television personnel wanted to expand on the story by clamoring for interviews with the other girls, the staff at Bacon College and the president himself.

Dr. Damond had used the press conference in recent months to get information to the media in a fair manner, so following all the inquiries the next morning, he scheduled a meeting with the media in the gymnasium but not before he met with the students again. Of course, there were many media already on campus but from afar came many more for his eleven o'clock conference.

Standing before the media surrounded by his students and his entire staff, he began his statement without notes that he usually carried with him on such an occasion. "Thank you all for coming this morning. I have received so many inquiries about the college's reaction to the story published in the Margone Magazine that was distributed yesterday. Let me start by saying to you that the story is totally false. There is not a shred of truth in it.

"Having said that, let me approach this terrible injustice in another way. I am older than most of you so I have a longer and probably a richer history of the emergence of the media as a force in shaping our society. During the last several years, it seems that the floodgate has been opened to stretch even the more zealous communicators' creative minds of delivering stories that whet the appetite of those who have learned well that 'if you want to do it, do it.' Responsible writing can't keep pace with smear print in our free enterprise program that is the backbone of our democracy that is driven by competition.

"Our nature is sin and anything in print that is demeaning or approaching derogation of people or concepts, we are attracted to it. The insatiable thirst for this kind of message causes all of us to lean in that direction. As I ponder the past, examine the present and look to the future, it does not look promising to have a balance of the guaranteed freedom of the press without disturbing the peace and tranquility we all should experience in this great land. Our forefathers certainly did not envision that our press would squander its responsibility just to be more competitive, and yes, to gain more income from its endeavor.

"Just turn in your newspaper, watch on television, or read your magazines, and you will see the level we have gotten. It's not a beautiful sight. Who would have ever thought that our precious media would be the dregs of our society by displaying scandalous behavior under the cloak of enjoying freedom of the press? At what point does the freedom of the press confront the individuals' rights? Has the media gotten so powerful it's out of control? Can misused words ever be retracted and removed from the minds of all of those who read them in the first place? A writer each time has the responsibility of making a first good impression, and this is repeated in each story or article. But the impressions many times are those similar to the story that so many people have read in the Margone Magazine, and the people rush to read, having confidence in the writer that it is accurate. It's my understanding that more people have purchased this publication than any other in its lucrative history.

"I know the young writer is proud this morning about the huge sales. In her mind though she has to have some empathy about those whom the story was written. We will all pray for her and please know that she has been forgiven.

"If you have questions, I will respond to them at this time," he stated.

With several wanting to ask a question at one time, he acknowledged a young reporter in the front. "Are you saying that this story in Margone Magazine is not true?"

"That is right," he emphatically stated. "There is no truth in it at all."

"Why do you think this story was written about your girls?" an elderly gentleman asked.

"It's my opinion that the writer was driven by a competitive spirit to prepare a story better and more popular than anyone else on the subject of the benevolent person who gives to the college," he pointed out. "I am sure that numerous stories are written by overzealous persons, but this one is so hurtful because it's about the most humble and kind group of girls to be found in the world."

"What do you plan to do about this story?" another reporter asked.

"I don't plan to do anything," he said. "To do anything would make us appear to be in the same category as the writer. I have heard all my life that two wrongs don't make one right, and to take any kind of legal action would only make the college as irresponsible as the writer of this terrible story."

Following many questions, Dr. Damond closed the conference as the reporters headed to transmit the stories to their editors. All the students and staff gathered around their leader and gave him many hugs of encouragement.

HEADED FOR TRAINING

In Charlotte Coach Anna received the briefcase
from a young man who discreetly sat near them in
the terminal while they waited for their flight.
Soon, without saying a word, he got up leaving his case for
her to take to their destination. On the flight to Chicago
Coach Anna and her team examined the contents of the
briefcase. There were several maps of Abedistan and
surrounding areas, much information about the people and
several documents advising of the type of government. A
long historical narrative of the whole area, which revealed
the origin of the hostility among the various factions that
were vying for control of the whole region, also, was
included.

Changing flights in Chicago without being detected,
they boarded for their last leg to Sacramento. Fearing that
they would be overheard, there was little talk among the
group, although Coach Anna could tell that there were many
unanswered questions for the team. It seemed like a short
flight as they arrived in the early afternoon according to
California time.

Obtaining a rental van they headed for Fort Santida to
the east in the Mohave Desert. It was nearly dark when they
finally approached the gate where two soldiers in full field

gear armed with assault rifles looked into their vehicle. With one on one side of the vehicle and the other on the opposite side, Coach Anna said, "I am Major Bosley of the green beret reporting with my team for training," as she handed the guard her official identification.

Checking the identification carefully, the soldier stepped back and saluted with a return salute from Coach Anna. "We have been expecting you," the young sergeant stated. "We are proud to meet you. I have a jeep escort arriving immediately to take to your quarters."

The young man in the jeep was very excited to meet the group because he had heard rumors of their being trained at their base. Soon they were taken to a small building with several rooms surrounding a large commons area. "These will be your quarters while you are here," the young soldier stated. "Colonel Samson will meet with you later this evening to discuss your schedule for the next several days."

"Thank you for your assistance," Coach Anna said.

Before he departed he smartly clicked his heals together, braced at attention and saluted Major Bosley, his superior officer.

Following a good meal in the chow hall, the group returned to their barracks to continue to examine the documents from the briefcase. "How long will the training last?" Dorothy asked.

"It is my understanding that our whole crash course will take three weeks," Coach Anna stated.

"What kinds of things do you think we shall need to learn?" Marsha asked.

"It would be my guess that because we are here in the desert, we shall have to learn to survive in this environment in the first place," Coach Anna responded. "Secondly, we shall be taught how to parachute out of an airplane, and thirdly, the most important activity will be to learn how to

conduct a rescue under different conditions and
circumstances."

"Have you ever done any of this kind of training?"
Mit asked somewhat excitedly.

"I received most of this training earlier when I was
on active duty in the marines, but only a little training
directly related to the desert environment," Coach Anna
answered. "We'll be learning this part mostly together."

"They call you major here," Hanna noted. "Should
we call you major or Coach Anna as we usually do?"

"I am an officer, a major, in the marine corps," she
stated.

"Why do others salute you?" Dorothy asked.

Chuckling just a little, Coach Anna said, "The
marines are made up of enlisted personnel and officers, and
all enlisted soldiers are required to salute all officers.
Because I am a major in the marines, enlisted personnel
salute when they see me."

"Do we have to salute you now that we are in
training?" Dorothy asked, while showing a wide grin on her
face.

"I don't think that will be required," Coach Anna
answered, chuckling just a little herself.

In a short while Colonel Samson came along with a
major, and two captains dressed in their field camouflage
uniforms, and each was carrying a briefcase. "My name is
Roland Samson, and these three men with me are Gregory
Livermon, Jimmy Steele and Landon Ettleton," Colonel
Samson stated, making introductions of the military players
at this juncture.

"I am Anna Bosley and my team members are Esther
Minold, Dorothy Buford, Maggie Morrow, Hanna Green,
Mit Travers and Marsha Gavanto," Coach Anna stated. "We
are all from Bacon College."

"We are so glad that you all volunteered to
participate in this very important mission," Colonel Samson

related, as he directed them to sit around the large table almost in the middle of the room. "From time to time in our unsettled world we find some of our citizens caught by those who want to do evil, and for us now we have three young missionaries being held captive by terrorists in Abedistan. This one is a little different from the others, because this country is harboring the most notorious terrorists of them all, so our government is planning a military assault on these evil people and those who would hide them. Our training will equip you to rescue these three people now being held for a huge ransom by this terrorist group."

"We have volunteered to be of service in this capacity," Coach Anna stated with much pride. "This group I have will do an excellent job."

"I have heard a lot about them during the last twenty-four hours," Colonel Samson stated. "I believe we have the right group to do the job."

"We will certainly do our best," Coach Anna responded.

"The reason why we are using women as you were told earlier is to effect a surprise of monumental proportions," the colonel said, as he looked directly at the team. "Women in this country have much less freedom to express themselves than what we have in our society, so you ladies can no doubt use the element of surprise to good advantage. I will warn you right off though that to get you prepared will be a grueling experience, because we want you to get maximum training such that you will be able to fulfill the mission successfully.

"Before I say anything else, I want to give you all a geography lesson of the area so that you will have it in mind exactly where you are going in the world." Placing several maps on the wall and two spread on the table, the colonel began his first lesson. "You will note that Abedistan is a very small country in southern Asia with one river located in the south. For the most part the country is desert; thus, our desert here will be your training environment for the next several days. Three million people live in this small country with most of them living in two large cities in the northeast. The troublesome area is to the west where a terrorist network resides and trains, and where several small towns are located that are inhabited by native Abedistanies of eastern European descent. They are very tolerant and are willing to live among the terrorists for fear of physical reprisals, if they show signs of discontent.

"In the last report we received on our captives, they were being held by these western terrorists in the small town called Moraba. Keep this town in mind as you continue your training these weeks. It is a desert village with sand everywhere. At this time of year it's hot in the day and very cool at night. While Abedistan is very small, there is a lot of territory that is barren or open that you may be able to use to good advantage. Not all of the people are terrorists because there are many peaceful citizens, but the terrorists are very militant and have control of this western sector of the country. The balance of power between the east and west has prevented general chaos until this point in time. The capture of the young ladies was a statement by the terrorists that our country must not actively get involved in the affairs of this part of the world.

"I want you to spend much time studying these various maps along with notes and demographic data of the area. Tomorrow you will begin your training, which will be an assessment of your current physical conditioning, and this will start at 4:00 a.m. Following our meeting, you will report to the quartermaster for field apparel for the training. Everyone knows you are here and will expedite all of your requests so you will have maximum training time. I will meet with you at the end of each of your next several days, but for now, do you have questions?"

"You have not mentioned the type of rescue we will be conducting," Coach Anna stated. "Is that already set or will we develop our own plan as we participate in the training?"

"You all will develop several different scenarios along the way and during your exit discussion, all of us will evaluate the various approaches."

After much questioning and discussion about the mission, Colonel Samson decided that they had enough for this evening so they could get to the quartermaster for training gear. But first he wanted Major Bosley to tell just a little about the astute and attentive young ladies she had chosen for her team.

"I would love to do that," Coach Anna happily stated. "Marsha here is from New Mexico, a freshman at Bacon who led her high school team to the state championship in soccer. To her left is Mit who is a native Virginian but grew up in the jungle area of the southern zone of Costa Rica. She led her jungle team twice to the country's Junior Olympic soccer championship, and prior to that, she did the same thing for her missionary kids' school, winning the countrywide high school championship. Sitting beside Mit is Hanna, who is our manager and also is from Virginia and is a very good basketball player and a good foul shooter. From time to time we use her in games even with her bad knee. The other three, Dorothy, Maggie and Esther, are from the Hollow in southwest Virginia, and they have never lost a basketball game since they began to play. Esther is the top basketball player in the country. All of these young ladies are excellent students and have outstanding character, very obedient, and strongly committed to meeting a goal."

"You have an excellent team," Colonel Samson stated. "We know you very well from your past record, and we have seen some of your girls play on television so we know too that they can get the job done. What an exciting and competent group you have who volunteered to execute this rescue! I applaud you very much. Let me remind you of something you already know that this is a very dangerous mission that will require patience, endurance and finesse."

The team was up early the next morning to dress and be prepared for the four-o'clock rendezvous in front of their quarters. They really looked sharp in their camouflage outfits including caps and light weight shoes. Outside they were greeted by a young drill sergeant who was superbly physically fit. "The initial phase of your training is going to be an assessment of your physical fitness to determine your stamina and will power to persevere under extreme duress," he related in a commanding voice. "We will be running five-mile segments with a short water break at the termination of each. Upon completion of this part you will have breakfast in the chow hall followed by a very brief respite after which more specific physical training will be conducted."

The running phase went very well as the sergeant was amazed how well the girls could run the long distance without appearing to be too tired. "You all are in excellent physical shape," he said, as they finished their objective around the running paths through the sand.

A delicious breakfast was served to the group as they went through the line and then sat in a corner area. Many marines were also present, and they all wondered who was this new group of young ladies. It didn't take long for them to discover that they were from Bacon College and being led by Major Bosley whom all knew because of her previous most excellent training records and earlier heroic exploits. Before breakfast was over, most of the other marines came over to speak to the group.

The remainder of the morning session involved all kinds of physical activities including rope climbing, wall climbing, crawling under and over logs, swinging on ropes and simulating parachute jumps from a tower. At the end of the day they were ready for quiet time in their quarters. But that would not be the case as Colonel Samson and his group came back to discuss the mission plan further and the characteristics of the environment in that part of the world.

"I am told that your team is very physically fit as you all passed the introductory phase with most outstanding marks," he happily reported. "No wonder you all never lose a game because you just over power your opponent with continuous effort."

"The girls really like to practice to get better and better," Major Bosley noted.

"Tomorrow you will run again in the early morning, and in fact for the next several mornings you will run before breakfast," Colonel Samson pointed out. "We don't have much time to get you ready so tomorrow after breakfast we are going to work more on the parachuting phase of your training. Your entrance into Abedistan will be by parachuting in during the night, so I want you to keep this in mind as you continue your training. This will be one of the most critical parts of your schooling here, so we will continue it until we are satisfied that you have become very skillful. I am told by our leaders that you all do not grumble or complain, and in fact, the drill sergeants tell me that you rarely spoke aloud all day long during your first day of training. Also, they have been surprised as to the strength of your group, because they thought when they first saw you that your group of young ladies would not be able to do the kinds of things demanded in this training. They have been very pleasantly surprised. Your first day of training has far exceeded the efforts of any group we have had come through this special program of military training."

"When requested to assume leadership in this mission, I knew my chance of success would be enhanced with this special group of girls," Coach Anna stated proudly.

"They are quick learners, very obedient and as you have discovered, a very strong group."

A much more detailed educational session was conducted by Colonel Samson and his staff, including showing a video about Abedistan and its people. "Try to remember all you can about this area," Colonel Samson pointed out. "This and other videos will be shown to you several times so that you will have a good understanding of that part of the world, and more specifically of Moraba."

This was a long session extending almost to midnight. As soon as the training team left, the girls prepared for bed but not before asking Coach Anna, "Have you ever jumped out of an airplane before?"

"In my previous training in the green beret I jumped many times," she replied. "After the first jump you forget about the fear because it's such an exhilarating experience. After we felt comfortable, we began to learn how to do more precision landing in parachute jumps. With what we are going to be asked to do, I am sure we shall be trained to guide our chutes to a specific landing target."

"It's going to be an interesting experience," Dorothy said, as they went to bed.

Following the marathon running and breakfast, they were back at the parachute jump training area where they took turns learning how to initiate a jump and how to land safely. Up the tower they went and down they jumped time after time until they satisfied their instructors that they were competent.

This day was a long period of training so when they entered the chow hall that evening, they were somewhat tired. Following a little rest after dinner, they were again faced with the educational phase of their training.

About mid morning the next day, they were loading the propeller driven aircraft with their parachutes strapped on for their first parachute jump. "On this jump the only objective is to follow through on all of your instructions and exercise supreme caution when landing," the young sergeant pointed out, trying to remove as many obstacles as possible from the minds of the Bacon team on this initial jump.

Reaching sufficient altitude, Coach Anna and the girls were instructed to hook up and upon command, Coach Anna led her troops out the side door. Coach Anna opened her parachute quickly and steered away from the plane to observe her girls as they fell through the air headed for the desert floor. "They look like professionals," Coach Anna thought, as she watched her girls settle in after their parachutes were deployed for a breathtaking journey to the sand.

After landing more skillfully than the training officials expected, they gathered up their chutes and headed for an enjoyable rendezvous with Coach Anna. "It was fun," Dorothy stated excitedly, as they grouped for prayer led by Esther.

"Did any of you experience any difficulty?" Coach Anna asked.

Seeing that all of them were sporting a wide smile told the whole story, as their first parachute jump was a time that all would remember all their days to come. "We need to go for a debriefing and later prepare for a second jump today with more specific landing instructions," Coach Anna related to her team.

"Precision jumping is a little more difficult," the instructor indicated. "For your team it's imperative that you land exactly where you have your target, because there is only a small window where it's safe." Spending much time on what to expect when the cords were pulled, they soon learned that they were capable of guiding their parachute to a specific target.

There was less anxiety on this second jump that was scheduled to evaluate their skill in landing at a specific location. A large white target was affixed to the ground so each one began to maneuver in that direction as soon as the chute was fully deployed. With the wind blowing a little stronger than usual, they were getting a good test of their knowledge at the early stage of their training. Coach Anna, Esther and Mit hit the target and Marsha, Hanna and Maggie came very close, but Dorothy's chute was caught with a sudden gust of wind, which caused her to miss the objective by several yards. Being pleased with their initial efforts, Coach Anna said, "You guys really did an excellent job in finding and hitting the target."

"Well, you might say all but one did a good job," Dorothy said with a huge grin on her face. "I'll know next time how to maneuver my chute against the wind."

The other girls hugged Dorothy and each other, and Coach Anna prayed to God asking that He continue to look after them during the remainder of their training and on the mission itself. All of the officials were delighted about the excellent progress of the team shown in their various activities during the next few days.

Soon they reached the night jumping phase, which resulted in some trepidation by the girls even though the instructors had said that their parachute training to this point was excellent. "An electronic homing device will be used on the ground that will send signals back to you as you descend so your target will be a listening location and not something visual as your previous targets were," the sergeant noted. "The beeping sound will be picked up by a wrist device, and in addition to beeping sounds, you will learn how to read the red signal emanating from your watch like instrument.

All strapped on their instruments and the leader placed the homing device near the side of the room. Walking toward the device caused their arm instrument to beep more frequently, and likewise, when they moved away, the frequency was reduced. "You will need to learn to let these signals guide you through the night sky to your destination," the sergeant pointed out.

Having a few minutes before they departed, Coach Anna got her Bible and read Psalms 121:

1 A song of ascents. I lift up my eyes to the hills-- where does my help come from?
2 My help comes from the LORD, the Maker of heaven and earth.
3 He will not let your foot slip-- he who watches over you will not slumber;
4 indeed, he who watches over Israel will neither slumber nor sleep.
5 The LORD watches over you-- the LORD is your shade at your right hand;
6 the sun will not harm you by day, nor the moon by night.
7 The LORD will keep you from all harm-- he will watch over your life;
8 the LORD will watch over your coming and going both now and forevermore.

"It is always comforting to read from the scripture to see what God has included in the Holy Bible to be our guide as we live on His good earth," Coach Anna stated before she asked Mit to pray for the group.

Boarding the plane for their excursion through the beautiful night desert sky, they aligned themselves in the usual manner. "You will leave the plane west of your target so the prevailing desert winds will help you toward your target," the sergeant explained. "Your compass on your wrist will provide guiding assistance as you move toward your destination. When you have landed, engage your sensor button on your wrist instrument and insert your earphone, and this signal will help you to assemble quickly with your leader."

The quietness of the night was eerie as the seven team members headed toward their target using their compass and listening to the rhythm of the beeps coming from their wrist instrument. "Knowing how to interpret the beeping sounds and translate them into distances was going to take a little time," Esther thought, as she tugged on her parachute cords to direct her descent. Each placed a marker where she landed, and then immediately hastened to a rendezvous point.

The next morning they flew over the landing area and examined the location of the various landing sites of each of the girls. Later, they assembled in the meeting room to show on a topographic map the distance of each from the homing device. "We will continue to address this part of your training until you all are landing within several yards of the target," the Colonel said to his trainees.

Night landings were really improving such that they were moving on to the next phase of their training. One night Colonel Carlton came to the meeting of the group and really surprised them with his request. "We have to step up our training such that the length of time is reduced by one week. Do you all think that will be possible?" he asked.

Colonel Samson immediately responded, "The team has expertly handled all facets of the training thus far so I believe this can be done."

"Our government has learned through our intelligence that there is some unrest in the western sector which leads them to believe that there may be an attack on the border country," Colonel Carlton indicated. "Their whole conduct has changed since they have begun to hold the three missionaries hostage. They believe that we and our allies will be reluctant to fight back in case of an attack, if they are holding these three young ladies."

"When do you think this team should be ready?" Colonel Samson asked.

"If they could be ready to fly out on Wednesday of next week, that would be great," Colonel Carlton stated. "I will get you all full details by Monday about their schedule. The air force is primed and ready to deliver the team to its target, and will be on standby to pick them up upon successful fulfillment of the mission."

Much discussion was generated before they concluded their session. Immediately following, Colonel Samson pointed out that they would begin a mock exercise on this night to evaluate not only their skills, but also to assess the viability of the strategies that they had planned to effect a successful rescue.

Following dinner in the chow hall, the team assembled with Colonel Samson again to go over the plans for this part of the training. "You will drop in tonight and move toward your objective before we pick you up," he told the group. "Starting tonight you will wear and carry with you the same things you will have in your possession when you parachute into Abedistan. Once you get on the ground, you will dig a hole to bury your parachute and don your full burqua, the typical dress of women when they are seen in public. This robe like dress is not what one would select to use in war games, but it is very important that you all wear them until you make the rescue. At this juncture Major Bosley will be the only one to carry a weapon, an automatic assault rifle that will be strapped out of sight on her side under her burqua. Each of you will be carrying tear gas canisters and a gas mask along with several other supplies that we shall discuss later. For tonight you will go through the exercise to learn as much as you can while thinking of other strategies that might be even more effective. This is just a 'walk through' this time, but starting tomorrow night, you will be situated in a more realistic setting. Best of luck to you all! You are doing a splendid job."

The night jump was conducted without a hitch with the entire group landing almost perfectly. Disposing of their parachutes and donning their new outfits, they assembled, checked their compass and headed stealthily toward the outskirts of the village. Traveling quietly over the sand dunes, they finally reached their destination. "Each of you did an excellent job," Coach Anna said, praising the group.

All during the next day they practiced dispensing tear gas and using their gas masks over and over again. A metal detector was used in their training to detect land mines, and they were schooled in how not to come in contact with these deadly underground explosives. The debate among the officials regarding the girls being issued a weapon was finally going to be settled by the team itself.

Meeting with the team just before lunch, Coach Anna asked the girls, "There is considerable discussion among our leaders regarding your welfare during this operation. Some seemed to think that you all should carry a weapon such as a pistol with you as we attempt to effect this rescue. What do you girls think?"

"I have never held a gun in my life," Dorothy indicated in a high pitched voice.

"Do you think you would like to have one on this mission?" Coach Anna asked.

"I was hoping that we could get the missionaries without hurting anyone," Dorothy responded, as the others listened.

"That is certainly our objective but in reality this may not be able to happen," Coach Anna stated. "These young captives may be confronted with all kinds of terrible treatment and even might be tortured as we speak to get them to make a statement in support of the captors' cause. Freeing them as soon as possible might prevent them from being subjected to further torturous behavior. When we confront the enemy, can we remove the young missionaries from their grasp with your using firearms or with my having the only weapon? This is the question you need to help me answer."

There was a long silence and then Esther made a statement. "Not having a weapon will cause us to think more creatively how to subdue the terrorists on the one hand, but on the other one might need some way to cause our enemy to follow our commands. It is through strength that others respond, not through weakness. Are we strong enough without external assistance to command obedience of those bent on doing evil? A weapon unto itself is benign until it's used by the possessor, but the threat of its use might be enough to cause one to change his course of action. I have never held a gun in my entire life, and if I had my way, I would never hold one, but I now find myself functioning in different circumstances and in a different environment. I volunteered for this rescue, and it would be my wish that the officials would equip us with whatever wherewithal to effect a successful rescue of our neighbors being held captive against their wishes."

"What a powerful statement," Coach Anna thought, as she waited for the reaction of the other members of the group who were strong individuals in their own right. Esther over the years seemed to know how to ferret out the components of an issue, and she had stepped up again on this day to do the same. Soon all the others were echoing her sentiments so it was unanimous that they would be equipped with whatever the officials believed would give them an advantage in the mission.

Nervousness was in vogue on the firing range, but soon they were showing more skill in handling their military pistols that would be strapped around their waist. Coach Anna really felt more comfortable with their having a pistol on this rescue, and as the group continued to train by shooting at targets, she could see that the girls were feeling more at ease with the weapons.

Their gear load was increasing such that a backpack was added to their wherewithal to carry all of their supplies. During the parachute jump, they were instructed to strap it in front until they were on the ground. On this night they were carrying sufficient sustenance for a three-day supply as they were going to conduct a mock rescue on the third day, including a helicopter rescue of the whole group. The signal beam would be picked up by satellite and transmitted to a ship in the Indian Ocean that in turn would relay to an air force unit stationed in a neighboring country. On this day this aircraft would come from the base.

"Check your bags carefully girls," Coach Anna rather loudly called out to the team. "Be sure you have water, high energy bars, and other things on the list so we will be adequately supplied on our three-day mock session." Coach Anna and the other team members knew that each time they were involved in another phase of their training, they were getting closer and closer to the real thing.

MOCK RESCUE

The night jump went well so after their rendezvous they quickly and quietly headed east this time to plan a mock rescue in the village. Entering the edge of the small cardboard town, they moved behind a tall wall and waited for the sun to come up. Coach Anna pulled out a map and they all examined it carefully. Marking their location on the map, Coach Anna used her finger to trace where they thought the missionaries were being held. Obviously, it was several hundred yards farther into the small village where they would encounter the enemy.

"I believe in Abedistan there will be many people, especially women, in the streets visiting the markets each day so we can attempt to walk among them to discover as much as we can," Coach Anna pointed out to the girls. "We'll need to remain hidden here to see whether or not this mock rescue includes people on the street. If not, we'll just stay here and after dark make our way to a location near the place where we believe they are being held captive. We need patience so just relax and wait for a time when we can move forward into the city."

The sun continued to boil down as it got higher and higher in the sky. It was during the afternoon that Coach

Anna thought, "They are really testing us on this training session to see how patient we are." From time to time soldiers pretending to be Abedistanies could be heard talking and sometimes singing across the sand street from the team. The team was really hunkered down such that no one was going to discover them on this day.

As soon as dark prevailed, Coach Anna led her team around the back side of the buildings feeling her way all the while. "It's really rough going," Coach Anna thought, as they quietly made their way through the mock village hardly making a sound. It was past midnight before they finally reached the point that Coach Anna believed was the location of those being held captive. Soon they slept while sitting up against a low wall to the rear of what they believed would be a high traffic area at daybreak.

Using binoculars as soon as the sun came over the horizon, Coach Anna could see several soldiers around a building near the site where they believed the missionaries were being held. Getting out the map, she further refined her thinking by pinpointing the building on the map, which coincided with what she thought was the one being surrounded by soldiers. "This one is it," Coach Anna noted. "I want each of you during the day to examine the building and surroundings so that we can develop our strategy for the rescue that will take place tonight."

Patiently and quietly they waited all day, and now it was time to solidify their strategy that would be used. "Based on our observation on and off all day, there are two soldiers on the roof area and two stationed out front of the chambers, I believe, in which the missionaries are located," Coach Anna stated. "I want you Dorothy to lead the team of Marsha, and Maggie to overpower the two on top, and Esther, you, Hanna and Mit will be responsible to overwhelm the two guarding the door of what I believe is the prison. It will be a secret attack wherein we should overcome our adversaries by being in their presence before they are aware that we are there. If you need to use your pistols, remember that they have blanks on this rescue but will contain live ammunition later."

At exactly one o'clock a.m. the group began to crawl toward their objective. The soldiers were weary such that they didn't suspect anything was taking place around them. Dorothy led her group quietly up the steps on the side where she peeked over the final step to see the silhouette of the two leaning against what appeared to be a guardrail. Pointing her laser beam toward Coach Anna, she indicated that they were ready for their part of the attack. Esther had done likewise so Coach Anna stood back with her assault rifle ready, as she flashed her laser beam signal to her two leaders.

Dorothy, Marsha, and Maggie quickly pounced on the two soldiers on the roof area and soon subdued them. All three ran down the steps and assisted Esther, Hanna and Mit in the actual rescue. Dragging the dummy missionaries behind them as they fled, Coach Anna turned and fired a long volley of rounds in the night sky just as they scampered behind the nearest wall. Making their way to the outside perimeter of the village, they were soon in the desert walking in a plodding fashion through the sand. Over the first sand dune they all lay on the slope with each in her own way evaluating the mock rescue to this point.

The search continued in the village for a long time, but the Bacon team was far into the desert, preparing to signal the rescue craft to remove them from the mock enemy this time. Safely back at the base, they were immediately whisked into the conference room to evaluate what had just taken place.

After passing out water and colas to the group, the officials began a critique of the morning's rescue. "What did you think of the mock rescue?" Colonel Samson asked Major Bosley.

"We had to ad-lib just a little because during the day there were no people in the streets so we turned to our map and our own observation to discover as much as we could," Coach Anna replied.

"All of us gave you all an excellent grade on this part of your training," the colonel said. "The make-believe Abedistany soldiers were most complimentary of your efforts. They were surprised how strong the girls are and the fierceness they went about their job."

"They did an excellent job and followed the directions perfectly," Coach Anna stated in praising the group.

"One thing that really baffled the mock soldiers was when you fired that volley of shots from your assault rifle," Colonel Samson said. "They wanted to know why you decided to do that."

"It was so very dark, and during the whole process of capturing the missionaries, not a single shot was fired," Coach Anna explained. "There were two reasons I did this. First, I wanted the enemy to know that we were armed with more than hand guns which might cause a short delay, giving us just a little more time to get away. Secondly, I thought it might be good for the girls to hear the sound of an automatic rifle up close in this make-believe activity, which might give us a little edge later on when we are engaged in the real thing."

During the final two days they reviewed all areas of their training, including assembling their equipment and supplies that they would need to take with them. Finally, they were given an itinerary, which included a brief stopover at Bacon College for them to say good-bye to their teammates and others.

"It was going to be good to be home," they thought, as they boarded their military aircraft to Mateland Air Force Base and then by helicopter to the college.

BACK AT BACON

There had been much activity around Bacon College during their absence. Not only had the various television personnel left the campus, but to get things back to normal, the Board of Directors decided to close the campus to the media except those who had specific approval from the president. All thought this was a good decision because the small campus had really been overrun by the media during the last thirty days or so. But this wasn't the big news.

The terrible story written by Jewel Throneberry had been retracted and a follow-up story in the popular Margone Magazine related the whole scenario of the writer's visit to the athletic dormitory. Not only did the follow-up story appear as its lead article, but announcements were placed in other media advising of the fabrication in the initial story. It was truly a strong effort on the part of the magazine to correct a grievous error. "The story that was written about the wonderful and charming group of girls and included in our Margone Magazine was a faux pas of mass proportions," she stated clearly in her magazine. "President Damond of Bacon College said it best when trying to determine why one, such as I, would write such an untrue story as he said,

'In our society sometimes we are driven by competition and greed beyond the scope of our integrity to write articles that are totally fabricated.' His description clearly describes me and my effort to elevate myself and that of our magazine.

"In a few days after the article was published and the congratulatory comments had ceased, I began to think about the situation. I had never stooped to this low level of journalism before so I was beginning to feel the agony of guilt that was overtaking my entire being. But it wasn't until the local bank called to advise me that money had been placed in a special account by the benevolent person to be used to renovate my house to make it handicap accessible so my make-believe arthritic mother could be independently mobile, that I reached the lowest level. My guilt spilled out in my living room of my apartment in the form of tears that flowed freely. From this time I began to attempt to expunge the words of the despicable article."

Trying to blot out the ugly tattoo of demeaning words was going to be impossible, but she was giving a good effort. Visiting the campus before the ban of the media, she went to apologize to the president and his staff, got an audience with the students to ask for their forgiveness and then visited the athletic dormitory to talk to the girls. With the girls, soon in her remarks to them she realized that they were not even aware of the ugly article so they were totally impervious to what she was trying to say to them. "How innocent and pure they are," she thought, as she hugged them over and over again. "All of you are not here," Jewel said.

"Some of the group are not here at the present time, but will return in a few days," Jonsie stated.

When the rescue team of girls arrived, they immediately went to see Dr. Damond in his office to tell about their training and to advise him of their schedule. "I am so glad that you are back," he stated, as he hugged each one of the rescue team. "How did the training go?"

"The girls did an exceptional job on every phase of the training, including the night guided parachute jumps," Coach Anna said. "We are genuinely prepared to attempt the rescue of the young ladies."

"They are still being held captive by the terrorists, and their demands are being expanded each day," Dr. Damond told the girls. "It's really a very unsettled part of the world where I would not want to be at any time much less now. I am so proud of you all for volunteering to do what needs to be done to save these three missionaries from what many believe in the end will be a sure death, if they remain in the hands of the terrorists."

"We have trained hard during these past several days successfully to effect a rescue," Coach Anna reacted.

"It was only during the last few days while the television personnel were present that several noticed that you girls were not present on campus," Dr. Damond stated. "I am sure that many questions regarding your whereabouts will be forthcoming later."

"We are sorry that you will have the burden of talking to the media," Coach Anna responded. "You do such a masterful job with this though."

"When do you leave for Abedistan and how long will you all be gone?" he asked.

"We leave tomorrow morning, and it's my understanding that the maximum amount of time to effect a successful rescue has been set at three weeks," Coach Anna answered.

Soon their conversation with the very affable and humble president was over, and the group went to the athletic dormitory before going to see Maudie and later visiting the Hollow. Reports from the hospital indicated that Maudie was improving slowly, and would be able to go home in several more days. Two by two the girls visited and found her to be sitting up and very alert. Her tearful eyes sent a strong message of love for each tandem, and when

Esther entered alone to embrace and talk to her dear friend, tears just rolled down their cheeks.

"It's so good to see that you are feeling better," Esther said. "We all love you so very much."

"I love you all, my only family," she replied. "I am the luckiest person on earth to have such a wonderful group of friends who could have any friends on earth, but you have chosen me."

"You are the best of the world's people," Esther said. "That's the reason we love you so much."

"Thank you all very much," Maudie said.

"I have been doing your benevolent work as best that I can," Esther told her.

"Thomas tells me each day what a splendid job you are doing," Maudie said. "I want you to continue with me in this capacity because you do such an excellent job in fulfilling the objectives of the benevolent person."

"I feel so inadequate trying to do something that you do so very perfectly," Esther noted, praising the impeccable character of her friend.

"Thomas was really elated over the latest benevolent act of genius you initiated which resulted in a change of attitude of journalists near and far," Maudie related.

"It was not a stroke of genius as you might think but one of being naïve of worldliness," Esther pointed out.

"I know that, but because of your naiveté, the outcome emerged that shocked the secular world," Maudie countered. "You are my precious friend whom I admire so very much."

"Several of us have volunteered to go to Abedistan to rescue three young missionaries who are being held hostage by terrorists," Esther stated. "Maggie, Dorothy, Marsha, Hanna, Mit and I join Coach Anna on this team."

"Oh! I can't believe you are doing that! I have read much about this abduction and have heard and seen much on television so you are really flying into very dangerous territory," Maudie anxiously related. "Their value of life is different from our culture so please be extremely careful. I never cease to be amazed at what lengths all of the Hollow folks go to meet Jesus' guidelines of helping your neighbor."

They both hugged ever so hard and warmly before Esther departed her hospital room to join the others waiting in the hall. "Maudie is doing so much better," Esther said, as she walked out with the team of girls.

In the Hollow after the greetings, Josh conducted a service recognizing the rescue team by commissioning them to assist the young ladies who found themselves in harm's way while fulfilling the command of Jesus as expressed in Matthew 28. He continued his message by including thoughts taken from the scripture that he read from Proverbs 11:

1 The LORD abhors dishonest scales, but accurate weights are his delight.

2 When pride comes, then comes disgrace, but with humility comes wisdom.

3 The integrity of the upright guides them, but the unfaithful are destroyed by their duplicity.

4 Wealth is worthless in the day of wrath, but righteousness delivers from death.

5 The righteousness of the blameless makes a straight way for them, but the wicked are brought down by their own wickedness.

6 The righteousness of the upright delivers them, but the unfaithful are trapped by evil desires.

7 When a wicked man dies, his hope perishes; all he expected from his power comes to nothing.

8 The righteous man is rescued from trouble, and it comes on the wicked instead.

9 With his mouth the godless destroys his neighbor, but through knowledge the righteous escape.

10 When the righteous prosper, the city rejoices; when the wicked perish, there are shouts of joy.
11 Through the blessing of the upright a city is exalted, but by the mouth of the wicked it is destroyed.
12 A man who lacks judgment derides his neighbor, but a man of understanding holds his tongue.
13 A gossip betrays a confidence, but a trustworthy man keeps a secret.
14 For lack of guidance a nation falls, but many advisers make victory sure.
15 He who puts up security for another will surely suffer, but whoever refuses to strike hands in pledge is safe.
16 A kindhearted woman gains respect, but ruthless men gain only wealth.
17 A kind man benefits himself, but a cruel man brings trouble on himself.
18 The wicked man earns deceptive wages, but he who sows righteousness reaps a sure reward.
19 The truly righteous man attains life, but he who pursues evil goes to his death.
20 The LORD detests men of perverse heart but he delights in those whose ways are blameless.

Josh told them in life in following the will of God by adhering to the commands by Jesus, we could not pick and choose to select only the safe and easier chores, but we have to be brave and move forward with talents God has so graciously given to us to overcome the forces of evil. Sometimes the challenges of life place us on the edge where our efforts are met by those who have interests not in keeping with those who seek peace and tranquility among mankind.

It was a very emotional time for all of them in the Hollow but especially so for James, Corbin, Jean, Josh and Charlene, whose children were on this secret mission.

Back at the dormitory they headed toward the dining hall for dinner where the other students greeted the rescue team by singing the school song and rendering several impromptu cheers to the embarrassment of the entire team. They were all surprised when Hanna's mom and dad came into the cafeteria to be greeted so lovingly by their daughter, a member of the rescue group. Later in the evening Coach Anna's mother and father drove down from northern Virginia to be with their daughter on the eve of their departure.

A festive evening for sure in the dormitory attended by several unexpected guests who had heard news of the clandestine rescue attempt by the Bacon girls was a good send off. The school district personnel including Glenn Colson, the amiable superintendent of schools, the curriculum supervisor and the elementary principal expressed their love for the brave volunteers on this mission. A last minute guest made her appearance near midnight, and her presence was a shock to the entire staff and students. Jewel Throneberry came anyway realizing that she had not fully apologized for her totally erroneous article that was published in her magazine. With tears of remorse running freely down her cheeks, she hugged each of the girls more than one time.

All wondered about Jewel now that she somehow discovered that the young people of Bacon were participating in this mission. She was an unusual journalist who could find out information where others would fall short. "Please know that I will not write about any of this until you are safely home," she told Coach Anna. "I am a different journalist from the one you first met. It is my goal to model my life after your girls you recruit for your teams. One of these days I want to do a story on your kind of recruiting."

"That would not be much of a story," Coach Anna said. "God has really blessed me with the Hollow girls who provide the standards for other girls I add to the list."

"Sometime I would like to talk to you about the way you selected the team to conduct this extremely dangerous pseudo-military rescue mission, and why you volunteered in the first place," Jewel said, as she hugged a good-bye to each of the group.

Early the next morning the helicopter broke the morning silence and landed on the small campus the second time in twenty-four hours. Making a lane all the way to the aircraft, the students and staff wished the team well, and just as they started to board, Dr. Damond rendered an eloquent prayer while all held hands asking God to hover over them and bring them back safely.

Back in his office Dr. Damond leaned back pensively in his executive chair and thought, "It's a good thing that the media have been banned from the campus until further notice because the news of the girls' pseudo-military rescue attempt would be disseminated by all of them. It is going to be such a quick strike in a short while that the question of media hopefully will be moot."

At Mateland Air Force Base the girls were whisked into a building near the runway for their final instructions before departing to their destination. They checked off the items one by one that they needed in their small backpacks. An electronics' specialist examined their wrist instruments to ensure that they were functioning properly. With all of the wherewithal in order, the officials turned to the maps and details of their entry into the country. "Once your rendezvous has been effected, Major Bosley, you will signal to our control center located on the USS Virginia in the Indian Ocean," Colonel Carlton stated. "From this point our military rescue team will be on the alert twenty-four hours a day to pick you all up. If conditions become unbearable, just give the signal and excite the homing device so we can find you.

"Because the western border is so well fortified by the terrorists, our military helicopter unit will get their attention by provoking them into a brief skirmish just long enough for you to make your entry without being noticed. There will be much shooting as you enter, but the guns will not be pointed toward the rescue team. There is an old saying regarding these kinds of missions that the quicker a team gets in and out the better. This seems to hold for your mission. Patience is very important and so is acting swiftly with appropriate caution. You will have to determine that balance.

"Our latest news about the three missionaries is that they are suffering from extreme anguish as their lives are threatened many times each day. One report indicated that they have been tortured to get them to admit that they were proselytizing Abedistanies to the Christian faith. In another report it was announced that they were being enticed to renounce their belief in Christianity in favor of the Islamic way of life.

"As you know, you have a generic strategy for this capture, but it's only a guide, and any solution you deem appropriate after you are on the ground will be your call. We want you to signal our control ship every twelve hours at least. Of course, all this does is to let us know that you are safe. Remember, we are only using beeps so at the initial rendezvous, your signal will be seven beeps which will tell us you are all okay. As soon as each of you is on the ground, you must excite your Personnel Identification Marker (PIM), which will provide the command center with your exact location during your entire operation."

The briefing was very informative and hopefully helpful. Now it was time to put their training into practice. The flight was long so it was good to feel their plane touch down on the pavement of Boraqi, an ally in the fight against terrorism situated about five hundred miles from their target. Hastily disembarking the aircraft, they were taken to a

domed shaped building to await their departure. "Eat and
drink well because this is our last stop before we enter the
territory of the enemy," Coach Anna said to the group, as
they sat eating their last meal together for a while.

Darkness came quickly and as the eleven-o'clock
hour approached, Coach Anna reached for her small Bible in
her backpack and turned to the Book of Ecclesiastes to read
these verses from Chapter 3:

*1 There is a time for everything, and a season for every
activity under heaven:*
*2 a time to be born and a time to die, a time to plant and a
time to uproot,*
*3 a time to kill and a time to heal, a time to tear down and a
time to build,*
*4 a time to weep and a time to laugh, a time to mourn and a
time to dance,*
*5 a time to scatter stones and a time to gather them, a time
to embrace and a time to refrain,*
*6 a time to search and a time to give up, a time to keep and
a time to throw away,*
*7 a time to tear and a time to mend, a time to be silent and a
time to speak,*
*8 a time to love and a time to hate, a time for war and a time
for peace.*
9 What does the worker gain from his toil?
10 I have seen the burden God has laid on men.
*11 He has made everything beautiful in its time. He has also
set eternity in the hearts of men; yet they cannot fathom what
God has done from beginning to end.*

"God has given us the ability to perform wonders in
helping our fellow men," Coach Anna stated. "We are
blessed with strength and wisdom to generate actions led by
the Holy Spirit that never ceases to hover over us. There is
no doubt that our mission is within the framework of the will
of God. He uses people like us to conduct activities on His

good earth. We will be safe in His arms during the next several days as we attempt to rescue His workers who have been thwarted by the enemy. I am so very pleased to have you all on this team," she said, as she touched each lightly on the head.

Paul H. Jones

TIME TO GO

It was time. They loaded the plane in silence with each trying to remember all that she was expected to do. A lieutenant explained the jump procedure from this aircraft, and a little later the pilot visited them to tell about the route he would be flying. "A guided homing device will be launched in advance of your jump so it will be in place as you all guide your chutes in that direction," the pilot stated. "I hear you have become expert in parachuting so I hope you have no difficulty as you leave the aircraft. You are reminded that there will be some shooting at the time you leave the plane. Don't let this bother you, because the terrorists will be shooting at two provoking Apache helicopters to the west of them while you are falling and guiding your chutes to the east."

At three minutes until eleven, the lieutenant opened the door of the craft while the girls held hands and prayed silently. The long free fall on this night was going to be very important to elude the enemy down below. Just as Coach Anna turned to look at her team once again, she said, "We can do it girls." Then she fell downward toward an unknown ground followed by the others. Suddenly the night sky lit up to the west as the Apache pilots were getting the attention of the enemy by flying up over the horizon and then darting below the mountainous dunes out of sight. The gunfire ceased very shortly.

Coach Anna had picked up the signal of the homing device as she soared so gracefully toward the landing site. All were heading to the rendezvous point except Mit whose parachute had gotten tangled, and she was falling swiftly to the ground. Cutting off the tangled chute, she held it firmly and tugged at her reserve parachute which opened immediately, but she had lost all means of maneuvering it toward their target. The instructor's words rang out in her mind as she finally stabilized her fall. "Remember, always to do what is necessary to land safely. That is the most important action on your part. Remember too, don't drop your chute or any debris that will help the enemy discover your whereabouts."

Mit had learned well, but the sudden jolt she received when she landed almost knocked the breath out of her. She was very far away from the homing device but she was alive. Pulling her two chutes toward her, she was starting to bury them when a volley of bullets struck the sand nearby, one close enough that it struck the side of her leg. Quickly she climbed the few feet to the top of the sand dune and partially rolled down the other side. With shots continuing and getting louder, she knew the terrorists had spotted her and were coming to her location. Finding herself in a small crevasse of sand on the east bank, she put one of the parachutes over her face and the other underneath her, and began franticly to pull sand over her whole body.

The shots had ceased, but she could hear the soldiers climbing up the west side of the steep dune. Somewhat breathlessly, they stood on the precipice shining their hand held lights to and fro. It seemed like an eternity as Mit was hunkered down under the sand just a few feet from the soldiers, and her oxygen supply was swiftly running out. As the men reversed their steps, much larger and brighter lights were beamed toward Mit's direction, but she was not detected, having ingeniously hidden on the east side of one of many sand dunes in the area.

Not wanting to be discovered, Mit did not use her small directed light to check her bullet wound. The best she could ascertain as she felt the area with her hand, it had stopped bleeding, but there was a hole left when the bullet pierced her leg. Leaving the one parachute buried behind, Mit checked her compass and moved to the east in the dark and all alone. "God, I am in your hands," she thought, as she stumbled along in the sand while checking to see whether or not she could detect the beeps of the homing device.

Their hearts were pounding as one by one the girls made it to the rendezvous point. When Maggie breathlessly arrived to join the others, she excitedly said in a low voice, "Has Mit made it yet?"

"Why?" Coach Anna asked immediately.

"I came out just before she did and when I got my parachute under control, I heard something flapping that I believe was a chute that had not opened properly," Maggie told the team.

"There was shooting to the west and a powerful light shone in the sky a little later," Coach Anna stated. "We'll signal our contact at this time and wait here."

The wind was beginning to pick up as daybreak approached such that the granules of sand cut into their faces. Before they buried their parachutes, each cut a large strip to use as protection over her face against the sand particles blown about by the wind.

Immediately, the report of their landing was transmitted back to Colonel Carlton at his base in North Carolina, and with only six beeps he knew that something had gone awry. He had told Dr. Damond at Bacon College that he would keep him apprised of their welfare.

"This is the office of the president," Dr. Damond's secretary answered.

"This is Colonel Carlton and I would like to speak to President Damond," he said in the usual military fashion.

Connecting the two, Dr. Damond stated, "How are you Colonel Carlton?"

Not answering his question, Colonel Carlton stated, "We received the message that the rescue team is on the ground with one having strayed off course. Our Personnel Identification Marker shows one of them far removed from the others."

"What happened to the seventh?" Dr. Damond immediately asked.

"We don't know because our signal only deals with the location," Colonel Carlton answered.

"Please keep me abreast with what is taking place in this mission," Dr. Damond pleaded, following their brief conversation.

"I will certainly keep you informed," the colonel responded.

In Abedistan the six who had successfully assembled at the rendezvous were extremely anxious about the welfare of their colleague. "We need to place our homing device on the highest dune in the area so that Mit can pick up the signal, Coach Anna said. "Because it's getting daylight, it's going to be necessary for us to position ourselves against the north side of the dunes in the shadows so that we won't be so very visible to aircraft flying overhead. Mit will not move toward us during the daylight hours because she too will be fearful of being discovered, so we won't turn our homing device on until it's dark. We'll just remain here through the night to give Mit time to catch up with us"

"Do you think those shots during the night came from the enemy shooting at Mit?" Dorothy asked.

"I don't really know, but they came from the vicinity of where she might have landed if she came straight down," Coach Anna answered.

"The fact that we heard shots could tell us that Mit landed safely and was observed by the terrorists," Esther pointed out.

"That is a very positive observation," Coach Anna responded.

Meanwhile, Mit had walked and crawled several hundred yards toward what she believed was where the others were located. "I'll need to hide from the enemy until nightfall," she thought, as she moved toward the shadowy side of a large dune. Except for the sound of the wind and small granules of sand hitting her face and clothing, the desert was very quiet.

Continuing to ruminate, she began to recall her training to handle situations such as separation from the main contingent of personnel on such a mission. "Don't panic, but remain calm, they told us over and over again. Become the leader of your own destiny, they would say."

As the lonely and scary day wore on, she thought more and more about her mom and dad in the jungle area of Costa Rica and all of her special friends she left behind. She was so glad that some of them were enrolled at Bacon College with her. "God has been so good to me over the years, and with the addition of the Hollow girls as friends, He has really given me a special bonus," she thought, as she opened her water bottle and took just a small sip, not knowing how long it would be before she got an additional supply.

Using the portion of her parachute that she had torn away as a canopy, she protected herself from the sun that still beamed down generating much heat. Suddenly, she noticed that her leg was bleeding profusely again so she quickly tore away a long strip of the remainder of the parachute to use as a tourniquet to stop the bleeding. Much blood was in the sand as she tightened the nylon strip around her leg. Because the blood had immediately soaked into the sand, she was not aware of how much blood she had actually lost.

Realizing that it was important for them to place the homing sensor on the highest peak in the area, Coach Anna stealthily climbed to the top of a high dune. She carefully placed it in position and slid back down with her other teammates. "Mit will be able to pick up the signal a good distance away with it being on this high point," Coach Anna told the other girls.

Mit was really surprised when suddenly she heard the beeping sound. "They must not be too far away," she thought, as she continued to evaluate the sound. The tourniquet seemed to be working, because there were no further signs of blood in the sand near her wound.

As nightfall came, Mit began her trek to the east. It was not a good sight as she walked, stumbled and crawled toward her destination. At the rendezvous point Coach Anna was planning a strategy for all the team members to travel west for several hundred yards to attempt to meet Mit. Moving toward the west, the team covered a very wide area to try to find their friend.

Going getting more difficult all the while, Mit continued slowly to make her way over the sand. "I believe I have lost more blood than I realized," Mit thought, as she struggled to move forward.

It was nearly three in the morning when Marsha heard movement up ahead. She lay very still, waiting to see a silhouette as the figure made its way atop a small sand dune. "It has to be Mit," she thought, as she watched the black shadowy figure roll helplessly down the side of the sand embankment. Generating strength beyond the fear of the moment, she decided to say something. "Is that you, Mit?" she said in a whispering voice.

"I'm over here," Mit joyfully stated.

Following hug after hug in this desolate land of sand, Marsha said, "Are you all right?"

"I am fine now," Mit replied. "It was a little scary being alone."

"Can you make it?" Marsha asked, realizing that Mit was struggling somewhat.

"I can now," Mit answered. "I was shot in the leg but have stopped the bleeding by using a tourniquet.

"I'll help you along," Marsha stated. "Let's meet up with the others.

"Is everybody else okay?" Mit asked.

"Everyone is fine," Marsha replied.

It was a happy reunion of young ladies on this morning in a foreign land so many miles away from the Hollow. Coach Anna immediately sent the signal of seven beeps to let them know that they were together again. Colonel Carlton let out a loud yell when he received the signal that all seven of the team were together again. Immediately, he called Dr. Damond.

"We just received the signal that all seven are together again," he told the president.

"I am so glad," Dr. Damond happily stated. "We have been worried to death."

"I don't know what happened," Colonel Carlton said, "but the important thing is that they are together now."

Back in western Abedistan, the rescue team assisted Mit as they trudged eastward to the small city where the young missionaries were being held captive. "We have about three hours before daylight so let's proceed as far as we can go before the sun comes up," Coach Anna instructed. "According to my best calculation, we should be out of the main desert area by morning."

They all took turns helping Mit along, stopping from time to time to check her bullet wound to be sure that it was not bleeding. About daybreak their footing was much improved as they walked mostly on solid ground so they could make much better time. Although the landscape for just a little way appeared to be level, the mountains several hundred yards farther were a genuine reminder that the terrain up ahead would be a challenge.

The first sign of life was a weather beaten mud brick wall that appeared to have been at one time a dwelling of some kind. It was well received by the team as they soon hovered against the north side in the shadows, which provided their best cover thus far on this mission. "We need to drink plenty of water," Coach Anna told the girls.

"I am on my second bottle," Dorothy stated.

"We'll be able to get more when we get in Moraba," Coach Anna noted. "Let me take a good look again at your leg wound, Mit."

Coach Anna slid closer to Mit and carefully loosened the tourniquet Mit had placed on her leg the night before. Pouring some water from her bottle on the wound, Coach Anna began to clean it gently, hoping not to start up the bleeding again. Following the liberal use of betadine, she covered the wound with gauze and tape. Upon completion, she said, "That should do it for a while."

"Thank you so much," Mit replied. "It feels so much better."

The Ab Didal, a militant terrorist group using Abedistan as its base, was "milking" the missionary captive situation for all that it was worth. Daily they communicated with the media about the three young ladies they were holding captive. Their demands changed with almost every exchange of talks, such that it was not really known what it would take to free the prisoners.

"They are really having a good time flaunting their power while holding the young missionaries captive," Colonel Carlton thought, as he listened to the nightly news. "They are so excited about having some leverage to get on the world center stage as they parade their young ladies to show them to their national audience," he continued to think. On a couple of occasions during the last several days, when their faces were exposed, all the world could see the stress and anxiety expressed so vividly on their faces. Many thought they had been tortured to attempt them to mock their present religion and their faith in a democratic form of government.

Bob had invited the Hollow group to Tiger Foods to watch the news from Abedistan, knowing that they were very concerned about the welfare of the rescue team. "The men with the guns are the Ab Didal, the mean spirited terrorist group, who are holding the missionaries," Bob told Josh, as he and the others got in position to see the television screen.

"We have been advised by the Better Television News (BTN) that beginning soon they will have a news reporter on site in Abedistan to give their viewing audience a close-up view of what is taking place," Bob said to the group. "They are trying to get in position to show us what Abedistan is really like during these days of terror, discontent and disbelief."

"How do they plan to do this?" Josh asked, realizing that the internal borders had been sealed days ago.

"That part of the situation has not been revealed yet," Bob responded.

"Won't that upset the Ab Didal once they discover the presence of the television media?" Corbin, Dorothy's father, asked.

"On the one hand they may be upset, but on the other some seem to think that this evil group wants a western news group to spread their venom more swiftly," Bob replied. "Holding center stage augments their position of power as they hold these young ladies hostage so with a credible news program recognized throughout the world on the scene, they will use it for all it's worth."

"Will the reporter on site cause any problems for the rescue team?" James anxiously asked.

"I am sure that the very small news team has been briefed on how to behave while on location," Bob answered, "so I don't believe they will do anything that might be harmful to the hostages. Keep in mind this news team has no knowledge whatsoever of a rescue team being present in the country. And likewise, I might add, neither does our rescue team realize that a news team will now be present. It's somewhat ironic that both parties will be arriving on the scene at about the same time."

"I wonder whether or not Dr. Damond would permit us to watch the television newscasts in the athletic dormitory," Josh inquired.

"I am sure he would love to have you all do that," Bob noted.

Following a call to the president, they were set to go to the campus each evening to see the news. "They will only be in Abedistan several days so we should keep up with the news very closely," Charlene stated.

"Before we depart, let us pray together," Josh stated as they joined hands, bowed and listened intently to the words included in this special prayer asking God's will be done on behalf of the girls as they developed strategies to fulfill successfully this dangerous rescue mission.

SUSPICIOUS YOUNG MAN

The elation of the rescue team shone on their faces as they were all together again and could proceed toward their target of the small city of Moraba, the hideout of the most notorious terrorists now threatening the world's tranquility. Night travel was slow, but they realized that daytime movement would arouse suspicion so they would have to remain steadfast to the plan.

In the early hours of the second morning of travel, they could see the lights from the eastern town of Moraba. "We want to find a spot up one of the mountainous slopes to look down onto the city," Coach Anna instructed. "We can learn a lot by just observing the movement of the people."

When daylight came, the rescue team was safely hidden on a steep slope in the shadow made by a craggy rock formation that was common everywhere. Using her binoculars, Coach Anna examined every breath of life in her view to learn as much as she could about the land and its people. Being several hundred yards away from the nearest person, they could talk quietly without fear of being heard.

"I want each of you to look through the binoculars to see the environment in which we shall be located during our rescue mission," Coach Anna stated. "Pay closely attention to the dress of the women, and you will see that they all wear burquas just as we do. Starting tomorrow, barring no setbacks, we shall walk among the people. The fact that all of us and all of the Abedistany women will be totally covered with our burquas, our presence will not cause any alarm. We will have to move about with confidence and emulate our Abedistany counterparts."

The novelty of their situation soon gave way to sleep for the group as they hunkered down among the rocks, blending in with the terrain, and got some well needed rest. It was late in the afternoon when Coach Anna observed a young man ten or so years old, acting rather curiously as he left the main street area. Looking all around as though he didn't want anyone to see him, he suddenly darted behind a weather beaten mud brick wall. Stopping momentarily to check to see whether or not he was followed, he continued into the rocky area glancing over his shoulder almost with each step. Getting a full view of his route to this point, he stood erectly and without a further hint, quickly disappeared behind two large rocks.

"He is trying to hide from someone," Coach Anna murmured to herself, as the others on the team grew more curious all the while. "Look at the young lad crouching down behind those rocks," Coach Anna indicated to Esther, while almost simultaneously handing the binoculars to her.

Getting the young man in view, Esther said, "I believe he is not only hiding from someone, but he seems to have something that he doesn't want others to see either. He continues to dig in the loose sand to retrieve something that appears to be valuable to him."

"Let me look," Dorothy requested, having been filled with suspense by Coach Anna and Esther. Taking the binoculars, she watched as the young man dug up a bag that he carefully dusted off before he untied the top. Inside he pulled out another bag that he unfolded and carefully held what appeared to be a book.

"What is he doing now?" Mit asked, as she and the others waited anxiously for their turn to hold their most exciting item on this afternoon.

Giving the binoculars to Mit, Dorothy said, "See if you can make out what he got from the bag that was buried."

"It does look like a book," Mit echoed, as she zoomed in on the young man's precious asset. "He is just sitting there very relaxed reading now as though he is impervious to his surroundings."

The binoculars were passed from hand to hand such that each girl had at least two opportunities to observe the action of their mysterious Abedistany lad. Reading for more than an hour until darkness was beginning to cover the landscape, the young man closed his book while Marsha got a close-up view of the book's cover. "It's the Bible! It's the Bible!" she excitedly announced to the group when she saw the inscription on the back. "It appears to be a bilingual translation of Arabic and English because there are two Arabic words and underneath the title, *Holy Bible*."

It had been a most interesting afternoon as the girls waited to move nearer to the center of the city.

Back at the command center, Colonel Carlton and his team were receiving continuous messages from the USS Virginia now situated in the Indian Ocean monitoring every move of the rescue team. "They are brave young ladies," he stated when he contacted Dr. Damond early in the morning.

"They certainly are," Dr. Damond responded.

"According to our report, they remained several hundred yards from the city, but during the night have made their way right to the edge of a popular activity area near the heart of the village," Colonel Carlton pointed out. "They are doing extremely well as they put themselves in position to learn more about the area wherein the missionaries are being held."

"Coach Anna is a very intelligent young lady and along with her courage and that of her dear friends and her athletic team, they have the wherewithal to pull this whole thing off," Dr. Damond proudly stated. "My confusion comes when I try to conjure up a response of why are they on this mission in the first place?"

"We are hopeful that their presence on this mission will cause confusion for the enemy," Colonel Carlton reacted.

"I hope so too," Dr. Damond replied. "On the personal side I have invited the Hollow parents and those of the others who can come to share my report from you each day in the athletic dormitory. Because it's their young people on this mission, I thought it would be nice to invite all of them"

"That's wonderful," Colonel Carlton responded. "I'll keep this in mind when I make my report to you each time."

The rescue team was still amazed at the sharp contrast in the temperature from day to night. The extra burqua layer was welcome at night to keep out the cold. While they had practiced working while wearing their burquas, they still did not feel comfortable in this garment that totally covered their body from head to toe. Obviously, they would have to wear them because this was going to be their continuous disguise all the while.

Having somewhat understood the lanes of pedestrian traffic gleaned from their lengthy observations using the binoculars, they stealthily trudged slowly in the dark to the south of the city where steep, treeless mountains covered the landscape. City noises could be heard from afar as they began to search for a more permanent roosting place near the building of which they would observe during the next few days. The winds during the night were a reminder that the Tamaran was on schedule wherein for a period of nearly a month sand would be swept up and carried eastward at times blocking the sun's rays for the majority of each day.

As soon as daybreak began, Coach Anna unfolded the map of the city so that each one could see it well. "When the street is full of pedestrians headed for the marketplaces, we want to travel among them in pairs," she stated. "Esther and Dorothy will comprise one subteam, Marsha and Mit will make up the second group, and Hanna and Maggie will be the third. I'll be by myself mostly remaining in the middle of the street. As you walk around, check to see that the money being used is the same we have, and secondly, see how purchases of food are made because we will need some food before too long."

Street noises became louder and louder as more and more people headed mainly to buy foodstuff on this morning. Realizing that the optimum time for their entry into their new culture was swiftly approaching, Coach Anna asked them to hold hands as they bowed together asking God to continue to be their deliverer, their shepherd and their provider as they continued their mission of rescue.

"Remember our guidelines this morning," Coach Anna cautioned. "Enter the street where there is highest traffic; don't remain more than two hours; stay with your teammate; be casual; and follow the lead of the Abedistany women."

Two by two they stepped into the street with their hearts really pounding. The small slit in their garment for them to see what was ahead didn't provide much of an opening. Every step was an adventure as they realized that the street floor was very rough under their feet. Soon though, walking more gracefully came easier, and they began to blend in with the native ladies, as they became quick learners on this morning. After they became more comfortable, more interest was shown in the behavior of those making purchases in the various markets, and too, the vendors and their tactics to make sales were most interesting. As time ticked away, the girls began to think about their real mission of rescuing the missionaries who had been held hostage for such a long time. As Esther and Dorothy wandered to the far side of the street, they glanced upward to see an Abedistany soldier holding an automatic assault rifle. "This must be the place where they are holding the young ladies as prisoners," Esther thought, as they walked with the crowd flow back to the other side of the busy street.

Maggie and Hanna had walked farther west than they had meant to go so they found themselves sharing the market scene with several women in that area. A young lad playfully ran after several other children in what they believed was some kind of tag game. "That looks like the young man who was reading the Bible earlier," Maggie thought, not wanting to stare at the youngsters while their Abedistany counterparts paid little attention to the young lads. She wanted to nudge Hanna to get her attention but decided that this might cause the other women to examine them more closely. To this point, they believed that they were just blending in with the crowd.

Their first excursion went well. The debriefing was mostly serious, but there was a sprinkling of humor also. Each of the groups observed the soldier holding the assault rifle near a corner building so they revisited their maps to see whether or not that particular building was the one that had been identified by their training officials as the place where the missionaries were likely being held. It appeared to be the target building so they quietly discussed the various characteristics of the whole area. Following a very lengthy debriefing regarding the missionaries, Maggie stated, "Did any of the rest of you see the young lad we observed through the binoculars earlier?"

"No," Coach Anna excitedly said. "Did you all see him?"

"We certainly did," Hanna stated. "He was playing with some of the other children in the far western part of the street."

"How many other children were playing with him?" Dorothy asked.

"There were several," Maggie answered. "In fact we didn't see all of them because many were playing between the buildings on the narrow streets adjoining the main market street."

"All of us seem to see something special about this young fellow," Coach Anna noted. "The fact that he was secretly reading his Bible in this almost totally Muslim country speaks volumes about this young man. As you all know, where we are presently located is very near where we saw him with our binoculars this morning, so if we position ourselves correctly, we shall be able to see him even more often."

The report from Colonel Carlton to Dr. Damond almost coincided with the arrival of the Hollow folks and other invited guests to the athletic dormitory. "Dr. Damond, the rescue team has been really active today as they have moved to a new location very near the main market street in Moraba," Colonel Carlton related on the telephone. "They spent nearly two hours in the street with the native folks, apparently not being recognized as foreigners as they walked around to the various vending centers."

"They are really brave young ladies," Dr. Damond couldn't resist saying.

"They certainly are," Colonel Carlton related. "At this point in the rescue mission everything is going well. I'll keep you abreast with their movements during the day and will contact you from time to time to give you a report."

The lead story again on this evening was about the three missionaries being held in Abedistan and what the reporters believed would be their fate. At the close of the primetime evening news, the anchorman stated proudly, "Beginning some time this evening, BTN will broadcast its first newscast from atop a small mountain not far from the main street of Moraba, the city most believe is harboring the strongest base of terrorism and where the missionaries are being held against their will."

It was ten o'clock with everyone glued to the television having high expectations that the news special report would be about Abedistan and particularly about Moraba. With only a brief narrative flashing on the screen and with no audio, the news camera revealed the topographical characteristics of this very small Muslim country as the television audience stretched to view the home of several thousand of the three million Abedistanies populating the country.

"Several years ago there was a tug-of-war concerning the official language of the country," the reporter stated who looked haggard with hair disheveled that blew in the wind that cast the sand from one area to the next. "Many of the old guard here wanted to use their native language, Orda, as the established language, but there were many of the governmental leaders who held firmly to their belief that English should be the language spoken by the people. In the wake of these differences of opinion came divisiveness in the country that has outlived its inhabitants. While this simmers all the while, this is not the main threat of the nation now. Through weakness in their governmental leadership caused by greed and plain power hungry groups of people struggling for control, the people find themselves outside the mainstream decision making. The advent of terrorists, who presently occupy and control the western sector where we are located as I speak, placed all of the other issues far down the list of priorities. The people in Moraba seem to be content to march to the drumbeat of the terrorists who call themselves the Ab Didal.

"I know you have raised the question in your mind as to how a television group could set up in this remote country to let the outside world know about them. Through lengthy discussions with the rebel leaders following their taking the three young Christian missionaries, they believed that a television broadcasting unit would work in their favor because they would have access to the world stage using their new assistance. We are told that tomorrow they will put their prisoners on display and will list their demands again."

With the camera zooming in on the various marketplaces on the street, those transfixed sitting before the large television screen back at Bacon College wondered whether or not the rescue team was among those shown on camera. The complexion of the environment had changed tremendously in Moraba as the small news team broadcast information several times each day.

Much time was spent by the rescue team in drawing the details of the prison that they believed was in the corner building. "We have got a good start so the next time we go on the street we want to add to our information," Coach Anna stated. "It appears that the heavy market traffic in the morning is the best time to move about."

"I noticed that several of the market sites where we visited, the vendors and buyers were speaking English, albeit broken for some of them," Esther indicated.

"When we go the next time, we can attempt to make a purchase, possibly of some food," Coach Anna related.

"We could visit a very busy market, and stick our hands out just like the others, pass on the money and move away quickly," Marsha suggested.

"We are really running low on food so this will be our way of getting nourishment," Dorothy stated, followed by a quick question. "What kind of food do they sell anyway?"

"They eat two or three different kinds of grain that you see them cooking on the ground with an open flame," Coach Anna said. "One is rice and the other I am not sure but it is a very small, round grain."

"I noticed the rice being cooked this morning, and it really smelled good," Maggie added.

"We won't be able to cook anything because the terrorists would discover us, so our best hope for market food at this time will be the vegetables and cooked food that is being sold by some vendors," Coach Anna advised.

Back in the hospital tears ran down Maudie's cheeks as the watched the news from Moraba where her precious friends were lying in wait to spring on the terrorists to secure the release of the three missionaries. From the tone of the reporter's voice Maudie could sense the strong feeling of danger lurking everywhere. "This young reporter has some immunity at this point, but what about later when the rescue is attempted," Maudie thought, as she lay on her hospital bed.

Colonel Carlton was raising similar questions to his team as they carefully monitored the activities of their rescue team. "We suddenly have a new dimension to our situation in Moraba," he stated. "Who would have thought that this war mongering group would negotiate a deal with the BTN broadcasting group to permit a reporter to be on site each day. Obviously, the news network is being used by the culprits to advertise their agenda to those around the world."

A young captain in the group commented, "The whole demeanor of the terrorists can change in a flash, and the reporter will be helplessly caught with no place to find cover."

"As soon as the rescue is underway, they will think the BTN television system is part of the mission, thereby making his life worth very little even though he would be innocent of any kind of betrayal," Colonel Carlton stated.

"Obviously, our scenario is a valid one so it's imperative that we include the newscasters in our plans as we approach the time when our rescue team carries out its assignment," the second captain noted.

"We can't communicate this to our team so it's going to be necessary for us at some time near the rescue date to advise the television unit what we will be doing, and prepare them for some kind of emergency rescue," Colonel Carlton pointed out.

With their food and water supply shrinking, the girls rationed what they ate and drank as the sun was going down in the west. Suddenly, they heard someone only several yards to their left, and quickly realized that it was the young man who hid behind a rock and again took out his Bible to read several verses before dark. Wrapping it carefully, and then covering it with sand, he paused on his knees and uttered an oral prayer that could be heard by the girls as they crouched behind the weather beaten wall of mud bricks.

Although they had limited maneuverability, they appeared always to be busy doing something regarding their rescue mission. Greeted again with considerable dust on this morning, they listened carefully to their assignment for the morning's walk in the market place. "Each pair should attempt to make one purchase of food," Coach Anna instructed. "Maggie and Hanna will again go to the far end of the market area to try to find out more about our mysterious young man. I want each pair to spend considerable time just examining the building wherein we believe the hostages are being held."

On the hill on the east side of Moraba the television reporter was beginning his first newscast which generally was a repeat of the report he made yesterday, except on this day his camera was focused more on the movement in the marketplace. All the way to Bacon College viewers glued themselves to the screen to try to see the girls. With hundreds of women shoppers in the area wearing full burquas, it was impossible to distinguish among them. But that didn't preclude the viewers from Bacon College straining to try to discover their love ones on the rescue team that they believed were walking in the marketplace on this morning.

Their excursion on this day was much less stressful as they entered the huge market area from different points and immediately blended in with the native people. More cognizant of everything as they moved about shoulder to shoulder with the Muslim women, they soon discovered that all kinds of items were for sale in addition to food. Joining with the other buyers, they soon were carrying their very thin plastic bags holding their vegetables. At the far west area Maggie and Hanna finally saw the young lad as he sat among several other youngsters in a walkway between buildings. Impervious to their presence, the boys continued their conversation in English but spoken with what they believed was a strong village accent.

Because of the large mass of people, movement was very slow so they just patiently went with the flow to make their way to the corner building where poorly dressed soldiers could be seen brandishing automatic firearms. No one seemed to pay any attention to their presence, indicating that this kind of scene was commonplace on this Moraban market street. Not wanting to be overly anxious to look in the direction of the building, each pair would catch glances from time to time as they moved around. Almost without any notice, the environment changed as the lads had conjured up a tag game and ran around and among the shoppers, giggling and yelling all the while. Suddenly the mysterious lad broke away from the group and ran up to the soldier guarding the main floor area. Comments were made by each, and then the lad was directed to go down the external hall between two ten-foot walls where he disappeared into a room that was unlocked by another guard.

"That was very interesting," Coach Anna thought, as she nonchalantly moved away from the area. "I wonder whether or not the lad knows the imprisoned missionaries."

As the time for their departure came, the area near the corner building became the focal point of those on the streets. Loud sounds were heard and chants of all kind were coming from several directions. Realizing that everyone was moving in deference to the men carrying guns, the rescue team did likewise, awaiting what would happen next.

Volley after volley of rifle shots fired straight up in the air was symbolic of some victorious situation, and for this morning the Ab Didal was reminding the citizens of their might. Immediately, a soldier dressed in combat boots and a half-length bubu displayed an American flag draped over his rifle barrel. With everyone's attention he lit the flag while they all chanted derogatory slogans about the United States. The orchestrated assembly got the attention of everyone in the area as all of those present gave them their undivided attention, really fearing for their life, if they failed to adhere to the numerous commands.

From behind the group stepped sharply Lada du Daba, one of the high ranking terrorists wanted in several countries for carrying out many grievous acts of terrorism. With assault weapon in hand he began to make a speech warning the United States about taking any kind of offensive action against Abedistan and its innocent people. "Imperialism has to cease," he yelled to the group. "The biggest threat to peace in the world today is the U. S., a country of greed, hate and war mongering. They have to be stopped."

The speech continued and on a particular cue, two soldiers came down from the corner building dragging three captive women with them. All three were tied with a thin rope that bound their arms and legs such that they could only take small steps without tripping. The crowd was pushed back so that everyone could get a good look at the hostages. Encircled by hundreds of men and women now involved in shouting demeaning statements, the young ladies were pulled back and forth such that they would fall from time to time.

"Our demands remain the same," Lada du Daba shouted. "If you want to see these women alive again, all demands must be met in a timely fashion."

Following this remark, the missionaries were almost dragged back to the corner building where they were taken down the hall to their secure cell. "What a scary morning," Coach Anna thought, as the group dispersed almost as quickly as it assembled earlier. Stealthily leaving the market area, the rescue team members soon were securely sitting in their home base preparing for a most interesting debriefing.

For the first time in days the missionary prisoners were seen. The television reporter had been invited closely enough for him to video the activities and capture the speech by the terrorist leader as well as getting good footage of the prisoners themselves.

That was a harrowing scene," Josh said at the end of the newscast from Moraba. "Obviously, they mean business."

"There were so many people in the marketplace, I couldn't tell one from the other," Corbin noted.

"The shooting took place near the area where the prisoners were being held, I believe," James indicated.

"There is considerable hatred toward the United States as indicated by the soldier burning the American flag," Dr. Damond stated. "If the rescue team is caught, I am sure death will come immediately."

Colonel Carlton was also alarmed when he viewed the telecast from Moraba. "I know that Major Bosley and her team were frightened with all of the firearms display and the hatred shown by the soldiers and Lada du Daba," he thought, while contemplating the various theoretical scenarios that might emerge before the rescue was over.

To this point no one had been seen near their hideout so when they sat down for their debriefing, they felt comfortable. All wanted to talk at once so Coach Anna became more of a director on this day. "Let's look at your purchases," she said.

Their plastic bags were filled with apples, oranges, cucumbers, carrots, two pineapples and several mangoes. "It looks like we have a good variety," Dorothy stated.

"Everything really looks very delicious, doesn't it?" Coach Anna indicated, praising the group for its marketing prowess. "Remember, before we eat this food, we need to wash it well."

"Were any of you close enough to see from where the gunmen came?" Coach Anna asked.

"They suddenly came from a very narrow side street to the north about fifty yards from the prison building," Marsha answered. "We were standing right in front of the entrance when they came barging out, pointed their guns in the air and immediately began to shoot upward. It seemed like a joyous occasion for them."

"We were nearly trampled during this time as the people tried desperately to move away from the group as far as possible, because they must have known that this was a raucous group," Dorothy commented. "I looked in the eyes of several women, and I could readily see that they were frightened."

"We learned much this morning," Esther related. "Seeing the young man come through the group and head directly to where we think the missionaries are being held was most interesting. His presence becomes more intriguing as time moves along."

"Did the rest of you see what happened?" Coach Anna asked.

With all nodding Esther continued, "The young man was apparently known by the soldier who is a guard because he permitted him to go inside what I believe was the prison room. If this is the case, our mysterious lad appears to be more interesting."

The debriefing continued for more than an hour, and the team added much to their drawing of the prison scene in the corner building.

Following an uneventful afternoon in their hideout, Coach Anna met with the group. "Suppose we speak to the young lad when he comes this afternoon to read his Bible," Coach Anna suggested

"That's a good idea," several said in unison.

"Keep in mind though that to this point no one knows we are here, so do you think we can trust him not to tell anyone?" Coach Anna asked the group.

"That we don't know," Mit stated, "but he appears to have some valuable information that would be very helpful to us when we make the rescue."

"The good certainly overshadows the bad in this situation," Hanna indicated.

"Just out of nowhere this young man shows up," Dorothy said, "and everything he does seems to be able to contribute to our rescue mission."

At the conclusion of the discussion of this issue, Coach Anna appointed Esther and Marsha to meet and greet the young man and find out as much as possible about him.

Colonel Carlton and his monitoring team were working feverishly to try to match the PIM with the newscast video to determine where the members of the rescue team were standing while the whole scary melee was taking place. Before too long one of the many electronic experts synchronized the two reports to show exactly where they were during each episode of the morning's market experience.

The automatic dialer had the college president's office immediately. "Hello. This is Colonel Carlton and I would like to speak to Dr. Damond," he stated somewhat anxiously.

"This is John Damond," the president replied.

"Did you see the newscast this morning from Moraba?" Colonel Carlton asked.

"I certainly did," Dr. Damond said emphatically.

"We used our PIM indicator during this video and pinpointed where each of team was located," the Colonel excitedly said. "They were situated right there as the gunshots were fired not more than a few feet away. One of the girls was almost burned she was so close when the soldier burned the American flag."

"They are all right now, aren't they?" Dr. Damond quickly asked.

"Yes, they are fine as they all are sitting behind the wall to the south of Moraba all together," the colonel responded. "This has been their hideout since they arrived."

"I know the group was excited when the missionary prisoners were paraded out in the street," Dr. Damond stated.

"A couple of them could have reached out and touched them," the colonel pointed out.

The bond of friendship was very obvious between the tough colonel who had many battle ribbons to show for his involvement in war, and the affable college president who typified the embodiment of humility in guiding one's decision making. "I'll stay in touch," the colonel stated, as they closed this most interesting conversation.

Paul H. Jones

SURPRISE MEETING

A ll the girls had their eyes focused on the area where the mysterious young man had come the afternoon before to read his Bible. Would he come this afternoon, and would their making contact be as fruitful as they hoped? A sudden noise alerted the team to some movement to their left and surely enough, it was the young fellow again. Concentrating on his digging, he failed to see Esther and Marsha approaching from his right.

To say he was startled when he looked up to see two women wearing burquas would have been an understatement of mass proportions. Trying to hide his Bible while at the same time wanting to leave the area caused much confusion in the young man's mind.

"How are you this afternoon?" Esther asked in a very pleasant and passive voice.

Not saying a word but attempting to complete the chore of hiding his Bible, he stared at both of them, never saying anything as though he did not understand. "Do you like to read your Bible?" Marsha followed, wanting to give him an opportunity to respond to something that was important to him.

Just as this question was uttered, he looked at Marsha with a quizzical stare as though the two of them had something in common. Then instead of trying to bury his Bible, he opened the bag again, took it out and then gingerly dusted it off, while raising his head toward them as if to say, "I have this special book to read."

"Could we look at your Bible with you?" Esther said, while the other girls looked on from the hideout to see what was going to happen next. Walking very slowly toward the young man, when they drew near, they both sat down beside him, and Marsha gently took the Bible from his hands. "Let me read a favorite passage to you," she said as she turned to Psalm 23:

1 The LORD is my shepherd, I shall not be in want.
2 He makes me lie down in green pastures, he leads me beside quiet waters,
3 he restores my soul. He guides me in paths of righteousness for his name's sake.
4 Even though I walk through the valley of the shadow of death, I will fear no evil, for you are with me; your rod and your staff, they comfort me.
5 You prepare a table before me in the presence of my enemies. You anoint my head with oil; my cup overflows.
6 Surely goodness and love will follow me all the days of my life, and I will dwell in the house of the LORD forever.

When she finished, he smiled and looked at both of them.

"What is your name?" Esther asked.

After a very long pause wherein they knew he was evaluating the situation after having been discovered with a Bible, he said, "My name is Madu Ommad."

"My name is Esther and this is Marsha," Esther stated to the lad.

"You speak good English," Marsha stated, as she put her hand on his shoulder.

"Could you tell us about yourself?" Esther asked.

"I live in Moraba with my uncle and his family," the young man stated. "I attend school and am in the seventh level. I am in level four in English and can speak two other village languages along with French and some Arabic." Then he paused and looked his two visitors over once again and said, "Who are you?"

Before we tell you this, why don't you bury your Bible and walk with us to meet our other friends.

"This is Madu," Esther told the group as the team hovered around him.

They learned a lot about Madu that afternoon. When they got on the subject of his friends, the missionaries who were being held captive, he balked somewhat and withheld further information.

After he departed to return to his uncle's house, they discussed why they thought he withheld information about the ladies now in prison. Also, there was some concern that he might divulge to others the presence of the rescue team. "I think that he is very much concerned about us more than we are of him," Coach Anna stated. "He knows we know that he owns a Bible and for that he would be severely punished, if anyone discovered his secret."

The BTN newscast dwelled on the missionary prisoners on this evening as the viewing audience saw the three young ladies roped together while being paraded and dragged before the people as a public display of the power of the Ab Didal. The reporter was so touched by what he saw he asked the viewing audience whether or not they could see any way that one might suggest to assist the captives. "Do we just sit back and observe our fellow countrymen being mocked and ridiculed, and just say I wish something would be done?" he pointed out in a pleading tone with tears seen welling up in his eyes.

The two-by-two guard shifts provided security during each night, and it provided a time of rest for the whole team.

The dawn shift was observing the arrival of the sun, when they heard some noise like a runner panting heavily. Soon they noticed the young man coming their way wearing a wide smile on this morning.

"Why are you out so early this morning?" Marsha said to Madu, which woke the others.

"I want to talk to you," he said. "I was not able to sleep last night thinking about you."

"What would you like to talk about?" Marsha asked.

"When you saw that I had a Bible, you didn't get upset," he stated. "You must not be Abedistany. Who are you?"

Deferring that question to be answered by Coach Anna, Marsha turned and asked, "Would you like to answer this question for the young man?"

Coach Anna smiled without answering Marsha and asked a question of her own, "Where did you get your Bible?"

"I have never told anyone before now," he indicated. "You know I have it, but you don't punish me so I'll tell you. The three missionaries who are being held by the Ab Didal gave it to me."

"When did they give it to you?" Coach Anna asked.

"Almost a year ago they slipped it to me and told me to keep it hidden," he noted, "so from that day forward, I have kept it buried here."

"Are you a Christian?" Coach Anna inquired.

Sporting a wide smile to show his shiny, white teeth, he responded, "Yes I am."

"When did that happen?" Coach Anna further inquired.

"I became a Christian in October, 2001 and was baptized later that month," he proudly stated.

"Does your uncle know you have accepted Jesus Christ as your Savior?" Coach Anna continued her probe.

"No," he said emphatically. "He would kill me if he knew because all of my people are Muslims."

All the girls were really enjoying this most unusual conversation with a very unique individual. Then Coach Anna returned to the unanswered question and stated, "We are from America and on a mission to Abedistan."

"Why do you all hide here and not go around our people?" he asked.

"Some things you want people to know about, and others you want to keep a secret very much like your Bible," Coach Anna told the attentive young man. "At this time we don't want people to know we are here."

It was a lengthy conversation taking up most of the early morning. Then Dorothy made an observation that would solidify their friendship. "The food certainly smells good that is being cooked nearby," she stated. "Do you think you can buy us some breakfast?"

"I would love to do that," he replied. "What do you want?"

Asking him to be a runner for his fellow Christians was a special request for him. He waited patiently to get their order which turned out to be whatever Abedistanies ate for breakfast.

He was a wise young man, who brought the food back on three different trips from different parts of the marketplace. Not having had "real" food in several days, the rice and beans were very tasty such that they consumed all that he brought. "I'll buy more next time," he laughed, as the rescue team drew even closer to their young runner.

Late that afternoon, the young man showed up again at their hideout. "Have you had a nice day?" Esther asked just as he arrived.

"It was a good day," he said. "I got to see my missionary friends again this afternoon."

"Do you get to see them each day?" Dorothy asked.

"Almost everyday I go by to talk to them for a few minutes," he related.

"Why do the guards let you in to see their prisoners?" Coach Anna questioned.

"These same guards have been here for many months, way before the young ladies were captured," he said. "Ever since the Ab Didal came, I have been somewhat of a runner for them from time to time. Now they let me do everything."

"How long have you known the missionaries?" Coach Anna asked.

"They came three years ago and spent most of their time here in Moraba," he said. "I began to go to their place where they lived to study the Bible. It wasn't long before I became a believer. One day they gave me a Bible so I hid it where you saw me the other day."

"What is the prison like where the missionaries are being held?" Coach Anna queried.

"They are usually kept in a small room up front," he noted. "They are tied together and sit on the floor in a room with no light."

"Do they get enough to eat?" Coach Anna asked.

"I don't believe they do," he replied.

"How many guards do they have around the missionaries?" Coach Anna further inquired.

"Usually they have three upstairs and two on the first floor near the prison room," he indicated. "A new set comes on duty at six in the morning and these five return for another shift starting at six o'clock that evening."

"Are they armed?" Coach Anna asked.

"All of them carry large guns," he responded, "and they keep large amounts of ammunition near them on the roof. They have hand grenades in a box in the corner on the roof."

"He is a very intelligent young man," Coach Anna thought, as their conversation headed in another direction from this point, but she knew that the team needed the information he had.

There was nothing unusual about the tenth day except that Coach Anna believed that their rich reconnoitering was very much enhanced by the involvement of their new Abedistany friend. Reviewing every avenue of their information gathering, they all concurred that they possessed a wealth of data that could help them overcome the enemy in their rescue attempt. "It would appear that our rescue will be undertaken in two days," Coach Anna informed the group. "Be thinking about the strategy that we shall use in this endeavor."

While the group had become very comfortable in their new setting, now that the rescue was only several hours ahead changed the whole demeanor of the group. Colonel Carlton knew that the time was near so he anxiously awaited the signal that the rescue was underway, that would be relayed from the USS Virginia. The nightly news from Moraba didn't reveal that any kind of rescue was underfoot, but when Colonel Carlton called Dr. Damond, he realized that the situation was not nearly as serene as he had hoped.

"Good evening, Colonel," Dr. Damond answered.

"We are approaching the final days so I'm expecting a signal that the rescue will be underway any time now," Colonel Carlton noted.

"It can't be too soon," Dr. Damond excitedly stated. "Reporters from everywhere are all over the campus inquiring about the girls and Coach Anna. They know something is going on and a few even suspect that they are involved in some kind of clandestine activity."

"I didn't know that," the colonel responded.

"To this point the students and the other girls are holding up," Dr. Damond indicated, "but how long I'm not sure."

LOCK-IN

Having Colonel Carlton, the leader of the whole operation as a sounding board helped a little, but it wasn't until after he hung up that he believed he had the right course of action. Because the rescue attempt was imminent and the students were so concerned, he staged a lock-in for all students and those from the Hollow in the coliseum for the duration of the rescue undertaking.

Early the next morning, he assembled all the students for a meeting in the huge basketball arena and advised them of his plan. "All of you who feel uncomfortable about this should not stay, but for the others who want to be in a continuous prayer vigil should remain in this area until the rescue is over," he told the group. When he asked how many would want to stay, all hands were raised high. "We now will be sheltered from the news media until our girls and Coach Anna are out of harm's way."

By noon the campus was like a ghost town with everybody in the coliseum, including the staff except for a small cadre of workers to handle the administration during this blackout of the media. In early afternoon an anonymous telephone call was received which advised Dr. Damond that food and drink would be provided for the entire group until the rescue was fulfilled. "The benevolent person is still at work," Dr. Damond thought with a wide smile, as he finalized administrative details for the lock-in.

Then the last door was closed which separated the Bacon students from the most aggressive media that swarmed the campus upon hearing many different rumors regarding the basketball coach and several of her team. Walking to the front of his large family of students and those especially invited guests, Dr. Damond told them about Elisha and the oil jars as included in 2 Kings 4 of the Bible. "God didn't really need Elisha, the prophet, to assist the woman during the time of need," he stated in his mellow, deep bass voice. "But He used him anyway, just as God uses us from time to time to fulfill some objective. 'Go get some jars,' he directed the woman. 'Get as many as you can.'

"Thus, the woman scurried about in the neighborhood and got several containers from those nearby. Having enough she thought, she closed the door and as directed began to fill the containers with expensive oil. Container after container was filled until there were no more jars. The woman sold the oil and received enough to pay the large debt of her husband who had recently deceased, and in addition, used the remainder of the money for her family.

"There are several lessons in this beautiful story. First of all God uses ordinary people like us to fulfill missions of different kinds. Secondly, many times God's blessings that He freely gives all of us are only limited by the energy we expend. And thirdly, God's help for all of us should be top priority and not down the list after secular measures have been attempted and failed.

"On this day God is using our basketball coach with Dorothy, Esther, Hanna, Maggie, Marsha, and Mit to perform a rescue. Tomorrow, He may use some of you for His purpose. God is truly our deliverer in all things as noted in Colossians 1:

10 And we pray this in order that you may live a life worthy of the Lord and may please him in every way: bearing fruit in every good work, growing in the knowledge of God,
11 being strengthened with all power according to his glorious might so that you may have great endurance and patience, and joyfully
12 giving thanks to the Father, who has qualified you to share in the inheritance of the saints in the kingdom of light.
13 For he has rescued us from the dominion of darkness and brought us into the kingdom of the Son he loves,
14 in whom we have redemption, the forgiveness of sins.

"Our job during these next several hours will be to remain secretive about this mission. From time to time I will be getting reports from Colonel Carlton from the command center and will keep all of you posted. Let me say at this time that I believe the attempted rescue will be undertaken within the next forty-eight hours."

The environment on campus changed so suddenly that it caught the media by surprise, such that this became the story on this particular morning. Those on national networks worked hard to make the campus scene a frontline story, but their executives did not believe that there was any kind of significance to the peculiar behavior on the campus that truly was beleaguered during the last several months. The general consensus was that this did not rise to the level of a national story of interest so mainly the news of the lock-in was communicated only by radio and print media.

Colonel Carlton and his command center staff anxiously awaited any kind of signal from the rescue team. Because he was not sure what the timing would be, he decided to make contact with the TBN executive and set up a meeting immediately. To delay might be too risky, particularly if the rescue was being conducted immediately.

Assembling a meeting with the leaders in the command center filled with all kinds of monitors and electronic devices, he immediately told them of his plans.

"Captain Nolte, I want you to call Gary Davidson, President of TBN, and set a meeting with him for one o'clock this afternoon in a restaurant in Halifax County on the Virginia and North Carolina border. It is called Ernie's Restaurant and is located on Route 360 toward Richmond. A car will be waiting for him at the small airport to take him to the restaurant."

It took a while but eventually Captain Nolte had the president on the telephone. "My name is Captain Dudley Nolte of the marine corps, and I am calling for Colonel Carlton," he stated. "Mr. Davidson, something is taking place as we speak that Colonel Carlton needs urgently to talk to you about. I can't talk to you on the phone about the situation so he wants to meet with you at one o'clock today in person about it. The meeting place is set at Ernie's Restaurant on Route 360 in Halifax County in Virginia. Upon your arrival by helicopter at the small airport, a car will pick you up and take you to the rendezvous point. Do you have questions?"

"I am so flabbergasted that I don't even know what to say," the president stated, "much less ask questions."

"Again, my name is Captain Dudley Nolte and my telephone number is 342 415-5559, if you need to reach me before the meeting," the captain advised.

A bewildered TBN president hung up and hastily prepared for a most unusual meeting in the southern part of Virginia.

Helicopters in the south side area were nothing new, but when two came in to land on the same day, some eyebrows were raised at the airport and later at Runt's Convenience Market at the intersection. "We have really become an important community in recent years," Gene, a long time patron and self-appointed political pundit, stated. "I can't believe that we have two helicopters coming to our area at the same time with dignitaries, including a military officer with so many medals he is almost stoop-shouldered," he related in humorous colloquial terms which elicited loud laughs from his usual audience.

Gary Davidson in recent years had been waited on by those around him, but on this day, he walked into Ernie's not really knowing what he was doing there in the first place. "I am looking for Colonel Carlton," Gary told the young waitress who smiled and immediately took him to a corner table where a military person was seated.

Military personnel were not often seen in this area, and especially one with so many medals, so the local folks were beginning to generate theories about his presence. Following the usual greetings and after having been served delicious thirst-quenching tea, Colonel Carlton got right to his message to the president of TBN.

"As you know, three young missionaries were captured and held hostage several days ago in Abedistan," the colonel told Gary. "Their fate was truly left in the hands of the Ab Didal who inhabit a small city of Moraba and other points to the west of the Muslim country. There has been much concern about their welfare such that television networks, such as yours, have included their situation in news programs on a daily basis. Many believe that some kind of military strike will be launched in Abedistan in the near future, especially in the western sector of the country.

"Having this in mind, our strategy team was urged to move forward with whatever we deemed appropriate to effect some kind of rescue attempt before the military skirmishes begin. After some serious discussion it was agreed that we would develop a unique pseudo-military effort as quickly as possible to remove the young ladies from harm's way. A crash course was devised and a team of seven was trained for the specific purpose of getting these hostages in advance of any military intervention to remove them from the land of the Ab Didal terrorist group.

"About two weeks ago this brave team parachuted into Abedistan and have been situated in Moraba since that time. Although we have not received the signal indicating their exact timing of the rescue, we believe that this will take place in forty-eight hours.

"A few days ago when your network sent a reporter to the area after negotiating with the Ab Didal, we all knew that you all needed to be informed before the rescue strike was undertaken. I know you see the danger after the young ladies are rescued. The Ab Didal will certainly think that you all were involved in the mission somehow, and your reporter's life will certainly be in danger."

"That is a powerful story," the president stated. "I am sure our reporter would wind up in the cross-hair sight of a rifle after the missionaries are rescued. Obviously, I want to keep him on location as long as possible, but on the other hand there is much risk of keeping him there too long.

"You have provided me with a wealth of information that if communicated would foil any rescue attempt, so please rest assured that I'll withhold any report that might jeopardize the safety of the rescue team. By the way, who is on this team?"

"You will never believe this, but the Coach of Bacon College and six of her athletes are sitting as we speak only a few hundred yards from your reporter and only a very short distance to where the missionaries are being held."

"I can't believe these girls from the small college are involved in this extremely dangerous mission," Gary stated so loudly that several people in the restaurant turned in their direction. "Are they trained well enough successfully to pull this off and not get killed themselves in the process?" he asked with eyebrows raised.

"During the training everyone was just amazed as to how well they did," the colonel answered.

"I have spent my entire life in television, and this is by far the most intriguing story that I have ever heard, and here I am right in the thick of it all," the president stated excitedly.

"I don't have to tell you this, but it's imperative that none of this information is broadcast such that it would put in jeopardy the welfare of the rescue team," the colonel seriously related.

"Please be assured that nothing will be said until after the mission is over, but after that time, will you permit me to divulge the whole scenario?" Gary asked.

"That will be fine, but be sure the team has escaped Abedistan and outside a hostile environment," the colonel requested.

Having completed their most important meeting and eaten a most delicious home-cooked buffet known throughout the area, the two leaders headed to their respective aircraft that had gathered several curious local inspectors by this time.

Paul H. Jones

SIGNAL

Back in Moraba the team members were just completing their morning excursion in the marketplace and were starting their debriefing session. "The activities around the prison seem to be routine, and the soldiers on guard utilize the same schedule each day," Coach Anna related. "With this kind of behavior we can predict their movements with more accuracy."

"I saw Madu moving among the guards with ease and without any obstruction whatsoever," Esther added. "He seems to know everyone and everybody shares with him all along the way."

"This afternoon we want to talk to him again about the prison area to be sure we are aware of all of the things in reach of the guards," Coach Anna stated.

"I believe we can trust him because if for no other reason than that we know he has a Bible," Dorothy indicated.

"Our time here is running out," Coach Anna pointed out. "It's time to effect our rescue mission. I am going to give the signal that we are ready." Pulling the electronic signaler from her backpack, she pressed the red button, giving three long beeps and then followed by sending three short signals.

The whole complexion of the unit on the USS Virginia changed, and when the signal was immediately relayed to the command center, the heart palpitation increased by several beats. Radioing the center commander, Captain Nolte told Colonel Carlton that the "go" signal had just been received and that preparations by every unit were underway.

"I want you to contact Gary Davidson of TBN television and have him on the line when I get to the command center," the colonel stated excitedly. "We'll be there momentarily."

Gary was surprised to receive news of the rescue so soon, but he immediately knew that he had to work fast. "Would he be able to effect the rescue of his reporter who was not imprisoned?" he thought, as he single handedly tried to take care of everything without arousing suspicion. "My situation is not like that of the Bacon girls' team that would be dealing with a hostile environment including gunfire and possibly even more battlefield exchanges," he continued in thought. "Those girls are really something to risk their own lives to try to save another."

Dr. Damond took the call from Colonel Carlton in the spacious coliseum. "Dr. Damond," the colonel said, "we have just received the signal that within forty-eight hours the rescue mission will be undertaken."

"I am so worried about the welfare of our girls," the president stated. "Please keep me informed."

"I'll do that," he replied. "I have also alerted the TBN president so he can remove his reporter in Moraba."

"That too is a serious problem for you to consider," Dr.Damond stated.

Moving to the middle of the gymnasium floor, Dr. Damond reported to the students. "The rescue team has signaled our command center that they are ready to launch the rescue. It will be done during the next forty-eight hours.

At seven this evening I have asked Reverend Josh Morrow, the father of Maggie, to conduct our service."

Colonel Carlton continuously met with his team to develop numerous strategies to fit the various scenarios. In the friendly border countries pairs of rescue helicopters were placed all along the boundaries to be prepared to pick up the rescue team and the missionaries. Each was totally equipped in the attack mode in the event shooting and bombing were necessary to get the team out safely. Once everybody was in place, numerous mock practice sessions were staged to work out the details. It was truly a professional military exercise of giant proportions.

In the hideaway in Moraba the rescue team was just completing its planning session when Madu came into view. "Come over here, Madu," Coach Anna requested.

Always a delight to be around, Madu with a wide smile hustled over to where his new friends were located. "How are the missionaries today?" Coach Anna asked.

"They are very weary and seem to be very weak," he responded. "They didn't talk very much when I was with them."

"Are they being guarded the same way?" Coach Anna inquired.

"There are always three guards on the second floor roof and two on the bottom floor," he stated.

"Which one keeps the keys to the prison door?" Coach Anna asked.

"The one who has a long beard always opens the door for me," Madu told her.

"Does he have many keys with him?" she interrogated further.

"The one to the prison door is tied on a short rope and it is the only one he has," Madu said, being pleased that he could answer her questions.

Coach Anna had a long meeting with her team after Madu left. "At three o'clock tomorrow morning, we shall

stage our raid to free the hostages," Coach Anna said. "I
want each of you to go over in your mind the whole scenario
from start to finish many times over before that time.
Dorothy, I want you to lead the subteam to the second floor
and subdue the three soldiers in that area. On your team will
be Marsha, Mit, and Hanna. To overcome the two soldiers
on the first floor area, Esther and Maggie will handle that
chore. I will be stationed near the steps to the roof while at
the same time in position to observe what is taking place
near the prisoners. Those of you with Dorothy must realize
that there is a case of hand grenades in the corner on the
second floor. It's imperative that you take control of the
three soldiers quickly and without their getting to the box of
grenades.

"Night sight equipment should be used again tonight
so that you will be familiar with night vision tactics when we
start the real assault. Patience is going to be critical, but our
actions must be simultaneous to be effective. Our cue will
come from Dorothy's group so when you start, the first floor
group will begin immediately. We will wear our sleek
camouflage uniforms with our lightweight shoes.
Camouflage dressing will be utilized on our face and hands.
Our weapons will be checked before we depart to be sure
they are fully loaded with ammunition. Gags and tie strings
will be carried in a convenient place. Remember, a strong
blow on the head might be the difference of victory and
defeat, and a brief reluctance might give the enemy the
advantage, so don't hesitate. Know that you are in
command. Be sure the soldier is totally aware that you have
a weapon. This could be a large part of the battle."

There were numerous questions as they honed their
mental battle skills for what lay just ahead. Their behavior
had changed; it was a time of serious pensiveness. This was
different; they had weapons; would they have to use them?
These were some thoughts along with many others as they

tried to rest during the night lying on the ground with sand covering their garments behind the weather beaten mud brick wall.

Nightly TBN news came on at the regular time with the reporter describing the scene in Moraba, going on to say that little had changed during the several days he was there. The schedule of the people was very predictable as they go about their routine each day. He spent a lot of time in his telecast about the three missionaries being held hostage in Moraba and from time to time paraded in the streets to show not only strength of the Ab Didal, but clearly flaunting their arrogance so as to say to the United States, "Here they are. Come and get them, if you dare."

He continued to revisit our country's stand regarding the use of hostages to obtain ransoms of all kinds. "We have always said that we would not negotiate with terrorists, and to my knowledge we have not in this case. It's an honorable position, but it does not bring peace to the minds and hearts of the victims' relatives and friends. Of course not, but what do we do about these situations, especially this one so far from our homeland in this remote country of people who are being led through fear? They cooperate with the Ab Didal because they want to live. Just down the street tonight are these lovely young ladies wanting so desperately to be free, but more is needed than just desire"

Using the philosophical approach with his audience this evening, he had touched many hearts during this telecast. He was really anxious himself and stood ready with a minute's notice to abandon his telecasting and be airlifted to safety. As the camera panned the area showing the mountains all around the small city, he thought, "My responsibility for safety is only to save myself, but the responsibility of the rescue team is not only for their safety but the safety also of the three missionaries." Not really knowing the make-up of the rescue group, he assured himself in his thoughts that they were seasoned military personnel in special forces trained well for such an undertaking.

In the scene all along the way from the USS Virginia to the command center to the coliseum at Bacon College, everyone was very tense awaiting the assault on the terrorists by the most unsuspecting rescue team ever assembled.

The media had gotten in such a state of frenzy with several theories being tossed about such that each of the major networks couldn't hold back any longer so they began to make the news themselves by suggesting reasons why the Bacon College girls and coach were missing. "No one around the college seems to be concerned about their welfare," one anchor stated. "Some seem to think that it's the college's way of paying back the media that have been so very disruptive of their academic program during the last several weeks. One even mentioned a meeting that couldn't be substantiated by anyone else of a high ranking military official and Coach Bosley a few weeks ago on the Parkway."

"I am glad to get through the evening's main news programs without any definite reporting of the girls' whereabouts," Dr. Damond thought, as he sat in the coliseum with his students and invited guests. "It's not going to be long now."

Standing before the group shielded from the menacing press, he told the students and others, "Preparation for this exercise began several weeks ago when our young ladies, your peers, volunteered to challenge the will of terrorists thousands of miles away in Abedistan. They have been waiting a long time for this moment. I am very excited as I stand before you in our very safe environment, and can only imagine what is going through the minds of our dear friends on the rescue team. Please hold hands and let's offer a sentence prayer each for this brave group as they too wait for their command to rescue those whose freedom was taken away from them."

The sentence prayers were so compassionately and beautifully stated by all present, after which quiet reigned supreme as the students were lost in their own personal thoughts. Spontaneously, all of the basketball and soccer players were taken to the middle of the floor where they were instructed to sit with all the others sitting around them.

RESCUE BEGINS

I t was two o'clock, and Coach Anna was preparing her team to meet the enemy. Checking off items one by one with positive responses, she reviewed the escape route one more time. It was a very dark night and with their camouflage, they blended right in with the night environment. They had removed all excess items including their wrist compass and PIM signaler. Everything was placed in their backpacks, which were carefully positioned to be picked up as they fled the area. Checking their weapons to be sure they were loaded, they tightened their belt so their pistol would remain steadfast on their side. Coach Anna could sense that the intensity she had gotten used to on the basketball court was evident as the group moved quietly to the edge of the market street, right across from their target. Dim oil lamps in the distance could be seen breaking through the dark.

Moving across the narrow part of the street in the dark, they soon were within a few feet of their enemy. "Please God help us on this night to fulfill our mission," Coach Anna prayerfully thought, as they got in position to make their attack. Quietly, she hugged each of them and while doing so realized that they were ready to do the job. "Let's go," she whispered, as Dorothy led her group of

Hanna, Marsha, and Mit quietly up the steps. Peering over the top step, Dorothy carefully assessed the situation. One soldier was asleep almost at the top step where she was located, a second one was sprawled on the concrete floor and the third was sitting in a chair around the corner with only his feet sticking out. Dorothy directed Hanna and Marsha to subdue the first soldier, Mit was advised to handle the second one and Dorothy would take the third. With pistols in hand they quietly moved in position standing over the Ab Didal guards.

Esther and Maggie were in position downstairs to overtake their sleeping soldiers. With Coach Anna holding her fully loaded automatic assault rifle in the port arms position, they were ready to do what they had planned for the last several weeks.

Back at Bacon a strong prayer vigil was underway, as they seemed to know that something important was going to take place soon to free the hostages. In the command center Colonel Carlton and his command team were watching the numerous monitoring screens and examining the pictures being sent by high flying surveillance aircraft. "We have a very good team on this mission," the colonel thought in just a last minute personal vote of confidence.

Dorothy suddenly pushed her guard turning over his chair, jumped on top of him and poked the barrel of her pistol in his face so he knew she had one. He made an immediate thrust upward to move toward his automatic weapon, and just as he did, she reacted by swatting him across the temple with the handle side of her pistol. He fell motionless to the floor where she began to tie him up securely and placed a gag in his mouth.

Hanna and Marsha kicked the weapon of their guard to the side while they sat on top of him as they held his arms behind his back. They were not swift enough to prevent his loud yells for help from his colleagues. Soon they were in

150

control having tightened a gag in his mouth to preclude further yelling. Mit was using some of her jungle tactics to subdue her guard with help later from Dorothy.

A shot rang out early on the first floor as Esther fired her pistol to get the attention of her objective. Maggie used her feet to kick her guard several times before he relented such that she could render him helpless with a good job of tying him up. As Coach Anna stood ready to use her automatic weapon to assist the girls amidst the activities on both floors, she felt a tug at her arm. Startled, she turned with her weapon when she heard a frightened voice, "It's me, Madu. I have come to help!"

Without hesitation he ran up on the second floor to help Dorothy and her group. Among other things he put the guards' weapons in a pile, and carefully examined the wooden crate of hand grenades, picked one up and brought it back down to Coach Anna.

Seeing the silhouette of Dorothy standing, Coach Anna hollered to Dorothy. "Roll the soldiers down the steps."

Esther got the key from the bearded guard who was now helplessly tied and gagged. Quickly, the door to the prison was opened, and she and Maggie rushed in to get the missionaries. The young ladies were really frightened because they were not sure who their captors this time really were. "We are a rescue team from the United States," Esther said, as she grabbed the rope that held them all together. Taking her knife, the rope was cut hurriedly, and the prisoners still stood in their tracks not believing what was taking place, having been in captivity so long and during that time severely being mistreated. One of the missionaries said, "But you all are just girls."

"Let's talk about that later," Esther said, as she directed the group to the street where Coach Anna was located.

"Get the two guards down on the first floor and pull them out in the street with the other three," Coach Anna directed.

The noise of the rescue had caused those nearby to come to the market area and watch the action as best they could in the dark, with shadows being cast by the oil lamps that were becoming more and more visible in the area. The whole team with the missionaries assembled in the street. Checking to see that everyone was okay, Coach Anna sent the team to the other side of the street where Madu was waiting for them. Coach Anna surprised everybody as she pulled the pin from the hand grenade and threw it on the roof near the case of grenades in the corner. Almost simultaneously, she ran to catch up with her colleagues. The rapid fire detonation of the several grenades caused a huge fireball to go up into the air as the whole building below that had served as a prison for the three hostages disintegrated as the rescue team got one final look.

"Follow me," Madu said in a commanding tone. With the missionaries in the middle there was a brief stop to get the team's wherewithal, and they were on their way to the south. The terrain was really rough, and the difficulty in walking was compounded by the darkness.

Coach Anna felt comfortable being led by Madu, who certainly had risked his life in helping them on this morning. Then too, they were being led by a young man who knew the terrain like the back of his hand, going in the same direction she was planning to go to make their escape.

Not too long in their movement, a helicopter could be heard overhead, and in the distance it was casting a bright and wide light beam as the Ab Didal searched the landscape for their prey. Soon they could hear the engines of several choppers canvassing the whole area with only one goal in mind, that of retrieving their missionary prisoners and severely punishing those who made the rescue.

"The Ab Didal is pulling out all stops to prevent us from escaping," Coach Anna thought, as she walked behind her special team that only moments ago performed a rescue without anyone being killed or hurt severely. "They always amaze me, because they seem to be so very mild mannered, and then to fulfill their objective, their entire comportment changes suddenly."

Helicopters crisscrossing the sky continued even with more intensity such that Madu directed the team toward a mountainside of craggy rocks where right at the base was a small opening. "Bend down and slide between the rock and the bank," he said.

Madu went first followed by Esther and the remainder of the team. Inside, a cavernous opening provided much room for the whole group comfortably to take refuge. Shortly, Madu scrambled deeper into the cave and came back with an oil lamp that he lit. When the light was visible, it was almost like one could hear a strong sigh of relief.

Speaking for the first time to the missionaries who still did not know who their rescuers were, Coach Anna inquired, "How are you three doing?"

"We are so thankful to you for rescuing us from the terrorists," one said.

"Let me introduce our group to you," Coach Anna said, as she looked around at her rescue team that really looked like an outstanding special forces unit in their camouflage outfits, with their face dressing and pistols strapped to their sides. "From my left we have Esther, Marsha, Mit, Hanna, Dorothy and Maggie. My name is Anna Bosley and they call me Coach Anna. We are from Bacon College. I am the basketball and soccer coach, and these young ladies are some of my athletes."

Crying all the while, the missionary seated closest to Coach Anna introduced herself and the other two, and the real hugging and crying for joy began. What a joyous scene tucked away in a cave in the remote area of Abedistan!

TBN was trying its best to uphold the promise made by the president so almost every half an hour he would call Colonel Carlton for approval to release the story. Finally, Colonel Carlton relented with specific restrictions.

Surfing the news channels the Bacon group saw on the screen, "Breaking News." A tired reporter advised the viewing audience that they had been on site in Abedistan for the last several days, but were forced to withdraw at the request of the government last evening.

"With cameras pointed toward Moraba, at three o'clock this morning an attack was made on the building thought to house the missionaries being held prisoner," he stated. "A gunshot could be heard and about ten minutes later a huge mushroom of smoke and fire billowed upward filling the sky with smoke seen many miles in every direction. Following this development, I was whisked away to safety in a helicopter, now being situated in a bordering friendly country. Let me show you the blast."

Watching while holding their breath, the Bacon group knew their girls were responsible, but were they safe now or were they blown up in the powerful blast? Then the reporter came back on the air to say, "Obviously, someone is responsible for this explosion, and the fact that Ab Didal helicopters are scouring the landscape as we speak means that the rescue must have been successful."

"They have just disappeared," Colonel Carlton said to his team. "Official calls were coming from everywhere. From the Office of the President of the United States came a call. "I'll call you as soon as we hear anything," Colonel Carlton sadly told the staff member, not having anything positive to report. Surveillance planes were discovering nothing on the ground.

"I wonder why Major Bosley has not sent us a beeping signal of any kind," Colonel Carlton asked his staff that had grown considerably as time ticked on. Conjuring up many thoughts, the colonel related several theories including one that raised serious concern about their welfare following the blast during the raid. "Our team was not equipped with any explosives so whatever detonated was possessed by the Ab Didal," he stated. "Could our group have been blown up by a suicide bomb strapped to one of the guards?"

"Further, if this theory is not acceptable," he said, "How do we account for the fact that they have not made contact? All Major Bosley has to do is to excite the beep sensor, and we immediately know they are safe. That doesn't sound like it's hard to do, does it?"

"But we have not heard a sound from them," he continued in an anxious tone. "Thirdly, they are equipped with PIM instruments that they have used during their entire stay, and now the instruments have been deactivated following the rescue attempt. What do you make of that?"

"But all of us envisioned that the rescue team would discreetly leave Abedistan on one of our helicopters shortly after the rescue was over," he continued. "Just look at the area on the monitors as we speak. The skies over there are filled with helicopters, not ours, but those of the Ab Didal, as they show unusual determination to seize our rescue team. If my previous theories were correct, do you think the Ab Didal would have launched such a massive military search. They have been embarrassed by it all following their boastful and arrogant behavior as they held the missionaries hostage. Wait until they find out the make-up of the team."

The meeting of Colonel Carlton was interrupted suddenly when there was news of an official report from the Ab Didal in Abedistan regarding the alleged invasion from the United States. The television network for years had been friendly to those with anti-American sentiment so it was no surprise that the terrorist group in Moraba would have access to the medium to convey their message. "We can learn much from their remarks," Colonel Carlton stated, as he looked around to a full contingent of interested command center personnel.

An official of the Ab Didal made a general statement indicating his and his group's hatred toward the "imperialists" from the west. "They have usurped our justice by taking our prisoners before they were provided a fair trial by our people," he said excitedly flailing his arms and hands as he displayed numerous gestures, which were supposed to reveal truth in what he was conveying. His loud dissertation continued for several minutes before the consensus most notorious world terrorist leader stepped before the microphones, with numerous armed soldiers brandishing new automatic assault rifles standing behind him.

The Ab Didal had terrorized throughout the world for decades and had moved their renegades to the poor and weak country of Abedistan a few years ago when world concern about terrorism was heightened as a result of more than a dozen attacks on the free world. After the United Nations failed miserably to fulfill its commitment to freedom and tranquility, the United States realized that it had enough of their terror so our country got on the offensive, with the goal in mind to rid the world of those bent on terror. Lada du Daba, their leader, was number one on the list.

"The team of militants from the United States entered our country several days ago, and their activities here were monitored closely," he said in a calm voice. "Little did we know that they were here to remove our law breakers and deprive them of Abedistany justice by our fair system of meting out punishment that befits the crime. This invading force on our sovereign land brought a different kind of battlefield tactic. The foreign invaders used a poisonous gas of unknown origin to kill our guards, all of whom had families to support." At this time graphic pictures of those allegedly killed in the raid and their families were shown for all the world to see on television.

"We are very disturbed regarding this matter and have requested the United Nations for assistance and also help from the Red Cross. These are warmongers cloaked in business suits and driving new cars on their streets looking down their nose at fledgling countries who happen to disagree with their philosophical approach to government. With all of their war toys we all here wonder why the self-proclaimed best country on earth would stoop to kill innocent men with a chemical banned from use by the world community. Please know that our search goes on for these culprits that we believe are still in our country, hiding in our mountains. We'll find them and give them the same medicine they gave our innocent governmental workers guarding our prison. If your country would like to help us, please contact our Chief of Homeland Security stationed in Moraba. These imperialists need to be taught a lesson. Their next attack may be on your country."

This venomous assault on the integrity of the United States was going to be difficult for the officials to respond. On the one hand the military was involved in this rescue mission, but on the other the private sector played a bigger role. Immediately, the press secretary was asked to answer questions of the ravenous media whose appetites had really been whetted during the last few minutes, as they were spellbound by the outspoken terrorist world leader.

Calls from the media to the White House multiplied after the statement made by Lada du Daba, such that a meeting was immediately scheduled for the press secretary to make an official statement as a response to the strong allegations earlier. Colonel Carlton received another call from the White House. "What do you make of the statement that was made by Lada du Daba?" the staff official immediately asked.

"I don't know how world leaders can get center stage and lie to the people time after time," Colonel Carlton responded.

"They can really get a sympathetic ear from the Muslim world such that no concern is given regarding establishing the truth," the official said.

"It doesn't matter what is uttered so long as it supports the terrorists' cause," Colonel Carlton replied.

"Have you all heard anything at all from the rescue team?" the official asked.

"It's been nearly four hours since the rescue was attempted, and we have not received any indication as to where they are," Colonel Carlton indicated. "The clearest message we have received came from Lada du Daba himself when he told everybody that they were searching for the group. With that in mind we know that they have escaped. You are aware that we have used two electronic systems to monitor their movement. One is the manual beeping system that gives us a signal that they are all right. The other system is one wherein our rescue team is identified on the ground by number so we can see and know where each of them is located all the while. Just before the raid this system went dead and nothing has been heard from them since."

"What do think has happened?" the official asked.

"We have been discussing this for the last three hours, and the only thing I can come up with is that Major Bosley is concerned that the system signals can be picked up by the helicopters flying overhead over there as we speak," he related.

"Do you think that is a valid reason for not keeping in contact?" the staff official asked.

"Recently there was a military informational sheet supplied to the various special forces' commanders advising them to realize that at times the PIM system was not fool proof and that the enemy could pick up the signal in certain kinds of environment," the colonel advised.

"Do you think that Major Bosley, who is really a civilian now, would have had knowledge of this flaw in the system?" the official inquired.

"We think this informational sheet was included in her training package when they went to the California desert training," Colonel Carlton responded.

"Would you tell me the make-up of this rescue team?" the official asked.

"Major Anna Bosley is the leader accompanied by Esther Minold, Marsha Gavanto, Dorothy Buford, Maggie Morrow, Hanna Green and Mit Travers," he stated. "Three of them play on the best basketball team in the country, two are on the new soccer team, while the sixth member is the manager who plays basketball from time to time when needed. Esther is the most outstanding basketball player in the country, and I am told that Mit is probably the best soccer player in college today. The other girls excel, also."

"Whew! That's a powerful team!" the official excitedly responded. "They too foiled the terrorist plot in Portland, saving the lives of all on board, didn't they?"

"That's correct," he noted. "You can see now why we were so optimistic regarding our rescue mission."

"Please keep me posted so I can keep the President informed," the official requested, as he closed the conversation.

Stepping out in front of a packed house of reporters, the press secretary said, "I have a statement to make before I take any questions.

"The report that you all heard from the leader of the Ab Didal from Abedistan was blatantly untrue," he firmly stated, as he looked at the numerous members of the press corps. "At this time we are trying to piece together why we believe such a statement was made at all, and secondly, why such an untrue statement was made at all. The psychology of this whole statement by Lada du Daba clearly points to his frustration as we defied his boastful threats to attempt to rescue our loved ones. Now let me take your questions."

"Are you admitting that the United States did attempt some kind of rescue of the three missionaries being held captive by the Ab Didal?" an older female reporter asked.

"That's correct," he replied.

"When did this operation take place?" a young man asked.

"The best way I can describe the time is to remind you of the television report of BTN when a loud blast was reported," he said.

"What kind of blast was that anyway?" a bearded reporter asked. "What kind of explosives did the special forces' team have with them?"

"Our special rescue team only had hand pistols and one assault rifle with them so we are at a loss at this time to explain the huge blast that rocked the area," the press secretary answered.

Then the serious questioning began. "There have been all kinds of rumors afloat regarding the make-up of the rescue team," a national reporter indicated. "Could you tell us what branches of our armed forces participated?"

"All four of major branches of military group were actively involved," he stated, just before he dropped the bombshell. "But the main thrust of the total effort came from the private sector or our civilian population?"

With sudden unrest in the journalists' ranks, a reporter blurted out, "Are you saying that members of the brave rescue team came from civilians?"

"That's what I am saying," he acknowledged.

"Who are these individuals who would risk their lives to free these hostages from the most notorious terrorists in the entire world?" an excited reporter asked.

"I can't divulge that information at this juncture, but will release it soon when the group has made contact," the press secretary stated.

"Have you heard from the rescue team at all since the attempt was made?" another asked. "Are they and the missionaries safe at this point?"

"There has been no signal from them whatsoever so far," he pointed out.

It had been a powerful press conference that was closed at this time realizing that the press secretary had been forthcoming with so very much valuable information, and further answers to questions might really jeopardize the safety of Coach Anna and her team as they struggled to safety.

By the time of the press conference a large national talk show had the parents of the rescued missionaries on board a flight to be guests on the morning show the next day. It was being advertised continuously.

HIDING OUT

S outh of Moraba the rescue team with their freed missionaries hunkered down in a large cave, waiting for a time when there was no helicopter activity in the air and darkness covered the area. After they had time to relax just a little, Coach Anna met with the group. "I know you all have really been mistreated during your days of captivity," she stated, as she reached to touch each of the three missionaries. "Please feel comfortable with the rescue team as we continue to make our way to safety. All of you remember to drink your water sparingly. Madu tells me that in one of the caves there is pure water to drink, and we'll be in that one before too long. As long as there are helicopter flights nearby, we won't be able to signal our command center. When we move out tonight, I am going to give the beep signal to indicate that we are safe, but no more because I believe the enemy might pick up other signals.

"Not being able to contact our rescue helicopters, we are going to travel from cave to cave until we reach the border country that is friendly to the United States. Upon arrival I will use our PIM sensor and notify our command unit where we are located." Following the meeting, Coach Anna encouraged everybody to get plenty of rest.

There was much interest in the news from the command post so the officials called constantly, but the report was always the same. "We have not heard anything from the group since the rescue," Colonel Carlton told caller after caller. "We think they are okay for now as we continue to pick up signals that the Ab Didal is still flying numerous helicopters across the country, hoping to find the group that captured their prisoners in which they had been so proud over the last several weeks."

Dr. Damond was always thankful for his report from the command center team, but each time wished the report was more positive. "The girls have been silent much too long," he told his group now remaining in the coliseum around the clock. "Each hour that passes elevates our concern for the team that are really in harm's way and probably at the moment struggling themselves to remain free."

The six parents of the three missionaries looked very tired as they took their seat in front of the popular morning show host. "I hope you had a good night's rest," he said.

"We tried to sleep but our concern, as always, for our child prevents us to rest properly," one mother stated.

"Tell us a little about your daughter," he said while looking at the older couple sitting to his left.

"Right after college, our daughter wanted to serve on the mission field for a couple of years, and following six weeks of training, she was assigned to Abedistan, a country I didn't know existed. "She was joined later by two other lovely ladies who had similar stories. As time passes and after reading the letters from my daughter, I realized that this country was becoming the hideout for a group of terrorists called the Ab Didal. Peace and tranquility were replaced with confusion and uncertainty as weeks passed. The people were suddenly subjected to rigid rules of conduct, and those not following the guidelines were severely punished, mainly to show the stranglehold the Ab Didal had on the people."

"During this time of change, did you try to encourage your girls to come home and remove themselves from the danger that lurked everywhere?" he asked.

"Obviously, we all did but because of the bond of friendship among the three, and their commitment to tell the world about the teachings of Jesus Christ, they never wavered in their commitment to stay," one mother stated.

"When do you think they realized that the situation was out of hand?" he asked.

"In the last uncensored letter from my daughter, she wrote a lengthy dissertation about the abusiveness of the leaders in Moraba, and how it was impossible to do anything without it being judged immediately by the gun carrying Ab Didal with punishment meted out by the accuser," the middle mother related. "All the people were really frightened and had little enthusiasm to thwart those who were taking their freedom away. They just cowered away and just hoped this new group now calling Moraba home would just leave. But this didn't happen."

"What did your daughters do under these conditions?" the host asked.

"Many young people and adults had become Christian brothers and sisters in Christ, but our daughters encouraged them not to continue to meet with them until further notice but to take their literature, including a copy of the Bible, and study individually in a very private and secret place.

"One day a young lady's literature was confiscated and was traced back to our three girls, and of course, you know what happened then," the youngest father said. "They were arrested and placed in prison. We believe they were abused and tortured to attempt to get them to renounce their citizenship and their Christian faith. To this point they have remained steadfast in their commitment to God."

"Have you heard the rumors about the rescue team?" he inquired.

"We have heard all kinds of things," one father said. "Someone knows but won't tell at this time because the safety of the whole group is at stake."

"We are so happy that someone made an attempt to rescue them," another stated, "because we knew their lives were in much danger as each day passed."

"There is one rumor floating around which indicates that some private citizens are implicated in the scheme to rescue your girls from the enemy," the host noted.

"We are so grateful to anyone who has dared to undertake such a very dangerous and risky mission," another father related. "Everyone has been so kind to us during this ordeal. Just as we came into your studio, we received an anonymous call from someone who had purchased airline tickets for us to fly to Roanoke, Virginia, and stated that Dr. John Damond, President of Bacon College, had invited us to the campus, awaiting the outcome of this rescue attempt."

"Why do you think he invited you on campus at this time?" the host asked excitedly.

"We are told that he is a very compassionate and humble man who treats his students as though he is their father," the oldest mother stated.

"Do you think your invitation to Bacon College has anything to do with the rumor we all are hearing more and more each passing hour that some of the rescue team is made up of Bacon students?" he inquired.

"I hadn't really thought of that, but what would a group of students know about a most dangerous rescue like this?" one asked the host.

"It really does sound bizarre, doesn't it?" he stated.

"It is somewhat too farfetched for me to believe it," the youngest father indicated.

It was nightfall so Madu crawled outside the cave and

then returned to give the go ahead signal to the others to follow him. They had planned to follow the ravines during the night going directly to the south. As soon as they had traveled about a hundred yards over rough and rocky terrain, Coach Anna stopped the group, opened her backpack and removed her beeper signal. Holding it directly in front of her she firmly pressed the red signal button eleven times.

The first signal from the rescue team brought a loud yell from the USS Virginia, and when simultaneously it was received at the command center, Colonel Carlton gave out a loud and continuous yell. Immediately, he was joined by the others.

Usually he had received these kinds of signals showing no outward signs of emotion, but he and the other strong and brave soldiers were overcome with emotion and tears flowed freely. "They are safe! They are safe! They are safe!" he shouted over and over again. "They pulled off the impossible."

Immediately, Colonel Carlton called the White House to report the good news, and he thought he heard shouts in the background. Shortly, he reported the good news to Bacon College where the students yelled and sang for nearly an hour when the good news was received.

"You have heard that the missionaries' families have been requested to come to Bacon College by way of an invitation by the benevolent person," Dr. Damond stated. "That will really be special because that way they will get timely reports on their daughters, as soon as you receive them."

Maudie was feeling much better now and was so much concerned about the welfare of her Bacon friends on this special mission. "Hello, Dr. Damond," she said after dialing the college. "This is Maudie."

"Maudie, how are you doing?" Dr. Damond asked.

"I feel much better now, but I am really concerned about Coach Anna and the girls. Aren't they something special?" she related.

"I never cease to be amazed at what they do," he stated. "They are far from safety at this time, but somehow I know that they are going to arrive home safely. They have the wherewithal to complete the dangerous task."

"You are such a kind man," Maudie said, praising him for all that he was doing for the students. "Thank you for being a person that would listen to the thoughts of a cleaning lady."

"You are a very valuable member of our wonderful staff here at Bacon College," he quickly responded. "We can't do without you."

"I really want to be present when the rescue team returns," Maudie said. "Would you mind having someone from the college to come to get me here at the hospital?"

"I would be so happy to do that," he gladly replied. "A homecoming would not be complete without you."

Back in Abedistan the rescue team was making very slow progress over the craggy mountain slopes, avoiding normally traveled routes because of the possibility of land mines. Within about thirty minutes of Coach Anna's sending the beeping signal, several Ab Didal helicopters converged on the area casting their bright lights all over the landscape. Coming so fast, the team had no time to take cover, as the light passed within a few feet of them. Realizing that as the helicopters crisscrossed the night sky, they would be discovered soon if they didn't hurriedly find a hiding place.

"Come this way," Madu shouted as he grabbed the hand of one of the missionaries. "There is a large opening in the bank up at the head of the ravine we are in now."

They could hear the helicopters turning around to head back their way as they stumbled and crawled about a

168

hundred yards to what they hoped would be a safe haven for at least a while. The timing was perfect. Just as the last one entered the large area underground, a chopper flew directly overhead casting a light up the ravine. "That was close," Coach Anna thought, as they all hovered around each other waiting for what was next.

With helicopters continuing to fly overhead, Coach Anna said to the group, "It was important that we send the message to let our folks know we are safe on the one hand, but obviously, our enemy picked up the signal. They realize that we couldn't have too many supplies, including water, so they are going to pin us down in these rugged mountains. I'm sure they will put forth their best effort here to stop us so as a warning, expect anything from them."

Before this statement was hardly completed a missile from one of the helicopters detonated just at the large opening, causing rocks and debris from the roof to fall all around the team. Luckily no one was hurt but now they were covered with dust.

"The rescue team is really taking a pounding tonight in the southern hills of Abedistan," the special forces commander stated to his group as they all examined the various monitors. "The Ab Didal must have picked up their all-safe signal about an hour ago and are now pouncing on the area to foil their escape. The Ab Didal has taken it on themselves to use this airspace for their wrongful acts, it appears. I believe Major Bosley decided to use this route because it was not controlled by the terrorist group, but little did we all know that this evil group would make its own rules to fit the occasion."

"We have fourteen pairs of attack helicopters to be used to rescue the team so I want to bring our brave team back to safety," Colonel Carlton stated. "They have done their most dangerous job, and it's now time for us to see that they get back safely."

Because the other television networks were making regular reports on the rescue mission, TBN got approval to go ahead with further coverage. Announcing about fifteen minutes in advance of the telecast that a very special report was forthcoming, they had garnered most of the viewers for its special telecast.

"I report to you today from a neutral country near Abedistan where I was assigned several days before the rescue attempt," the reporter stated at the inception of what would be a most interesting program. "It took several days for me to understand even just a little of their governmental situation. There was a president who lived in the eastern part of the country, and in the west of this sovereign land lived the terrorists, or the Ab Didal, led by Lada du Daba. This man was known all over the world for his terrorist attacks, and here I was each day seeing him in the streets of Moraba, a small town where he was holding his prize prisoners, three young female missionaries.

"To say that I felt safe there would not be a true statement. Then I received the shock of my journalism life. My network president contacted me to advise of an impending attempt to rescue the young missionaries. How could that be done I thought? Were they just going to swoop down and shoot up the place and hope that no one on the team would be killed? With soldiers brandishing the most modern assault rifles as they guarded what was believed the prison, it would take a miracle to rescue these people from the determined Ab Didal.

"During my last couple of hours on location in Moraba, the president of our network talked to me again about the situation, and he told me that the rescue attempt would be made during the darkness in the early morning. I was really scared. The president knew I had great compassion for my assignment and had made many

Abedistany friends so he said he wanted further to reveal to me information about the impending rescue.

"The rescue team is made up of females, the athletes and coach of Bacon College." When this statement was made the whole viewing audience gasped, and after they caught their breath began to cry. In fact tears could be seen in the eyes of the reporter. "I was told that the girls had been in Moraba for several days in preparation of the rescue attempt, having parachuted in during the night from the west. They walked around in the streets wearing their burquas and blended in with the native people. Many of you were watching TBN when the loud and powerful explosion rocked Moraba during the rescue. I still do not know what happened to cause such a blast. Lada du Daba was really embarrassed that a team could free his most special prisoners and get away with it and not get caught. He will stop at nothing to kill them so that is the reason all of us are concerned today for the welfare of this brave group of young ladies from Bacon College."

It was a compelling report that really had shaken the viewing audience. Because there were so many calls to Bacon College, Dr. Damond had his students to take turns answering the telephones. Now the media, who were still being deprived access to the students and staff of Bacon, knew why there had been so much secrecy during the last few days. There was some solace though; they did recognize that some of the group was missing and tried to fit them somehow in the puzzle. Now they knew what part they were playing in this whole ordeal.

Jewel Throneberry had never been bashful in seeking out a story for her magazine, and now that she was trying hard to undo that ugly article that had really changed her entire life, she continued with the same zeal.

"Dr. Damond," she said, when the president came on the line. "This is Jewel Throneberry, the author of that despicable article that was printed in our magazine several days ago."

"Oh! I remember you well," Dr. Damond stated. "You really did a good job in relating your apology to the girls. We all were impressed."

"I would like to provide a catered dinner for your students and others participating in the lock-in on campus," she said. "Please know that I have no ulterior motives whatsoever."

Realizing that she was still groping for an even deeper act of contrition, Dr. Damond consented for her to provide dinner for the group. All the students got very excited when Dr. Damond mentioned to them that the evening meal included pizza.

The White House had been brought up to date such that they were ready to hold another press conference as the table was being set to bring the rescue team and the rescued out of Abedistan with or without force. The Pentagon was now in charge with the Commander-in Chief at the controls.

Walking out into a full house of reporters, the press secretary, Morgan Stacy, said, "I know that you all have been clamoring for more information regarding our rescue attempt in Abedistan. A signal was made about two hours ago indicating that all eleven of them were safe. At this juncture we are not sure who the eleventh one is because the rescue team is made up of seven, and they rescued three missionaries being held prisoner there. We think they are hiding in the mountains south of Moraba where, as we speak, there is shooting taking place. Our surveillance aircraft and other devices show several enemy helicopters hovering over a small area where we believe the team is located. We are reviewing the situation carefully and are ready to take whatever action is appropriate to bring this group back to us safely. Now I will take your questions."

"Is the President aware of the situation, and if he is, what is he doing about it?" an older reporter bluntly asked.

"He is aware of every aspect of this situation and is making the decisions regarding a rescue attempt even as we speak," the young man answered.

"How on earth did college girls get involved in such an undertaking?" a young man asked.

"Now as we look back on a successful rescue, we can get a better picture as to why we used females on this endeavor," he stated. "These girls led by Major Anna Bosley, their coach and a decorated green beret marine, made an imposing team that received strong plaudits all along the way in their training, mainly in the Mohave Desert a few weeks ago. In any challenge it's important to send your best. The United States did in this case."

"We have heard of Coach Bosley, but who are the others on this successful team?" a lady reporter asked.

Pulling a note from his pocket, he read, "Dorothy Buford, Hanna Green, Marsha Gavanto, Esther Minold, Maggie Morrow, and Mit Travers. They are all athletes from Bacon College. Esther, Dorothy, Maggie and Hanna are part of the basketball team, and Mit and Marsha are members of the newly organized soccer team. As you know regarding the basketball program there, these girls are very exceptional players, and I am told that Marsha and Mit are unusual soccer players with many believing that Mit is the best player in the United States. Most of you now know Esther whose name is synonymous with women's basketball in our country. You see, a better team could not have been found."

"Could you tell us a little about their training and what weapons they used?" an older, bearded man asked.

"Their main training took place in the Mohave Desert where they learned how to jump out of planes at night and guide their chutes to a designated target," he responded. "In addition they did all kinds of training on obstacle courses, and participated in many endurance runs. A mock city was established with soldiers used as guards, and they successfully freed the make-believe hostages. In every aspect of their training they made excellent scores. Regarding their weapons, the major carried a military assault rifle and her team members had pistols strapped to their side."

"What caused the explosion in Moraba at the time of the rescue?" a man in the rear asked.

"We are not sure about that, and no one has generated any viable theory to this point in time," he candidly answered.

The questioning continued for nearly an hour as the news conference was carried live throughout the country.

At the various command centers strategies were being planned to rescue Major Bosley and her team. "The helicopter activity we see on our screens now is strong," Colonel Carlton advised the special forces units now poised on the border. "With all of the strong attempt to flush out our rescue team, the Ab Didal is not holding back and throwing everything into this endeavor."

"What do you suspect will happen next from the Pentagon who are now making the decisions?" his counterpart in charge of the attack force near Abedistan asked.

"In our last discussion it was agreed that the reason Major Bosley doesn't more closely identify her position is because the enemy picked up the earlier signal," Colonel Carlton noted. "I believe, and so do many in the Pentagon, that she will signal again soon because right now it couldn't get much worse for them as the enemy aircraft are trying to blow them out of the caves."

Two other blasts had come really close to the cave openings but no one was injured. "They are really honing in on us," Coach Anna said to her group. "As soon as there is a let up in the attack on us, I am going to excite the beeper

again with three long beeps asking for assistance in our
rescue. This is going to be a time when we shall have to
trust our military that they are ready to pounce on the enemy
immediately. Both our enemy and hopefully our leaders will
hear the signal simultaneously, and of course, the faster of
the two who come to our position will have the advantage."

The team sat quietly absorbed in their personal
thoughts knowing that their defensive weapons could not
match that of the Ab Didal, as helicopters still hovered
overhead. Coach Anna was sure they wanted to land but
because of the rough terrain it was not possible. "The only
reason they don't permit their troops to repel to the base of
the ravine is because they didn't bring ground soldiers along,
and they don't have repelling capability on the craft," she
thought. "When they leave we can expect them to return
with the soldiers and equipment."

As the sounds of the helicopters diminished, the
group sat quietly in the dark not saying anything. Then
Coach Anna felt for her backpack and said, "I am going to
try to climb the other side of the mountain to place our
signaling device as far up as possible with a direct beam to
the south," she said. "Esther, I want you to go with me, and
Dorothy, I am placing you in charge of the group until we
return."

The night sight equipment was really helpful as
Esther and Coach Anna moved down the ravine and up the
craggy side of the other mountain. Helping each other climb
a few feet at a time, they soon reached a plateau where there
were several large rocks covering the area. One was a rock
pile with three on top of each other. "I'll put the signaler on
the top rock, excite it, and we can move as swiftly as
possible back to our hideout," she said to Esther.

Soon the job was completed, and she and Esther
moved quickly down the rough mountainside. Just at the
time they thought they were safe, they heard the helicopters
and knew it must be the enemy because U. S. forces had not

had enough time to get to them. Overhead soon with the large and bright light beams moving about on the ground, Esther and Coach Anna hid in the shadows under a rock shelf against the bank. "They have located the signaler," Coach Anna whispered to Esther.

The go ahead was immediately announced to the armed helicopters of the special forces. "We have got a fix on our target area by satellite from the rescue team," the commander stated "Move out to perform the rescue. Don't hesitate to fire on the enemy. Be careful not to injure the rescue team."

All twenty-eight helicopters moved out and headed directly north. Coach Anna knew that it was important to keep the rescue signal activated, and the enemy knew it would serve them best to silence the beeping device. Coach Anna slid out from the rock shelf to look almost straight upward to see the helicopter hovering near the signaler, and suddenly a rope was thrust out the side door. Almost simultaneously, a soldier was repelling down the rope to destroy the signaler. Stepping back just a little, Coach Anna aimed and fired her assault rifle straight toward the helicopter that caused the soldier to change his course, but not before she had emptied her whole clip at the massive machine overhead. "We need to keep the signaler activated as long as possible, and they are bent on destroying it," Coach Anna said to Esther. "They are really mad now so we had better make our way to our group and stand by for what comes next."

During the absence of the enemy chopper, Esther and Coach Anna made it back to their group. "Are you all right?" Dorothy asked. "What was the shooting all about?"

"They were trying to destroy our signaler," Coach Anna said. "I shot a few times into the body of the helicopter to scare them away. They will move more cautiously now and hopefully much slower to give our troops a chance to arrive."

Realizing that her team was very anxious, Coach Anna had all of them to hold hands as they recited Psalm 100:

1 Shout for joy to the LORD, all the earth.
2 Worship the LORD with gladness; come before him with joyful songs.
3 Know that the LORD is God. It is he who made us, and we are his; we are his people, the sheep of his pasture.
4 Enter his gates with thanksgiving and his courts with praise; give thanks to him and praise his name.
5 For the LORD is good and his love endures forever; his faithfulness continues through all generations.

In a short while the whole sky was filled with Ab Didal helicopters, and two fired missiles near the spot where Coach Anna and Esther were hidden earlier. "Their blasts toward the signaler certainly rendered it ineffective," Coach Anna thought, as she checked her assault rifle to be sure that it was ready, if needed. "Check your weapons," she said to her team.

It was like daylight as the enemy lights from the sky covered the ground as the Ab Didal searched the area for the rescue team. Not being able to see what was happening above them, Coach Anna knew that as they steadily hovered overhead soldiers were preparing to repel to the ground. As Coach Anna slid to the opening, she could see what she suspected was taking place. "I believe we are going to have to fight to survive this ordeal," she thought, as she had her armed team members to join her at the entrance of the huge opening. "They don't know where we are located so just remain calm and out of sight. Be sure you have your ammunition with you. It may be a long battle."

About twenty yards away a soldier was struggling to get out of his harness and eventually fell a few feet before he jumped up and hid behind some rocks. Others were coming down nearby. "They appear to be wanting the soldiers to capture us and not just shoot into the mountainside," Coach Anna surmised, as she watched six soldiers trying to assemble on the ground. "If they do get together, we won't have to protect but only one area."

Soon the Ab Didal soldiers began to shoot in several different directions trying to provoke the team to return fire, but they remained silent. Two of the soldiers headed their way quietly slipping up the hill to check the cave opening. Within a few feet of the entrance as soon as one displayed his light, Coach Anna stood and shot several rounds at their feet, frightening them so badly that they scampered back to their hiding place while the other four were pelting the cave opening with bullets. Although not wanting to shoot any of the enemy, Coach Anna still continued her assault of the six men such that they left the area and headed rapidly down the ravine.

TEAM RESCUED

S uddenly, the complexion of the battle scene changed as daylight came along with numerous friendly attack helicopters that immediately forced the Ab Didal to retreat. Several soldiers were captured in the process. Having put their wrist devices on, the PIM sensor gave direct information regarding the whereabouts of the team who by this time had been spotted by a pilot. Landing several hundred yards down on a flat area, two of the helicopters were going to be the rescue vehicles for this brave team of young ladies. Soon, hugs were commonplace because the American special forces' teams were so happy to have made the rescue without bloodshed.

Before they boarded, one of the captains stepped up to Major Bosley, saluted, and said, "I am so very proud of you all. Thank you so much for what you did."

Returning his salute, Coach Anna said, "We are so pleased that you all were able to come to get us from the Ab Didal."

The team looked haggard on the one hand but strong and committed on the other. "Would you mind introducing these young ladies to our teams?" the second captain asked.

"These are my special girls who play for me at Bacon College," Coach Anna stated with a smile that had not been visible the last few days. Walking up to each one and putting her hand on the team member's shoulder, Coach Anna stated, "This is Dorothy Buford, Maggie Morrow, Hanna Green, Esther Minold, Mit Travers and Marsha Gavanto, and these three are our special missionaries who were held captive, tortured and abused. And finally, this young man's name is Madu, and he was the commander of our earlier escape mission."

As soon as they were airborne, one of the captains got on his radio and said, "This is Captain Hassel, come in command post."

"This is command post, go ahead captain," a voice responded.

"All of the rescue team are accounted for along with the ones they rescued, and all appear to be doing well," the captain reported. "They appear to be somewhat undernourished but strong."

"They have performed a miracle and we are so proud," the commander said. "Let me speak to Major Bosley."

Receiving the radio, she stated, "This is Major Bosley."

"We are so very proud of your team and you for what you all have done," he said.

"We were successful only because of the strength and commitment of my girls," she said. "God has blessed us all on this day. Thank you for asking us to participate in this activity."

"What a great job!" the commander said, as he closed the conversation.

Soon they were in friendly territory where the fleet of military helicopters landed, and immediately the whole group was whisked away to a larger transport chopper to be flown to Rome where an air force transport plane was waiting to carry them back to Mateland Air Force Base in Virginia. As soon as they were all situated on the transport plane, several military personnel brought many boxes of food along with water and colas for those on board. Following the blessing by Esther, the group ate ravenously until they were filled. Madu was still with the group of his friends, and they all knew that he would be killed if he returned to Abedistan because of the active role he played in the escape of the prisoners from Moraba.

Before they were airborne, Colonel Carlton came on the radio to speak to the team. "We are so very proud of all of you for what you did for our country," he stated. "Everybody wants to meet and talk to you as soon as possible, but we have planned your return in the way we think you would want to have it done. Upon arrival at Mateland Air Force Base, you will remain there about an hour, and then you will be flown directly to Bacon College where all of your parents will be located. Your debriefing will be conducted later after you have had a chance to be reunited with your loved ones."

In the coliseum at Bacon College all became very quiet when they were advised of breaking news on the large television screen. "Would this be about our girls?" Josh thought, as he held Charlene around the shoulders.

The news of freeing the young missionaries was carried by all the networks. One photographer had gotten a video of the rescue team as it changed helicopters in the border country. "Let me show you our rescue team as they are being transported to a larger airport," the reporter proudly stated.

The students all held hands as the helicopters' engines were shut down, and the doors were opened. The crew unloaded first and then out jumped Coach Anna still carrying her assault rifle, which brought a loud and continuous scream from those watching at Bacon, including the coach's mom and dad. Maggie came next in her military uniform with her army pistol strapped around her waist, and everyone turned to Josh and Charlene who were both so happy they could not hold back their tears. It was James' turn to join the others when Esther jumped down and walked over to where Coach Anna and Maggie were standing. The Bufords yelled when they saw their Dorothy, and Mr. and Mrs. Green cried openly when Hanna joined the team. Marsha and Mit followed and stood with the heroic group.

"They really look like special military troops wearing their uniforms and having their pistols strapped to their sides," Jonsie said to the other girls.

"I believe they are very tired and hungry," Diane stated. "They really do look like a military rescue team with their faces covered with dressing and all of the gear they have with them."

Joining the rescue team were the three missionaries who had been freed. When they walked over to be with their heroes who rescued them, a loud and continuous applause came from every corner of the coliseum. The parents of the hostages were escorted to the center of the coliseum floor, and with everyone holding hands around the group, Dr. Damond said a beautiful prayer that included several special verses of scripture that befitted the occasion.

Afterward Dr. Damond told the group that he had heard from Colonel Carlton and that the whole group would be flown directly to Bacon College to be with their parents and loved ones before they had any kind of debriefing.

In the meantime the President's press secretary announced to the world that the rescue of the three missionaries was successful and everyone was safe. He warned the Ab Didal that future acts of this kind would not be tolerated, and if it did, expect the results to be the same. "Terrorists can't be allowed to hold innocent people hostage, and if it's done, we will take the lead to wipe them off the face of the earth even if it's done one at a time. Peace and terrorism can't coexist so the Ab Didal must understand that the peaceful part of the world had a zero tolerance for terrorism of any kind."

Further, he stated that the President was so grateful for the bravery and courage of the rescue team, and he looked forward to their visit to the White House sometime in the near future.

With this announcement and the breaking news of the return of the team, the campus was inundated by reporters, such that Dr. Damond and others believed that the best course of action would be to permit the media to have access to the girls, if they concurred, after all of them spent some time alone with their parents and others in the coliseum. The parents of the three missionaries who had been freed were very appreciative of the way this special homecoming was being conducted because they too felt right at home at the college with the students and the Hollow folks.

The personnel at Mateland were ready for the special rescue team when it arrived as they lined the walkway when the squad disembarked the aircraft. Shouts and yells along with encouraging comments were heard, and most of those in the receiving line just wanted to touch the group as it walked toward their rendezvous building. Sharing more of their experiences, the rescued and the rescuers were enjoying the building of a permanent relationship, as Madu looked on still sporting that wide smile. "Madu was very important to us in prison," one of the missionaries mentioned.

"We got acquainted with him several days before the raid when we discovered him reading his Bible secretly," Dorothy said. "But we didn't know that he was going to show up the night of the rescue to help us escape."

"Were you happy that he helped you escape?" another missionary asked.

"We certainly are," Maggie replied. "He knew about the various caves in the area which were very important for us to hide from the Ab Didal."

The conversation was discontinued when they heard a captain tell them to prepare for a trip to Bacon College. Having changed into their Hollow clothes and turned in all of their military gear, they looked normal again as they headed for a large troop helicopter.

The loud noise of the props failed to diminish the singing of the group as they were going home. After several hymns Dorothy led the group in singing, "She'll Be Coming 'Round the Mountain When She Comes," to the delight of everybody, including the pilot. Even the young missionaries appeared to be becoming plenary participants in the group activity following their terrible experience with the terrorists in Abedistan.

Emptying the coliseum early, the students, staff, Hollow folks, and several guests of the college assembled around the softball field awaiting the arrival of their loved ones, joined by numerous media who had faithfully remained on campus. From the east in a short while could be heard the whirring sound of the huge helicopter props that got much louder as the aircraft descended on the small campus.

The engines shut down, the side door opened and out climbed Coach Anna as the applause and shouts started. Maggie came next followed by Dorothy, Hanna, Mit, Marsha and finally Esther along with the three missionaries and Madu, and they all joined hands and raised them over their head. Just then the other basketball and soccer team members broke away from the group and met the brave rescue team for joyous greetings as the other people watched beyond the fence. But that didn't last long because the rest of the students headed to welcome the rescue squad home. So on the softball field somewhere in the middle were the young ladies who were rescued and the courageous athletes who liberated them from their terrorist captors.

The massive media had a field day witnessing the arrival of America's heroines, but they were refused entry into the gymnasium at least for a short period of time. "As soon as these young ladies have had time to relax just a little, I'll permit you all to meet with them for a short period of time," Dr. Damond stated in a loud businesslike manner to the large group of reporters who waited anxiously to talk to the missionaries and the athletes.

Dr. Damond had developed a specific plan to welcome the group home. First he had them to sit in chairs on the side of the playing surface while all the others sat on the floor in a semicircle. With the three missionaries sitting in the middle with Coach Anna, Dorothy, Mit and Hanna on one side and Maggie, Marsha, and Esther on the other, the students sang the school song followed by several hymns led by Charlene. After these were sung so beautifully, the students and parents were permitted to make statements which included comments regarding their concern for the group during this dangerous undertaking. It was an emotional time as students after students voiced their love for their peers, and their happiness over their return home to safety. Maudie, who had gotten out of the hospital for this special homecoming, joined in the celebration as she too was filled with joy. Tears continually streamed down her cheeks as she sat near her beloved athletes.

Following this emotional time of sharing, the parents of the missionaries and the rescue team reunited again with their girls surrounded by all of Bacon College. It was a private time for the various families, as they seemed to be impervious to those around them. The coliseum was filled with love and joy on this day, as the little college family was whole once again.

Later, setting the stage for the media, Dr. Damond had the parents of the missionaries and the rescue team to sit together up front surrounded by the others so he made space for the extremely large number of media. "During the last several days," he said, "we have locked out the media because we believed that if they discovered that you all were participating on this rescue mission and made that information public that you all would be in much danger. To my knowledge the media, who have remained on campus, never learned of your endeavor."

After the media were seated, Dr. Damond established the ground rules for their interrogatories. "Because the group has been requested to limit their responses to specific questions regarding their rescue, you should understand the reluctance of this group possibly to respond to some of your questions," he stated. "The missionaries who were freed will not answer any questions until they have completed a thorough military debriefing in the near future."

With his strategy in place the popular president assumed the role of moderator to act as buffer between the media and the rescue team for this unusual session. "All of us in the media and everybody else couldn't believe that female athletes from small Bacon College were involved on this rescue team," a television reporter stated. "Could you tell us how you all were selected?"

With numerous television cameras pointed her way to telecast all over the world, Coach Anna stood to answer the inquiry. "My name is Major Anna Bosley, and I am a member of the marine reserves and more specifically a member of the green beret special forces," Coach Anna said. "Several weeks ago I was approached about leading a team to help free three young missionaries, and without much thought I agreed to do it after I had an opportunity to get approval from our college president, Dr. Damond. After his approval and very encouraging words, I moved forward with putting a team together. Having been given approval to select anyone I pleased, of course, I utilized the members of our basketball and soccer teams because I wanted the best to fulfill such a job successfully. I wanted to use all of them but only could select six."

Quickly, a young female state newspaper reporter asked, "How is it that this team to participate in this very dangerous mission was made up of females?"

Continuing to answer all inquiries, Coach Anna said, "Strategists implement a plan in all cases that gives the team members whatever advantage it can, and for this case females were the better choice because of the type of rescue. I knew I had the best team possible all the while, and the fact that it was successful and without injury to the group, others too would concur, I believe."

"I know you all cannot tell us much about your training, but could you relate just a little about your involvement and what was considered the most difficult experience," a veteran reporter asked.

"Earlier you were told that I would answer all of your questions," Coach Anna stated, "but I am going to deviate from our plan just a little. One of the areas of training that caused the most discussion was an area that upon our live attempt to rescue the young missionaries caused the most chagrin at the inception of our rescue attempt. I would like to ask one of our rescue team members to tell about our training sessions for parachuting and also to relate her experience in entering Abedistan. 'Mit, would you mind telling the media and others about yourself and your parachute training and its use in the rescue attempt?'"

A hush came over the entire group because everyone was going to hear from one of the team about a part of the dangerous undertaking. Mit, a very strong, dark skinned, blonde young lady, stepped up to the microphone where Coach Anna held her around her shoulders. "My name is Mit, originally from the Piedmont section of Bassett, Virginia, but spent most of my years in the beautiful country of Costa Rica in Central America with my missionary parents. My home was in the jungle where I lived with my special friends, three of whom have joined with me on the soccer team of Bacon College.

"Coach Anna wanted to take the whole group of Bacon athletes but had to limit the group to six so I was very fortunate to have been a member of the rescue team. Others of our athletes could have done what I did and even better. For our training in the Mohave Desert we had the most apprehension about the parachute jumping and the training leading up to it. We jumped many times, improving all the while in meeting the demands of our perfectionist instructors. Soon we graduated to night jumping where we attempted to guide our chutes to a sound target. Even in this experience we gained expertise and soon completed that phase of the training.

"Flying into Abedistan, I would clearly be untrue if I told you that I wasn't concerned. Coach Anna jumped first followed by the rest of us to maneuver ourselves to the east near our rendezvous point. Suddenly, I realized that my chute did not open so I quickly pulled it back under my arms, and while tumbling in the dark, I fumbled to find the hook to release my emergency parachute. This chute opened, and immediately I was jolted in an upright position headed for the desert below. Not being able to guide my chute, I dropped straight to the ground, cut both parachutes off and moved for cover a long distance from the others."

While the media had her up front, they didn't want her to get away before they asked more questions. "What did you do to get back with the other team members?" a young lady asked.

Looking to Coach Anna for approval to answer the question, Mit continued, "It was so very dark, and the sandy terrain made it difficult to maneuver very comfortably, but I checked my compass and headed east to join my other team members. Making slow progress, I crawled up the side of a huge sand dune only to realize that bullets were striking the sand all around me. Quickly, I climbed to the top and rolled over the other side in a crevasse in the sand when I realized that I had been shot in the leg. After stopping the bleeding, I used parts of the parachutes to put over me and then covered myself with sand, just in time not to be seen by a group of soldiers holding a bright light who could be heard talking as they stood right over me. After breathlessly waiting covered with sand, they moved back to the west, and I continued immediately to the east. Much later I picked up the signal of the homing device and joined my special team members."

"How is your leg now?" a newspaper reporter asked.

"It soon healed well," Mit responded as she showed the scar on the calf of her leg.

Coach Anna thought it would be appropriate for Mit to tell this story that really mesmerized everybody in attendance, but that they would limit other remarks until they had talked with their officials. Answering only general inquiries the remainder of the session, everything was going well until Coach Anna was asked an interesting question that had really begged for an answer since their rescue.

It was an older gentleman who prefaced his question by saying, "The whole world was so engrossed in the capture of the missionaries by the terrorists that anything even remotely mentioned about them brought about a wide viewing audience. All of us were so much concerned for them that we wanted to report all the details we could. On the night of their rescue we knew something was taking place in Abedistan, but when a large explosion was shown on television, we all were really concerned about the welfare of everyone. Up to this point only you all know what transpired to cause this explosion. Would you be able to explain what happened during the rescue?"

"I will relate this story to you as the conclusion of our media session," Coach Anna said. "We had spent much time around the prison each day so we learned much about the environment in the daylight so we would not have difficulty during the night of our rescue. Wearing our burquas, we blended with the other women in the market, so as time passed we walked freely among the people each day. In addition Madu spent time talking with the guards so he provided valuable information for us including a report of the explosives being stored in a box on the roof of the prison. This was a very important discovery because we now knew that the soldiers possessed these powerful tools of destruction. After the guards were overtaken that morning, Madu brought me one of these explosives, a hand grenade. I held onto it until we had completed our task, and the captured guards were removed from the building, and then as we departed, I pulled the pin and tossed the grenade on the roof near the other explosives. Of course, when it detonated, the whole night sky lit up and could be seen for miles around."

The media's thirst seemed to be quenched following the news conference such that Dr. Damond was really pleased. "I hope now we can get back to normal here at the college," Dr. Damond stated to Coach Anna. "We are so happy that you all have returned safely to our campus. So many, many people were praying for you and your team."

"I know they were," Coach Anna responded.

"We still have a lot of visitors with us including the three missionaries you all rescued," he said. "Would you mind taking them to the athletic dormitory, and after dinner would you mind conducting a basketball program in the coliseum for our students and others?"

"I would love to do that," Coach Anna replied.

The girls were really excited about the news of the basketball clinic when they were told in the athletic dormitory. At the evening meal the rescue team volunteered to help serve to the delight of everyone present. Following a brief respite after dinner, the girls headed to the beautiful basketball arena to play their favorite sport as all the others followed.

It had been several days since the rescue team had practiced, but just watching them, one didn't know that they had not been on a basketball floor in over a month. They really had fun observing Esther carrying her group through their drills as though she had been practicing all the while. Marsha and Mit continued to fit into the program, although Mit still was just a little unsure on her gimpy leg that was somewhat tender because it still was mending from the gunshot wound. Following the preliminary program, many of the other students were invited to join them on the floor to participate in short games, including the three missionaries who really enjoyed their experience. Later, the parents of the girls showed their skills in a hilarious display of basketball prowess. Even Maudie moved up and down the side of the floor in her wheelchair in a refereeing mode to the delight of all of those present.

All remained on campus over night and prepared to leave after breakfast the next morning to their various homes. It was hardest for the missionaries to say good-bye to their rescue team as they hugged each of the girls several times, crying all the while. To soften the good-bye, they all agreed that they would return to see Bacon College play in one of its earlier games.

Meanwhile, the media had left the college site, and those at the LBC television network were wrapping up their unique program that had been advertised liberally during the last several days. It seemed that little Bacon College couldn't get out of the news. Having been dubbed the program of the year entitled, "Unveiling the Mystery," everyone was poised and ready to view the first of three episodes on the following Tuesday evening.

Dr. Damond was elated when Coach Anna talked to him about holding a soccer clinic in the coliseum on Saturday. "It will be so good for our students who have been very tense the last several days awaiting the safe arrival of the rescue team," he stated with a wide smile. "This will get their minds off this dangerous mission and onto campus related activities."

"It should be fun on the one hand and should present a message to the benevolent person that we are making progress in having a quality soccer program starting in late February," Coach Anna stated.

"It's amazing how the benevolent person knows all about what we are doing on campus," he jokingly said.

"The activity should be fun for everyone," Coach Anna indicated. "Even for those who don't know anything about soccer will know that they are in the presence of a very outstanding player when they see Mit play."

"You know, I sat in disbelief when I saw her play basketball," Dr. Damond continued. "I want to come to watch her play soccer when you hold your clinic."

On Friday afternoon Maudie was released from the hospital, and the girls with Coach Anna picked her up and brought her home along with the numerous flowers, gifts and cards people had sent to her. She still needed some assistance so the girls took turns helping her during the initial days following her long hospital stay.

Although Maudie could walk without assistance, she elected to come to the coliseum on Saturday morning in a wheelchair. Mit, her grandniece who had really been a blessing during her siege of sickness during the last several weeks following their trip to the jungle area where Mit's parents were missionaries, was very responsive to her needs. There was much love between the two.

Both arriving somewhat early for the soccer clinic, Maudie asked, "How do you like it here at Bacon College with the other girls?"

"I really love it here so very much," Mit stated excitedly. "The Hollow girls and the others are such special people. God has been so very good to me to permit me to go to college in the first place, be able to play with these girls, and finally to be with you here on campus each day."

It seemed that every time the girls practiced on campus almost all of the students came to watch, joining many local people who had adopted the team as their own. This Saturday was no exception.

The clinic went well. Several girls from Central High School were on hand to watch and to learn from Mit and Marsha who were leading the program. Although Coach Anna was a very skillful soccer player herself, she let her students present the entire activity. It wasn't until the end of the whole affair that those in attendance saw why Mit was held in such high esteem in the soccer world. With Mit playing on one of the two teams engaged in a game at the conclusion of the program, the people sat on the edge of their seat as she kicked four straight balls into the net on consecutive trips down the floor. It was a sight to behold! Coach Anna still couldn't believe the skill level of this beautiful young jungle girl who was so much like the Hollow girls. Marsha too dazzled the spectators with unusual footwork, making two goals herself.

SPECIAL REQUEST

Following practice, they all headed to the cafeteria for lunch. Just as they went into the door, Dr. Damond met Coach Anna and asked to have lunch with her so he could talk to her about something. They both got their tray and walked to a corner table to eat delicious spaghetti and talk after the blessing was rendered by the president.

"We had a good soccer clinic this morning in the coliseum with several girls and their leader from Central High School on hand," Coach Anna stated. "As always, Mit really showed those present why many think of her as being exceptional."

"She is really a good soccer player," Dr. Damond responded.

"You know," Coach Anna continued, "she is a carbon copy of the Hollow girls and so is Marsha. They all are just exceptional young ladies."

"I haven't told you this but since the Hollow girls arrived, I have had no discipline problems whatsoever," Dr. Damond stated with pride.

"They just set the tone without any fanfare at all," Coach Anna related.

"I want to talk to you about a telephone call I just received from one of our senators representing us from Virginia," he stated in a businesslike voice. "So much has happened in the last several weeks here on campus that it has been difficult to sort everything out. Being a private person by nature, the events of this recent period have been difficult and certainly different."

"You do such a masterful job handling everything," Coach Anna responded quickly. "You always seem to know what to say and when to say it."

"You have said that you have learned a lot by observing Esther and how she responds to situations," he noted. "Well, I too have been very observant of her conduct and have learned much from this special young lady."

"She is truly an exceptional model," Coach Anna proudly said.

"Our senator has invited the rescue team and others to be present for a Congressional Hearing for Monday afternoon at 1:00 p.m. in Washington," he stated "It didn't seem like there was a choice so I indicated that you would be present. He then advised me that our legislators would like to talk to many of us in and around Bacon College. At first I thought it would be impossible to do because it would not be fair to you all, having only been back just a day or two from your rescue, but then it dawned on me that maybe this meeting with our representatives in Washington might bring closure to this chapter of our very turbulent school year."

"I think you are right," Coach Anna responded. "The girls have gotten all of their make-up assignments from their kind and gracious professors. They were so supportive of the actions of the rescue group."

"The senator said that they wanted all of the basketball team, all from the Hollow, the rescue team, and anyone else involved in the mission project to Africa," he pointed out. "They are planning for a large contingent of people, including those three missionaries who were rescued and their parents."

"That's going to be an unusual hearing," Coach Anna noted.

"It certainly is," Dr. Damond replied. "Would you mind advising the Hollow folks of the invitation when you go to see them this afternoon?"

"I would be glad to do that," Coach Anna replied.

"I'll get in touch with Bob Waters to ask him to get transportation for us," Dr. Damond said. "Also, please invite Maudie to go, if she is well enough, because she has been an active part of our entire program. I know that Bob will want to ask Devin and Jim with their wives to go. It will be a large group."

At 3:30 a.m. on Monday morning two large buses pulled up to the side of the coliseum to load the congressional hearing group for their trip to the nation's capital. As the girls rushed to get to the buses, Jonsie saw a brown envelope pinned to the bulletin board in the foyer addressed to the girls' teams, attention Esther. Quickly Esther opened the envelope to find several large bills, which totaled five thousand dollars.

Dear Esther and Girls,

I am so glad you are going to Washington, having been invited by our legislators. Please use this money to pay for the buses, food and whatever else is needed for the group.

An Admirer

Esther passed the money to Coach Anna as they hastily headed to the buses, and before they departed she was named treasurer. Many students and town folks were present as they had heard of the unique invitation and wanted to see them off. Maudie and others were already on the bus so Esther went to her seat and hugged her very warmly and thanked her several times by whispering in her ear. Tears of joy in their eyes went unnoticed as everyone was finding a

seat on the buses for the long trip. On separate buses Josh
and Dr. Damond rendered eloquent and heartfelt prayers
asking God to shield them from harm during their unusual
trip.

Like old times, Charlene led the singing on one of the
buses, and on the other a new song leader emerged. Mit had
led many songs in the jungle so she volunteered to direct the
singing on the second bus to the delight of the whole group.
Maudie was a proud lady watching her grandniece leading
the singing. Following I 81 to Roanoke and up the valley
was a very scenic route. Turning east on I 66 toward
Washington, the traffic increased considerably, but the
professional drivers maneuvered the buses along at an
excellent pace all the way to the Capitol where they parked.
It was approaching noon so the legislative assistant led them
to the snack bar where they purchased sandwiches and
Mountain Dew Colas. Following this quick lunch, the
assistant put name tags on each and then took them on a
whirlwind tour of the Capitol, arriving at the hearing room at
12:45 p.m. When the double doors swung open, the
legislators seated up front stood and applauded the group as
others in attendance, including numerous reporters, stood
and did likewise.

What an embarrassment for the group! With red,
blushing faces they followed the direction of the assistant
and just stood in place for what they believed was an
eternity. Finally, they were asked to be seated.

Standing and looking so proudly out at the group
from his state, the Virginia senator was the first to speak.
"As you all know this is my last term of office because I
shall be retiring after twenty-four years as a Virginia senator.
I have observed many occurrences during these years but
nothing like those I have experienced during the last few
years. I know all of you folks here today, but my colleagues
wanted to meet you. Thus, the invitation was made, and you

all accepted on a minute's notice. Thank you for doing that. The agenda we all agreed to follow with which not to overburden you all was to attempt to get to know you, and just thank you for what you have done for our country. At this time we would like to have the Hollow adults to come up front to sit before the congressional committee to make a statement and then answer questions."

Josh and his group really looked the part as Hollow folks as their dress would attest. Bashfully they moved to the front, as directed, with Josh being led to the seat in front of the microphone.

"Mr Chairman, this is Josh Morrow, the pastor of the Hollow Church and with him is his congregation," the senator from Virginia stated.

"Thank you very much," Josh said.

"Please tell us your name and a little about yourself," the chairman requested.

"My name is Josh Morrow," Josh stated and continued to tell them about himself.

"Would you mind introducing the Hollow group who went to Africa to distribute food?" the chairman asked.

Josh had each one to stand as he or she was introduced to this special group of legislators.

"Would you mind taking several minutes and just tell us about your mission to Wasi, and how you all got involved?" he requested.

Following a lengthy dissertation by Josh that heaped much praise on the Hollow folks, a member of the committee from Ohio started the questioning. "As soon as I discovered that a group of private citizens had undertaken this mercy mission of distributing food to the Wasian people, I was really concerned about their safety each time I would hear that the president of the country had vowed to take care of their own problem without outside interference. With that in mind and the fact that he threatened to severely punish any who did try to interfere, weren't you all frightened as you went about doing your job there?"

"At the inception of our discussing the mission, the term danger was utilized many times, but as soon as we all agreed, we knew the circumstances and the consequences so it was never introduced again for any serious discussion," Josh stated, as the legislators were beginning to understand more and more why he was the leader of this brave group of folks from the remote Hollow. Carried live on national television, everyone was seeing and hearing this Baptist preacher who was included in the top news stories only a few months ago.

"We were so busy during this period that we had little time to be concerned about any harm," he continued. "The Wasian people were very friendly and helpful as we developed strategies for further deliveries. I would be in error if I didn't mention to you that we were reminded of danger each day, because we could hear gunshots both day and night for several weeks before the country defeated the rebel forces."

Another committee member stated, "Over the years our country has been involved in food delivery to countries where people were starving, and we have felt good about our efforts, but you all changed the system of distribution and really established another standard for handling the movement of foodstuff to people in need. Would you mind telling us about your way of distributing food?"

"Our initial goal was to start slowly in getting the food to the starving people so we could learn how to do it effectively for much larger groups," Josh said, as the committee members leaned forward to hear every word. "This was a most difficult problem for us because people were dying daily, and yet, we knew we had to remain steadfast to our plan or stand a good chance of spoiling the entire program. Very early in our distribution we discovered that it would be a good idea for those whom we had helped to be utilized as distributors themselves, thereby doing two things: expediting deliveries and permitting the native people to share in the process and feel good about themselves. Utilizing this method, the distribution of food really was enhanced, and all the while we were gaining more and more the confidence of the Wasian people."

An older legislator leaned up to his microphone and said, "During the time of your mission to Wasi, I faithfully watched the news in amazement that private citizens would be driven to undertake such a dangerous mission. The news reporters indicated that you all were mistreated a couple of times, and there were rumors of other occasions wherein your people were physically abused. Would you tell us about the times when you all found yourselves in harm's way?"

"The first night we got off the big transport plane in the middle of the night, we knew that the country was unsettled because we heard gunshots all the while which reminded us to be careful," Josh said. "We made the distribution to villages in the bush country without incident, but all of us realized that the environment was more volatile in and around the more populated areas, so we needed to handle distributions there differently. As we prepared to go into our first city, three of us took one of our trucks into the city through a secondary route. While reconnoitering with much caution, we suddenly arrived at a point wherein a fierce battle was raging between two rebel forces. One group shot up our truck and took us as prisoners. It was during this ordeal that we made many friends who were truly instrumental in making food deliveries to this city and to others later."

At this point the legislator continued to probe to get a definitive answer to his inquiry. "You have failed to mention to us that you all were physically beaten, and three of you were nearly killed and left to die in prison."

"Experiences, such as those you mentioned, helped us immensely to remain strong and committed to our goals and objectives," Josh stated, while all of them could see that he was not one to talk about things which would direct attention toward himself.

"I want you to be more specific in responding to my inquiry," a young legislator from Indiana stated while smiling. "All of us understood the plight of Wasi and respected the decision of the president that his country would handle its own problem of famine. Yet, you all defied this command and brazenly slipped into his country under the cloak of darkness, delivered food to those starving, and when discovered, he was not upset. How did that happen?"

"Obviously, we thought about this all the while, but the response of the people in need of food seemed to overshadow his threat of reprisal to any who interfered," Josh said. "God works in so many different ways. While in prison we gained a large number of new friends, and when we all were captured and marched to the capital city and held prisoner in a mud brick compound, our friends came to our rescue by requesting assistance from the military. It was because of this that we were brought before the president to answer questions about our presence in his country. These meetings were most interesting, and the ultimate outcome was his approval of our continuing food distribution with a special twist that his government not only would support, but would assist in whatever way we deemed appropriate. With this new beginning food distribution to those starving in Wasi was greatly increased with other countries sending food for us to get to the people."

"We understand that you have become a best friend of the president such that he has invited you all to visit and has asked you to help train his women's basketball team for the next Olympics. How is it that you all developed a lasting friendship during your several weeks there, when we as a

202

nation have tried hard to develop a viable relationship with the president and his country and have failed miserably?" a female senator from Louisiana asked.

"The president of Wasi is such a fine gentleman," Josh said. "When we left after our food distribution, he came to the airport to say good-bye to us, and he reminded me that he wanted us to come back for a visit. You all know that he did invite all of us from the Hollow to visit during the summer, taking the Bacon College girls' basketball team. It was a marvelous trip that the president directed which kept us busy all during our most special visit with this warm and loving group of people."

Questioning continued for a very long period of time such that a brief recess was called for those in attendance to take a short break. A legislative assistant assembled the basketball team with Dr. Damond and Maudie included in the group and directed them to sit before the large congressional committee. Reporters and photographers were everywhere and during this short respite, most were hovering around Josh who had just completed his question and answer session with the committee. Bob was making his rounds getting and making pictures to pass on to his good friend, Devin, the owner of the local newspaper in southwest Virginia.

When the chairman rapped his gavel signaling the continuation of the hearing, everyone suddenly got very quiet. "I am so grateful to all of you for coming here today to be with us. It's been just such a delight to have you all here because we usually deal with issues arising from conflicts, confrontations and confusion but not today. You are such a nice and humble group of people."

Continuing, he stated, "Our next group comes from the Hollow also by way of Bacon College. They are the women's basketball team that has never lost a game since they started playing several years ago. We all would like to address so many different things with this lovely group of

young ladies, but for today we want to hear from you
regarding a trip you all took from southwest Virginia to
Oregon. Their coach, Anna Bosley, will address us at this
time. Miss Bosley."

"Thank you so very much for inviting us to be a part
of the proceedings for today," she stated. "It is truly an
honor."

"Would you tell us a little about yourself and your
team?" the chairman asked.

"There is little to tell about myself, but there is much
to say about my excellent team of girls," she said excitedly.
"I was once a high school coach before I was employed by
Dr. Damond to lead the Bacon College team. Having never
had a women's team before, my job was to recruit a whole
new group to start a program. The day after I signed my
contract, I went to a remote area even for southwest Virginia
for my first recruiting trip. I met this very humble looking
group of girls whom I knew had never lost a game of
basketball all through high school so I wondered about the
veracity of the stories I had heard about their basketball skill
level. It wasn't until we played a game together on the strip
mine in the Hollow that I knew this was an unusual group of
athletes. They truly have been exceptional young ladies."

"Would you mind telling us just a little more about
your college and the years immediately following your
graduation?" the chairman asked.

"Really, my college years were very normal as I
participated in sports and settled on soccer as my emphasis,"
she answered. "Immediately, after college I joined the
marines and later enrolled in officers' candidate school,
graduating later as a second lieutenant."

"There is much more to the life of Coach Bosley than
she is telling," the chairman pointed out. "Let me tell you a
couple of things she left out in her brief statement about
herself. First, she was a two-year All-American in soccer for

her junior and senior years in college, and she holds the rank of major in the marines and is a member of the prestigious green beret. She still holds the distinction of being the most outstanding graduate from this special forces' program, and her picture still hangs in the main building on the base for all to see. Now with much less brevity, we would like for you to tell us about this unusual trip to Oregon a few months ago."

"We arrived at the Roanoke airport early in the morning, and just as we headed for the ticket agent, three men of Mid-Eastern descent got up from their seat and walked along with us. It's unusual for anyone to be in the airport this early in the morning, and to be Mid-Easterners even made it more intriguing. They boarded our plane to Dallas sitting in three different areas. All so far could have really been just coincidences, but when I read in the newspaper that there was credible evidence of a terrorist strike in our country in a couple of days, I began a higher level of consternation.

"Not advising the girls, I gathered as much information as possible because I knew if I made a report, many questions would be asked. On the plane I moved and sat for periods of time near them clearly to see their facial features. But, it wasn't until they changed to our same small commuter plane to Tempe that I really knew that they were bent on doing some kind of harm. The Bacon team was the only common denominator besides the terrorists themselves."

With everyone spellbound by this time Coach Anna continued to relate her story in this eerie quiet chamber. "In Tempe I called my good friend Maudie Graves, who is with us today, and she suggested that I should call Dr. Damond, the president of Bacon College. I did this and he in turn called the FBI. After playing in Tempe we headed to Denver the next morning, and surely enough, the three suspicious persons got on board with us, seated as always in three different places on the plane. When they continued with us to Portland, I knew that the probability of this occurring just by coincidence was very remote.

"At the game in Portland I was discreetly approached by an FBI agent dispatched to assist us so when the three Mid-Easterners suddenly showed up at the game, he had an opportunity to see them. We had been advised that an agent would be present as we departed from Portland the next morning, but that failed to materialize so our last hope for protection was going to be that which I had been trained a few years ago, and what I had taught the team in our hotel room the day and night before. As you all know, the hijacking took place the next morning

"There we were sitting on the hijacked plane with all the other passengers at the mercy of the terrorists. Obviously, they were bent on doing more evil than just parading the captain and two older passengers before all of us to show their might, but that is what they did for a long time. I had divided my girls into two teams, and had their seating assignments changed so that one of the teams was seated adjacent to the terrorist in the rear of the plane, and the other team was seated near the one in the middle. I was seated up front near the first class section. We just waited.

"It was during the morning hours of the next day that the whole scene changed, and the environment deteriorated immensely, such that we could see the time had come to consider some offensive action. I raised my fist in the air to alert the two teams to prepare themselves for the attack. Following their reciprocated fist in the air, I raised both fists, which signaled an all out attack on the hijackers. You all know the outcome. We had some scrapes, but there were positive results. Everyone escaped with just minor injuries so God really blessed all of us."

"Your group was so very brave," the chairman stated. "Would you mind having your two teams of girls stand so we can see them? And too, would you permit each of these leaders to say something to us today? We are so very proud of their heroic efforts."

Coach Anna had Dorothy's team to stand to her right, and Esther and her group moved to her left. "Ladies and gentlemen," Coach Anna said, "I want to introduce to you my two guards at Bacon College who led these two teams who attacked the terrorists on our plane in Portland. They, along with the other girls, are exceptional students and very obedient and humble young people. The first to speak will be Dorothy Buford followed by Esther Minold."

"I would like to say to you today that I wasn't scared during this ordeal but that would not be true," Dorothy stated. "While our training to undertake this mission was very brief, our attentiveness to the details really paid off. All of us joined together to get the job done such that the passengers were saved from unusual harm. I am so thankful to God that He provided safety for us during our attack."

"I am too thankful to God that he gave us the wherewithal to fulfill our mission on that fateful morning," Esther said. "The misdirection of this trio of earthly brothers was indelibly set such that in their lives evil was spawning more evil each day. Placing little value on life, they used the innocent passengers as ransom for other wherewithal to inflict further destruction on God's world. While these were thwarted on this day, scores of others will follow brandishing their ugly philosophy to spread more havoc on the landscape, especially around the pools of tranquility. I do not envy you all in your difficult job to maintain a safe environment for all of us here in the most blessed country on the face of the earth. May God and His holiness continue to reign supreme!"

The questioning continued such that another break was called after which they convened for the final session of the day. It had been a most interesting day for everyone present.

Coach Anna and her rescue team took their seats before the very important congressional committee with the coach sitting before the microphone. As before, there was total silence.

"Over the years I have always been very impressed with our military personnel who have done numerous heroic things to keep us safe," the chairman stated. "In our free and safe society we have come to expect this kind of behavior from our men and women in our various armed services. While they go about their duties and responsibilities, we find ourselves totally depending on them for our security. But that all changed a few weeks ago when our citizens participated in an unusual act of bravery such that I have never witnessed in my entire life. We have these brave citizens with us today so I want you to meet them now. First I want to introduce to you again Anna Bosley, who is the coach of Bacon College's outstanding basketball team and also a major in the marine reserves. Coach Bosley, we would like for you to tell the committee about your latest experience in rescuing the three young female missionaries."

"Thank you again for permitting us to appear before your congressional committee," Coach Anna said. "I was contacted by a high ranking officer to meet with him to discuss an important assignment. He told me in the meeting the next morning that he wanted me to lead a rescue team to Abedistan to free the three young missionaries being held captive by the terrorists. With some reluctance because of my job as coach at Bacon College, I did agree pending approval of Dr. Damond, the president of the institution. It was further stipulated that I could select my own team so I picked them from my athletes at the college.

"All of my athletes volunteered but because only six of them could participate, I selected Esther, Dorothy, Maggie and Hanna from the basketball team and Marsha and Mit from the soccer program. We were sent to the Mohave

Desert to train for this mission so we could learn desert tactics. Following a very rigid training exercise including precision night jumping from an airplane, we traveled to Abedistan. Jumping into Abedistan in the still of the night, we experienced our first difficulty when Mit had to use her reserve chute after the primary one failed to open properly. Escaping her enemy but not before she was shot in the leg, we assembled joyously in the desert to move farther east toward our objective.

"During the next several days, we moved about in the streets of Moraba with all the other people, wearing our burquas covering our face. Each day we gathered more information that we compiled for use when our rescue would begin. Hiding out on the outskirts of the small city, we soon discovered a young man reading a Bible as he hid behind rocks. This young man became a valuable helper as we developed strategies to free the missionaries.

"Wearing our military apparel for the night assault with pistols strapped to our side, we initiated our rescue effort at three o'clock in the morning. Successfully removing our subjects from their prison after subduing the five guards, we headed to escape following the lead of our Abedistany youth. An all out effort was launched by the Ab Didal to seize us, but with the help of our very alert guide, we disappeared in the caves of the mountains. Of course, we were rescued ourselves soon when several apache helicopters engaged the enemy in combat. We are so very much grateful for the assistance of our brave military forces."

Everyone stood in awe of these brave young ladies who risked their lives to save the three young missionaries. When Coach Anna concluded her remarks, the committee stood and applauded for several minutes, and then asked the group to stand which started the applause all over again. Not through yet, the chairman asked all of the others to move to the front where they too received a very loud and warm applause from everyone in attendance including the media.

Tears could be seen running down the cheeks of Maudie and many others on this special occasion.

Following a joyous trip back home and soon getting back to normal in southwest Virginia, the girls continued to prepare for the basketball season which was just around the corner. The Hollow folks opened the new orphanage, Devin published a special insert in the newspaper about the Washington trip, and the television program regarding the benevolent person was begun. Shown on three episodes, the attempt to discover the person who had given so much to small Bacon College turned out to be less exciting than the television network envisioned at the inception. In the end they broadly intimated that the benevolent person could be one of the five wealthy people in the area who had received the most votes by a large audience of viewers.

AET SCORES

B ut there was not all peace and quiet in the area surrounding the Hollow. Glenn Colson, the amiable school superintendent in the area, was faced with a group of constituents who demanded his resignation because of the poor showing of the students on the Achievement Expectation Tests (AET) administered to the students each year. It seemed that the other school divisions were doing some better so many parents were demanding more of the school division regarding their children.

It all started right after the Hollow girls graduated wherein students were required to pass a battery of state prepared tests along the way in school before the school itself could be accredited. The school district wound up in the warning category, which caused many of the people in the area to become almost hostile toward the superintendent, the teachers and other administrative leaders in the school division. The school board had really panicked such that they were meeting to demand an explanation of the sorry report.

Following the lengthy newspaper article divulging the scores, the superintendent's telephone continued to ring from parents who wanted an explanation of why their children failed to meet these standards, and others chastised him because the whole school division failed to meet the minimum requirements. It was truly a difficult period for the school chief who previously had been held in such high esteem by the whole community.

Many thoughts went through his mind during this time. From time to time in the past he had contemplated moving to another school division, and now might be an appropriate time because in all honesty, most teachers thought that the school division personnel were doing all they could to teach the children. Low scores had always been the case for the students in these mountainous schools, but now that they were made public and more was at stake, the whole landscape had changed.

While he was winning all basketball games, he was approached several times to lead other districts, but at that time he failed to entertain any thought about leaving. Little did he know that in a short few months his whole relationship with the community would have changed.

The school board was set for its normally quiet annual organizational meeting to elect officers, when about a hundred very angry parents showed up for the meeting demanding to be heard. One by one they paraded before the board revealing their feelings regarding the dismal AET scores. They had truly caught the school board off guard such that they were really embarrassed, because they knew that what was said in the meeting would be read in the morning newspaper.

The demands were so great on the board that they held a second meeting that month to hear the irate parents again whose number had really grown by this time. Glenn Colson just sat in disbelief, thinking all the while that he was doing what the parents wanted to provide their approved teaching-learning environment for the teachers and children.

The school board thought the problem would go away after the parents had been given an opportunity to express themselves at the previous meeting, but that wasn't the case at all. When the chairman gaveled the meeting to order, they immediately could see that the number had grown tremendously, and when a parent stepped before the microphone to speak and introduced herself as the leader of the parent group, they knew that the problem was far from being resolved.

"My name is Elizabeth Turnbull and I have two children in the school division. Informally, during the last few months several of us parents have been meeting to discuss the plight of our young people in the school district. We have become concerned that our children will not have a fair chance to compete for employment with others who have attended more affluent school divisions. When the report of the miserable test results was published in our local newspaper, we read the report and sat back in disbelief. The problem, as we saw it, was even more devastating than we had imagined. We all wondered what was being done or wasn't being done in the schools to cause such a dismal showing. Can you imagine how we felt after all of these years putting our faith and trust in our schools that we had worked so hard for over the years when we read these most horrendous achievement scores made by our children?

"We truly expect more and obviously we demand more from our tax dollars. We expect you all to effect change such that our children will successfully fulfill the requirements established by the state. I want you all to know that we are so distressed over these AET reports that we are examining home schooling, Christian schools, or enrolling our children in an adjoining school division. Please don't take this as a threat, but please know that our children's education is very important to us, and we are going to see that they get the best there is with or without this school board as their leader."

Then the parade began wherein the parents pointed out specifics and at times naming teachers. One parent stated that her child never had homework whereas another pointed out that her son always had too much homework, and a third indicated that her children had the wrong kind of homework. Complaints came easy on this evening as the parents bombarded the beleaguered school board and superintendent. The teachers were the earlier thrust of their complaints noting that some spent too much time away from the classroom, many failed to report to parents, and others didn't seem to be enthusiastic about their work.

Soon the subject of administrators entered the fray with an idea presented by the group to get rid of all the administrative staff and add teachers for the classroom. Several indicated that all the highly paid central office staff just rode from school to school or just sat in their office all day. It was time to make changes, and this would be a good start several stated. Some of the group talked about how the teachers complained about all of the paper work they had to do which interfered with their doing all they needed to do for the children.

Being very attentive during their presentations, when it was over the board gave a sigh of relief, but no closer to a solution to this monumental academic problem. Among those present from the school system besides the school board were several who made their way to the office meeting room even at such a late hour to discuss what they had heard from the hostile parent group. "Obviously, the parents are really upset that our achievement scores are not any better than they are," the superintendent stated. "There were many complaints from them, but during the entire evening I didn't discover one point that I believe would be helpful to correct the situation. They are really mad and their expressive behavior at times left much to be desired."

"You know you employed me to be the school
division's curriculum and instructional leader," Mrs. Brown
said. "It doesn't take a rocket scientist to realize that I have
let you all down as indicated by our test scores."

"Don't feel like you have to handle more than your
share of the blame," the superintendent indicated. "As we sit
here tonight, there is much blame cast our way, and we all
should share in it and try to move forward with a positive
thrust to elevate our position. All of us will go home tonight
and have a good cry before we go to bed. Tomorrow is
another day, and we all know that everything is possible with
God."

After a sleepless night the superintendent arrived
early to his office, took out a piece of paper and began to
make notes regarding the school division. "Sometimes in
life what one has been doing all the while is not appropriate
any more," he thought, as he sat pensively at his desk before
others had arrived to begin the day of work. "I have always
thought of myself as being a good educator, but something is
wrong as shown by the dismal AET scores of the students."

As the morning passed, he ground out more thoughts
of the school division including a happy time when the
school division was winning all of its basketball games. A
shallow grin could be seen on his face as he reminisced on
this morning. "The Hollow girls were really good basketball
players," he thought. "In addition they were outstanding
students who were at the top of their graduating class. It fact
they have been the highest achieving group of young people
who ever graduated from our school division."

Following these thoughts, he headed for the Hollow
to talk to Josh and Charlene about his situation and about
their earlier schooling for the Hollow children.

"Good morning, Mr. Colson," Josh said, as he
answered the rap at the church door.

"Good morning to you Josh," the superintendent said.
"Please call me Glenn."

"It's so good to see you again," Josh stated. "Charlene and I think of you often."

"Please know that I often think of you two," Glenn responded.

"What brings you to these parts this cold morning?" Josh asked.

"I guess you all are aware that the parents in the school division are really upset because the AET scores are so very low," Glenn replied. "Not knowing how to respond to their total disgust of the schools and our personnel, I thought it would be helpful if I came and talked with you about it."

"Why don't we go into the house to include Charlene in this discussion, and we shall make some coffee," Josh stated.

Charlene was totally surprised to see the superintendent, but following greetings put on a pot of coffee for them. "How have you and your family been doing?" Charlene asked.

"Everyone is fine at home, but in the school division a lot is desired so that is the reason I came to the Hollow to talk to you and Josh," he answered.

Seated in straight back wooden chairs beside a small kitchen table covered with a blue and white checkered oil cloth, they began a most interesting conversation.

"Again as you all probably know, the parents of the school division are really upset because the AET scores of the students are very low, and they are demanding immediate changes to effect better achievement of their students," the superintendent told them. "Last night in an especially called meeting, approximately a hundred parents expressed their concern with many loudly proclaiming that the school personnel were not doing a good job. Obviously, I disagree with that but on the other hand, achievement results really are the proof of the success or failure of our schools."

"How long have you known that the achievement level of the students was low?" Josh asked.

"For many years even before I became superintendent achievement scores were not satisfactory," he retorted. "Over all these years it didn't seem to matter what our test scores were like because no one really paid any attention to them. There really has been no change in the school division's output for many, many years, and with no overt demands on the schools I have fulfilled my job just as all the others have done, I'm sure. Because of the background of their children in other school divisions being more affluent, they reap good test scores not because of what the school division is doing but the affluent backgrounds of their students. You all know what I'm trying to say."

"Have you thought about any strategies that might help the young people perform better?" Josh asked.

"Over the years I have really been interested in the academic part of a school division so I have taken many notes and put them in a little green notebook that I look at from time to time," he stated. "When I was appointed to lead this school division, I immediately began to set in motion some of my ideas included in this green notebook. The reforms were very simple but truly academically sound."

"Did you discover that the children learned better using your ideas?" Josh inquired.

"Well, we implemented these simple changes for just a short while, and both parents and teachers became very frustrated and strongly balked at the measures to enhance the learning of the young people," he sadly replied. "The teachers could not handle the disturbance of the curriculum landscape that they had grown accustomed for all the years it had been in existence, and the parents were suddenly thrust into the fray as plenary partners in schools, and they too were ill equipped to deal with their new duties and responsibilities."

"What happened then?" Josh asked.

217

"Because there was no immediate clamor to improve the quality of learning of the young people by parents and the teachers, I abruptly abandoned the program and permitted the instructional personnel to revert to their usual method of classroom management. That was more than a dozen years ago. On two other occasions I revisited these fertile ideas but they were rejected each time."

"Do you think the climate is right now for you to revisit these practices included in your green notebook to get the teaching and learning on track in your school division?" Josh asked.

"I really think so on the one hand, but on the other I remember too well the bitter reaction of both the parents and the teachers when these basic educational practices were introduced a few years ago," Glenn noted in a surrendering tone. "I knew that our children were not learning at a satisfactory level when these innovations were included in the school division, but no one seemed to care. They do care now, it seems, so you may be right that they would be more receptive today for any new undertaking that would improve the achievement of the children."

"How long do you think it would take you to put your plan in writing?" Josh inquired.

"I have everything already in writing that I would need to implement this program," Glenn stated. "I never thought that I would ever think of using my educational ideas again, but would follow the usual practices that are used by educators that are passed on and repeated year after year in all of our schools here and beyond."

Glenn had a good feeling as he left the Hollow following a long talk with Josh, whose judgment he cherished. Now would be the time for him to get on the offensive, and attempt to do something about the dismal achievement of the children in the area.

When the superintendent called the school board chairman to call a special meeting so that an improvement plan could be presented, the chairman was happy to hear that something was going to be done. His telephone had not stopped ringing, as it seemed that every parent in the whole school division had called at least once. Realizing that the tone of the callers was becoming more and more hostile, any kind of suggestion by anybody was looked on with much favor.

Because the crowd was so large, the meeting was held in the auditorium of the high school to accommodate everyone. It was Glenn Colson's night to present an educational plan to make positive changes in the way children were being taught in the area such that parents could see immediate results. It was a beleaguered school board and superintendent who sat before the large audience watching every movement as the people took their seat for this most important meeting. There was an agenda with one subject.

Glenn had heard years ago that when a group of parents got involved, and the group grew to large numbers that their whole agenda sometimes would get lost, and any solution would be very elusive. "I hope this is not the case tonight, but it does appear that the people already have their minds made up, and it will take a miracle to right the listing boat that seems to have tilted too far," he thought, as he sat behind the table on the stage.

At promptly seven o'clock the chairman called the meeting to order and announced that the purpose of the special meeting was to hear a presentation by the superintendent, noting suggested reforms for the school division which would enhance the achievement of the young people. It had been a long time since any kind of major reform movement had taken place in the school division because everyone had gotten complacent with the status quo. Always being optimistic, Glenn carried this feeling with him as he waited to step behind the microphone to deliver his talk, the most important in his long career. Not only did he want the people to hear what he had to say, he also wanted them to see his plan in writing so he had an overhead projector and numerous transparencies to reveal his plan of action.

The superintendent tried not to let the hostile environment of the evening interfere with the presentation he had for the school board who was really pulling at straws just to do anything to appease the vehement group of people who had ugliness on their minds. He realized that he was the main target of their complaints because they wanted something different for their children in the school division. Awaiting the time when he would be making his most important presentation, he thought about the reforms that he suggested several years ago when they were promptly rejected by teachers and parents alike. "This time it will be different from before when many of the same suggestions he had in mind for tonight's plan are presented even though they were rejected several years ago," he thought, being really at peace just before stepping to the microphone so all could hear what he had to say.

"I have been your superintendent for more than fifteen years," Glenn stated, "and I have enjoyed it very much. All of you parents have been most cooperative and helpful, and our teachers and other staff members have provided exceptional wherewithal for an excellent learning environment. I would hasten to add that these provisions have not effected a program of action wherein our children have satisfactorily fulfilled the requirements of the AET administered each year.

"Several years ago when I first was appointed to be your superintendent, I presented to you several reforms that I believed would provide a teaching-learning environment that would produce optimum results in the classroom. As some of you may or may not know, these suggestions for curriculum and instruction revisions were rejected, and shortly the whole innovative program was scuttled. Let me start afresh tonight.

"Education is like many of our modern movements that are carefully defined by its pursuit of educational correctness. For those of us involved in the pursuit of excellence in the classroom, many find themselves jumping on each new colorful bandwagon that comes by. In the meantime, in response to criticism from all fronts, schools find themselves jumping from one bandwagon to another to try to elevate their delivery by utilizing frills and gimmicks to arouse and hold the interest of parents while they attempt to fix their system. Of course, many are hampered by those set against change, which preclude utilizing many innovative expressions that would cause a stronger and different effort on the part of educational personnel.

"It is my guess that many of you are trying to discover what are the components of a good school. Even in our school division you have probably said to someone that your child attends a good school, but now you ask yourself, does he really? You note with enthusiasm how nice your child's teacher is, how nice the school looks, and the many extracurricular activities scheduled during the year.

"With this description of a good school so far, let me ask you, what is the main purpose of the school? Wouldn't it be how well the students are taught reading, writing, and mathematics? Isn't the learning of the students the main reason for the existence of a school for the young people?

"There are so many 'moving parts' to a school with some being important and others having little impact on learning. One may discover that most schools do not possess the right ingredients to provide an adequate learning environment; therefore, year after year the level of performance of the students falls very short of what it should be. Yet, these same people will declare their school as being a good one because of emotional reasons and not because of the true production of the school.

"A friend once said to me that one could not tell a book by its cover, and the same holds true for a school, because our evaluation of a school is made based on areas that most of the time have little to do with the learning of students. A good start on most people's judgment of a good school is to have a new or very attractive school building including landscaping which they translate into a good school. Yet, in another state a few years ago the best school as measured by the achievement of the students was a very old, unattractive school, but it had the right program inside. Today, if you ask several people why they consider their child's school a good one, they will generally give you the same answer with all having little effect on learning.

"The emergence of demeaning reports on education has brought about a bevy of literature regarding the demise of public education with some that produce a collection of data and statistics that support their findings. To combat their failing institution, many educators have been searching feverishly to find ways to improve their effectiveness and in so doing have jumped on every bandwagon imaginable regardless of its proven qualities. To discover the 'fountain of excellence,' some school districts have gone to great lengths with a steady diet of elaborate innovative programs that they believe will assist young people to improve their achievement. There are some that believe that there are school districts that introduce new programs mainly as a smoke screen to mask the poor achievement results of their students so that the school level clients will think that they are attempting to improve the learning environment for the children. For the most part whatever the school district decides to do regardless of how bad, untried, and ineffective it is, the parents will accept it based on the good faith and respect that they have for their children's teachers.

"Usually, the new and innovative educational programs in our schools will only last for a short time. Shortly after disparaging remarks are heard about an innovative program presently in use that has been ineffective, parents are told of a better 'mousetrap' and the cycle for another program change gets underway. Over the years I have seen many instructional techniques and programs come and go.

"I have grown up in the work place uttering the terms accountability, learning at own pace, acceleration, collaborative learning, grouping, cooperative learning, units of teaching, reading across the curriculum, site based decision making, manipulatives, learning centers, whole language, readiness, thematic learning, ungraded primary, open space classrooms, team teaching, meeting the needs, multiage grouping, and so on. We are always involved in seminars, conferences, workshops, staff development, curriculum development, developing instructional strategies, selecting textbooks, and so on. Children are placed in grades and nongrades, in classrooms with walls and some with no walls, groups as in birds, as in heterogeneous and homogeneous, as in multiage, as in reading ability, as in teams, as in committees, and so on. If we haven't thought of doing it for just a little while, it's probably not worth mentioning tonight because over about thirty-five years an educator goes through the cycle more times than a raccoon has rings.

"Usually, each year there will be some kind of 'educationally correct' activity that trickles down from 'above' that should be emulated by the school. One year it was whole language that was sold to all of us, and then in a couple of years this practice was 'unsold' and in its wake came something else, thematic learning. When some mentioned that thematic learning was only revisiting unit teaching that had been around a very long time, their comments were sufficiently squelched because we were told that thematic learning was different, if for no other reason than that it was the 'educationally correct' thing to do at the time. All of this has been fun because there has been little time to be idle as we have been loyal educators and have followed the cue and have marched to the cadence of many a different undertaking only to have it sent to the glue factory and a new mount acquired to ride in equestrian style down the educational brick highway. All, of course, has been done in the name of progress.

"Obviously, for some educators it is believed that innovative programs will elevate the achievement level of youngsters, and for others new programs will place them into an 'educationally correct' category which seems to be very important for some school districts' own self-concept. One can always count on an innovative practice done by the 'educationally correct' school being emulated by others as educators place a lot of emphasis on visitation to discover a new program and to see how it functions. Some travel so much to observe programs in action that they are called the 'jet set' because they fly all over the country to look at all types of school programs and at times introduce the new program in their school district. This is done in the name of advancement that will place them in an 'educationally correct' posture, a position generally well received by parents. It seems that there is a positive correlation between the distance traveled to see a program and the excitement generated by educators as it is added to the school district.

"For many years I have heard it said that in the world of business 'time is money' so if this is good enough for business why wouldn't it be appropriate for school except that it would be stated as follows: 'Time is achievement.'

Knowing of the feeble attempts of schools to protect the precious time in school for instruction and learning, I thought that it was only fitting to include the subject of time so that parents in search of the good school would not lose sight of the importance of actual classroom seat time on the learning task. A serious searcher will look closely at time as a friend of the good elementary school, and the examiner will discover that the weaker the student the greater protection there should be on his or her time in the classroom. In addition to the protection of time there should be available, particularly from those students who are not working at least at grade level, greater utilization or extension of time than that normally scheduled for the student.

"Let's assume for a moment that the average student attending school for the entire school year with no absences, class interruptions, or school activities that cause him or her not to be present for classroom instruction will make exactly one-year's achievement. Everything being equal, one would assume that instructional time has value, and if the student is deprived of same, would suffer as a result of not being present. In other words the classroom learning environment is important, and when a portion of it is removed from the grasp of the student, learning will be hampered.

"Time is one of the most precious commodities in education, and when used efficiently and effectively, it can help to make the difference between a good and a bad school. I have often heard teachers and principals say, 'Where has the year gone?' It's very much like mercury as it just slips away, and in its wake we sometimes have little to show for it. Because of the complexities of schools and the demands on the program, all kinds of activities compete for school time so it's important that a school's well-planned program be given priority.

"When the children from the Hollow were enrolled in

our school division, I often thought about why they could play basketball so much better than their opponents as they won every game by a lopsided score. You see, they spent a lot of time on the task of basketball and became extremely skillful in playing the game."

The superintendent had really spent a lot of time up to this point and had not unveiled anything about his plan of correction. He wanted the parents to realize that they had contributed to the demise of AET scores because of their unwillingness to permit change when reformation was introduced by the superintendent several years ago. It was no secret that the school board members were becoming more impatient as he continued his eloquent presentation to what he believed was not a receptive audience. Although he was sensitive to the atmosphere of the board and the parents during this unusual meeting, he knew this was his opportunity for them to hear his points of view as preliminary statements before he introduced his plan of corrective action, so he continued.

"The teachers in each of the classrooms in an elementary school usually create the daily class schedules, and they are mostly similar in that they will have included all of the subjects in which there are textbooks. A school day will include a schedule of reading, writing, mathematics, language, social studies, health, science, physical education, art, music, and lunch. The set schedule is for all children in the classroom regardless of their strengths and weaknesses, so during the course of most days each student will be exposed to some form of instruction on each of these subjects. Time for each of these classes and whether or not they are taught each day is left to the discretion of each teacher.

"Most teachers are very faithful to follow their schedules; however, when there is a shift in the utilization of time during a school day, it usually leans toward the interest of the teacher. For example, a teacher who does a lot of unit teaching in social studies will devote more class time on this subject at the expense of the fulfillment of the regular daily schedule. The 'jury is still out' regarding whether it's worse to follow a rigid schedule or 'go with the flow' in utilizing a more relaxed approach to scheduling wherein there is the freedom to extend the time for instruction whenever the teacher deems appropriate.

"In many schools there are itinerant teachers who have emerged in recent years who teach subjects, such as art, music, and physical education, so a teacher's daily schedule will be adjusted so as to provide a specific time for these teachers. In other words itinerant teachers' schedules will be given priority so that they can teach the various classes of the several teachers in a school. For example, an itinerant physical education teacher will schedule classes all day on one-half hour intervals so the teachers in the school make their schedules with this in mind. With alterations being made for all itinerant teachers in addition to the many interruptions, such as field trips and school programs, a teacher's schedule begins to look very much like 'Swiss cheese.'

"There are many different philosophies regarding class schedules with one being that reading should be taught every day as the first subject. Others believe that language arts should be taught the first thing each day because the students are freshest during the early part of the day. There are some teachers who believe that students concentrate on mathematics better so they schedule this subject for the final class period of the school day. In spite of all of the different beliefs that they have in making their schedules, most teachers fail to experience the genuine fulfillment of providing instruction in their schedules because of a grievous ogre that lurks the halls of our schools each day. It is the 'big foot' of our hallowed halls--class disruptions. They tend to kill the enthusiasm in trying to meet the needs of the children.

"It is believed that with specific expectations of fulfillment by each student and a program of continuous accountability, the school day would be protected as the teachers who are expected to fulfill certain tasks with their students would not stand for too many class disruptions during the school day. Then too, if the principals were strongly held accountable for the achievement of their students, they would resist class time interference. Also, the principal would work closely with the teachers to ensure that the instructional time was meted out in accordance with the needs of the students.

"Early grade intervention has been around a long time as a solution to problems experienced by students, but the impact of the intervention rests on the quality of the prescription and its implementation. Many times ineffective actions are taken under the guise of early intervention that leave the deficiency unresolved. To correct a reading deficient effort that produces a heavier burden as the student moves up the grade ladder, one must look for strong fixes to the most serious of the educational woes. Expunging fear of a radical change can be a good start in eradicating the 'school yard illiterate' from the playgrounds of the schools. A major change can be made so that young people with serious reading problems can be enrolled in more than one hour of reading each day. If the student is only a month or two behind in reading, a two-hour reading program may be prescribed, and for one who is farther behind, there could be as many as three hours of instructional time scheduled for reading each day. For those students with a very, very serious malfunction in reading, the schedule probably should include four hours of reading each day.

"This is a simple but radical move and educators, boards and parents who hear this immediately are trying to develop a rationale to suggest failure of such a program. The truth is that tradition is difficult to give up, so to assist educators and parents in accepting this type of scheduling, it is suggested that they put the pupil in the middle of every decision, organize for the student accordingly, and provide a program that will give each young person equal access to a high quality educational program. Multiple periods of quality reading instructional time can reduce the number of school yard illiterates found on the school campuses today and will begin a basis for reducing the 23,000,000 adult illiterates who are struggling in our society, also. Many of these are in our neighborhood.

"Time on task is such a simple solution to many of our educational woes that when the subject is brought up it is considered more humorous than serious. The maxims of time are overlooked and pale when compared to educators' 'far out' suggestions and ideas of programs that they wish to replicate from other educators who have tried these new gimmicks without any shred of evidence of improving achievement of students. Having been involved in education for thirty-five years, I have seen these bandwagons loaded with those 'educationally correct' programs and educators who always want to be on the cutting edge of new programs. Educators have been taken in by this type of behavior year after year and have failed to find the elephant in the haystack to solve many of the critical problems now prevalent in our educational institutions. We have been guilty too.

"The answer to this immense and complex reading problem has been right before our eyes all the time, as educators have frantically looked for new, meaningless programs that have been used in far off places to stop the 'bleeding.' Usually they are wrapped in colorful 'paper' and are described as unique, innovative, motivational, etc., and are generally accepted without question by parents. Yet, there is a hue and cry for educational systems to return to the basics.

"I know you all are sitting here tonight thinking that I have been the superintendent over the years, and if I am so strongly convinced that what I am suggesting would have enhanced learning, why haven't I done it before now? Well I introduced this same concept earlier for more than one time to you all, and it was flatly rejected by both parents and teachers. When our state legislature approved site-based decision making for each of the schools utilizing a committee composed of parents and teachers, my concept for reform had little chance of approval. Secondly, in the modern day schools the education associations carry a lot of clout, but over my many years as superintendent, I have never had a group from the education association to want to meet and discuss achievement of students. With this information I want to continue.

"Deficit reading starts probably at home but becomes recognizable at the start of school as a sneak preview of things to come. The student's weak progress in kindergarten and first grade is not viewed with serious regard so the student innocently moves along with the others. This is a classic case of deficit reading, but because of the innocence of the child at this age, strong measures are not taken to bring children up to a normal reading level at an early age because it is thought that they will catch up later in school.

"There is an old saying, 'a stitch is time saves nine.' No truer statement has ever been made regarding most activities of life. One person indicated the best way to remove morning glories from a garden was to pull them up one by one. Certainly, this is an admirable thought and a realistic approach if one began pulling when morning glories started to grow or were few in number. Teaching of reading is not too far removed from these parallels. The earlier the start and the handling of each case independently for reading instruction, the better chance educators have for success. In other words the lack of success in reading begins to snowball, and the farther along the poor reading student gets in the program, the less control there is of the situation.

"There is little disagreement about when to strive for success in reading. The early grades have it hands down. In many instances deficit reading takes place immediately with the shortfall being compounded so rapidly that severe problems are characteristic in the middle grades.

"One can be reminded of the subtlety of a growing reading deficiency in many other situations in life's experiences. It is known by some as creeping educational paralysis. I am reminded of my thoughts one afternoon not too long ago while at a meeting at the University of Kentucky, and one of the professors and I were sharing small talk at the termination of the activity. He stated that he needed a new pair of glasses and inquired about the quality of the frames of my glasses. It was interesting to discover that his poor eyesight came on so gradually that he thought his vision was normal because he believed that everyone had difficulty seeing the blackboard from various points in the classroom. As I drove home that afternoon, I thought of the subtle vision deficiency and how it parallels the gradualness of deficit reading in school such that it is considered by the at-risk child to be normal.

"There seems to be not enough concern for the young student in the first grade who is reading at the first year, fifth month level at the end of the year and seems to be doing all right; however, the same child several years later in the seventh grade will be as much as 2.8 grades behind if the student continues at the same pace. A reading level of 2.8 grades behind would mean that the student was reading at the 5.1-grade level at the end of the seventh grade.

"I am sure that you will agree that a student reading on the fifth grade level will not function well in the eighth grade setting. The innocent months lost each year along the elementary school road leaves a student with not enough skills to face the future. The student truly becomes a misfit, a dropout probably. In deficit reading young people get farther and farther behind in their reading, and down at the crucial time in their lives they realize that they cannot function with the limited skills that they have obtained.

"Early grade intervention is a must for students to have a reasonable chance of success of overcoming reading deficiencies. Identifying and preparing individual and personal educational programs for each student gives new meaning to a school as standardized test scores take on personalities, and subsequent planning provides a route for the school that will produce optimum achievement in reading. Even schools that have praiseworthy percentile scores of more than the 60th percentile find that large numbers of young people still are functioning at a much lower level. These young people fall short of the mark and need more time on task to overcome their malfunctioning in reading."

The superintendent was really relating his points to a less than genuinely attentive audience on this night, but he believed he had to forge ahead. He firmly believed that he had a remedy for what ailed the school division, but would the parents be receptive this time? It wasn't like he was pointing fingers at the parents or teachers but was trying to soften up the parents and get the teachers' attention to effect positive changes that would bring about quality results. "Would the parents remain at this meeting long enough for me to present my entire case?" he thought, as he continued his preliminary remarks before unveiling his simple but effective plan of reform.

"A reading curriculum provides a vehicle for everyone to know what is involved in the most important subject area in a school so that the teacher and the student can be held accountable for its fulfillment. School districts can go in several different directions regarding a curriculum in reading, but generally there is no curriculum at all, and the results of the reading program depend solely on the textbooks and energy expended by the teacher. The principal has no way of keeping track on a consistent and continuous basis of the progress of the young people as growth is mostly determined by where a child is in the reading textbook. In the good schools there is a way that the principal can follow and check the achievement of the young people on a day to day basis. To do this, some districts may decide to set up a specific curriculum that goes into great detail whereas others may wish to use broader learning objectives.

"Regardless, there should be some kind of curriculum so that if the student fulfills it satisfactorily, he or she would be reading on grade level. It has to be strong enough to challenge the students so it's always been my recommendation to have the curriculum developed at a little above the average level. With a high goal students will have to meet the standard, and the school will not be guilty of 'moving the finish line' so that students are able to reach a lower level and be given a feeling that they have accomplished all that is expected.

"Many times curriculum guides are written in such a way that they are complex and very difficult to understand and herein lies a big part of the problem, if curriculum guides are found in the school. Those that are direct and to the point stand the best chance of being utilized by school personnel. But regardless of the format of curriculum guides, they all usually fall short because of poor utilization. For school personnel to use any kind of guide for their instructional program, it must be simple, direct and easy to manage. A curriculum guide must include a schema that indicates succinctly what is expected of a child and what is expected of the teacher.

"Handling school curriculum and reporting matters in this manner for reading can place the principal in the educational leadership role where he or she belongs, gives the parents a full understanding of what is expected and what has been done and how well, and it gives everyone an opportunity to compare the progress with others. The principal can tell exactly where every child is in fulfilling his or her curriculum.

"On a trip several years ago to discuss a problem about a standardized test, I had lunch with a member of the staff of a testing company in a massive business complex. Trying to be a good guest, I wanted to contribute to the conversation, but when I began to understand what the staff person was saying, I became a very close listener. Approaching retirement age, she indicated that over the last several months she had done much reminiscing about the past, especially as it related to school. At this time she warmly told a story about her favorite teacher, and one of the things that the teacher did that made the staff member's life easier.

"Each day she said the teacher assigned the class a writing exercise. The teacher checked the paper for errors and at the start of the next day's writing class, the students would receive that paper which had been corrected, and promptly would receive another assignment. Students were required to write a paper each day of the one hundred eighty days of the school year. She said that it was amazing how much she learned about writing that year, and that the skills had been extremely helpful in her career.

"Her eyes just twinkled as she continued to explain

how the teacher handled the writing assignments each day along with all of the other subjects she had to teach. First of all, it was indicated the first day of school that the students could expect to write each day, and by the next day she would have read all of the papers, made corrective markings, and affixed a grade on each. The staff member went on to say that the students were overwhelmed with the requirement and found the experience rather threatening to the degree that it affected the quality of their work in the beginning. She recalled the stiffness in which her classmates and she undertook the writing chore during the first few days and the utter disdain that they had for writing anyway.

"There would almost be a sigh of relief as the students completed their papers as one could almost hear a collective 'whew!' The very next day at the same time the previous day's paper was handed out that had been corrected by the teacher, and then after the general improvements and shortfall were discussed with the class, there would be another writing assignment. Needless to say, most looked at this kind of thing as being a nightmare.

"Looking back, she tried to determine why it was such an ordeal for the youngsters to accept a mere writing assignment each day. The students had to be in school each day so why not do writing as well as anything else. It was her belief that much of the grief came not from writing but from fear of an expectation each day, as the students in their first three years in school had no predetermined expectations as they went to class and attempted to learn what was exposed to them. Their writing assignments in their first three grades were more conventional practice of penmanship that was prescribed by the school district. Practice of this kind was a 'piece of cake,' the teacher did not grade the papers, and the students just followed what the book stated for them to do.

"But this teacher was different. In the other subjects

she would ask essay type questions and would want the students to write about different things. There were only a few times during the year that the students had objective questions on tests, such as fill in the blank, multiple choice, or matching. This was the type of test that the students wanted because most of them really had gotten good at selecting the appropriate answer.

"To start the writing class each day, the teacher gave the students a blank piece of paper with only lines on which to write, and then an assigned topic. For approximately twenty minutes the students would write their paper, fold them, and hand them to the teacher. It was interesting what the teacher did the rest of the day. Every spare minute she had she would grade the papers so that by the end of the day she would have several completed and would remain after school to do the others.

"As the year wore on, the papers were easier to write, and there was almost anticipation for the writing class. The students improved immensely from what was a horrible start, and the class's grades were showing signs of remarkable improvement. The 'practice effect' worked and the faithful teacher who did 'stay the course' led the class to outstanding heights in writing. Because of the teacher, the staff member indicated that she loved to write and had written much over the years. This joy was made possible because a teacher stated what the expectation was, followed through to see that objective was fulfilled, and made the students practice their writing.

"The blank page is probably the most under used supply that is found in the schools. Each year school districts purchase the plain paper by the train carloads not to be used for writing but to be used in what I believe has done much to damage the educational system. Plain paper copiers are in most of the schools now, having replaced the spirit duplicator, so that all of the blank paper is run through the copiers to produce tests, class assignments, and whatever else. Education would take a giant step forward if schools would limit the use of copiers and use the blank page for writing. In the real world there are usually only blank pages to use. I always like to ask how one writes a letter by using the 'fill in the blank' method or how students learn to express themselves on paper without being given the opportunity to practice.

"Not too long after my visit to the testing center and having heard what the staff member said about writing every day, my wife and I took our youngest son to college orientation which included some testing. It was at this time that the use of the blank page and the practice of writing again came home to me. We had traveled down to eastern Virginia the day before so that he would get a good night's rest before taking the preliminary tests that were used to determine his skill level so the college officials could place him in the appropriate classes based on his secondary school experience. The morning session went well so at lunch time he talked to both his mother and me about his success in this early session of testing and looked forward to the assignments for the afternoon. It was a hot day so the air-conditioned environment was met with considerable favor with him as he experienced his first glimpse of college.

"After a good lunch he departed to his assigned room to begin the afternoon session. As he turned the corner, he made a short waving gesture to tell us that college was just a 'piece of cake' and that we as parents had made too much to do about nothing as far as he was concerned. His mother and I just wandered around the campus awaiting his dismissal from this last session so we could travel back home which was approximately four hours away.

"After about three hours we could hear voices from the hall and noticed that the students were departing the

classroom and were being greeted by their parents who were
waiting in the hall. Almost at the tail end of the line came
our son who looked as though he had been wrestling a bear
and lost. Hair disheveled, shirt tail out, perspiration running
down his face, and a very damp shirt, he 'grunted' something
like, 'It's time to go.' It was such a change since lunch when
everything looked so bright, and the ease of which he was
entering college was so upbeat, and now to be down so
dismally was incomprehensible. And yet, there he was, a
walking and living example of a plan gone awry.

"Being parents of four children we could read the
mood enough to know that it wasn't the time to pry at all into
what caused the change from morning to afternoon. Keeping
quiet and talking about other things to each other, his mother
and I proceeded to the car along with him and made the
appropriate turns in heading west to our home. Down the
road many miles with a very quiet son, it was time to deal
with the mystery of the sudden change in demeanor.
'Talking around' the subject just a little prompted the first
audible sound that indicated that we could continue but not
to pry too deeply.

"Soon though the three of us were talking normally
about a very 'abnormal' situation. Do you know what it
was? The college officials had 'thrown them a curve' as
they had given them blank sheets of paper and had requested
that they write an essay using same. The students thought
that this was unfair because in their various high schools,
they had not been given practice as they always filled in the
blanks, so they were not used to writing on sheets of paper
like this. We just said to him, 'Welcome to the real world.'

"For a school to have an effective writing program
there has to be accountability on the part of the teacher and
student to ensure competence. First and foremost in the
good program is the requirement that writing be done on a

daily basis. Every time I mention this to other educators they almost fall out of their seats followed by some laughter. They see problems in this, one of which they don't talk about much, and that is the administrative intrusion on the teachers' turf which, by the way, is rarely done. So making fun of writing each day is caused mainly because district and school leadership feel uncomfortable about requesting teachers to do this. There is a feeling among administrators that teachers are overworked and they should not be asked to do more.

"But it's my contention that if writing is weak then additional structured practice is needed to make improvement. The teacher's schedule must be altered to accommodate the additional instruction, and additional training, if necessary, should be given to most teachers to assist with this type of instruction.

"Scope and sequence of objectives are very important to develop an effective mathematics curriculum. What a youngster ought to learn and at what point along the vertical ladder should it be learned are integral parts of the mathematics program. Usually, young people do a better job in the computation part of the curriculum than they do in learning concepts of mathematics so it's necessary to keep this in mind because it's so easy for the mathematics program to shift toward computation mainly. However, a strong curriculum that covers all aspects of mathematics will give balance to instruction and learning.

"In the good school the student achievement manager will have a computerized system to keep track of all to the 'moving parts' of the educational program so that at his or her fingertips comprehensive reports of magnificent quality can be produced for each of the students. Teachers in the school will continuously feed information on a daily basis into the electronic system that indicates the progress of the young people in their charge. The principal may enter information concerning the achievement of students in the form of checkpoint tests and tests administered when pupils fulfill objectives to a specific place in the curriculum. Teachers determine what to teach, when to teach, how to teach, and whether or not students learn what is taught in almost all of our schools; however, in the good school the principal as the student achievement manager determines whether or not the curriculum is taught by administering different kinds of tests and examinations to ensure that all students learn that which is expected. A higher level of accountability is evident when such a program is incorporated wherein the principal monitors the learning of students closely.

"The electronic system of the good school should have a data base of students that will be matched with the approved curriculum such that any progress in completing objectives in the curriculum is entered into the system indicating permanently what was completed, when it was completed, the quality of the performance of the student (grade made), and how the other students fared who have completed the same task. This efficient and effective system will produce unique information so that the student achievement manager can have achievement data to use to make wise decisions concerning each student. With just a click on the computer all kinds of information can be retrieved, sorted, compared, and utilized to produce statistics in printouts in easily understood charts, graphs, and many comprehensive reports that reveal the status and progress of the individual students and groups of students.

"Included in the massive computerized system in the good school, the principal will have a SPA Center, Student Performance Access Center, that should provide access to the daily record keeping of the school for the parent and student. The Center should be set up in a convenient location so that parents can have easy access upon utilizing a password to retrieve up to date information about the achievement of their children. A Center such as this can have the capability of telephone accessibility from the home so that continuous records of performance can be obtained without leaving the house. Having a SPA Center with these and other capabilities available, parents can state with confidence that they truly have a genuine 'open' school.

"In summary the student achievement manager sees that a curriculum is in place for all concerned, monitors closely the progress of the students in fulfilling the expectations of the curriculum, and organizes the teaching-learning environment to maximize learning. The importance of effectively fulfilling this triumvirate of duties cannot be overstated.

"I know you are tired and many of you are disgusted at my remarks, but let me encapsulate all that I have said tonight in a brief summary of a guide that I believe will immensely augment the achievement of our students. Please know that what I am presenting generally was presented several months ago and was rejected by you all. Listen again to my plan that will certainly remove the dark shadows from our school division.

"First I want to reveal the responsibility of the various personnel in the school division. At the forefront the school board approves the curricula employed by our teachers, and it monitors school division achievement. It is my responsibility as superintendent to implement the curricula, monitor school achievement, and be the overall division achievement manager. Having a major chore, the school principal implements school curricula, monitors class achievement, and is the school's achievement manager.

"The classroom teacher teaches the curricula, monitors student achievement, and is the classroom achievement manager. The student learns the curricula and the parent monitors student achievement.

"All of this takes place in a school environment with no frills. Reading will be taught as long each day as the individual needs instruction to ensure that he or she is reading on grade level. Students will write each day and will be evaluated accordingly. The school will not permit interruptions, such as class programs or those from outside, and there will be no field trips permitted.

"To give you an idea what the new school will be like, I have made a copy of a brief story I wrote entitled, *Miss Huston*, of such a school that will be handed to those interested following the meeting. I have spent a lot of time tonight, and I appreciate your indulgence to hear my ideas on the new direction of the school division. If we all work together to implement the various components of this plan, I am sure it will bring swift quality results. Thank you again for coming and for your attentiveness this evening."

MISS HUSTON
By Glenn Colson

Awaiting the start of her third year of teaching at Crafton Elementary School, Ginger Huston was spending much of her time during the summer examining the needs of the students assigned to her class for the coming year. It was only a few days after school terminated that she and the other teachers of her grade met with the principal for a lengthy and productive meeting to assess the status of the third grade group of children. The meeting dealt with the accountability as the principal and teachers knew from past experience that they would have all of the students on grade level in reading at the end of the year. The pressure of dealing with education in this manner had subsided somewhat since Ginger's first meeting two years ago when she started her teaching career. What a difficult time she had following that first meeting!

Ginger thought that teaching school was going to be just like it was when she did her practice teaching in college, so after her first meeting with the principal during the summer preceding her first year, she almost panicked. And now here was Mrs. Ellen Neal standing before the third grade teachers with all of those charts and graphs spouting off so many statistics so fast that Ginger could hardly keep pace with her.

She said that the staff at Crafton Elementary prided itself in seeing that all of its students could do the basics, reading, writing, and mathematics, and that the third grade teachers were the last net to catch all of the students to ensure that they would be competent students for the next grade. Ginger remembered her years in school and also, her class that she taught for six months in college, and she knew that many of them were not on grade level at the end of the year. As she recalled, having about a third of a class working below grade level at the end of the year was not considered that serious, so the students, for the most part, were "passed" on to the next grade. Furthermore, little was said about it either way as though it was something that was expected.

After being a part of the staff at Crafton Elementary, Ginger had gotten used to the accountability staff meetings conducted by the principal and had begun to accept her role with more ease. As she approached her year for tenure, she felt like she had become part of a very special program and pridefully accepted her position as teacher with such a dedicated staff. All of the teachers marveled over the progress that had been made by this group of children since they started school in kindergarten and quietly congratulated the kindergarten, first, and second grade teachers for having done such a good job. When the current third grade class was in kindergarten, more than thirty percent of them had achieved below grade level in reading at that time in their educational program. There was a little improvement in the first grade and some more by the end of the second grade wherein nineteen percent were reading below grade level.

The principal went over all aspects of the achievement of the new third graders, and emphatically indicated that the staff at Crafton Elementary only had one more year to reduce this nineteen percent not on grade level. She noted that during the last seven years the school had met its goal, and with a strong effort she didn't see any reason why the school would not meet its goal during the coming year. The grade level distribution of standardized test scores showed the number of students achieving at various levels, and the principal had prepared a list of students and scores of those who were working below grade level. It was indicated by the principal that there would be one hundred three third grade students, and that two of the classes would have a normal daily schedule. Students who would be enrolled in the other two classes had been involved in summer school, and starting this school year they would be scheduled for extended time for reading. One of the classes would have three hours of reading scheduled each day and the fourth class would have four hours of reading.

Each year the principal assigned teachers to the various classes in accordance with the expertise of each of the staff members for the various grades. For the third grade classes Ginger was assigned to the class that would have three hours of reading so she had a special challenge to help the young people to make good growth during the year. Everyone knew the conscientious effort made by the principal to place teachers and students in the best environment possible, and they also knew of the achievement record of the school during the last several years so there was nothing ever mentioned about her way of making the assignments. They, too, fully internalized the strong statement by the principal several times each year that it was a moral obligation of the principal and teachers to see that children learn the basics, especially reading. None of the teachers ever complained about the students assigned to them, or the specific reading schedule because all seemed to be strongly dedicated and genuine professionals.

Ginger spent quite a bit of time studying the curriculum, and the progress of each of the children assigned to her in fulfilling the curriculum. From the report cards that showed grades by objectives she could tell exactly where the children were in completing their curriculum so young people could just begin their work at that very point that they left off last year. The Student Performance Access Center provided plenary wherewithal for Ginger in gaining knowledge about each of her class so she spent much time at school using the computer setaside for this purpose. The comprehensive reading passages, library books to be read, and word lists made up a big part of the curriculum that she was studying as she focused on her responsibility in being fully accountable.

The teachers' work day started the challenging school year. Ginger's classroom was ready because she and others had spent a lot of time at school working on their rooms and meeting periodically to solidify the team effort. The clerk placed copies of each segment of the curriculum in each teacher's mailbox accompanied by a letter that the teachers, including Ginger, signed and sent home to the parents. Parents were instructed to place the curriculum in a conspicuous location, such as on the refrigerator door, and become assistant teachers in helping the children to fulfill all parts of the curriculum.

The principal called two staff meetings during the three teachers' work days prior to the children coming to school. There were coffee and doughnuts served at the first meeting in which she spent much of the time talking about where the children were in fulfilling the objectives at the end of the last year, how much progress those enrolled in summer school had made, and how the progress of this group compared to the others of previous years. According to Mrs. Neal, that with a good effort on the part of everybody, the school should have all of its students on grade level by the end of the year and would not have to attend summer school. The teachers felt good about this statement, and one of them commented that possibly none of the students would be below grade level at the end of the year. All agreed that it just might be possible.

Following the lengthy meeting with the principal who touched on every statistic imaginable and clearly outlined the expectations of the children for the year, the four third grade teachers met to discuss their mission. One of the things that was discussed was the use of the time before and after school to increase the time on task for reading so they invited the librarian to meet with them. As usual, the librarian indicated that she was going to keep the library open from the time the first bus arrived until the last one departed in the afternoon. She further stated that she would assist the students in their reading from the third grade list in their curriculum, and would meet with the third grade teachers from time to time to ensure that she was assisting in a responsible manner. The third grade teachers planned the utilization of the other times before and after school in such a way to enhance the achievement of the students who were enrolled in three and four hours of reading each day.

During the second staff meeting Mrs. Neal related the philosophy that had made Crafton Elementary School the popular school in the area and even in the state. Historically, she said that many of the teachers presently on the staff met several times about eight years ago and raised many questions and then proceeded to set up a program in response to the questions that were raised. One of the questions raised was why did schools tolerate such a high number of students not functioning on grade level, and another was could a school with its regular staff substantially reduce the number of low achievers? During this period the staff discussed the reporting system and how the grading system could be linked to a curriculum in each of the basic subjects. It was during this time also, that it was agreed that if the staff worked together, the school could bring all of the young people up to grade level. There would be a high degree of accountability based on objectivity and very little, if any, subjectivity, and all attention would be on the child's performance. To take the lead, the principal was to become the student achievement manager and would direct the program with the support and cooperation of the staff.

Following the lengthy talk to the teachers, Mrs. Neal told them that she was very proud to be their principal and knew that all of them would have to do less work in another school but was proud to have them to continue on the staff at Crafton Elementary. She concluded her remarks by saying that there would be no frills again this year which precluded their having parties, field trips, itinerant teachers, duty free lunches, class performances and anything else that would interfere with the learning process. As they were dismissed, she handed out the calendar for the year which indicated all of the staff meetings, grade level meetings, and accountability meetings scheduled for the year.

Ginger met with many of her parents during the work days, and they had already been informed that they were enrolled in three hours of reading each day. Being aware that their children were achieving below grade level in reading, the parents wanted the students to start their program during the work days before the official start of the school year. One of the activities during this period was reading library books on the curriculum list. Ginger requested library book quizzes from the clerk so she could quickly test the comprehension of each child. Further, she gave each child from time to time a blank sheet of paper, gave a topic, and collected the papers that she graded and returned. The number of students participating in this early bird program increased as each day passed.

Crafton was an interesting place for learning because it was unique in so many ways. One of these ways was that there was no bell in the morning because all the teachers were in their classrooms at the time of arrival of the first bus and began the day at this time. As others arrived, they, too, joined in so that by the time the last student entered the classroom the instructional program for the day was well underway. Because the program was individualized and provided a way that students could work at own pace, it was easy to utilize time wisely in this manner. The teachers were so concerned about reaching their goal that they used every spare minute to augment the learning environment of the students.

As the students made progress in fulfilling their curriculum, Ginger would supply the Student Performance Access Center (SPA Center) clerk with that information. The students seemed to understand that they had a lot of work to do so they worked hard and completed a lot of objectives, thereby causing Ginger to furnish a lot of data to the Student Progress Access Center clerk. From time to time in the afternoon Ginger would see her parents at the Center retrieving information on their children so that they knew exactly how they were doing in school. After she had gotten used to forwarding her grades to the clerk on the transfer sheets it became easy because she did not have to keep a grade book herself for the basic subjects. Ginger thought it was very interesting and most informative how the grades that the clerk entered could be retrieved in such comprehensive reports of magnificent quality for parents and her at any time.

Ginger remembered two years ago that parents had a little difficulty accepting report cards that actually indicated progress on substantive curriculum objectives instead of the usual subjects, but after they began to understand what the school was doing they wouldn't change the system for anything. Since, they often wonder why it took so long for the school to make such an important change in its reporting.

The initial accountability meeting was very well attended as there was a packed auditorium with only the principal up front with all of the statistics and information on charts, transparencies, and handouts. Ginger sat with some of her parents about middle way back and watched as Mrs. Neal made some general remarks that advised that the school's mission was to teach young people and to get them well equipped to continue their education at the next school. To do this, she said that the school would not schedule any activity that interfered in any way with the teaching-learning process so at Crafton Elementary there would be no frills. She went on to say that in her earlier days as principal she did not have this philosophy, and that she was not too concerned about young people "graduating" from her school who could not function well in reading, writing, and mathematics. She indicated that she had fallen into the trap as most principals do that it's inevitable that many students fail to perform satisfactorily, and after some time she changed her philosophy by seeing that all children, if possible, read, wrote, and did mathematics at a satisfactory level before they left her school. She said that it was a moral obligation that the school do well in educating the children, and because of this, the staff wanted to keep the parents well informed regarding the status and progress of the children during their four years of enrollment.

Ginger was always impressed when the principal conducted the accountability meetings. There was nothing hidden as Mrs. Neal told the parents the number of children on grade level, above grade level, and below grade level. There was always a higher number at the end of kindergarten, but she would always say that this was not that important because the staff at Crafton Elementary had three more years to help them improve their achievement to a satisfactory status. One could almost hear a sigh of relief when she advised those in attendance about the number on grade level at the end of their third grade. Mrs. Neal said that the school had reached its goal each year of having all of its students on grade level when they "graduated" each year.

Meeting the demands of such a successful good elementary school was made easy because all the staff members believed that they were contributing, and each knew that the most important thing was that the students achieved the curriculum that had been established for them. Everybody worked so hard each day, but it did not seem as though it was all that tiring because Ginger and the others felt so good about what they were doing.

Although the parents were so well informed about the progress of their children, there was still a parent and teacher conference night setaside in early October. To prepare for this meeting, Ginger requested that the clerk prepare the following for each of her parents: conference report; standardized test report with comparison of other students; reading, writing, and mathematics reports for the year; writing and mathematics work from beginning to present; level of each student and, if behind, what was required to be on level and, if ahead, how much was required to enter scholars' program; and numerous other statistics furnished by the clerk.

Ginger had become a strong proponent of practice being a big help to students, especially in reading. She remembered her first year of employment at Crafton and the principal calling her in the summer to come to the school and meet with the other third grade teachers about library books. Mrs. Neal lead the meeting and stated her concerns about children's deficiency in reading and would like to proceed in a different manner by developing a reading list of library books that were on the level of the students in the third grade. The librarian was in attendance and agreed to prepare a list for all of the grades. Mrs. Neal indicated that she had a computerized program wherein questions could be listed for each book and a randomly prepared test could be generated for each book that would be administered to the students when they completed each book. What she wanted each of the teachers to do was to read several books and prepare five to ten questions on each that could be entered into a computerized item bank, retrieved when needed, given to student, graded by the teacher, and finally the grade recorded by the clerk. The use of library books in this manner could be done easily with a high degree of accountability, with little additional work on the teacher, and a permanent record of the reading of library books for all the years in school. For her third graders Ginger could print out the full list of library books read by each of her students, grades made on each test, and how this compared with others.

Some of the teachers in other schools in the district and surrounding area teased Ginger about being part of the staff of such a drab school. They would always boast about the conferences that they had attended, and it seemed that each of them had a big meeting of some kind that would take them away from their school for three or four days. Field trips would be brought up in conversation as they told of those scheduled for the year and how important they were in the learning of children. Usually, a conversation with those from another school would soon touch on the "educationally correct" teaching technique, and the one for this year was thematic learning so all the teachers from the other schools wanted to know whether or not her school used this method in teaching. Of course, she said that she did not, and in fact, she was not sure what such a program entailed, but seemed to be certain that she was not using it in her classroom. One teacher asked in the presence of others about Ginger's not taking her two breaks during the day and especially about not having duty free lunch. Another wanted to know how early she arrived at school and when did she depart in the afternoon. The final comment was made to Ginger that what the teachers were doing at Crafton Elementary made the other teachers look bad and was noted in such a way that it was a hint that the teachers at Crafton Elementary should approach their work as the others.

About midway through the school year several prominent people met with Mrs. Neal and the staff about the "closed school" concept that precluded business leaders from participating at the school as speakers and as business partners. In the group were members of the Chamber of Commerce and other leaders who held responsible positions in the area including local government. They indicated that in all of the other schools the principals cooperated with them and that there were all kinds of activities sponsored by businesses and companies that the children seemed to enjoy. Furthermore, the other schools visited most of the businesses in the area during the year on field trips, and it was so exciting for the children, businesses, and the parents. There were so many ways that the community and the school could cooperate that augmented a wholesome relationship that improved the quality of life for its citizens.

Following the powerful and persuasive comments with just a tinge of a threat, Mrs. Neal was asked to respond to the group. Ginger had gotten nervous and was so glad that it was Mrs. Neal and not she who had to do the talking. In Mrs. Neal's initial statement she thanked them for their concern and agreed with them regarding the place school ought to play in school community relationships. Mrs. Neal indicated that she had heard rumors of their concern so this was a welcomed meeting so that she could express the views of the school. First of all she wanted to say to them that the staff took their responsibility of teaching the children very seriously, and in so doing set up specific standards that they had to meet each year to be considered successful. They discovered in order to do this it was necessary not only to utilize all the time during school day on the specific tasks of learning, but to enlarge the day to include before and after school along with summer school. She said that there was concern about what the media, including our local newspaper and radio, were saying about the ineffectiveness of our schools, and agreed with them that much more could be done above the present output. That's when she and the staff at Crafton Elementary decided to change and provide the best teaching-learning environment possible to ensure maximum learning so that they could be proud of what they were doing and become true professionals. One of the things that they changed was the elimination of the many interferences and interruptions that were plaguing the school each day of the year. With that Mrs. Neal showed several transparencies filled with statistics of learning, and some showing the impact of class time lost on learning. The group was very attentive as she showed the improvement made at Crafton Elementary over the years, where the students were now in their work, and where they were expected to be at the end of the year.

Mrs. Neal then turned to the subject of the "closed school" and said that she was a little offended that anyone would suggest that Crafton Elementary School was closed, because she believed that this school was the only one that she really knew that was "open." In this school parents have open access to the learning of their children from day to day and the report cards show fulfillment of objectives and not just subject grades. Parents in this school know everything the teachers know about the progress of their children and have all of this at their fingertips. Also, she advised the group that there were three accountability meetings scheduled each year for parents, and she used the occasion to invite the fact finding group to attend all of them. At the conclusion of this lengthy session wherein Mrs. Neal "held court," she stated that it was the school's moral obligation to ensure that all children learned at least to a satisfactory level so it was important for the school to plan and implement a program for that purpose. School had to come first and could not effectively compete with so many other activities that seemed to be important, but interfered with the teaching-learning process. Her final statement to the group was that Crafton Elementary's record would speak for itself regarding the kind of program provided for the children.

Following the meeting, there was a feeling among those in attendance that they had experienced a different attitude about school, and that with achievement being first and foremost in the minds of school leaders, they had a better understanding why nonacademic programs were not included during the day that utilized valuable instructional time at this particular school. One person asked Ginger why it was that other schools did not protect the school day in the same manner as Crafton Elementary. Of course, Ginger's response was that she didn't know about other schools, but that she did know that what was done in her school was very successful even though it was not considered "educationally correct" from the standpoint of being innovative. Ginger further indicated that the teachers were used to the 7:30 a.m. to 4:00 p.m. work day, enjoyed their challenge, and took pride in being innovative in the sense that they had a program that met the needs of all their students by the time they completed their last year in the school. They knew that they were doing something special because no other school in their area could make this claim. In fact, Ginger answered their inquiries with considerable pride.

As the school year swiftly was coming to an end, Mrs. Neal met with the third grade teachers to discuss reports of progress that she had generated from the computer. She had produced a list of students who were believed not on grade level as of the date of the meeting, and their rank order from high to low in achievement. The numbers were much smaller than they were at the beginning of the year; however, there still appeared to be several who needed to attend summer school to fulfill the requirement of the grade level before they moved on to the fourth grade. Two of the classes had no students with unsatisfactory achievement in reading, Ginger had seven and the other teacher who had extended reading time had eleven. In all there were more than seventeen percent of the students reading less than grade level; therefore, to get below the goal of ten percent some work was needed to be done, yet. After the standardized test results were received another assessment would be made.

Mrs. Neal held her last accountability meeting on the evening of the last day of school. After she finished her report she advised parents that in the mail in a few days they would be getting their children's report card and the school report card with all of the statistics she had reviewed at this accountability meeting. Following the completion of her remarks, Mrs. Neal was embarrassed when a parent asked an approving packed auditorium to give Mrs. Neal and her staff a standing ovation, and thanked all of them for providing such an extremely powerful program during a time when other schools were having difficulty "staying the course."

A reporter attended this meeting because he had been at the earlier meeting when business and community leaders and others had requested that the school permit things, such as field trips, partnerships, speakers, and other programs to be conducted during the school day. The reporter was very much impressed by the accountability meeting, the response of the parents, and the genuine wholesome relationship of the teachers and parents. The newspaper the next day had a picture of Mrs. Neal in the midst or her accountability meeting with the headline stating: "CRAFTON, THE REAL SCHOOL." In addition there was a lengthy article with interviews of several parents and teachers that presented the program of the community's elementary school in such a way that all felt more proud than ever that they were part of such a valuable teaching-learning environment.

After the standardized test results were returned the

number of summer school students was reduced to sixteen. After a very comprehensive summer school none of the students failed to meet their goal of being on grade level in school.

One day during early summer while Ginger was busy preparing for another school year, she received in the mail a letter from the district which indicated that she had achieved tenure. She had been so busy that the issue of tenure was pushed aside. Shortly, Ginger got a call from two teachers who were employed at the same time as she but were assigned to other schools in the district. They wanted to meet for lunch one day to talk about school. Ginger got to the restaurant early on the day of the meeting, so she had an opportunity to hug them as they arrived.

Following only a bit of small talk, they wanted Ginger to tell them about Crafton Elementary School. She didn't really know what it was they wanted to hear because it was not innovative with "frilly" types of activities. She stated that there were no field trips, plays, programs outside the class, parties, and the like; in addition there were no breaks, duty free lunches, and planning periods. Further, she noted that there were long work days from early morning to late afternoon, a sound principal, outstanding co-workers, and a strong sense of accomplishments. With a little beam in her eye she said that the principal does not look at my plan book, there is a schoolwide grade book, everything is open to the parents, and the principal does not visit my classroom for observation and evaluation. Ginger's final statement to them was that school was fun and she was a professional.

ASSESSMENT

The superintendent realized all the while that he had not said the educationally correct things to the parents, school board and many others on this extremely auspicious gathering of people in the school division. They had all heard him speak for such a long time, and through it all, their mindset was not altered; in fact, it appeared that they were solidly against anything that he suggested. "It is the age old problem in education today," he thought, as he sat in his chair while everyone left the auditorium. "The people want the best for their children, but because they are used to hearing about new innovative programs to be the lifeline for their children, so what I said tonight was far removed from being innovative."

Getting back to the basics never was understood and certainly not by the people who were in attendance on this evening. When the board members paraded quietly by not looking his way, he knew that they too failed to understand his message. Certainly the parents didn't, or else they didn't show any indication that any of them understood what he was talking about on this evening, and if they did, they didn't show it.

A visible sign of their total disdain for what he spoke about on this evening was the story, *Miss Huston*, copies of which were strewn all over the auditorium, in the hallway, and wadded up and thrown in the wastebaskets. With his limited optimism changing to pessimism, he slowly walked alone and dejectedly with his head down to his car. It had really been a long evening.

Devin, the local newspaper owner, did a good job on the lengthy story in the morning paper. According to his estimate approximately eighth hundred people attended the meeting held at the local high school with about one hundred having to stand in the hallway. "The die was obviously cast much before the group arrived to hear the division superintendent present his plan to correct the dismal AET scores," he stated in the article. "While the superintendent of fifteen years so eloquently and articulately told the group what he believed was wrong in the school division to cause less than satisfactory achievement results, there appeared to be no indication that they were listening for any solution. The fact that this poor achievement occurred on his watch caused all the hostility to be directed toward him.

"I talked to several parents after the meeting and many others by telephone before writing this article, and it appeared to be unanimous that the superintendent should have provided the leadership to ensure that students achieved at the expected level in their school work. When I mentioned to them about his having presented more than one time his unique plan of teaching and learning over his fifteen years as superintendent, none of those to whom I spoke wanted to speak on that subject.

"I asked several parents. 'What do you think the achievement level of the children would be if the school division had not rejected his plans that he presented to the school division earlier?'

"Several answered that they believed that the children would have even achieved much less in school. It was clear that during and after the lengthy meeting last evening the comments of the parents indicated that they had lost confidence in the school chief. A couple of parents brought up the subject of the Hollow girls when they played basketball for the high school and how much time the superintendent spent running all over the state during this period. More than one noted how embarrassed they were to see his loud and boisterous behavior at the games. 'If he had spent this time on trying to correct this achievement problem, we would not have this problem now,' one parent explained."

The newspaper owner concluded his very lengthy article by writing that the issue of poor achievement of the students is far from over, but the superintendent provided a revelation by means of a powerful historical review in his presentation. It was obvious to all who were present that his talk to the group went for naught except for the superintendent who feels much better now that he has had time to state his case. "Regarding his plan for correction," he wrote, "almost to the parent, nothing he would have said last evening would have made any difference at all. The die was cast and is still cast. As for me, I thought his plan was a good one which really could be summed up in a few words: tell the child and parent what it is the student should learn, monitor progress closely, and for the students, provide whatever instructional time is needed. It's the most innovative idea I have heard since the days before we got away from the basics."

Paul H. Jones

LET THE SEASON BEGIN

Meanwhile, the Bacon College team was practicing each day to prepare for the new season of basketball. Mit and Marsha were strong additions to a most excellent team already. They really did have fun not only playing together as a team, but because of their warm and loving relationship off the court. Wanting to be a part of this special team, the students and the people in the neighborhood came to watch them practice twice each day in the new coliseum.

Coach Anna scheduled fourteen home games, but there were two practice games that she had not revealed to the girls until following practice on this Friday. As they were preparing to go to the Hollow for their usual and most exciting dinner with the folks there, Coach Anna said, "I have a special surprise for you. Tuesday evening we are going to play our first practice game of the year at Central High School. On Thursday we travel to Norfolk to play at Hanna's high school where the coach there tells me that the game has been sold out for several days. These games should really be fun for all of you as we stage a genuine practice with an intrasquad game. I hope you all like the schedule."

Hanna was speechless as she walked over to Coach

Anna with tears running down her cheeks to give her a big hug. This started an avalanche of hugs of Hanna by the entire team. "What an exciting time this will be," Esther thought, as she wrapped her arms around her good friend, Hanna.

For the trip to Central High School all of the other students who participated in games last year, and in addition the new soccer players were included. Maudie had become such an integral part of the team that she was invited to come along. The short ride was fun. Arriving early, the group was met by pompom carrying cheerleaders in the parking lot along with many high school students from Central and from several other schools in nearby school divisions. Numerous pictures were made, and scores of autographs were gotten by the excited group who had waited several hours for the arrival of their favorite team.

The Hollow folks had arrived early and were greeted warmly by Glenn Colson, the superintendent, who was the host for this special event at the high school. In the center of the welcoming committee for the girls, he stood helping to hold one of several banners which stated: "WELCOME HOME, HOLLOW GIRLS."

Seeing the superintendent in such a joyous and festive mood, one would not realize that only a few short days ago the whole community of parents had suddenly turned against him and his leadership of the school division. It was ironic that some of the same parents who spoke such negative statements about the cause of the low AET scores a few days ago now joined with him to welcome the pride of Central High School back on campus.

When they walked into the gymnasium before a standing room only crowd, the team paused and looked around before proceeding to the dressing room. Mit was really struck by the large number of banners hanging overhead indicating what was won by the Hollow team during their years in high school. "It's so hard to believe that the Hollow girls have never lost a game since they began to play," Mit thought, as she put her arms around Esther while the spectators continued to applaud, whistle and yell. All were really showing their special love for the girls.

On this day the superintendent had put aside his serious problems with the school board and parents and was enjoying every minute, just as the others in attendance for this special event. Sitting near Josh, he felt very comfortable because this appeared to be old times when the young ladies from the remote area of the community dominated basketball all their years they were enrolled in school.

Following prayer by Esther, they departed the dressing room to be received by loud greetings as they made their way to the floor. Even Hanna was dressed for practice after she had begged Coach Anna, and the two new girls, Marsha and Mit, were the topic of discussion of several in the stands. The crowd was not disappointed as Esther skillfully led her team through intricate maneuvers in the warm-up drills.

It was a full afternoon of fun with several contests for those in attendance, especially the current high school students. Not being able to control herself, Maudie hugged Coach Anna several times during the afternoon, always thanking the coach for including her as a part of the special group of young ladies.

Being thrust suddenly in a different role when Coach Anna asked him to coach one of the teams, the superintendent was overjoyed such that a tear or two could be seen in his eyes. This would provide well needed relief from the enormous pressure he had been under during the last several days. His counterpart would be Josh, his very best friend and former coach of Central High School.

"This is going to be the day you are going to lose

your first game," Glenn said jokingly to Josh, as the two huddled with their team.

"You won't get upset if we run up the score, will you?" Josh countered, laughing all the while.

Esther and Dorothy led their respective teams in the special game on this afternoon in their alma mater with Marsha on one team and Mit on the other showing their expertise in playing basketball. Seeing both of these players for the first time, one fan leaned over to another and said, "The new girl Mit, who they say came out of the jungle in Costa Rica, is extremely fast going up and down the floor."

"Marsha, the other new girl from New Mexico, is very methodical and extremely patient all the while," the other responded. "They are an awesome tandem to be added to an already invincible team."

A catered dinner purchased personally by the superintendent was served in the cafeteria for the team, the Hollow parents and many community leaders. Following the dinner, several people spoke praising the Hollow girls for their excellent basketball skills in addition to their special efforts to make the world a better and safer place in which to live. Near the close of this most festive occasion, the superintendent introduced the boosters' club president who announced that the jerseys of the entire team that never lost a single game throughout their career at Central High School were going to be retired and hung in the gymnasium for all to see now and for years to come.

The presentations were not over as Mrs. Joy Brown, the school division instructional supervisor and Mrs. Sally Dunden, the elementary school principal, gave each of the girls and Coach Anna a special plaque. Following this activity, the chairman of the board of supervisors presented beautiful plaques to the Hollow folks in recognition of their efforts to assist their neighbors in their community and in other parts of the world.

"What a special event!" Coach Anna thought, as she and her phenomenal group headed back to Bacon College.

Hanna had a hard time believing that the team was going to conduct its next practice at her high school in the Norfolk area of Virginia. It had been advertised well in the area and a large crowd was expected to be in attendance. Just as they were preparing to leave to Hanna's high school, Dr. Damond received a letter from the women's collegiate athletic association office in Denver, as follows:

Dear Dr. Damond:

Over the last few weeks my office has received several complaints from individuals who state that your women's basketball team has failed to adhere to the guidelines as set forth in the American College and University Women's Athletic Association's manual for women's athletics.

The main thrusts of these alleged infractions are as follows:

Pursuant to Section II, Paragraph 1, it is reported that your students failed to meet the minimum SAT score for admittance to participate in collegiate athletics. Those students who failed to obtain a score of 900 or more are not eligible to participate in any form of intercollegiate athletics.

Pursuant to Section V, Paragraph 3, some of these serious allegations deal with money much above the limit being given to the women on your basketball team. Specifically, it is alleged that your team members have received funds from an unknown third party.

Pursuant to Section VI, Paragraph 2, students are required to be enrolled in a minimum of courses leading to a degree. It is alleged that some of your student athletes fail to meet this standard.

As required by the Association's guidelines, you are directed to forward a response to these allegations listed above within sixty days of receipt of this correspondence. My office will be in touch with you following receipt of your responses to set a timely schedule to investigate these serious allegations. Following the Association's on-site-visit, a full written report will be forwarded to you and your staff.

Sincerely yours,

Mary R. Green, Director
American College and University Women's Athletic Association

Leaning back in his executive chair, Dr. Damond muttered to himself, "How many more things can happen to the college?" he thought, as he laid the letter on his already full desk. It wasn't the fact that all of these allegations were absolutely false that bothered him as much as not understanding why someone or some people would make up such outlandish stories about this very beloved group of young people. He knew that they hadn't received any money from anyone because they didn't have any money. To his knowledge, they had not spent one dime in the school store.

To verify this, he called the store manager. "This is the Bacon College Sundry Shop," the manager answered.

"This is John Damond," he stated.

"How are you today, sir?" the manager replied.

"I am fine," Dr. Damond indicated. "Would you answer a question for me?"

"I'll do my best," the manager answered.

"Have the basketball team members bought much from our store?" the president asked.

"You know," the manager said, "we were talking about that the other day. We all agreed that the Hollow girls had not bought anything from the store since arriving on campus, but that Hanna buys some small items from time to time that we believe are being shared with the others, such as small snack items. To our knowledge, the Hollow girls themselves have never purchased anything. It was our thinking that they don't have any money."

"Isn't it refreshing to know those students who don't need money to make their way here on campus and elsewhere?" Dr. Damond said.

"When they come into the shop with others, they are so very mannerly such that the other students appear to be trying to emulate them," the manager noted. "The conduct and behavior, including manners of students on campus, has been excellent since the Hollow girls arrived. By the way the new soccer players seem to be from the same mold because they too display outstanding conduct."

"I concur with all you have said," the president stated. "Thank you for your information."

Dialing the filing clerk, he asked her to bring him a list of classes being taken by the basketball players and their SAT scores. In a short while the filing clerk, who had been employed for nearly twenty-five years, brought the information to his office. Giving the information a cursory examination, he noticed that the range of SAT scores started at 1150 to more than 1500, and the girls were majoring in several different areas including engineering, biology, education, psychology, mathematics, computer science, foreign language, English, and archaeology. Each was enrolled in six courses each semester to fulfill requirements for their bachelor's degree in four years.

Following his preliminary perusal of the information from the filing clerk, he asked his secretary to bring him the statistical data regarding the various colleges and universities throughout the country. Retrieving the large paperback book of statistics and data on all institutions of higher learning, she began to search for more specific information requested.

"What is the mean score of all students entering college for the first time?" he asked his secretary.

Turning to that category, she then replied, "The mean score of those students was 1011."

"Can you find the mean score of all athletes?" he asked.

Flipping through the pages hurriedly, she soon found the information and said, "The average for athletes in 943."

"Thank you very much," the president stated. Leaning back in his chair, he wondered aloud how such allegations could be made against the college and especially about the basketball team of outstanding scholarly and God fearing young people. "To attack the sender of the letter or to attack anyone, is not the Christian thing to do," he thought.

Greetings were received from numerous sectors of the Norfolk area when the girls disembarked on the campus of Hanna's high school. Hugs were generous as the people mobbed her as everyone stood in a parking lot filled with cars. Several large banners welcoming Hanna and the team could be seen on the building and others hanging on poles just for this auspicious occasion. A large number of young people stood by just to get a view of the best girls' basketball team in the country. "Can you believe they are here at our high school today?" one said to another, as greetings continued for a long time before they all headed for the gymnasium.

Hanna was so excited when she dressed to participate in practice before her home community, including her parents who had invited the whole team for barbecue at their palatial house in an exclusive area on a private golf course. Every time Hanna touched the ball in practice the crowd applauded. Not only were their eyes fixed on Hanna, their hometown favorite, the capacity crowd of spectators began to applaud them all for their unusual skill level playing basketball. In the intrasquad game they stood for the entire game shouting and applauding both teams, especially Esther, who quietly passed and shot brilliantly, as usual.

The entire team marveled over the luxurious house of Hanna, such that Hanna took them on a tour of the large dwelling. Mr. and Mrs. Green were such gracious hosts for the evening. Following a delicious dinner and delightful visit, the group headed west up Route 58 back to Bacon College with thoughts of love still ringing in their ears from the wonderful people in Hanna's community.

The sports world was shocked the next day to read the headlines of a New York newspaper as follows: "Bacon Breaks ACUWAA Rules." Widely circulated, the story was disseminated to thousands of readers in the early morning, and by midday the letter and another article were forwarded all over the country by way of the Information Express News to all state and most local newspapers. Within one twenty-four-hour period this distasteful story was distributed throughout the wonderful country permitting freedom of the press. What a horrible scene!

Jewel Throneberry read with interest this article carried in a New York newspaper which contained verbatim the letter received by Dr. Damond outlining the alleged infractions of the Bacon College basketball team. "After all the college has gone through in recent months regarding the media, I don't see how they can withstand much more," she thought. Soon she had her secretary to call a meeting of the magazine staff.

With the staff assembled around the large conference table, Jewel made some preliminary remarks to the attentive group. "Several weeks ago, as you know, I wrote a scathing article in our Margone Magazine about the Bacon College basketball team which was untrue and later retracted with a heartfelt apology," she told her group. "I talked to the president of Bacon College this morning, and he told me that he was shocked regarding the article about American College and University Women's Athletic Association (ACUWAA) infractions while informing me that he had only received the letter yesterday. He immediately pointed out emphatically that the alleged infractions cited by the American College and University Women's Athletic Association were absolutely false, but he didn't want me to write anything at present about the situation. Almost as soon as the letter was received by the president of the college, the contents of the letter were included in a New York newspaper article. Obviously, this is a devastating blow to an already beleaguered institution of higher learning."

"This certainly adds more salt to the wound made by your ugly article earlier," a young lady stated.

"That's so very true," Jewel responded. "Somehow, I feel very much responsible for these allegations being made in the first place. I am now obligated to right the ship regarding these lovely young and naïve ladies who make up this team. I am sure that they are not aware of this latest hateful assault on them and their very special college."

"How did this confidential letter from the Association to the president of the college get in the newspaper in the first place?" a young man queried.

"I really don't know," Jewel replied. "Obviously, someone from the Association leaked it to the press."

"It is my understanding that all correspondence to member colleges and universities regarding infractions of rules is handled confidentially until there has been time for the college or university to make an informal response to the allegations," an older man indicated. "Let me look at what it says on the internet."

Keying in the appropriate request on his powerful laptop computer, he found the information. "It says here that all matters related to any allegation will be handled confidentially until the institution was permitted sufficient time to respond to the inquiry or sixty days, whichever came first," he stated.

"If this did leak out from the Association, it is in huge trouble," Jewel noted. "Lawyers throughout the country will be calling the president to represent the college."

Bacon had been invited to participate in the Preliminary Season Tournament so they were scheduled to play a pair of games in St. Louis followed by two in Atlanta, if they won the first two. If they continued to win, the finals of the PST would be staged in New York City.

Grieving all the while, Dr. Damond realized that the story had massaged the imagination of basketball fans throughout the country, and many other derogatory media reports would follow. On this ugly period in the life of Bacon he turned to his Bible to read Psalm 8:

1 A psalm of David. O LORD, our Lord, how majestic is your name in all the earth! You have set your glory above the heavens.
2 From the lips of children and infants you have ordained praise because of your enemies, to silence the foe and the avenger.
3 When I consider your heavens, the work of your fingers, the moon and the stars, which you have set in place,

*4 what is man that you are mindful of him, the son of man
that you care for him?
5 You made him a little lower than the heavenly beings and
crowned him with glory and honor.
6 You made him ruler over the works of your hands; you put
everything under his feet:
7 all flocks and herds, and the beasts of the field,
8 the birds of the air, and the fish of the sea, all that swim the
paths of the seas.
9 O LORD, our Lord, how majestic is your name in all the
earth!*

His human side told him to fight back and clear his
college's name by refuting the articles that one by one
defamed his institution. He knew it was time to talk to
Coach Anna so he called her to his office for a long
conference with the only subject being that of the letter and
the terrible articles.

"I know you have heard about the derogatory articles
being written following my receipt of this letter," he said, as
he handed her the letter from the ACUWAA.

After reading the letter Coach Anna looked up and
said, "These allegations are not true, not even one word,"
Coach Anna vehemently stated with total denial. "How
could anyone suggest such things?"

"They are all untrue," he followed. "However, the
media throughout the land now have this letter and will write
stories about it. In my opinion this will continue for many
days ahead, so you must prepare the girls for all that will be
coming by means of the press. My telephone has been
ringing off the hook ever since the story was written in the
New York newspaper. I am not making any kind of
statement, except a brief comment to Jewel Throneberry,
because this was supposed to be a confidential
correspondence to the college and not for use by the media.

She is not reporting my refutation, but she is preparing an article to be released later."

"I admire you greatly for not responding to these allegations at this time," Coach Anna stated. "I know it must really be difficult not verbally to disprove these accusations of infractions of rules."

"You may want to tell the girls before you play your first game so they will understand if someone says something," Dr. Damond suggested. "It seems that all of their lives they have had something to prove all along the way. It behooves me that in our society that people accused have to defend themselves while the false accusers just remain silent."

Marsha and Mit were so very excited as they stood with their teammates for their pep rally before they departed the campus. Coach Anna had spent much time the previous evening relating the story written about the team, and they had a few questions to ask, but when they understood the situation, it was business as usual with the group. Always enjoying these sendoff rallies, Coach Anna thought, "Nobody here at Bacon seems to be concerned about these horrible allegations about the team." In fact, it was not mentioned at all until one young zealous student made up a cheerleading yell:

> Jealousy, jealousy is your name,
> We have America's team,
> And you have the shame.
> On the floor we play our best,
> Not sending letters,
> To the world-wide press.

Dr. Damond hugged each team member before saying a wonderful prayer to start the new season. "Remember that we are so very proud of you, and so very proud that you are part of our educational community. May God continue to bless you as you represent Bacon College so well."

"If there were no external distractions, the girls retreat unto themselves and not be cognizant of their surroundings," Coach Anna thought, as they headed for the Roanoke airport. "I have a feeling that this special characteristic of theirs will soon come in handy when they play before coliseum crowds now that the fabricated charges have been spread throughout the country."

Coach Anna could tell that the atmosphere was somewhat different in the airport terminal, but there were still a few who wanted autographs. Mit and Marsha fulfilled this chore rather awkwardly at first, but soon became more comfortable with this part of playing on the Bacon College team.

Purchasing a newspaper as usual, Coach Anna and the girls headed to board their direct flight to St. Louis to play Barton University, and if they won, they would play the winner of the game between Roan and Oakin Universities the next evening. Seated on the plane, Coach Anna sensed that the demeaning article in the newspaper caused the passengers to examine the Bacon team with a jaundiced eye. Soon on their way with the girls just as impervious as ever regarding their surroundings, they headed for their first game of the season.

Unfolding her state newspaper, the first thing Coach Anna saw was the headline: "Bacon Submits No Denial." Reading further, it stated that Dr. Damond had refused to respond to the article regarding the allegations of multiple infractions of ACUWAA rules. The writer of the article couldn't understand why the college chief would not make some comment to the reporter's numerous telephone calls to get a comment from him.

This was not the only article in this vastly circulated newspaper. An editorial was included entitled: "The Pure Are Not So Pure." It seemed that the editor had a field day making derogatory statements with numerous innuendoes laced with sharp sarcasm about the "make-believe tramps secretly living as royalty among us, gaining our sympathy all the while." The writer continued, "Never in my years in journalism have I witnessed a group so pure on the outside who captured plenary love from all they met, and underneath were like so many in our secular society who are bent on greed and personal gain. The bubble is burst for these basketball players who have been participating on an uneven playing field. We should all applaud the ACUWAA for it's astute discernment when the rest of us could not see through the veneer displayed by the 'puritans.'"

"What an ugly editorial by this respected newspaper!" Coach Anna thought, as she leaned back and thought how wonderful it would be to live like the Hollow girls. "They never seem to be concerned when derogation is thrust their way. After many years of being butts of jokes and ridicule, they have grown to be strong warriors for peace and tranquility as they follow closely the teachings of Jesus Christ."

Coach Anna didn't expect anything like this when she was employed as coach of the small mountain college. For this moment, as she lay her head back on the seat near the window, basketball didn't seem as important at this time with the totally contrived charges whirling around by everybody. "It would only take a cursory examination of each of these alleged infractions included in the ACUWAA letter to be refuted," she continued her thoughts. "Dr. Damond is very wise so his silence on this matter at present has some meaningful purpose that will be revealed later."

As they walked through the airport terminal in St. Louis, Coach Anna saw the headlines of several newspapers in the vending machines. One stated: "The Cheaters Play Tonight."

"No wonder the people in the airport are snubbing us here," Coach Anna thought.

The girls playfully walked along as happily as they could be enjoying each other's company all the while. It was much like the environment now was very similar to that described in Esther's short story: "Life in the Shadows." She had described their earlier public school period as being a time when the Hollow girls could not avoid the ugliness displayed toward them by the other pupils in school. She had clearly described their school atmosphere as that of shadows, and the difficulty the children from the Hollow had to remove themselves from the derision. The Hollow girls were better equipped to handle this miserable climate that Coach Anna expected them to experience during the weeks ahead than she was, so she would follow their lead as she had done so many times before.

Having not been in St. Louis before, they all looked out the window of the shuttle bus as it traveled near the Golden Arch headed for their hotel. Several young people near the entrance made some comments to them with one saying, "Would you mind lending me fifty dollars until Saturday?"

Walking through the menacing group, Coach Anna quickly went to the desk for their room keys, and they went up the elevator without further incident. "It's going to be a difficult time," Coach Anna thought, as she waited in her room until the time for them to leave for practice.

Everywhere the Bacon College team played there was a sellout crowd, and this one was no exception. Many people were standing at the entrance when the team approached the coliseum. Being a cold day, one person loudly yelled, "Why didn't you all wear your fur coat today?" Others hollered many disparaging comments including, "How many Bacon girls do you need to count to ten?"

Coach Anna had a fighting spirit and her red faced showed it, but just looking at the peaceful demeanor of the girls as they moved through the hostile crowd, she followed their lead. The ugly cheering throng followed them into the coliseum to watch practice and to conjure up as many derogatory comments as possible while the girls went through their season opener practice session.

"The whole world seems to be against our team," Hanna said to Coach Anna.

"I have never seen anything like it in all my life," Coach Anna responded. "I knew it would be somewhat difficult until the ACUWAA investigation is over, but never in my wildest dreams would I have thought it would be like this. We just can't get away from it."

"There are no peaceful corners," Hanna replied.

"I know what Esther and the Hollow girls felt like when they were enrolled in school," Coach Anna stated, as she spoke to Esther when she came by.

"How many papers did you write for the girls, or can you write?" one of the hecklers yelled to Coach Anna through a huge megaphone.

Having dodged the reporters when they came into the coliseum, Coach Anna made her way to answer their questions at the termination of their practice. "How do you respond to the serious allegations about breaking numerous ACUWAA rules?" a young national reporter immediately asked.

"You are asked to direct all questions regarding the ACUWAA rule infraction allegations to our president, Dr. John Damond," she calmly stated.

"Watching practice today, your team took a lot of

abuse," another reporter pointed out. "How much can the team withstand and continue to perform at a high level?"

"The team, as always, will separate itself from its immediate environment and play the basketball game without outside interference," Coach Anna answered. "Their test of situations comes from the heart that is guided by their Christian principles they learned in their conservative families in a remote area of western Virginia."

"You have two additional players on your squad," an older female reporter stated. "One is from a very isolated area in New Mexico and the other from the jungle of Costa Rica of all places. Some say that these two girls fail to meet any of the minimum standards set by the ACUWAA for entrance into college. How do you respond to those allegations?"

"Again, I respectfully ask you to direct this question to our college president," Coach Anna answered.

"The human side of Coach Anna wanted to tell the world that these allegations were wrong and that the girls on the team were genuine and pure, but on this day she left this message to be delivered by the president.

Thinking that the girls had been exposed enough to this hostile environment for now, Coach Anna had their pregame meal delivered to their room. It was always fun to eat in their room so they really had a good time on this day teasing one another but never mentioning what took place at practice. "Following the game, we shall have pizza," Coach Anna announced to an approving group of young people.

When they arrived for the game, a local policeman met them and escorted the team through a side door away from the maddening crowd who had come early to harass the team. "I have been assigned to protect you this evening before, during and after the game," the polite officer told Coach Anna. "I will be present with you so anything that you need, just let me know. This crowd tonight has been preparing for this occasion for a some time now after reading reports about your team in the newspaper and seeing them on television and radio."

"Thank you for being our protector during this game tonight," Coach Anna said. "If we win tonight, will you be present for our game tomorrow evening?"

"I'll be there with my partner," he happily stated. "Our chief thought that if you all won, tomorrow evening would even draw a more hostile crowd."

Soon they were dressed, and Coach Anna asked the players to say a sentence prayer or even more than one, if they wanted to do so. Bowing while holding hands in a circle, their prayers included praise to God for His abundance of provisions, His grace, and everlasting love. It wasn't until Esther's turn that any mention was made about the hostility shown toward them by the people. "Please forgive those who falsely accuse us just as You were falsely accused two thousand years ago." Prayer time was special and more so on this evening in St. Louis.

A very large crowd was in place at Bacon College, including the Hollow folks, the president and students along with Maudie, and numerous community folks. An anonymous donor had paid for pizza for all of those present to be delivered at half time.

"Do you want to wait for the whole team to go on the floor instead of going out alone?" Coach Anna asked Hanna, the team manager.

"The team never backs away, so I don't want to tonight," Hanna told her coach.

"You and I both are learning from the group, aren't we?" Coach Anna said with a grin on her face.

It seemed that all in the capacity crowd saw Hanna entering the floor area at the same time, and what came forth was a unified "boo" that continued on and on. This was followed by all kinds of deprecatory comments, some she could discern and many mixing with others such that they were difficult to understand. "These are really ugly comments that they are making toward Bacon," Hanna thought. Many in attendance wondered whether or not the young team could hold up under the pressure generated by this pugnacious and rancorous crowd on hand on this evening in St. Louis. Soon they would find out as the girls were headed on the floor led by Esther.

With the air filled with taunts and unique statements of derision coming from all corners of this capacity crowd, it was business as usual as Esther and the other girls were impervious to the ugly and hostile environment. "They amaze me," Coach Anna said to Hanna, as they went through their drills masterfully.

"When I think that the team has met its match, I look up and Esther has the ball encouraging the others to follow her lead," Hanna pointed out while leaning over and loudly speaking in Coach Anna's ear so she could hear over the crowd noise.

Broadcasting from near the Bacon bench, Coach Anna could hear what the announcer was saying as he too sided with those in attendance. "Why would the ACUWAA permit the Bacon College team to continue to play when they have broken so many of the Association's rules," he pointed out. "In the survey taken this afternoon more than eighty percent of those responding thought that it would be in the best interest of the ACUWAA to remove the team from participation until it abided by the guidelines like the other colleges and universities."

"Based on what he is reporting, there are only a few people who are supporting our institution at this time," Coach Anna said to Hanna.

"From what I can gather this is the kind of world that the Hollow girls grew up in," Hanna said. "You noticed that they have taunted both Marsha and Mit in addition to the Hollow girls."

With the St. Louis police officer standing near their bench, Coach Anna decided to remain on the floor and not go back to the dressing room through the hostile crowd for their final meeting before the game. This new season of basketball would now begin under very abnormal conditions.

Just before the game started Coach Anna left the bench to go to speak to the Barton coach where she received a less than warm greeting. In fact the opposing coach barely shook her hand and almost simultaneously turned her back on Coach Anna to the delight of those in attendance. It was a long walk back to the Bacon bench.

Looking at the team who seemed to be impervious to the horrible things being said to them, Coach Anna hugged each one before sending the initial five players to the center of the court to begin the game.

Everyone was standing. There were no handshakes by the Barton players. Pejorative yells filled the air continuously. Opprobrious loud comments from fans near the bench rang in the ears of Coach Anna and the other team members. It was a terrible scene.

On the jump ball Dorothy retrieved it and headed immediately down the court only to see Coach Anna standing to call a timeout. This was so unusual for the Bacon team because timeouts were hardly ever called.

Huddling together on the sideline, Coach Anna said, "I just wanted to tell you all how much I appreciate being your coach. Remember that God is always with us regardless of the situation."

Esther passed the ball in to Dorothy who dribbled toward the center of the floor, and suddenly whipped a sharp pass to Jonsie1 who flipped a lob pass to Diane who made a bounce pass to Esther who made a smooth jump shot near the foul line. A Barton player passed the ball inbounds where Dorothy and Esther smothered her and forced an errant pass which gave the ball to Bacon. Dorothy took the ball out of bounds and passed a long arcing pass to Esther who laid it in off the backboard.

Bacon calmly went about its business of playing a very strong defense that was their trademark last year, and Esther was leading the charge on offense, as usual. The powerful Barton team with optimum support from the fans couldn't muster any offense against a determined Bacon team. Early in the game Coach Anna inserted Maggie, Marsha and Mit, her three-M team speedsters with Vivian and Mabel. Fast breaks were commonplace as Mit showed the crowd her jungle speed racing up and down the floor. With two minutes left in the half the score was Bacon 47 and Barton 23.

Name calling by half time had reached a fever pitch. Fists were raised in the air by many fans as they shouted ugly remarks toward the team, including obscenities and vulgarity. The whole environment was so hostile that Coach Anna walked to the end of the bench to speak to the police officer.

"Because the actions of the fans are more vicious now, I am going to keep our team here on the floor and not walk near the crowd to go to our dressing room," Coach Anna said.

"I'll just remain on the floor with your team," the policeman responded.

Back at Bacon College those watching the game on television had really heard much ugliness from those in attendance at the game. "The ACUWAA allegations of wrongdoing by our college has caused our team to be taking a lot of abuse," Dr. Damond said to Josh who was sitting near him watching the game.

"I really can't understand why the people, including the announcers, would be so hostile toward our girls," Josh said.

"It will take a wide scale, thorough investigation to clear our good name," the president noted. "At this time I am not making any statements whatsoever because the people throughout the country are going to believe what they want without regard to what I have to say. Their minds are made up."

"It's a difficult time for everybody, but in all instances God prevails," Josh said.

"I have such a hard time trying to be patient," the president noted. "It's so hard to be still and wait on God as found in Psalm 37."

"The ugly taunting has not affected the basketball team as far as I can determine," Josh said.

"All things are possible with God, even a revelation of truth regarding the ugly allegations," Josh stated, as they turned to watch the second half on the wide screen.

Even with the wide margin in the score, derogation was continued to be expressed by individuals mixed with collective yells of hatred from pockets of fans throughout the coliseum. Following a long tradition, Coach Anna inserted Esther back into the game with just under two minutes to play. For a moment the group of spectators discontinued their belligerent conduct, pausing to recognize the outstanding basketball game played by Bacon College and particularly by Esther. It seemed that as they watched the game clock tick down, they just stood serenely, reflecting on their conduct for this evening.

Leaving the hotel in the early the morning after having won the first two games in the preseason tournament, one would have thought that the team had contracted a terrible contagious disease when no one attempted to associate with them along the way to the waiting area in the terminal. Matching conduct of the passengers and crew was duplicated on the aircraft itself. Media accounts had supplied the public with total misinformation, having drawn from the initial article quoting the letter from the ACUWAA. Each one included the statement, "All efforts to contact and get a comment from Dr. John Damond of the Bacon College had failed, and Coach Anna Bosley quickly requests that all questions regarding the charges be addressed to the president."

The campus was absent any media, resulting from a decision of the college's Board of Directors the previous evening. As soon as the team entered the athletic dormitory after returning from St. Louis, the telephone rang, and it was Dr. Damond. "I know you have just returned from a long and most tiring trip, but would you mind coming to my office for a meeting?" he asked.

"I would be happy to do that," Coach Anna replied, as usual, but this time responding to a sense of urgency in his tone of voice.

His efficient secretary quickly whisked her into president's office as he got up from his executive chair and came around the front to sit adjacent to Coach Anna. "First of all, how was your trip to St. Louis?" he inquired.

"We had a very good trip that the girls loved very much," she said. "Mit and Marsha really have added much to our basketball family."

"It was really a difficult road trip, wasn't it?" he probed. "As we watched the game and heard the announcers expounding continuously about the ACUWAA letter, we all knew that you all were under much pressure to perform well and especially in a Christian like manner. I was so much concerned for you all."

"At this point in my life I don't really have sufficient wisdom to loose myself from those things that might be nagging hindrances to success," Coach Anna said, "but I have the best teachers so I should learn soon. The girls seemed to be totally impervious to all the taunting, name calling and just outright ugliness at each of the games and elsewhere. God has given them a special gift. I hope to learn how they do it."

"I am glad that they could remove themselves from that derogatory environment," he added. "The Board of Directors wanted me to meet with you as soon as you returned to apologize to you for the situation surrounding the basketball team. They have been adamant from the beginning about responding to any media inquiries because they believe to say anything would only legitimize the terribly false charges by the ACUWAA. To this point no official from Bacon College has addressed any question from the media, and according to their stance at this point in time, there will be no statements in the future until this has been resolved with the ACUWAA."

"When do you think the ACUWAA will be on campus to do their investigation?" Coach Anna asked.

"At this juncture, I don't know," the humble president indicated. "You do remember Jewel Throneberry, who is an executive of the Margone Magazine, don't you? She is really trying to do her best to redeem herself with the college after she wrote the completely erroneous article several weeks ago. She has advised me that she is doing an investigative article responding to each of the charges of the ACUWAA and is going to be on campus in a few days to begin her personal probe."

"When will this article be released?" Coach Anna asked.

"That will be up to the Board," he indicated. "It

probably will not come until after the preseason is
completed. With that in mind can you all endure the abuse
you will get for the next few games?"

"The confrontational environment provides a
different landscape for the players, but they adjust easily,"
she pointed out. "Obviously, this is an unusual group who
can remain focused on the task at hand."

"The Board of Directors discussed several options:
holding a press conference, submitting a written response,
inviting all the media on campus to make a discovery for
themselves, or taking the offensive by inquiring of the
ACUWAA why the letter sent to the college wound up in the
newspaper almost before it was received by my office," he
stated. "But the board members failed to take either of these
options as they decided to remain silent and just be patient."

"It certainly is a viable option as it has churned up the
media to a frenzied state," Coach Anna reacted. "Many
articles have already been written and more will come, I'm
sure."

"It is my opinion that responding to such a very
negative document of charges only affirms its believability
so that not reacting at all at this time will soon be discussed
by the media as a separate issue altogether," Dr. Damond
said. "Going about our daily schedules in a businesslike
manner may cause the press to turn its thoughts in a different
direction to determine the veracity of the charges in the
ACUWAA letter in the first place."

"Will Jewel Throneberry's investigative report
provide a healthy revelation of the situation?" Coach Anna
said.

"You know," he replied, "I think that it will be the
catalyst to change the direction of the inquiries. Some may
mistake my reticence in this grave matter as weakness, but I
have learned that waiting and patience are very important in

decision making."

"I always stand in awe of your wisdom," Coach Anna said. "Thank you for letting me be one of your faithful and loyal employees."

"I thank you for wanting to work here in Bacon College," he said, as he stood up which was Coach Anna's cue that he was through, and it was time for her to leave.

For the next couple of days the girls were preparing for the trip to Atlanta to continue in their quest to win the Preliminary Season Tournament by playing two other formidable foes. As they practiced with time passing, the massive media charge continued to crash down on the small Christian college tucked away in southwest Virginia.

BELEAGUERED SUPERINTENDENT

But beleagueredness was not only confined to the college in this small community, because the superintendent of public schools was still being bashed by irate parents whose group was growing larger by the day. Everywhere the superintendent went, he was faced with the same issue regarding the low AET scores. In spite of all of the pressure he believed he could handle it, but for the school board that was a different story. They were really upset over the whole matter.

Although the telephone rang constantly at his office as well as his home, he seemed to be holding up under the pressure of the parental demands. This could not be said for the school board who from the outset were really upset with the superintendent for not providing a program that would produce good results. Having made several attempts to get back to the basics in the schools with innovative programs from his green book, the board had always sided with the education association. As usual, the entire matter would always become political and not what was best for the student.

The superintendent had really been at peace with the whole sordid matter after he had the opportunity to speak to the large group of parents and teachers in the auditorium of the high school. No encouragement had come from anybody so his posture was now one of professional loneliness and isolation. Being a very devout Christian became his armor plate during this period in his career. With all of the meetings being held by parents in the schools and those conducted regularly by the school level site based decision making units, he knew that the remedy to this malady would not include his expertise.

Having pondered his position at present and his work to effect improvement of achievement in the past, he felt comfortable after weighing all aspects of the dilemma. What a terrible period! "At the edge of adversity comes learning," he thought, as he leaned back in his chair behind a desk filled with papers of all kinds.

His telephone rang again. "Hello," he said, knowing that the secretary took all his calls.

"The chairman of the school board wants to talk to you again, and he still appears to be really upset," his secretary excitedly noted.

"This is Glenn," he said immediately. "How may I help you?"

"What have you done to get the parents off my back?" he loudly inquired.

"I haven't done anything subsequently to the meeting at the high school a few nights ago," he said calmly in response to a very irate and demanding school board chairman.

"You need to do something else because the parents are continuing to worry me to death," he said. "I don't have a minute's peace here at the bank or at home. "They call all the time."

"I am sorry that is the case," the superintendent stated. "There is a lot of activity among the parents during the last several days so I guess what I had to say to them the other night fell on deaf ears."

"But they want to hear something substantive from you, and not some educational jargon that we hear all the time," he vehemently stated. "They want specific change and not a litany of vague ideas that have little effect in bringing about better achievement of children."

"Please know that achievement woes of the school district can't be overcome in a brief moment," he said emphatically now getting on the offensive. "As I have earlier indicated and as you know, I presented a plan of commitment of quality for the school division more than one time. On each occasion it was not approved by the school board as it became a political issue with the education association winning out each time. I firmly believe that if my proposed plan of action had been implemented our school division would be leading the area and possibly the state in achievement of its young people."

"I remember these times that you would try to convince us to approve a different way of teaching," he admitted, "but the teachers were so adamantly opposed to any change that would disrupt how they were doing it."

"I realize that teachers want the status quo, and to have complete freedom in determining what to teach, when to teach and how to teach such that any intrusion on this precept is frowned on by the association and individual teachers alike," he continued. "Teachers work hard each day, but because of the organization itself in the schools, children are advanced along the way not based on achievement but because of time in a setting. Let me ask you, what percentage of the students leaving our elementary school moving to the middle school can't read on grade level?"

"What difference will this make to solve our present crisis?" he immediately said. "When they are declared graduates of our elementary schools, they all will be reading on grade level."

"That is what everyone thinks," the superintendent stated with a tinge of victory in his voice. "In some instances as many as fifty percent will not be functioning satisfactorily on grade level. It's the age old problem in our schools that I have been trying to correct, but have failed to convince my employer. Everybody is in charge in a school, and at the same time nobody is in charge overall regarding curriculum and instruction."

Instead of the school board chairman listening to what the superintendent was saying, it was déjà vu as again the chairman thwarted his suggestions, this time to attempt to discover a quick fix to a very complex problem. "This is a very hostile group of parents who are really scalp hunting and will soon lose their focus on achievement of children," he pointed out. "They have demanded that the board call another meeting and not one where you do all the talking. They want to vent their demands for the board to consider."

"As always, let me know the time and place of the meeting, and I shall make the necessary arrangements," the superintendent stated, as they closed their conversation.

There was much being written about the massive mobilization of the parents in addition to the continuous discussion on the talk shows.

A Friday evening meeting was not what he expected, yet, here the superintendent was preparing the usual meeting room to accommodate a large group by adding many chairs and hooking up the microphone and speakers. The agenda only included one item, that of providing a time for the many parents to vent their frustration to the board regarding the weak showing of their children on the AET's.

Soon the meeting chamber was inundated with parents and the press. Glenn Colson just sat in his usual seat beside the chairman facing the large throng filing in for the meeting. Shortly, everyone was settled, and the chairman gaveled the meeting to order and then established certain generic ground rules for speaking. Then he sat down waiting to recognize the initial speaker for the evening. They all began to hear the sound of a hymn being played that got louder and louder. Suddenly, the main doors to the meeting room were opened and in marched six parents carrying over their heads a black wooden casket. "What on earth is this?" Glenn asked himself as he sat, joining the board in full incredulity.

The six "pall bearers" walked in unison down the aisle while the old hymn, "Amazing Grace," was being played on a tape player carried by a lady dressed in white, including white gloves. Placing the homemade coffin in the front of those in attendance, they stepped back a few feet, stood at attention with eyes forward when the second coffin made its way into the meeting area lifted over the heads of six parents. Soon a third coffin came forward as another six men solemnly carried it to the front near the school board.

Total silence crept over the body of people in attendance as the leader stepped forward. "Many have already expressed their view about the school district as they have made their statement that it is dead, and that they were notifying the world that a resurrection is needed to transform it to life again," the group leader announced to a flabbergasted school board. "The bandaids you have applied over the years to cure its ills have not worked. The time has come for real action which I hope you will generate to lift our once proud school division up by the bootstraps."

While the messages of the group were succinct and to the point, it wasn't until later that the speakers began to point fingers, mostly at the superintendent, but the school board was not spared in the vicious attacks on the character of the county officials. Glenn sat looking at each of the parents who came to the podium to speak, some he knew by name and others he had seen before but couldn't remember their names. Either way, he knew he was the target and in the crosshairs as they spoke about the lack of achievement of their children.

As the evening wore on, objectivity of the comments slowly converted into direct condescending remarks about the superintendent, even calling him by name. "I listened to the long oratory at our last meeting rendered by the superintendent trying to figure out what he was saying to all of us grieving parents, and it was at almost the close of this boring talk that I realized that he was claiming that we parents were the ones at fault," an emotional lady stated who indicated that she had attended school in the division and now had two children in attendance. "I have thought a lot about his statements since the meeting, and it was hard for me to get off my mind his huge salary you all on the board are paying him to see that our children receive a good education. Making six times more than my husband, I would think that he could earn his big salary by providing good schools so our children can learn like other young'uns in the surrounding area."

Following the comment of the lady about the salary of the superintendent, several followed to include what the beleaguered superintendent was paid in their remarks. This subject had been the defining moment for the hostile crowd as now the focus was solely on the school chief. "I have to wonder what our school leader does each day when the children's achievement is so dismal," one father pointed out. "If he were minding the store, nothing like this would have happened."

"I am told by the teachers that he requires so much paper work that they do not have time to do an effective job each day," another pointed out, revealing that the teachers were now pointing fingers and joining the parents against the superintendent. "I am told that every time the teachers turn around, there is another memo from the central office requiring some kind of report."

It had become obvious that everyone was trying to distance himself or herself from the superintendent, and even the principals had their own emissaries to speak positively on their behalf. One older man stated, "A principal of one of the elementary schools had really gotten frustrated because he felt that he no longer was in charge of his school with so much interference from the superintendent and his supervisors from the main office. The main job of the principals is to make it comfortable for their teachers so they are able to do a good job teaching. Usurping the power of the site based decision making body is a grievous error that minimizes the probability of the success of each of our schools. The school board years ago appropriately fashioned the school division such that the power base would be at the school level. For the superintendent to attempt to by-pass these decision making bodies to insert his own agenda makes the whole process contrary to the wishes of the school board itself."

Numerous speakers stepped forth to make their thoughts known to a very attentive school board who had been spared sharp criticism on this evening as the knockout blows were hurled clearly toward the superintendent. It seemed that the school board, parents, teachers and principals were delighted that they had discovered someone to blame, and as the evening wore on the obvious candidate was Glenn Colson. For whatever reason there appeared to be a sigh of relief by those in attendance, including the school board, that they had determined who was to blame for the achievement shortfall. Discovering this mystery was tantamount to correcting the problem, one would have thought just listening to buzz sessions after the formal meeting was adjourned that evening.

DERISION CONTINUES

Meanwhile, the Bacon College team was headed to Atlanta for their second leg of the Preliminary Season Tournament. The topic of choice for all media was the story of the alleged ACUWAA infractions by the Bacon team, including theories as to how it was done and all kinds of remedies to correct the problem and to see that it never happened again. The support for the team had really soured after the country had been inundated by vicious reports from all corners of the sports world. The two newspapers purchased by Coach Anna in Roanoke contained four stories, several letters to the editor and one editorial column. While sitting in the waiting area, the television station carried a lengthy story about the situation going so far as to indicate that there had been an informal interview with an ACUWAA official who corroborated the charges announced earlier.

"This is our first time to move through the Roanoke terminal without congratulatory comments or signing autographs," Coach Anna thought, as the team waited for its flight. Sitting with the girls, she realized that they were not even cognizant that they were being snubbed by everybody in the terminal. They just knew how to enjoy life within their own little circle just as they had done in the Hollow only a short time ago. Growing up with abuse and derision from the outside world really provided a shield and an armor plate for them as they participated as genuine ambassadors of little Bacon College.

Realizing that bitterness and hatred toward the Bacon team had increased since their last game when the terrible atmosphere surrounding the game was almost unbearable, Coach Anna was developing a worst case scenario in her mind so she could plan as best she could some defensive maneuvers. Although the girls seemed to be impervious to the ugliness of the game environment, Coach Anna didn't want to subject them to any more derision than possible. "They are a special group of girls with loving hearts," she thought, as she looked around while they were descending to the Atlanta airport.

They were totally disregarded as they walked swiftly through the terminal to the shuttle bus area. Waiting for an empty bus beyond earshot of others, soon they boarded a small van type bus with no other passengers to go to their quarters. Upon arrival they were faced with banners and signs held by students containing all kinds of derogatory comments. "I need some money," one stated, while another student waived one affixed to a stick saying, "Can you spell Hollow for me?" Four students were holding a large banner saying, "Can the Hollow team give me money for lunch today? I am so hungry." Several students dressed as cheerleaders yelled, "Give me a C; give me an H; give me an E; give me an A; give me a T; give me an E; give me an R; and give me an S. What does that spell? Cheaters, cheaters, cheaters."

Everything was happening so fast such that the team seemed to be thwarted totally by the large group bent on abusing them. Quickly, Coach Anna herded up her group and moved around the throng of students to a side door to check into their rooms. Many followed them inside where a security guard finally ordered the hecklers to leave. It was not a pleasant scene, but the desk attendant offered no apology to the team so Coach Anna thought that he too harbored similar sentiments toward the group.

Many more waited at the coliseum for the team to arrive for its practice time set for one o'clock, but Coach Anna decided that it would be best to forego the afternoon session. They just remained in their rooms to study, awaiting the game scheduled for seven o'clock.

During the afternoon, Coach Anna discovered a back door exit to the hotel so promptly at five-thirty, the team stealthily exited the rear door to board a taxi van that was waiting, having been called by Coach Anna earlier. As they approached the entrance of the coliseum and seeing hundreds of fans at the main gate, Coach Anna instructed the taxi driver to take them to a side door to avoid the mass of people awaiting their arrival.

Inside they dressed and immediately headed to the floor as a unit, not sending Hanna to precede them as they usually did. Just as they arrived at the large opening leading to the playing area, two policemen met them and advised that they would escort them on and off the floor and would remain with them all the while.

"Thank you so very much," Coach Anna said to them, breathing a sigh of relief.

Loud and ugly yells met them immediately such that the team somewhat was frightened momentarily as the unexpected jolt of derogation even made them show a sudden sensitivity to the rowdy reception. With one policeman in front and the second behind them, they moved directly to their seats to the left of the scorer's table. Hanna distributed the basketballs and the players started their warm-ups. Soon Coach Anna was about to learn that this was not going to be an ordinary pregame program. Without any warning, a student came dashing on the floor running among the girls while they were practicing waving a sign that read, "They wallow in the Hollow in squalor?" Then immediately, a female student hurried to the middle of the team and flashed her signboard, "Follow the money to the Hollow."

Two security guards escorted the two brazen students out of the building at variance with the vociferous crowd that became even louder and more rancorous upon seeing the two being led away. Now with no interference on their end of the court, Esther continued to carry the players through their usual drills before the game. Coach Anna could tell that Esther and the others had tuned out the crowd, and were ready to meet Taliton University that was warming up on the other end of the floor.

With the tumultuous conduct continuing as indicated by the ugly yells from the spectators, the announcer cautioned the fans about their behavior, but his comments seemed to fall on deaf ears. Coach Anna didn't take the team back to the locker room for its pregame meeting but chose to remain on the floor. As the game time approached, she had the group to form a circle and she told them, "We have such a loving God who sent His Son here on earth to us years ago, and He left behind before returning to heaven a set of guidelines for all of us to follow. Thank you all for being followers of Jesus Christ, and always remember that regardless of what happens, we are not to be judgmental. Forgive those who transgress against you. I know you will. Esther, would you pray for the group?"

Following a beautiful prayer, the starting five moved to the center of the floor to meet their opposition. The team was shunned by the Taliton players to the supreme delight of those present. The harassment would continue.

Just as the ball was tossed in the air to begin the

game, five pairs of old worn out basketball shoes were tossed on the floor. Stopping the game to remove the shoes, the chief referee was really angry such that he quickly ran over to the announcer to advise that such behavior would not be tolerated. The announcer stated, "Please do not throw debris on the floor because it could endanger the players."

Coach Anna had heard the old saying for years, "When the going gets tough, the tough get going." This thought continued to ring in her ears as Esther made basket after basket and assist after assist in a way that Coach Anna had never witnessed before.

"Esther is really not holding back anything tonight," Hanna said to Coach Anna.

"I have never seen her this way before," Coach Anna responded. "She doesn't seem to be mad because her facial countenance appears to have a glow of serenity. I believe she is enjoying every minute of this game as she moves about on the floor always playing hard, but taking time to pick up an opponent who has fallen or even to encourage an opponent."

Frustration set in on the other team as the fouls were more flagrant with pushing, shoving and undercuts becoming commonplace. Coach Anna had to remove two of her girls because of injuries incurred by the rough play of the Taliton team. It wasn't until Jonsie was undercut viciously going in for a lay up that there seemed to be a surge of civility in the crowd. Lying on the floor bleeding from the head and mouth, all present knew they had contributed to this injury that could even be life threatening. Silence filled the building.

Coach Anna and Hanna ran quickly on the floor passing the referees who knew they too were participants in this tragic situation, having loosely called fouls and generally permitted the rough play. Leaning over Jonsie, Coach Anna could not get her to respond.

"Is there a doctor in the building?" the announcer asked.

A young man seated about midway in the coliseum rose from his seat and quickly walked to the gate leading to the floor. Through the gate, he ran across the floor to where Jonsie was lying motionless. Just as he began to check her vital signs, Jonsie moved her legs just a little, and then she tried to sit up but was restrained by the young physician. "She took a hard spill," he said to Coach Anna. "I believe it would be best for her to go to the hospital for a thorough examination."

"Could you help me in this matter?" Coach Anna asked, realizing that she couldn't be in two places at the same time.

"I would be happy to see that she gets the best of care at the hospital," he responded. "You all have really taken a beating from everyone here tonight. Please forgive us all for prejudging you and your team."

"We are so grateful to God to be able to play in this tournament," Coach Anna responded. "We thank you for being present to help us now."

"I'll go with Jonsie to the hospital so you can stay with the team," Hanna maturely stated. "You will be needed here for the remainder of the game and to assist the group as they depart."

"That's a good idea for you to go with Jonsie," Coach Anna replied.

"I don't think you and your team will receive any more abuse from anybody here," the doctor said. "I believe all here are so ashamed that they will not say or do anything else tonight to harass you all. You and your team have suffered enough from the derogatory comments and crude acts by the fans tonight."

The spectators applauded as Jonsie was placed on a stretcher to be carried to a rescue ambulance. Joining the fans were the Taliton team members who lined up near the gate to render their apology to her.

With Esther sitting near Coach Anna and the game clock winding down to two minutes, she put Esther back into the game as she had always done. Scoring fifty-three points on this evening, she revealed a determination that certainly Coach Anna had never observed before.

Although the bellicosity of those attending the game had disappeared, it was not replaced by congeniality and affability. It was a different atmosphere, but all the same the two policemen escorted them to an awaiting large yellow taxi van to go to the hospital. On the way Coach Anna's cell phone rang and it was Hanna. "How is Jonsie?" Coach Anna asked, while the others listened intently.

"She is fine now," Hanna replied. "She has five stitches in her head and two under her chin, but otherwise she is okay."

"We'll be there in a few minutes to get you both," Coach Anna told her. "Is the doctor there who helped us in the coliseum?"

"Yes, he is," she said. "Do you want to speak to him?"

"I would like to do that," Coach Anna replied.

"Jonsie is as good as new now except for a couple of places I had to close up on her head and chin," he indicated. "She will be able to play tomorrow night."

"Thank you so very much for helping us," Coach Anna stated.

"Before I hang up, let me apologize for the conduct of the fans for tonight's game," he said. "I believe that they just got carried away, and when you come to play tomorrow night, they will be much more civil as they watch the game."

The next morning following breakfast in a small restaurant around the corner from the hotel, Coach Anna took the team to a practice session in the coliseum to an entirely different atmosphere from that of the previous day. Even the reporters seemed to be more gentle in asking their questions.

In the game that evening before a much more serene capacity crowd, Esther was more of a facilitator in the contest, a whole different approach from the game the night before. The results, however, were the same as Bacon won the game beating Grand View University eighty-seven to fifty-three, with Esther sitting out much of the second half.

Arriving back at Bacon College early in the afternoon of the next day, Coach Anna was immediately requested to come to President Damond's office.

"Coach Anna, please have a seat," he immediately stated, as he again walked to the front of his executive desk to sit alongside her. "You all really were pummeled with much verbal abuse in Atlanta, weren't you?"

"It really was a different kind of setting," she said, "but by the end of the game the adversity turned to learning for everybody. The players handled themselves so admirably during both games."

"Jonsie is okay, isn't she?" he asked.

"She is fine," Coach Anna replied.

"I want to bring you up to date on the ACUWAA charges," he immediately stated. "I have not heard a word from them regarding the matter while all the media are writing speculative reports using all types of outlandish theories. All the while the Board of Directors remain steadfast in their position of not responding to the ridiculous allegations whatsoever."

"It was really interesting at our first game in Atlanta to see the whole environment change around us as the girls refused to fight back but remained focused on their mission of playing basketball," Coach Anna pointed out. "By game's end the entire demeanor of the group had changed very positively."

"We sensed that here as we watched the game on television," he stated. "Is it your thinking that our silence is beginning to pay dividends?"

"I believe so," she immediately responded with just a little victorious tinge in her voice.

"I want you to read something and tell me what you think about it," he noted in a different tone, as though they were now changing gears. "It's the article written by Jewel Throneberry, the only reporter we have permitted to have access to any campus information. I want you to take it with you to read and then return it to me this evening with your comments."

"I would be happy to do that," she replied.

Late that afternoon with all the girls in their room studying, Coach Anna opened the large envelope to remove the article written by Jewel Throneberry.

The Web of Jealousy
By Jewel Throneberry

Several weeks ago I got caught up in the same kind of mindset as many of you who have really focused on the Bacon College women's basketball team during the last several days. I just couldn't believe first of all that any team could win so consistently and at the same time so overwhelmingly with such ease. In the history of the women's basketball program, no team had ever been so dominant over its opponents. When examining the

team that was so very powerful, one would soon
begin to conjure up reasons why it was so very much
more superior to other teams including the perennial
powerhouses. "One team cannot dominate like this,"
most of you thought. Yet, Bacon College was doing
just that last year and ready to continue this year.

Rumors were beginning to surface last year
but had not reached beyond the walls of the
coliseums where the Bacon team played.

Many of you watched in total amazement as
the Hollow girls, as they are called, marched into
your home turf, proceeded to trounce your favorite
team and move on to the next site. "But there must
be a reason for their winning so handily," you all
thought all the while.

They are such a popular group of young
people not only for their basketball prowess but for
their handling of the terrorist plot and their rescue of
the three missionaries. Many of you started and
contributed to the rumor of the girls not really having
assisted in foiling the hijackers, but just happened to
be at the right place to receive unmerited praise. You
all wanted to believe this because many would accept
any kind of derogatory expressions to fill your minds
that yearn for anything that would bring the team
down. "Cut them down to size," can be heard by
those bent on letting jealousy rule their beings.

Several years ago a professional baseball
team called the New York Yankees won several
World Series over a short period of time. During this
time many people became ardent fans of the Yankees
while others supported other teams that longed to
become a World Series winner. Many baseball fans
decided that they were just against the Yankees

because they won all the time, and when they talked about the issue, one could sense more than just a tinge of jealousy. A winner in any sport begins to operate under a magnifying glass with all of its components being examined closely by the followers.

We used to play a game in primary school called "gossip." The teacher would whisper something in the ear of the pupil sitting on the front row, and that pupil turned and whispered the statement to the next child in the row until all had been told the statement. It was fun, but I never could understand how something told to a student on one side of the room could be so distorted as it made its way from one student to the other. If you are a women's basketball fan, I am sure you have heard comments that would be considered gossip that you have passed on to another. Being highly touted as Bacon College, the gossip alongside the rumor mill have kept many fans busy during the off season. It is a deliberate attempt to bring this most superior basketball team down to be at a level with others instead of discovering ways a team can improve to the existing level of the Bacon College team of young ladies.

Jealousy is such an interesting concept. How long did anyone expect before fans and officials began to nibble away at the heart of these pure and precious young people who learned to play basketball in the remote area of a mountainous mining community made up of twenty-four families? You see, the more affluent neighbors didn't want anything to do with the parents or their children so this group of children found themselves isolated from other parts of the whole area. For entertainment they played among themselves, starting to play basketball using an old bicycle rim nailed to the side of a building as their goal and an old deflated ball. They didn't have the luxury of a gymnasium.

A young pastor, his wife and daughter moved into the Hollow many years ago to fulfill a call from God to minister to this community of descendents of the miners after the mining industry collapsed. Their daughter became an integral part of the group, now playing on the basketball team at world class level. She was not a native of the Hollow; yet, she has become one of the top basketball players in the country. She, along with the others, reached this level through continuous practice and plenary dedication.

According to a New York newspaper, Bacon College has allegedly failed to comply with several rules as set forth in the manual of the American College and University Women's Athletic Association. The letter received by Bacon College contains the following:

Pursuant to Section V, Paragraph 2, some of these serious allegations deal with money much above the limit being given to the women on your basketball team. Specifically, it is alleged that your team members have received funds from an unknown third party.

Pursuant to Section II, Paragraph 1, it is reported that your students failed to meet the minimum SAT score for admittance to participate in collegiate athletics. Those students who failed to obtain a score of 900 or more are not eligible to participate in any form of intercollegiate athletics.

Pursuant to Section VI, Paragraph 2, students are required to be enrolled in a minimum of courses leading to a degree. It is alleged that some of your student athletes fail to meet this standard.

During the last three weeks I have been on the Bacon College campus to investigate these allegations so I want all of you to know what I discovered. Before I include my findings in this report, let me say to you what I said when I first read the article in the New York newspaper: "This is the most ludicrous set of allegations that I have ever heard, and in the end, the ACUWAA will be changing its entire procedure in the way it receives blind allegations without furnishing any proof whatsoever regarding the source."

Examining the allegation about money being received by the girls on the basketball team, this is what I discovered. The girls have no money and have not received any money from any source. They do not carry any money whatsoever with them. None of the team members have bank accounts, either savings or checking. An Esther Fund is administered by a committee of Hollow parents and is not available for any personal or private use. The manager of the campus sundry shop told me that during their entire time at Bacon, not one of the eleven girls had made a single purchase. One young lady associated with the team gets a modest monthly allowance.

Upon entry into Bacon College the range of SAT scores for the girls was from 1150 for both verbal and nonverbal to 1579. The average score for all students entering all colleges was 1011. As one can readily see these young ladies came into college academically superior to their counterparts from much more affluent areas.

Because of their academic excellence, they were permitted to enroll from the onset into more challenging courses in an advanced program of study. Taking courses in the curricula of engineering, biology, foreign language, English, computer science, architecture, mathematics, and other difficult programs makes one want to tip his or her hat to them as they excel in their daily courses. None of them has a course average of less than a 3.2. For classes, as one would imagine, they have perfect attendance and are always punctual. All of their professors make numerous laudatory comments regarding the behavior of the members of this unusual basketball team.

As many of you read about these young ladies and the serious allegations of the ACUWAA, I challenge each of you to compare the SAT scores and grades of your institution with those of the girls on the basketball team from a remote section of Virginia.

"Could it be that jealousy of this extremely small college winning all of its games from much larger institutions has precipitated these false allegations to harm the integrity of these precious young people? Obviously, they don't seem to be from the same mold as many of our athletes today. Being devout Christians, they follow the scripture to establish the ground rules for life. Having grown up in a very conservative atmosphere with very limited wherewithal, their needs are much less than those who have been reared in a more affluent society. Their assets are in the heart that they open each day to assist others who are facing trials along the way.

I know many of you will find it hard to believe, but I had an opportunity to examine the clothing closets of each team member. Each girl had three skirts and three blouses that they told me came from the Good Deed store near the Hollow. For shoes they had an old pair of worn out tennis shoes and a "Sunday" used pair, some of which were patent leather. Seeing these meager clothing items, tears ran down my cheeks for two reasons: first, that the girls had so little and secondly, that they would be accused of breaking any of the ACUWAA rules.

Thinking about these concocted allegations of ACUWAA rules infractions for several days now, it is my thinking that these young ladies are so much different from the average young people of today that many have a very difficult time understanding the situation. Beyond reproach to such a very high degree and playing basketball with skill never witnessed by basketball fans before, they become suspect because they are so different. Having established a new standard or morality and integrity, the secular society looks on with amazement, always searching feverishly for chinks in their armor. Finding none but still desperately wanting to take them down a notch or two after having failed on the basketball court, false accusations find their way to the ACUWAA office.

Could it be that this confidential letter was made pubic deliberately because even the ACUWAA has been caught up in a move to bring down the "'nobodies" at the very small Bacon College headed by their coach who had never coached a college game before coming to the small school in the mountains of Virginia? In spite of all that has transpired honesty and integrity will prevail. My mother used to tell me, "Do you see that regardless of how you drop a cat, it will always lands on its feet?" The Hollow girls too will land on their feet, and because of these harmful allegations will be stronger young ladies. Tracing back in their history, one finds them often times being falsely accused. Living beyond these untrue claims, they have developed an armor plate to ward off the sting of jealousy and deceit, thereby becoming impervious to a hostile environment.

What did Jesus really mean when he said, "The last will be first and the first will be last?" Does this statement apply to the Hollow girls?

I leave you with these thoughts that all of you can ponder for yourselves. These young ladies are so pure that our present society has a hard time dealing with the situation. Fold in the unusually superb skill in playing basketball, and the result is jealousy. You see, in spite of winning all games the young ladies from the Hollow continue "to keep the main thing, the main thing." They are truly Christians following the specific guidelines found in the Scripture that they read each day. If these characteristics are detrimental to the ACUWAA, we all should examine this powerful organization to determine its fitness to direct our young people in collegiate athletics.

Reading the article several times, Coach Anna left her room to ask some advice from Maudie who was moving about in the dormitory commons area. "Do you have a minute for me to talk to you?" Coach Anna asked.

"Why, certainly," Maudie replied, now moving to sit near her on the couch.

"Do you remember Jewel Throneberry?" Coach Anna inquired.

"Surely I do," Maudie quickly replied. "She is the Margone Magazine executive who wrote the scathing article about the team earlier, and spends much of her time now trying to make amends for her transgression."

"The only reporter that Dr. Damond has permitted on campus in several weeks is Miss Throneberry who has fashioned an article that, if given approval, she wants to disseminate to all media as well as Margone Magazine," Coach Anna indicated. "I have that article that I have read three times, and I want you to read it also to help me respond to Dr. Damond about it."

Seated in the chair near the corner under the lamp, Maudie began to read Jewel's proposed article. When she had completed the task, she walked over to sit by Coach Anna.

"What do you think of the article?" Coach Anna asked.

"Obviously, it's to the point," Maudie quickly responded, as though she was set with the answer before the question was asked.

"There is no doubt about that," Coach Anna retorted.

"Someone has to tell the world the true story, and she has done that in her article," Maudie said. "In some respects she has approached it differently from the way I would have done it, but she is a professional working in a very competitive market. That has caused her to sharpen her thoughts that have been put in print."

"I thought the same thing," Coach Anna noted. "She wants to get a message out to the people who have accepted the New York newspaper article as being the truth. The journalism she practices calls for getting the readers' attention, and I believe she has done that in this article."

"What does Dr. Damond think of Jewel's article?" Maudie asked.

"I think he has mixed feelings about it," she responded, "but he knows that someone is going to have to respond to these allegations soon before the ACUWAA comes to investigate. I think he sees the purity in Miss Throneberry's actions since she wrote the article earlier, and wants to give her this opportunity to redeem herself. I don't believe the letter is written the way he would have prepared it, but I think he is going to give his approval unless we voice a complaint."

"I think he is doing the right thing," Maudie said, putting on her stamp of approval.

Following some additional discussion between the two friends, Coach Anna headed to Dr. Damond's office to return Jewel Throneberry's article. In the brief meeting he informed Coach Anna that he was going to advise Miss Throneberry to release the article, using whatever dissemination she deemed appropriate.

It was late afternoon on Friday about the time the Bacon girls were going on the floor in New York for the semifinal game with Satterfield University that Jewel Throneberry elected to release her story defending the college, following the ACUWAA report. This was the first information from the college so to say that it was not voraciously gobbled up by all media would be an understatement of vast proportions. Jewel knew how to get news out to the media, and for this article no holds were barred. All of the national distributors of news gave priority to her story so it was passing through the electronic connections to every point along the route, including the huge basketball arena in our largest city. During the team's warm-up period, a zealous reporter cornered Coach Anna to request a statement from her regarding Jewel Throneberry's story. Of course, she continued to refer all questions to Dr. Damond.

"Jewel Throneberry has certainly pricked the consciousness of the sports world," Coach Anna thought, as she watched the girls on the floor going through their warm-up drills.

"The behavior of the spectators is much different tonight," Hanna said to Coach Anna.

"It's interesting how people's thinking is swayed by something in print," Coach Anna responded. "They believed the ACUWAA article in a local newspaper, and now as they realize that there is a second article refuting the first, they believe this one. At least they have taken the posture of reexamining the charges."

It was obvious that those in attendance were giving Bacon College a free pass from derogation, so at this time the spectators would just acquiesce, support Satterfield, but not cast disparaging comments about the small college from the mountains of southwest Virginia.

Esther had become a distributor for this game, passing time after time to the other players. Even in this role the results were the same as the margin grew between the two scores. Watching from the bench, Coach Anna leaned over to Hanna and said, "The players had better be ready to receive the ball tonight because Esther is really dishing it out to all of them."

"She always enjoys playing this role as point guard where the opponents converge to stop her, and with more than one defending her, she just passes off to the open girl," Hanna replied. "I believe she has more than a dozen assists at this time."

Although Satterfield was not overly friendly, still harboring a bad attitude toward Bacon because of the many ugly articles written about them, they did remain complaisant during the game. It was believed that the worst was over for the team regarding the ACUWAA report, but the issue had not been resolved because the ACUWAA had not made its own investigation.

By the next night the atmosphere at the game was more tranquil. The coach of Dorand University even came over to speak to Coach Anna before the game. The powerful local newspapers carried several stories about the ACUWAA situation with the main thrust of their articles centering around the rush of trial lawyers wanting to assist Bacon College in a lawsuit against the ACUWAA. Several of the lawyers even commented on the amount that should be requested in such a suit. "The character and reputation of this innocent college has been demeaned to such an extent that it will never be pure again in the minds of everybody," a lawyer stated, but asked for anonymity. "The recovery for the college could be in millions."

Playing before a capacity crowd as usual, Coach Anna decided that she would insert the selected student to start the game. All the while the Bacon students had been so very supportive of the team so this would be a small way to thank them. So up jumped Bonnie when her name was called by Coach Anna. Very much surprised, she walked with the other four to the center.

A different night altogether from the previous one, Esther was in charge swishing basket after basket. Trying in vain to stop her, Dorand fell victim just as all the other teams before them during the long history of participating in basketball. Esther and Dorothy made the Preliminary Season Tournament all-tournament team, and Esther was unanimous choice as most valuable player.

Flying back to Roanoke after the game, the team arrived at the college at an early hour of Sunday morning. Following breakfast, the group went to the campus chapel where their biology professor, Dr. Aubrey Noland, led the service. The spiritual atmosphere filled the campus, as usual, especially on the Sabbath when the group worshiped together.

At lunch Dr. Damond sat with Coach Anna to hear about their trip to the "Big Apple," as he jokingly called New York. "The team did so very well, as usual," he said. "We all here chuckled about the way Esther passed the ball to everybody on Friday night."

"She really enjoyed doing that," Coach Anna said, while laughing just a little.

"The students here last night really appreciated your starting Bonnie in this terribly important game," he said with a special gleam in his eye.

"She did a good job in the game," Coach Anna replied.

"Now let me tell you the latest," he stated. "Jewel Throneberry's article has really created a story. It seems that the attitude of the whole world has just flipped flopped since her article was released last Friday. It was truly the best psychological moment. She had to know this was the best time."

"The atmosphere at our games was so much different in New York," Coach Anna indicated.

"All day Saturday I received numerous telephone calls from lawyers who wanted to represent us in a lawsuit against the ACUWAA," Dr. Damond said. "They too believed Jewel Throneberry's article. Late yesterday, the director of the ACUWAA indicated that they would be on campus tomorrow to make their investigation. Please advise the girls that they will have company probably all day, and tell them to answer all questions that are asked."

"Thank you for sharing this with me," Coach Anna said. "We'll be good hosts for the ACUWAA team of investigators."

Early the next morning a whole cadre of eight persons from the ACUWAA joined the students and faculty on this cold morning on the small campus. One could detect the arrogance of the group as they fulfilled their obligation of conducting an entrance interview with the president. "We

don't have a large staff of personnel, but all of us here today
are at your disposal to assist you all in your investigation,"
Dr. Damond stated in such a gracious and kind tone. In fact,
his affable demeanor caught the team off guard, because they
suspected that all of those on campus would be showing their
anger toward the ACUWAA.

With the preliminary greetings completed, Dr.
Damond summoned Coach Anna to his office to meet the
group. As soon as she walked in, she could detect that the
ACUWAA team was under much pressure to discover
wrongdoing so they could save face. The world was
anxiously waiting. Jewel Throneberry's article had jarred
the consciousness of everyone, especially the ACUWAA
whose burden it was to find the "smoking gun."

"I am glad to meet you all," Coach Anna stated. "I
will be available to assist you in any way you see fit, being
stationed in the athletic dormitory except lunch, and two to
four this afternoon and six to eight this evening when the
team will hold its practice sessions. The girls will be
available to talk with you after their classes and their
basketball practice. If you all wish, we could visit their
parents in the Hollow either this afternoon or tomorrow."

The director split the ACUWAA team into four
subgroups with one interviewing the president and coach,
another checking the academic records of the players from
high school, a third examined the course load of each player
and a fourth checked the financial wherewithal of the team
as well as the coach. It was a busy time for the whole group
and as the day wore on, the various investigators could be
seen hovering together as though in a mesmerized state of
mind. By lunch time they had completed their investigation
which revealed that the little college was pure as wind blown
snow.

"I have never been on an investigation that nothing
awry was discovered," the director stated. "We have made a

mistake of monumental proportions, and I am sure that a huge lawsuit will be forthcoming. This afternoon I want all of you to continue your investigation closely scrutinizing all areas of the college's athletic program. There is much at stake here so we must discover some wrongdoing, or else we face a devastating lawsuit that we certainly can't win."

Late in the evening the ACUWAA team left the campus quietly without any kind of exit interview to meet together at the motel to develop further strategies. "Did any of you discover anything that would be helpful to us?" the director asked.

There was total silence until one member stated, "I thought I had run across something when I discovered the large sum of money in a bank account bearing the name "The Esther Fund," but soon I realized that it was sealed and not available to her individually. It really belonged to their parents for other than personal use."

"Did any of the rest of you find anything?" she asked.

Following a long period of silence, she stated, "Did any of you hear anything from them that might indicate that they were going to sue the ACUWAA?"

"I never heard a word," a young lady answered. "I led the interviews of the president and the coach, and they neither gave a clue whatsoever that a lawsuit was forthcoming nor did they say anything that appeared to be uncomplimentary to me or about the ACUWAA. I know that they have taken much abuse during the past few weeks; yet they don't show any signs of anger toward the Association."

"I have never seen anything to beat it," a middle age man stated. "During my many years working for the ACUWAA, I have been on many teams to investigate allegations of wrongdoing, but I have never experienced anything like this one. It's almost like we have been invited to be here as their guests, and they are trying to do everything possible to be sure that we are comfortable.

Refreshments were available all day yesterday, and I know they will be today, also. Their behavior defies logical reasoning."

"Unless we discover something tomorrow, the ACUWAA is in for a huge lawsuit," the director stated in a tone to try to challenge her cadre of investigators. "Our office has learned much from this ordeal that will be long remembered. I thought we were going to be in big trouble when someone in our office leaked the letter to Bacon College to the press in New York, but even then I believed we could rectify the whole thing. It wasn't until the leadership of this small college decided its course of not responding to inquiries that I knew we were in serious trouble."

"The president here is truly an intelligent southern gentleman, and not a 'country bumpkin' as many would think," an older lady pointed out. "Many mistake his slow speech as revealing ignorance, but to the contrary, he is very bright and most eloquent and articulate when he speaks."

"They have had so much media attention during the last months that I'm sure the whole group is ready to have some privacy," the director stated. "I hope that we can find some wrongdoing today on the one hand, but they do seem so pure that I would be somewhat heartbroken to discover anything awry. To this point they seem to have the most correct program that I have ever seen."

An exhausted team gave up their search for misdeeds by noon the next day, and as they made their way to the president's office to report their findings, the president's secretary met the team to invite them to a special luncheon on their behalf attended by the Board of Directors, Coach Anna and Dr. Damond.

Following a wonderful prayer by the college chief and a delicious meal, the director stood to make her report to the college officials. "Our office has made a grave mistake in sending you all a letter citing alleged wrongdoings in the first place," she related. "We have learned much from this experience that rumors and gossip about wrongdoing do not always indicate that a college is doing anything wrong. In your case here, we had received so many inquiries from people, we thought that surely you were breaking specific rules of the ACUWAA. With our staff being convinced, we mailed you all the letter noting certain allegations of wrongdoing. From our investigative visit during the last two days, we have discovered that these allegations are absolutely unfounded, and that your program is error free. In fact, according to our thorough investigation, your program here is the best with which we have ever checked.

"With that said and later presented in an official report to the media, let me address the copy of our letter to you that was sent the newspaper in New York. Obviously, that was an error of great proportions such that we hope that it will never happen again. You all have been punished greatly not for doing wrong, but for having an exceptionally good basketball team that has won all of its games. Jealously is a strong emotion.

"Because of this huge debacle, the ACUWAA will be stronger. All we can do now is to apologize to you all and ask for your total forgiveness for putting you all through this whole, ugly ordeal."

Following the brief exit report of the director of the ACUWAA, Dr. Damond reminded the team what Jesus had taught all of us in Matthew 5.

8 Blessed are the pure in heart, for they will see God.
9 Blessed are the peacemakers, for they will be called sons of God.
10 Blessed are those who are persecuted because of righteousness, for theirs is the kingdom of heaven.
11 "Blessed are you when people insult you, persecute you and falsely say all kinds of evil against you because of me.

*12 Rejoice and be glad, because great is your reward in
heaven, for in the same way they persecuted the prophets
who were before you.*
*13 "You are the salt of the earth. But if the salt loses its
saltiness, how can it be made salty again? It is no longer
good for anything, except to be thrown out and trampled by
men.*
*14 "You are the light of the world. A city on a hill cannot be
hidden.*
*15 Neither do people light a lamp and put it under a bowl.
Instead they put it on its stand, and it gives light to everyone
in the house.*
*16 In the same way, let your light shine before men, that they
may see your good deeds and praise your Father in heaven.*

"All of us make mistakes on the one hand, and all of
us on the other should practice the precepts found in the
scriptures to balance the scales when dilemmas, conflicts and
confrontations arise. Even the most complex situation can
be solved with a handshake or over a nice meal. I sincerely
hope that we all have done that today."

"What a delightful attitude!" the director stated, as
she emotionally shook the hand of each person around the
table. A happy ACUWAA team left the campus on this day
with a feeling of triumph only because of this wonderful
group of people who applied the teachings of Jesus Christ to
their everyday living. "We have learned much from these
people many call country louts. It has truly been an eye
opener for me to see humility and integrity at work in the
lives of people as they deal with circumstances of life. I
believe we have discovered a standard of behavior for other
institutions of higher learning "

The complete presentation of the ACUWAA findings
left the negative media desiring something reflecting
wrongdoing, but on this day the Association had done all it
could to deliver a report telling the world that Bacon College

was pure as wind blown snow. It was obvious that the ACUWAA was apologizing for its grievous error in the first place. To augment its contrition, the ACUWAA took out full-page ads to exonerate Bacon College of any wrongdoing in the major newspapers in each state. Closure was brought to the whole misunderstanding.

Paul H. Jones

INVASION

For years the people from the place called Bacon worked hard not to be called a town so it could hold onto its status of being rural, having a heritage that they cherished so dearly. Its relationship was excellent with the small Christian college that had become the centerpiece of not only the community itself, but in all southwest Virginia where everyone supported the basketball team made up of girls from the Hollow. With this unusual relationship reciprocal love flowed from the college to the community and vice versa.

Quiet and tranquil could be terms that described the setting now that the ACUWAA allegations of rules infractions had been resolved, and the superintendent had stepped down as the chief of the local school division. The whole community was basking in the serenity of its closed status such that it somehow had shut out the other part of the world as they just related to one another inside their comfortable little circle of local folks.

Any time there was talk of even a hint of some form of intrusion into their domain, the whole group fought solidly to stop any and all efforts. Several years ago they lost one long and extended battle with the Department of

Transportation when they vehemently opposed an interstate
highway a few miles to the east of the center of their little
community. Although losing out in the end to this well
traveled four-lane roadway running through the beautiful
mountains, the whole process created a more cohesive group
of folks and increased their pride of being mountain people.
In the end their defeat in many respects was a victory in that
the inhabitants of the area grew so much closer together.

Not too far up the interstate was one of many
underpasses where on this night Jim Baldwin was ascending
up the side to find a place to sleep for another night. It was a
strange kind of night that produced a serenity that Jim had
not sensed before even though he had been in the night air
most of the last five years following a collapse of everything
that was good in his life. It was only his fault he knew as
alcohol had caused him to plunge to the depths of despair,
and on his way down his wife of twenty-one years and his
two lovely children had given up and separated themselves
from his terrible behavior. Having really not gotten used the
horrible loneliness, he continued to drown out the
unpleasantness of his situation with the same thing that
caused his demise in the first place. It was no secret that he
was an alcoholic because each day he seemed to require
more and more to fill the void of emptiness so the main
thrust of his activity each day was centered around getting
enough money to purchase more wine and whiskey. It had
become a genuine armor plate to insulate him from his own
emotion of being alone, without friends and without
direction.

Curling up under the bridge over the interstate
highway with his bottle nestled close to his side, he settled
down for another night of sleep and rest. A breeze caused
the night air to cut through his well-worn clothes as he lay
there on the concrete in the mountains many miles from his
home. Lying in the shadows and shielded from the

numerous cars and trucks that traveled unceasingly during the night, he felt better about his situation for this night than he had in some time. Before too long he was asleep as the night noises seemed to make a very restful environment.

Waking to a cool morning breeze, Jim began to plan his day of sitting at a light post holding his "homeless" sign to beg for money to support his alcoholism. Having spent all of his previous day's money for his nightly bottle, there was nothing left for breakfast so he had his work cut out for him. In a dream of the previous night he found himself going to a small community making his way to his favorite corner near a light post and sitting there to solicit those people for money. Walking several miles, his hunger needs were taken care of when a family stopped and gave him part of a picnic lunch they had prepared. In fact during the day, two other cars stopped to give him food and wished him well, and in fact one of the drivers gave him a lift to the outskirts of the community of Bacon. As he walked toward the main part of the sparsely populated community, his thoughts wandered to the previous evening when he had the very vivid dream, which seemed to be guiding his efforts on this day. Now that he was here, what was he supposed to do?

Having put church in the background for several years, Jim was still in a state of wonderment as he continued to act out his dream so indelibly in his mind. "Why should I be doing anything caused by a dream?" he thought, as he moved on being led by the revelations discovered during the nightmare. His mind filled with mixed thoughts, Jim noticed that there were several churches in this little community that had a population of 1694 according to a sign that also included that the people in the area welcomed newcomers.

He felt safe as he made his way along the neat streets with well groomed and comfortable houses lining both sides competing for space with the aged trees that provided shade and beauty to this quaint community. His knapsack bounced on his back as he trudged along with all of his belongings to

share life with this special group of people who were
apparently a churchgoing lot, as a couple more attractive
churches with tall and conspicuous spires were noticed along
the way.

The trek was ended when Jim came to the corner of
Main and Church Streets, and after he surveyed the area he
got a piece of cardboard from the side of an old box, and
found a piece of coal that he used to scribble "Homeless.
Will work for food." Quite obviously, by far the most
unattractive thing in the town was Jim as he sat there near
the new light pole that was installed only a few weeks ago.
He could tell that the "radar" was operational even as he
walked into town, and now that he was situated, he could
almost see the "rivets" from the numerous eyes coming from
the various retail stores that were constructed on the corner
to vie for the valuable customers. His being in this little
town was causing some concern as he noticed a couple of the
merchants pointing his way as they talked to one another.
Overall though, he felt very comfortable and safe in this
Christian community with more churches than he had ever
seen in such a small area.

It was Friday afternoon shortly after 4:00 p.m., and it
seemed that the entire population converged on the
marketplaces found in this little two-block area. The local
citizens looked at him with obvious disdain with the
exception of only a few who gave him $4.82 for the entire
evening. After all of the stores were closed and the people
returned to their comfortable homes, Jim had to make a
decision about the place of sleep for this cold evening.
Walking north he saw First Baptist Church with the tallest
steeple in the area, and he noticed that under the thick shrubs
along the front of the building there was a heavy layer of
mulch where he decided to bed down for the night. It had
been a long day in a place that he was led by the previous
night's dream. Feeling comfortable and secure in this special

neighborhood, he crawled under a thicket of shrubs to retire for the night.

Jim was awakened early the next day by one of the church leaders who asked him several questions, and then reminded Jim that Bacon did not allow vagrants and freeloaders in its community. "What are you doing here?" the church deacon said in a disgusted tone clearly detected by Jim.

"It got cold last night so instead of sleeping in the open air I got protection from the weather under your beautiful and full shrubs," Jim responded, as he sat up wiping his eyes so he could focus better.

"Didn't you see the 'No Trespassing' signs we have placed here to keep vagrants from coming around our church?" he immediately asked.

"It was after dark when I came here so I didn't see them," Jim replied.

"We don't tolerate freeloaders in our quiet community," the deacon continued. "I just knew that the new interstate road would bring up the trash of the secular world before too long, and with your presence, I realize that what I suspected all along is taking place now."

"I really didn't mean to upset you all at the church," Jim stated apologetically.

"But you did," he quickly responded. "Today you are the one and tomorrow those like you will come wanting to receive our wonderful hospitality. Tell them that we are aware of their game, wanting to live off others and just be a scourge on any community. Why don't you just get up and move on out of our community, and bygones will be bygones, or I will call the local sheriff?"

"I'm going to move on now," Jim stated, thinking that he was bringing an acceptable end to their conversation.

But the deacon had the last word. "Let me give you some advice. Why don't you move on to the large cities wherein you can blend in with the surrounding environment and not be noticed as much as you are in this small community?"

When the church leader entered the building, he warned the minister about the sorry person who had slept near the front of the church, and that he had told him to move on and not bother this special little tranquil community. The pastor assured the deacon that he would be on the lookout for this vagrant so that he would not be visible where all could see when they came to church on Sunday. They both agreed that they could not understand why anyone could not have a productive job with the jobless rate at its lowest in years.

Jim knew that he was being guided by that unusual dream to fulfill a mission that he believed was for God in this quaint village so he proceeded again to the corner of Main and Church Streets contrary to the suggestion of the church leader. As soon as he sat down with the sign he made the previous day, one of the merchants hurried to his position and said, "Why don't you just move on and not bring inner city problems to this well meaning Christian community?"

Jim did not respond to the request of the merchant as he remained at the spot and continued to solicit aid from the citizens in the area. Just about two blocks away was a McHarburger so he headed in that direction to get something to eat because his last meal was nearly twenty-four hours earlier. Entering the modern fast food restaurant, he got in line with others who quickly moved to another line for service, and shortly the manager was beckoned in a quiet voice by one of the clerks.

Whispering, she said, "A freeloader is in line to get something, and he's really upsetting the other people standing in line."

Quickly, the manager came out and asked Jim, "Would you mind coming with me?"

"Sure," Jim said, standing there in his shabby dress, reeking with alcohol and emitting offensive body odors.

"You have really offended many of my customers this morning so I would be much obliged if you would leave quietly," the manager stated, while holding Jim by the arm to direct him to the door.

The smell of the food cooking and seeing what the others were eating in the restaurant caused his gastric juices to flow mightily, but now he was walking away from the only local fast food eatery still with an empty stomach. Turning back, he noticed that everyone was looking at him with some pointing fingers, others laughing, and a few frowning in disgust.

A child on a bicycle shared the sidewalk with Jim as he walked back to his corner.

"My name is Bobby Damond," the outgoing young man stated immediately.

Trudging along coughing all the while, Jim responded without looking at the young lad. "My name is Jim."

"Are you hungry?" Bobby asked, which caused Jim to turn alertly toward him, not believing what he had said.

"Yes," Jim faintly responded, as he sat down near the light post.

"I'll be back just in a minute," Bobby told Jim, and off he went on his old bicycle toward McHarburger, the fast food restaurant that refused Jim service a little earlier, purchasing a big burger and a Pepsi Cola. Upon the lad's return, Jim ate the hamburger in a jiffy and gulped down the cola in almost one swallow, which brought a smile to the boy's face.

The two shared small talk as Jim learned the young man's interests, and that he was in the fifth grade in Bacon Elementary School. An interesting bond was beginning to take shape.

Everyone seemed to avoid Jim during all day Saturday except for Bobby, the young man who bought him the hamburger and cola, and came back later in the day to see how he was doing.

"How do you feel this afternoon?" Bobby asked, while listening to the continuous deep cough.

"I feel good," he said. "How are you?"

"I am fine," Bobby replied. "Tomorrow is my special day of the week when we go to church."

As the stores closed for the day, a sign was left on each door indicating that it would not open on Sunday. The cough that had begun during the day had gotten worse so Jim pulled himself to his feet and began his nightly search for a place to sleep. The previous night's sleep was the best in a long while so he thought that he would sleep again under the shrubs at the First Baptist Church even though a church leader had warned him about hanging around Bacon. Realizing that Sunday school did not start until ten o'clock, he would be gone much earlier so he would not bother anyone.

His deep and persistent coughing prevented a good night's rest so he was awake when the men of the church parked their cars in the lot in the early morning to attend a Brotherhood breakfast that was scheduled once each month. Jim scrambled to his feet, coughing all the while, and tried to leave the premises without being noticed by any of the men of the church. Seeing the tramp, the church leader who saw Jim the previous day told the group that he would take care of the situation.

"I warned that same vagrant yesterday that if he tried to sleep under our shrubs any more, I would call the sheriff," he stated.

Walking over to where Jim was located, he stated, "This is a warning for a second time about loitering on church property, and if you are seen here again, we will have no recourse except to call the sheriff and have you arrested for trespassing."

Leaving the church property and making his way to his corner post, he met Bobby as he delivered about fifty newspapers to families in the community. It wasn't too long until he found his comfortable sitting spot near the light pole, coughing all the while and feeling somewhat weak from what was believed to be a minor sickness accompanying the little cold that he had gotten from sleeping in the night air. Observing Bobby as he returned up the street, he noticed that he stopped in front of the hardware store and stared through a window at a beautiful bike with all kinds of gadgets attached.

Then coming directly to Jim, he asked, "How are you getting along?" as he sat down beside him.

Jim indicated, "I am doing fine." He was very happy that Bobby would spend time with him during the day, and thanked him for getting him some food. It seemed that there was a lot of love between the two with little or no inhibitions as they shared stories of their lives.

"In my early years I played a lot of baseball, football and basketball," he told Bobby. "I became a star in each of the sports." Then he paused and bowed his head and waited for nearly a minute before he looked up to relate his story in more detail. "I was offered my first beer when I was a sophomore star on our state high school basketball championship team. It was offered by a senior so I took it to be sociable. Just barely making it through college because of a drinking problem, I still managed to make good grades in the field of engineering and to play two sports of football and basketball.

Following marriage, my wife and I had two special children, but because of the pressures of the job and my weakness for alcohol, I began to drink more and more until it interfered with my job performance. Soon I began to be very obnoxious and irrational at home, and later it spilled over

into the work place. Before too long at age thirty-eight, I
was without a job.

"Looking everywhere to secure a similar job, my
reputation preceded me at every corner, so I took several
menial jobs, only to be fired because of incompetence as an
outgrowth of my serious drinking habit. Soon there were no
other places to work, and by this time my wife and children
had given up on me for good reason, so I resorted to
vagrancy and bounced from one community to another.
How I got to Bacon is another story for another day."

Having listened intently to his friend's brief story of
his life, Bobby excused himself and indicated that he would
return after he attended Sunday school and church. As
traffic picked up, Jim knew that he was being scoffed at, as
cars loaded with family members came by with parents and
children looking his way and some making different kinds of
gestures of disapproval. None stopped to give him money
for food or offer him a job as they were in a hurry to get to
Sunday school. When Bobby came by, he almost fell out of
the window to tell Jim that he would be by after lunch to see
and talk some more. Jim noticed that Bobby's parents
reprimanded him for talking to a stranger, but as they drove
away, he believed that Bobby was presenting a good case for
himself.

Sitting quietly except for the coughs that came more
frequently, Jim decided to go to the morning worship service
at the First Baptist Church and sit on the back pew. Arising
from his comfortable position, Jim made his way about two
blocks to the entrance of the church, looked momentarily to
where he had slept the night before, and proceeded
cautiously and carefully up a large flight of concrete steps,
holding firmly onto the rail all the while. With each step
there was more uneasiness among the morning greeters,
ushers, and deacons who were stationed near the front door
and inside the vestibule. In fact by the time he made the last

step, two of the deacons had approached the pastor and asked for his advice as to what to do. Their immediate verbal response to this most unusual occurrence was to encourage him not to attend, and if this did not work for the ushers to have him to sit on the back pew, and advise everyone who came just to ignore the vagrant. By the time that Jim was seated on the back pew, the whole church was buzzing with whispers, some even loud enough comments for Jim to hear.

"Can you believe the dangerous tramp who has stationed himself in our community is now invading our church and is now sitting on the back pew?" one older lady turned to say to another who looked back to see the poorly dressed man with long and disheveled hair.

"Just ignore the vagrant who is on the back pew," the ushers told the members, as they filed into the sanctuary.

One man was really upset such that he volunteered to escort Jim out so they could have their usual church service without disturbances. "I'll go over and take him by the arm and lead him out the side door," he loudly told a deacon standing in the back assessing the entire situation.

"Everybody has water to wash his body and his clothes," a woman leaned over to tell her husband. "His condition is despicable, and I get nauseous just looking at him."

Jim felt good being in church for the first time in nearly five years, and wished that he had clothes that would blend in and not make him look so different that he was being ostracized by the faithful members of the most popular church in Bacon. The whole back pew was empty and immediately in front, that pew, also, was vacated. The congregation was large and the music was so beautiful that a little tear came into Jim's eye. When the minister asked for all of the people to turn around and give the person near them a big First Baptist welcome, it was over before Jim greeted or was greeted by anyone. Sitting down more slowly than the others and continuing with what seemed to be a disturbing cough, Bobby turned from near the front of the sanctuary and just literally beamed when he saw his friend, Jim.

"Mama," he said excitedly, "my friend, Jim, is at church today."

"Where is he?" she asked.

"He's sitting on the back pew all alone," he said. "May I go and sit with him?"

"Just sit here with us," she replied. "The service is almost started.

"Please, Mama," he begged. "I won't disturb anyone."

After much begging, finally, his parents gave in because of his persistence, and Bobby came to the back of the church sporting a wide smile and sat with Jim. Sitting there together, the whole church seemed to be focusing on them with few people listening to a very powerful message of brotherhood and the Christian community.

"I wouldn't let my child sit near a perfect stranger and a tramp at that," a mother of two said to a lady sitting nearby. Obviously, many others voiced their total disapproval of the actions of the young man.

Several Bacon College girls attended the Sunday morning service, and they thought it was interesting to see the grandson of the president of the college sitting beside this poorly dressed and unclean man on the rear pew. After church Bobby introduced Jim to them as his new friend who had just arrived in the community.

Following church everybody scurried about with pockets of parishioners here and there talking about the unwelcome visitor and that young Royal Ambassador "whippersnapper" Bobby, befriending this strange tramp who made his way to this peaceful community. Having only arrived Friday, the whole community was in a genuine frenzy because of Jim who really didn't want to come to this town in the first place. Bobby, who had already made a big scene, encouraged his parents to permit him to walk with Jim back to his post at the intersection of Main and Church Streets. They walked slowly as Jim's cough and cold seemed to be taking its toll on the little energy he had in the first place. Bobby enjoyed the conversation with Jim very much and hated to lose any of the valuable time with his new found friend, but he left immediately, running to McHarburger to buy two double burgers, large French fries, an apple pie, and a large Pepsi Cola for Jim. Upon his return he sat there and watched Jim eat all that he had bought in a brief period, while he told him of his family, friends and the special activities in which he was engaged. Time to go came too soon so with a warm good-bye, Bobby hustled home to eat lunch with his family.

It was late in the day before Bobby returned to his friend and found him slumped over the concrete base of the light post. Many people passed by, and some had gestured that the vagrant had gotten some money from the naïve and unsuspecting public, had gotten drunk and passed out for all of the world to see. Jim's breathing was rapid, he was perspiring freely, and seemed to be chilled as he was shaking all over. Bobby rode his bike at break neck speed back to his home and got an old coat of his dad's and a blanket from his R. A. camping gear, and returned to aid his most treasured friend. There were many onlookers riding by as Bobby helped Jim to his feet, put on his dad's coat, wrapped him with the blanket and coaxed him to sit on his bicycle after which Bobby began to push him toward his house three blocks away. As he made his way, there were many neighborhood watchers who couldn't believe what they were seeing, and the parents along the way warned their children about talking to and especially befriending people whom they did not know.

Arriving at his home, Bobby helped Jim off the bike, and when he was situated comfortably on the ground, he went into the house to get his mom and dad.

Breathlessly, he said, "Mama and Daddy, my friend Jim has nearly frozen on the corner, and I have brought him home to get warm."

"What do you want to do with him?" his father asked.

"Could we put him in the small room off the porch?" he asked, revealing a sense of urgency.

His parents reluctantly agreed to let the stranger stay in a back room off the porch that had been used mostly for storage. They proceeded to help their son get Jim into the room and onto the small cot, and Bobby's mom went to the kitchen to make some chicken soup for their son's friend.

All the while Bobby cleaned up the room so by the time that his mom had prepared the soup, the room was beginning to take shape. Jim was almost listless so he had strongly to be encouraged to take the soup one spoonful at a time. Bobby sat by Jim's side all night, feeding him a little soup from time to time and being sure that he had cover on him all the while.

Jim slept most of the next day, remaining awake for brief periods of eating a little hot soup, and by nightfall he was showing signs of recovery. For the first time Bobby saw a smile on Jim's face so he began to generate some humorous stories to continue this welcomed change in demeanor.

"My scout troop went on a camping trip this past summer," Bobby related, "and before bedtime two boys put sections of rope in another camper's sleeping bag. When he crawled into his bag that night, he screamed and jumped out of his sleeping bag and began to beat it with a shovel thinking the ropes were snakes."

"Do you have fun in the scout group?" Jim asked, laughing just a little.

"I really do," Bobby responded.

After two more days of rest Bobby insisted that Jim
use his bathroom facilities to clean up, and in addition Bobby
wanted him to eat meals with them. It had been many years
since Jim felt such personal concern by anyone, and with
supreme regret he declined the invitation to become a part of
his family at meal time for a little while. He told Bobby that
he would decline, and for now he would go back to the
corner of Main and Church Streets to continue his work.

In the meantime in the small community of Bacon,
the mayor had been approached about the sorry looking
vagrant that had been "roosting" at the corner of Main and
Church Streets. At the night's council meeting several
prominent citizens, including some charter members of the
First Baptist Church, wanted to know what the community
council was doing to rid itself of the dangerous and
obnoxious freeloaders who were invading their fair
community. One person raised up and said, "The filthy one
in the community now is frightening everybody to death, and
the women and children could not walk near the main
section of business area for fear of being molested."

"Why do we have to put up with the likes of this
shiftless man now causing havoc in our most excellent
community that so many of us have worked to get to this
level, and now find ourselves being invaded by people such
as the one who lurks in our neighborhood?" a red faced man
related to the council.

"We are trying to raise our children in a Christian
environment, but the big cities' woes have now stretched to
our little community here," a well dressed lady stated. "This,
no doubt, is the beginning of a wave of undesirable people
who will soon call our area home. I heard one time that to
get morning glories from one's garden, the way to do this
was to pull them up one at the time. With that said I want to
strongly charge our leaders to remove this terrible blot on
our landscape as quickly as possible."

Obviously, no one was in favor of letting the vagrant remain in the community. While everyone agreed on what should be done, how to do it was a different story. Wranglings over this issue consumed the entire time of the monthly council meeting with the final outcome being that they wanted to get an interpretation from the state attorney general of an old vagrancy ordinance to see whether or not it applied to someone like the present freeloader polluting their beautiful streets and wholesome neighborhood.

As Jim sat on the ground leaning up against the light post, he felt much better, and with Bobby's dad's blue plaid flannel shirt and the dark blue athletic sweater with an eagle logo, he felt very good indeed. All area people seemed to look his way with an unfriendly smirk on their face, but only one or two on this Wednesday offered to assist Jim with any contribution of money. Jim thought it was time to move on to a more lucrative area, where the people would be more generous and more accepting of his plight.

Not too far away the local women were meeting to discuss what to do with the tramp that seemed to be causing havoc for the whole community, and in addition was making people so fearful that they could not walk downtown. The group was extremely upset that the city council had deferred any action on the matter until they got a response from their inquiry from the attorney general's office.

"I don't believe our elected officials examined carefully our plight against this terrible scoundrel and decided that inaction would be the course at this time," a fiery young lady stated. "My young children are scared to death when they see this drifter sitting near the light post begging for money."

"They have reason to be frightened," another older lady pointed out in support of the young mother.

"Waiting will only entice others to follow the lead of this one," another woman added. "They have ways to communicate with one another so others will head our way. You see, they too want peace and tranquility even at the expense of scaring us all to death."

"Many Bacon College girls walk near where this dreadful man perches each day," another stated, "so I'm sure they will be wary of continuing that route to school. It's a shame that we have to adjust what we do because we have a dangerous man in our midst. Why can't he adjust and just leave us alone? I am really disappointed at our leaders for not coming to grips with the situation and nip it in the bud immediately."

All the women concurred that if they didn't nip this situation in the bud that every tramp in the area would think that he could come to Bacon and destroy everything in which they had worked so hard to accomplish. Frustrated, they decided that they would request that the citizens boycott the merchants on the block where the freeloader always sat until they were willing to take strong measures to see that it was safe for women and children around their stores. It was agreed that they would use the copier of the First Baptist Church where five of them were members to print the announcement that would be distributed to all of the taxpayers of the whole community.

As the evening approached, Jim decided to go to the Glade Baptist Church about three blocks to the south and again sit on the back pew. Having no cough and feeling much better as a result of Bobby's good care, he began his walk toward the church. It was a relatively new church that was not as tall as the other churches he had seen, and had a well groomed lawn that appeared to have been professionally landscaped. His arrival caused a flurry of conversation among various groups standing around waiting for the midweek prayer meeting to start. It was church supper night so each family took its dishes to the fellowship hall to share with all of the others. It was very much like Jim had remembered several years ago when he and his family attended these kinds of dinners very regularly before his terrible physical and spiritual demise that caused him to plunge to this level of begging for food just to exist. Finding his back seat, he was almost impervious to the behavior and reaction of the church members to his presence in their midst. He knew that he was disruptive and wanted to apologize to all of them, but he thought that he should attend this church so they would just have to put up with him.

The pastor made some announcements after the congregation sang a beautiful hymn with Jim participating, and then he asked whether or not anyone had a prayer request for the evening wherein several verbalized their petitions with others withholding any comments as they seemed to be intimidated by the presence of a frightful tramp sitting right in the midst of the congregation. No one sat near Jim so he had plenty of room. The pastor read from James 2 in the Bible.

James 2:17 In the same way, faith by itself, if it is not accompanied by action, is dead.

Following a brief but fiery message by the pastor on local missions, all of the ones who brought food were invited to come to the fellowship hall. As it turned out, everyone went to the fellowship hall except Jim and one other person who was directed to "take care of him." To avoid an awkward situation, Jim advised, "I am leaving now and really had not planned to eat at this time of day. Would you tell the pastor how much I enjoyed the service?" He wished them well in presenting the Word of God to the community.

Each day Bobby would come to the light post and talk for long periods of time about all kinds of subjects with his friend. Because Jim was not getting enough money from the people to buy food, Bobby was using his paper route income to purchase food each day for Jim. His friend's well being was more important than the money any day, and besides, each time that he brought him food, Jim would tell him that he would be repaid some day.

As their friendship grew, Jim became a bigger threat to the well being of the community because he kept attending the various churches and receiving the same results in the area on Sundays and Wednesdays. After the last church was visited and after he returned to bed down for the night in an area near an old fence row, he decided that he would follow further the directions of the powerful dream he had several nights ago. According to this dream, he had fulfilled all aspects of his visit to Bacon and now would proceed to Chartanta, a very large metropolitan center some five hundred miles to the south.

Waking early the next morning, he made his way toward Bobby's house to advise him of the sudden shift of plans. Bobby had almost completed his paper route when he saw Jim. They hugged each other as usual, and when Jim told Bobby that he had to leave, they both cried together standing in the middle of the sidewalk. Jim asked Bobby to sit down in the grass with him so he could tell more about himself. Before Bobby sat down he said that the had something to get for Jim at home first, and he sped away on his bike to return in about six or seven minutes with a small night deposit money pouch. He gave the pouch containing $84.27 to Jim and told him to use it for his needs during the next several days until he was settled in his new community.

Jim was very grateful for the money that he knew Bobby was saving for the new bicycle that he always looked at in the hardware store window with all of the gadgets. Bobby told him that he had changed his plans about the new bike anyway, because he was so used to the old one, it would be hard to give it up.

After a little while Jim said, "The reason I came to Bacon in the first place was because of a dream that I had. Since the dream, I have used it to guide my life while here in your community. Last night I had a continuation of the first dream, and because of it I am going to Chartanta."

"What are you going to do in that large city?" Bobby asked.

"I really don't know so I'll just go there totally on faith just as I came to Bacon," he responded.

"Do you feel like you can make such a long trip?" Bobby inquired.

"I feel just great now," Jim answered. "I have not had any alcohol in more than four weeks, and the way I feel now, I'll never go back to that terrible habit that nearly destroyed me, and it did cause my family to leave me."

"What makes you think that you will not return to alcohol?" Bobby asked.

With conviction shown in his eyes, he quickly turned and replied, "It is just so very good to feel the freedom from the dependence of alcohol that has enslaved me during so many years of my life."

"What will you be doing in that large city after you get there?" Bobby continued with his questioning.

"What is being asked of me in this large metropolitan area so far away, I am not sure, but I am willing to fulfill whatever mission that I am called on to do," he responded

Trying to discover what he should do, Bobby asked, "May I tell others what you have told me about your being led by dreams?"

Jim stated, "It is up to you as to whom you would relate the story of my experiences."

Following another big bear hug with some heavy tears from each, Jim departed down the street to get to the main thoroughfare to head for the large metropolitan area to the south. Nearly out of earshot, he heard Bobby calling to find out when he would see him again. Jim's response in a very clear voice was that it may be sooner than you think.

With a tramp like appearance Jim made his way passed the intersection of Main and Church Streets with a little bounce in his steps, waved at some merchants in front of their stores, and said good-bye to others who were on his side of the street. As he continued, he even thought he heard one of the men wish him well. There was a triumphant feeling among those watching Jim's departure, as they realized he was leaving by his own volition and would not have to be evicted because of not meeting a community ordinance.

Jim's thoughts were clearer as he made his way to the interstate highway leading south, and he began to use some of his engineering mathematical skills to compute the time it would take to walk five hundred miles, if he could walk at least thirty miles each day. The answer was easy. Jim knew that he would be less than twenty days on the road so the generosity of Bobby to give him food money was very special and meaningful, as he would have enough until he reached his destination.

Not too long on the road a state trooper stopped to talk to him about being careful as he walked along the highway, and particularly when he had to cross because the speed limit was sixty-five miles per hour and some drivers had a tendency to go even faster. The trooper wished him well and hoped that he had a pleasant trip. The weather changed during the afternoon of his first day as the temperature dropped considerably followed by a torrential downpour of rain mixed with snow and ice that lasted through the night. It was nearly midnight when he crawled under a bridge to find a dry place to sleep for the night.

Except for a few yells from passing cars, the next several days were uneventful. The weather had improved and his pace had picked up just a little so he was sure he was making at least thirty miles a day. The clarity of his thoughts was surprising, and his not having a desire for alcohol was a welcomed improvement over his previous sordid life. He thought of his special young friend in Bacon and couldn't understand why he would give up all of his savings to a drifter, who had wasted much of his life. "I know that his parents and grandparents were really concerned because of his befriending me as it caused him much grief among others in Bacon," Jim thought, as he trudged along.

Meanwhile, in Bacon Bobby was harboring a most unusual story about the vagrant who had genuinely upset the entire community by only his very presence. He pondered considerably over the time to tell the story to his parents and grandparents because he knew that they would be skeptical of such a wild story. It was obvious that his parents had not fully accepted Jim, and they were aware of the unrest he had caused in the neighborhood. At times when visiting his grandfather at Bacon College, he could tell that his grandfather was accepting of what he was doing, but he knew that he was not totally satisfied with him regarding the friendship he had developed with this stranger who was so much older than he. At times Bobby thought that he would just keep the special story to himself so that he would not have to face the scrutiny of his loving, yet, doubting parents.

Money running low and the weariness brought on by nineteen days of travel, Jim found himself within a day's journey of the city to which he was being led. His weight loss because of the unusual physical strain on his already frail body coupled with a rationing of food because of lack of money, Jim bedded down for his last night of sleep before entering the appointed city. It was with blind faith that he was going on this mission, which at this point was not understood at all.

With $3.47, his knapsack on his back, and with dirty clothes Jim looked very much the part of a vagrant, a position that he had held for several years. It was in the evening before he trudged near the maze of interstate roads that converged on Chartanta, a sprawling metropolitan area.

The skyline was filled with very tall buildings that made dark silhouettes, and a round building had a revolving roof line. With his mind clearer than it had been in years, Jim soaked up the beauty of God's creation and man's handiwork in adjusting the environment for his own purposes. It was this inner feeling of newness that caused Jim to press forward even though he knew that his body was beckoning him to rest.

TRAGIC ACCIDENT

Plodding on, his movement got more difficult because of the "banjo work" in the numerous highways and streets that made pedestrian travel very precarious indeed. The stress of dodging between cars and trucks began to take its toll as he got closer and closer to his destination right in the center of the city. Nearing a large and tall building that he had judged to be in the center of city, his legs would hardly move as he was going to make his final street crossing before going to sleep for the night. Midway across the street, the screeching tires told all in earshot that brakes of a car were being applied. It was too late for Jim as the vehicle struck him on his side, hurling him about one hundred feet into a parked car where he lay unconsciously. Bleeding profusely, all who witnessed the scene knew that he was dead.

A rescue vehicle came rapidly and with tourniquets and bandages, they prepared Jim to be moved to the nearest hospital. From time to time in Chartanta alcoholics stumbled in front of cars so the emergency room crew at Gardy Hospital took this case in stride as they worked to preserve another life. With many life enhancing attachments affixed to Jim's frail body, a clerk came and asked, "Do you all have personal data on this accident victim?"

After searching through his meager belongings, she replied, "We have found nothing that would reveal his true identity."

"Why don't we just call him H. L. for homeless," she said, while laughing about the name they had given to this wretched soul as she returned to her station and conveyed the information to her colleagues who had a good laugh, also. A reporter from the Chartanta Observer and Journal shared a chuckle with the group as he departed to go back to the newspaper office to write his story about another drive-by shooting that took the lives of four of the city's citizens on this evening.

Jim's condition remained critical as he lay motionless in the hospital bed. One could hear the nurses and aides asking about how H. L. was getting along, because all of them somehow had become enamored over this case which really had the same modus operandi of so many similar cases they had over the last several years in this thriving metropolis. All of the hospital personnel had grown very fond of this unknown vagrant who had been given the nickname H. L., and they were hoping that someone would come to visit him so they could really find out who he was. They had given him a haircut, shaved his face, and washed him up so that he looked like a very different person from the one who was brought into the hospital several nights ago on a stretcher near death.

The young fledging reporter who covered the night beat at the hospital was experiencing a lull in crime situations that made good stories for the major newspaper in the city, so he again approached his editor to get approval to do a human interest story. He had wanted to do such a story for some time. To his surprise, he was granted approval because the editor was busy and really just wanted to get him out of his hair. Now was his chance to make a good showing in writing about his favorite subject. As he searched his memory bank for topics to be included in the massive Sunday newspaper, he thought of the homeless character who had been admitted to the hospital whom the staff had named H. L., because they could not determine who he was.

The reporter enjoyed writing the story, and if he had to say so himself, his story was a good one and might just catapult him to this department for full time writing. The story was received by the editor with little fanfare and was published without any changes. The response to the article was swift as the telephones rang continuously from people who were concerned over the well being of this homeless person. Likewise, extra workers were employed at the hospital to man the telephones as they were receiving a record number of calls from concerned persons all over the region covered by the newspaper. Several Sunday school classes at First Baptist Church in Bacon mentioned the warm article about the poor old homeless person that was on the verge of death and friendless.

An on duty state trooper patrolling the interstate picked up a newspaper after getting a cup of coffee as he was winding down a very busy and tiring shift. Arriving home, he followed his normal habit of reading the newspaper before preparing for church. The last section to be read was the page entitled, "Life's Interest" with an article called "Who's H. L.?" Reading about a homeless character was not what he wanted to read, but he continued and came across the clothing description of an eagle on a dark athletic sweater and a plaid shirt. It dawned on him that this fit the description of the drifter with whom he spoke two or three weeks ago on the interstate near the Bacon exit.

The response of the people regarding this story about H. L. had caused almost everyone to talk about it in every place where at least two people gathered. The brief mention of the story on the Monday evening's prime time news on the major networks, caused the reaction to mushroom to a level beyond the memory of anyone at the hospital and newspaper office.

It was the call from the state trooper that gave the first substantive lead to identify the unknown patient as he told the reporter that he had talked to a drifter who fit H. L.'s description near the Bacon exit on the interstate some five hundred miles from Chartanta about two or three weeks ago. The reporter listened intently at every comment being made by this articulate trooper who seemed to remember every detail. As a follow-up, the trooper said that he was going to Bacon to see whether or not anyone in that small community had ever seen H. L. The reporter said that he would await his call from Bacon.

When the trooper arrived at the heart of the community at Main and Church Streets, he went directly to the merchants to ask them about a drifter who might have been in the area during the last several weeks.

"Have you all seen in the last few weeks a homeless person in the area?" the state trooper asked.

They all agreed that one had been in Bacon and had disrupted the whole community. In fact the people were scared to death as the women and children could not come to Main Street for fear of him as he sat by the light post to which they pointed. One stated that it was disgraceful how a young man, the grandson of the Bacon College president of all people in the neighborhood, befriended the vagrant and how upset the community was of the boy.

The trooper took the newspaper article with him as he walked up to the door of the young man's house. Bobby's parents were startled to see the trooper and were perplexed when he asked to see Bobby about the newspaper article he had in his hand. He was invited into the living room, and Bobby was called in from the back yard. The trooper showed them the article and told Bobby and his parents that he believed that H. L. was Jim, Bobby's friend. When Bobby was shown the clothing description in the article, he knew it was Jim, and he went to his room and cried. Upon his return the trooper asked Bobby whether or not he wanted to call the hospital to tell them the name of H. L. Declining, the trooper requested to use the telephone to make a call to the reporter of the newspaper who in turn would call the hospital.

Receiving this information and disseminating it to the various callers to the hospital and newspaper, there seemed to be an explosion of activities as the story began to swell beyond even the wildest imagination. As the wires were filled with this major breaking story, the news vans were headed northwest from Chartanta to the little community of Bacon. It was more than the small community could handle as media van after media van, accompanied by a large staff, in conjunction with the extremely large contingent of visitors, came to the little community to glean from its citizens the real story of the most popular person in the country at the present time, H. L. Inundation of vehicles prompted the mayor to seek assistance from the state troopers to handle traffic control, similar to that of a basketball game.

Bobby was the center of attention and he handled it well. His numerous interviews by all of the networks were beamed all over the country. There were so many questions. Dr. Damond, Bobby's grandfather, teased Bobby when he said, "For the last several months I have had a lot of experience with the media. Seeing the way you conduct yourself with them, I should have employed you as my consultant."

Bobby related his experience with Jim so many times with each reporting group adding its own touch to generate additional excitement. Through all of this, he still held within himself about Jim's activities being guided by his dreams, and with all of this interest in Jim now removed any doubt Bobby had of the situation. Bobby was pleased that the First Baptist Church was conducting a prayer vigil on behalf of H. L.

People from everywhere and all walks of life encircled the modest house on Elm Street, and among those were Bobby's many neighborhood and school friends who were so proud to know him. Bobby knew that they would have done the same thing as he for Jim, if they had understanding parents such as his. In the meantime the city council met and passed a touching resolution, which indicated how proud it was of its young man who had the courage to extend a helping hand to a homeless person. Of course, this resolution found its way to national news on the major networks.

Early the next morning Bobby was asked by a major network commentator where he would like for the money that they were receiving to be deposited. After conferring with his parents, he suggested that the First Baptist Church be in charge of any contributions if the deacon board approved the matter. The flood of T. V. programs vying for "one-upsmanship" filled the screens of homes all over the country by midday   Bobby and his parents began to make plans for him to visit his friend in the hospital. As they were discussing this visit privately, a messenger brought an envelope to the door, which prompted reporters to inquire of its contents. Inside were three airplane tickets to Chartanta from an anonymous donor who thanked Bobby for his genuine love for a "have not." After being told of the contents the reporters inquired about the family's intentions regarding a visitation, and Bobby's parents admitted that they were planning a trip soon.

One of the major media furnished the taxi service to the airport so that it could get a first hand interview with Bobby during his trip to Chartanta. Others followed in a motorcade, which was longer than even the longest of the funeral processionals that ever could be remembered by the

old-timers of Bacon. Theirs was truly a celebrity-type trip
with all kinds of media personnel on hand to get a last
glimpse of the little family before they boarded the plane.
As they struggled through the airport terminal, a well known
book publisher approached Bobby's father and told him that
he wanted to write a book about this experience and would
talk to them at a more convenient time.

It was as though Bobby was being interviewed all the
way to Chartanta as reporter after reporter on the plane took
turns talking to Jim's very special friend. Bobby maintained
his silence about two things that only he knew which were
concerning the fact that Jim's mission was prompted by his
dreams and that he had given Jim all of his savings. It just
didn't seem to be the appropriate time to tell these parts of
his relationship with Jim.

The crowd that had encircled Gardy Hospital made it
difficult for traffic to move in and around the perimeter of
the several blocks of the building, so the limousine driver
had to blow his horn several times to get the people to move
aside so they could get through. Everyone wanted to get a
look at this country lad who had stolen the hearts of so many
people these last few days. With flash bulbs blinking Bobby
and his parents got on the elevator to the ninth floor where
Jim still lay unconsciously following the tragic accident. By
this time Jim had been moved to a room that was only
reserved for V.I.P.'s. Pausing at the door with all eyes glued
on the little family, they huddled and agreed that Bobby
should go in first alone.

Almost being overwhelmed by the numerous tubes
attached to Jim's body to assist him during the period of
unconsciousness, Bobby slowly made his way to his friend's
bedside. With the new haircut and a clean shaven face,
Bobby had to get really close to realize that it was truly Jim,
his most precious friend. With tears streaming down his face
he touched his arm and squeezed his hand as Jim remained
motionless. Bobby noticed too that Jim was frail looking,

yet, there seemed to be a peace that filled all features of his face. The athletic sweater with the eagle and the plaid shirt lying on the chair caused further tears.

Getting control of himself, he surveyed the hospital room filled with beautiful flowers, stuffed animals, candy and cards that had been sent to Jim from all over the country. Bobby was pleased that so many people had expressed the same love for Jim during the last several weeks that he had shown during their good times together in Bacon. He sat in a most pensive mood on the side of the bed thinking of what the future held for his injured friend, without any regard for the frenzy of activities surrounding this whole ordeal that was commonplace in almost every community. The news of this person nicknamed H. L. had penetrated almost every household, and the human interest story encompassing it all made everyone feel that he or she had become a player in the whole episode.

After a very lengthy private visit Bobby went outside and beckoned his mom and dad to come into the room to see Jim. They too cried as they looked at Jim lying there motionless with all of those life enhancements attached. Bobby's dad rendered a beautiful prayer asking God to look after their special friend who was receiving without his knowing it the plenary expressions of love of so many people throughout the country. After they looked at many of the things in the room that had been sent to Jim, they said good-bye to him saying that they would return in the morning. Hearing this, Bobby requested to stay in the room with Jim for the night, and his parents gave their consent. A nurse got a cot and moved it into the room after moving the reporters aside and relating to them what the young lad wanted to do.

The evening and late night news covered the story that was unfolding in Chartanta as its lead item, and across the country people were transfixed as they held onto every word that was said. When the T. V. news was completed, many would resort to radio to continue with the story. Those with cable could hear continuous coverage as one channel had decided to cover all aspects of the saga around the clock except for breaks to bring people up to date on other important news.

Meanwhile, back in Bacon the members of the First Baptist Church had a candlelight prayer service for Jim, and had invited all of the citizens to participate. They were so proud of their Bobby who was one of the leaders in the R. A. program in the church. Bobby's church and school peers were present for the service with their parents, the governmental leaders related their love for the family and to Jim, and the visitors expressed their emotions on this unusual occasion. The outsiders who attended indicated that they wished that their neighborhood could be as compassionate for a drifter as they believed Bacon was. It was a spirit filled evening of praises to God for His love that was being played out by the people's love to one another.

The Bacon community had taken on a totally different complexion as it was the focal point of thousands of people as they converged onto the scene of the story of the love of homeless man and a little boy that had captured the hearts of the nation. There were banners, balloons, signs, music, food everywhere on the street, church bells ringing periodically, patriotic attire, wide smiles, and much laughter. The community council had requested that the maintenance department erect a beautiful marker where Jim had sat on the corner holding his sign: "Homeless. Will work for food." In fact, that was in the inscription on the granite marker. Within minutes after it was placed near Jim's favorite light post, flowers were placed on and around the marker. It became a most popular spot for making pictures, as car after car, many with out of state license plates, would stop and make a picture.

Bobby's mom and dad finally made it to their hotel room about three blocks from the hospital to get some well needed rest. It had been a long day for the quiet little family, so the anticipated rest was welcomed. They talked about their schedule and agreed that they would stay two days even though Bobby's dad was told that he could take all the time off work as needed. They could not believe what was happening as the media covered every aspect of their day's activities, and the television news was fraught with any event that would add to what they had dubbed as "America's Love Story." The flood of telephone calls prompted the hotel to move the couple to a suite of rooms where there were two telephones, and the manager told them that there would be no charge to them and that they could stay as long as they wanted to stay. Room service was provided on a gratis basis, also, to protect them from the mass of media filling the hotel hallways, lobby, and parking lot.

Late in the evening there was a rap on the hotel room door, and standing at the door was an official messenger from the governor's office with a letter from the state leader. It was written to Bobby stating that the governor wanted his family and him to be guests at a special session of the legislature being conducted in the state house at ten o'clock the next morning. Further, he wanted Bobby to address the assembly, telling about his friend and some of their activities. Knowing that the news of the assembly meeting attendance might be upsetting to Bobby, they decided not to tell him about this until morning.

Bobby's parents and he had exchanged calls several times during the evening with his parents telling Bobby about the kindness expressed by the management of the hotel, and Bobby telling of the love expressed toward him by the people at the hospital. His parents could tell that he was holding up well under the strain of all of the attention, and was the same humble young man in which they were so proud. It was he who was showing the world what love was really all about, and it seemed that all of the world was trying to emulate the style of a child. Both parents agreed that the Bible was replete with messages that all people should act as children.

Following a V. I. P. breakfast in their hotel room, Bobby's parents dressed and made their way through a media mob three blocks to the hospital to visit Jim and to advise Bobby of what was in store for the morning. Bobby calmly received the news, and then began to relate that to his knowledge Jim had not moved since he was brought to the hospital, yet, his facial expression seemed to indicate that he was conscious and alert. He excitedly told them that the hospital had received so many things for Jim that they were using the front lobby so that well wishers could see them. They had told Bobby that they had received by far more telephone calls on Jim's behalf than for any other patient in the history of their existence.

Being time to depart for the capitol, they left Jim's room as Bobby received many hugs from the hospital staff as they wished him well in his speech to the general assembly. Bobby's parents were surprised that everyone knew about Bobby's meeting with the general assembly. Reaching the outer lobby, three state troopers assigned to the capitol indicated that they would assist his family as they walked to the capitol. They were a welcome sight because it had become very difficult to move about with all the media at every side.

As soon as they entered the capitol, a man dressed in a light colored suit and a tie with white stripes, eased beside the state troopers and said in a low voice, "I will take it from here." Without hesitation the man took Bobby's hand and told his parents to follow him as they proceeded toward the double doors covered with well shined brass plates leading to the assembly chamber. The man seemed to know what to do and everyone made way for him, even the aggressive media.

Pausing momentarily at the door as he waited for his cue, he then turned to the little family from Bacon and said, "It is time to enter."

As the large doors spread to both sides, all of the legislators turned to watch this caring lad who had changed the behavior of so many during the last several days, come down the aisle of this hallowed room. A thunderous applause sprang forth filling the chamber with clapping from all corners of the building. With each step it got louder and louder as the man who was dressed in a light colored suit and a tie with white stripes guided them to the podium near the speaker's stand. With flash bulbs blinking, news reporters scribbling, and the several television cameras pointed to the front and from time to time panning the record assembly attendance, Bobby and his loving family stood before the group. For whatever reason Bobby was the calmest of the three even though he was the one with the most difficult job of speaking to the body of people.

After several minutes the man dressed in a light colored suit and a tie with white stripes who had escorted them to the front leaned over to Bobby and whispered in his ear that it was time for him to tell the whole story about Jim and that it was important for him to tell that he had given Jim his bicycle savings of $84.27. Bobby was shocked that the man knew the exact amount of money that he had given Jim and that it was his bicycle money.

Everybody was seated. Bobby's parents took their seats, and the man dressed in a light colored suit and a tie with white stripes led Bobby to the speaker's stand and helped him on the special box to increase his height. Having done that, the man bade farewell to Bobby, wished him well and stood among the massive crowd getting ready to hold onto every word of the country's little hero.

Bobby was surprised at the ease of talking before this distinguished group. He told them about how he just

happened to have run across Jim the day he arrived in the
Bacon community, and that for whatever reason it was love
at first sight. They had spent much time together at his
favorite "roosting place" as Jim called the light post on the
corner of Main and Church Streets in Bacon. As they got
closer, Jim related his story of alcoholism and how with his
demise lost everything, his job, friends, and his lovely wife
and two children. Jim blamed no one except himself. It all
started when he was a sophomore as he drank his first bottle
of beer to be liked by the seniors. He managed to make good
grades in college, play two sports, and earn an engineering
degree. Bobby jokingly told them that Jim would say to him
that he was using his engineering degree from the state
university as he would count the money he received each day
as he begged to support his drinking habit.

Bobby had been talking for what he believed was a
long time, and one could hear a pin drop in the assembly
chamber. He was having a hard time getting enough courage
to tell about their most intimate experiences, but he knew
that it had to be done. He went on to tell them that during
Jim's stay in Bacon, he had gotten sick and that his parents
had permitted him to become a part of his family for several
days. Upon his recovery though he declined the gracious
offer by Bobby's parents to become a part of their family.
Bobby said that it was during this period of time that Jim
began to drop hints that he was on some kind of special
mission that he said he would reveal at a later date.

Choking a little when he broached this subject,
Bobby paused a moment and took a deep breath and noticed
it was 10:45 A.M. by the large clock on the wall so he had
been talking for a long time. Continuing, he told of Jim's
sleeping near fence rows and under shrubs, and how he didn't
get enough money to sustain his needs. Bobby stated that he
had a paper route and earned some money so he shared his
income with Jim by buying him food from the fast-food
restaurant in Bacon. He indicated that Jim could do the best

job of eating a hamburger that he had ever seen. For the first time considerable laughter broke the silence of the audience so Bobby paused and laughed with them.

Bobby said that he was surprised when Jim told him that he had to leave. With tears flowing, he sped home on his old bicycle to get something for him to take with him. Returning he gave Jim a bank deposit pouch containing $84.27 that he was saving to buy a new bike to use on the paper route. Jim tried to refuse the money, but Bobby had insisted because it was more important that Jim have enough food to make the long trip to Chartanta, and furthermore, his old bike was in good shape anyway. It was at this time that Jim revealed to him his secret.

With tears in his eyes Bobby took several deep breaths, got down from his little box and went over and hugged his mom and dad and whispered to them that Jim was on a mission directed by his dreams. They all three cried together momentarily. At this time the Speaker of the House came forward and told Bobby's family that he was going to call a brief recess so that they could compose themselves. He told them, "Bobby is doing such a marvelous job."

In a while the Speaker gaveled the group back to order, and Bobby resumed his position before a most attentive and curious audience. He stated that as he looked back on his relationship with Jim, he could see signs that Jim was a different kind of person, one with numerous warts but one with great potential. There was a radiance about his face that produced a countenance that Bobby had never witnessed before, but it appeared that he was the only one who recognized the positive qualities of the person that others dubbed, drifter, tramp, freeloader, vagrant, and more.

As they sat on the grass prior to his departure from Bacon, Jim told him that he was being guided by his strong dreams he had had during the last several nights to come to

Bacon. With this statement there was considerable murmuring among the crowd to such a degree that Bobby had to stop speaking until those in the assembly chamber would get quiet. It was as though they could not believe what they were hearing. Bobby looked at the clock and it was exactly 11:00 A.M.

Having lain in a coma for several days, suddenly Jim opened his eyes. Soon the improved condition was discovered by his nurse who turned on the TV and showed him that every network was carrying a speech being made by his friend Bobby in the general assembly.

Resuming, after pausing for several minutes, Bobby continued to relate the warm story about how Jim had not taken a drink of alcohol since he started having these special dreams. Bobby went on to say that individuals like Jim were beautiful people and that all of us had to see the good qualities in them as they, like all of us, fall prey to wrongful acts from time to time and that God was so forgiving to us; therefore, we should emulate His style by forgiving others who are struggling.

As he got ready to continue, there was a telephone call to the assembly chamber from the hospital indicating that Jim had regained consciousness at 11:00 A.M. and was watching Bobby speak on television. At this time the Speaker came to the speaker's stand and told Bobby of the call and that Jim was watching on television. Bobby who broke out in a big smile and couldn't help himself, but he waved to Jim and wished him well. Those in attendance couldn't contain themselves any more so they stood, cheered, clapped, whistled, and did everything else to made a joyful noise with Bobby and his parents crying at the speaker's stand. In Jim's hospital room filled with nurses, reporters and well wishers, they were crying for joy because they too had become a part of the "America's Love Story."

Bobby and his family remained in Chartanta for a few days watching Jim make progress in his recovery all the while. Really a homeless person, Jim was invited to their home when he was released from the hospital to live with them until he was fully able to take care of himself. Those close to Jim were surprised when the hospital received money from an anonymous donor to pay all medical expenses after the hospital board had told Bobby's family that it would waive all of Jim's expenses. The story of the drifter's life had stirred the consciences of so many people throughout the country.

Bobby's grandfather stated to those close to him, "Jim Baldwin's life has really impacted on so many people."

"He certainly has," Josh said, responding quickly to the college president's comment.

"It's really something how an outstanding young person can let alcohol ruin his entire life," Bob Waters noted. "I believe he has conquered that strong ogre in his life."

"The whole basketball team is so proud of your grandson, Dr. Damond, for seeing beyond the dirty clothes and unkempt hair to see a heart yearning for help," Coach Anna said.

"The road to full recovery is going to be long for Jim," Dr. Damond said. "It will take all of us to be encouragers to him as he operates on a day to day basis. For the time being, I am going to employ him as an engineer to help us on campus to upgrade the mechanical functions of our various buildings."

"I hear that he was once an excellent engineer, possessing a brilliant mind," Bob Waters added. "I can use him some to help us at Tiger Foods."

"This spring I can get him to help us in our youth basketball program in the Hollow," Josh indicated. "According to his college yearbook, he was really an exceptional player in college, and still holds many records in intercollegiate play."

Following the meeting, each went his separate way, but all had grown greatly in applying God's word to an earthly matter. Jim Baldwin soon entered the community of Bacon triumphantly and began to live among the folks who earlier failed to see what a young lad observed that caused him to move his life in a different direction.

Paul H. Jones

MINISTERIAL MEETING

Josh just loved to attend the ministerial association meetings each month so on this cold December morning he fired up the dilapidated old van and drove out of the Hollow. Leaving puffs of dark smoke behind, he chugged eastward to the association office where he was greeted by other pastors in the area. Not subscribing to a newspaper and not having television, his main source of information besides that he received from Bob Waters came from the association of pastors.
On this day there was much talk in the group about the sudden resignation of the school superintendent who had served the community for so many years. "I guess he thought that the public wanted a change so instead of waiting until the end of the year, he decided to leave now," a young pastor indicated.

"I attended the first meeting when the parents were so upset because the children failed to do well on the AET's," another cited. "The parents were almost uncivil that night."

Another said, "There have been several meetings just with parents, and my wife attended one of them. She was appalled at what was brought up during this meeting such that she failed to attend any further meetings."

"I was there when the superintendent gave his lengthy speech that only a few listened to," an older pastor told the group. "What he said made a lot of sense, but no one was in a receptive mood on this evening so they just tuned him out. I believe that after there was little interest in what he said on that evening that he decided to resign so they could move ahead with their agenda."

"What is he doing now?" Josh asked.

"No one seems to know," the director responded.

Josh really admired the superintendent very much, having been the high school coach for four years. He was a learned man with much energy expended to provide an excellent teaching-learning environment for teachers and pupils. Following the meeting he stopped by Bob Waters' office to talk to him about the superintendent. As always, it was a good visit with his most treasured friend who had been such a faithful servant of the Lord over the years.

Following warm greetings, Josh asked, "Have you heard anything from Glenn Colson since he resigned as superintendent?"

"I have talked to him a couple of times, and one of those times he came by here for a visit."

"How is he doing and why did he resign?" Josh quickly asked.

"As you know, many parents were upset because their children's AET's were low," Bob replied. "Obviously, they were blaming Glenn for the shortfall, but his response to them was that over the years he had proposed changes in the curriculum, but in each instance the parents had disapproved of his ideas."

"Glenn is really a nice gentleman," Josh stated. "He came to the Hollow to talk to me about the parents' concern over the low test scores, but I never thought it would lead to his resigning. How is he doing and what is he going to do now that he is retired?"

"He seems to be in good spirits, and to answer your second question, I really don't know what he has in mind. I am sure he has several options. It was rumored that he was going to teach at Bacon College, but he didn't mention that to me," Bob indicated.

Before he left he talked to Glenn on the telephone to invite him to the Hollow, especially on the Friday evening affairs that had been held for years using the food brought faithfully by Bob each week. "It was really a good visit with Bob, as always," Josh thought, as he drove the old van toward the Hollow.

SURPRISE VISITOR

Two days later Bob made his usual delivery of surplus food to his friend. In their conversation Bob told Josh about a report he had read and had seen on television regarding a missing small airplane. "According to the report, a man, his wife and two children had departed from a small airport in west Ohio on Tuesday traveling to Myrtle Beach, South Carolina," Bob told Josh. "No one has heard from them since they were in the air."

"What do you think happened?" Josh asked inquisitively.

"It was really foggy in the mountains during the last several days," Bob said, "so it could be that they lost their way over the mountains."

"This is a long and high range of mountains, and if you are not familiar with them, I can see how pilots of a low flying aircraft might misjudge their height," Josh pointed out.

"If the plane did go down into a mountain and there are survivors, there is something else getting ready to take place that will certainly impact on their situation," Bob said excitedly. "There is a large snow storm brewing from the south and should be arriving here early tomorrow morning.

Accompanying this storm will be very cold temperatures with high winds lasting for more than a day. People have already been warned to remain inside except for emergencies."

"I'll warn all of our Hollow people about this impending storm," Josh indicated. "Thank you so much for coming and bringing the news of threatening weather."

"Let me know if you all need anything to get through this period of cold, snowy weather," Bob said to Josh. "I'll check on you all later."

"Thank you so much for all you do for us, Bob," Josh stated, as he put his arm around him, as the two walked toward his truck.

Pulling away, Bob yelled out of the truck window, "The family had a brown and white beagle with them on the plane."

By morning snow had blanketed the Hollow, leaving several inches on the ground with much more to come. Watching the snow come down all day, late in the afternoon Josh said, "You know, Charlene, this could be the deepest snow we have had in years, and if it keeps on, it could possibly be a record for the area."

"I hope the other families are okay," Charlene said. "They have been advised to go to the orphan home to stay, if they wanted to get warm on cold days so I'm sure many of them will head that way soon, if they are not already there."

"I believe we should go there too before it gets completely dark," Josh advised.

"I'm going to round up all the warm clothing I can find for us to wear outside," Charlene said, as she hurried around their two-room house for coats, sweaters, caps and gloves.

Closing the damper on the wood stove, Josh began putting on heavy clothing laid out by Charlene. Just as he had pulled over his second sweater, there was a sound at the door. "I wonder who that could be," Charlene said, as she turned to look at Josh.

Josh quickly opened the door to welcome their visitor, but was startled to discover a brown and white dog nearly frozen to death. Picking up the dog in his arms, he closed the door and carried the beagle immediately to where the stove was located. "Charlene, are you aware that in the plane with those missing there was a brown and white beagle dog?" Josh excitedly pointed out. "Do you think this is their dog that survived a crash in the mountains?"

"I don't know about that but he certainly is a very cold animal," Charlene replied, as she patted his frozen fur."

Charlene wrapped the very cold dog in an old shirt and held him in her lap near the stove, petting him all the while. His eyes looked up to her as though watching her every move without any sign of fear. After he appeared to be warm, she checked his legs and paws to determine whether or not they were responding favorably to the warmth from the stove. "He is really excited about getting warm," Josh said, as he patted their new guest on the back as his tail wagged back and forth.

"It certainly has been a quick recovery," Charlene stated with a smile. "He really likes to sit in my lap."

Suddenly, without any warning whatsoever, he jumped out of Charlene's lap and ran directly to the door where he turned his head back toward his two new caretakers and began to scratch on the door. "He wants to get out," Josh commented. "I'm sure he remembers how cold and snowy it is outside, but it appears he wants to go anyway." Josh responded to his request and opened the door, and immediately he ran out of the warm house onto the porch.

Stopping at the edge, he looked back and seemed to be waiting for them to follow him. "I believe he wants us to go with him," Charlene said. "He seems to be telling us that he is going to lead us somewhere."

"Do you think he wants us to follow him to where the airplane is?" Josh asked.

"I believe that is the case," Charlene said, "but if that's the case, we had better regroup and take more with us than just the clothes we are wearing. If he is going to lead us to an airplane wreckage, we need to carry items to effect a rescue."

"According to what Bob said, the airplane disappeared about three days ago," Josh pointed out, "so we had better take some food. I am going to get the tent that was given to us following the African trip. The other emergency items also will serve a good purpose, such as rope, flashlight, matches, first aid kit and a couple of sleeping bags to keep us warm if we are out very long."

"We haven't used the backpacks since we returned so this will be good to get them out," Charlene noted, as they quickly were putting their emergency gear together.

"The dog seems to be agitated with us as he moves back and forth in front of the door," Josh said while smiling. "He has not learned that it takes humans a little longer than dogs to get ready."

"I am a little skeptical about the dog's wanting us to follow him," Charlene stated, "but I have heard stories about dogs that do unusual things to save their master."

"Obviously, he wants us to go somewhere with him," Josh said, as he pulled his pack on his back.

"We have got a lot of stuff in these packs," Charlene said, as Josh helped to get her pack situated comfortably on her back.

As they moved toward the door, the dog jumped up and down, displaying joy that they were now ready to follow him to an uncertain destination in the snow and cold. Their faith and confidence abounded in this brown and white beagle dog. Before opening the door, Josh grabbed Charlene's hand and prayed to God for safety during their travel that they believed could assist the aircraft passengers one way or the other. Continuing to ask God for courage and direction, the two stooped down and held their guide as he tried to communicate with them that it was time to go.

Unwavering in their commitment to God, Josh recited, following his prayer, one of his favorite passages, Psalm 19:

1 A psalm of David. The heavens declare the glory of God; the skies proclaim the work of his hands.

2 Day after day they pour forth speech; night after night they display knowledge.

3 There is no speech or language where their voice is not heard.

4 Their voice goes out into all the earth, their words to the ends of the world. In the heavens he has pitched a tent for the sun,

5 which is like a bridegroom coming forth from his pavilion, like a champion rejoicing to run his course.

6 It rises at one end of the heavens and makes its circuit to the other; nothing is hidden from its heat.

7 The law of the LORD is perfect, reviving the soul. The statutes of the LORD are trustworthy, making wise the simple.

8 The precepts of the LORD are right, giving joy to the heart. The commands of the LORD are radiant, giving light to the eyes.

9 The fear of the LORD is pure, enduring forever. The ordinances of the LORD are sure and altogether righteous.

10 They are more precious than gold, than much pure gold; they are sweeter than honey, than honey from the comb.

11 By them is your servant warned; in keeping them there is great reward.

12 Who can discern his errors? Forgive my hidden faults.

13 Keep your servant also from willful sins; may they not rule over me. Then will I be blameless, innocent of great transgression.

14 May the words of my mouth and the meditation of my heart be pleasing in your sight, O LORD, my Rock and my Redeemer.

With total trust in a young beagle dog Josh closed the door, and Charlene and he began their trek as their guide went directly up the ravine to the point where the two tall mountains joined. With renewed energy the dog made its way through the deep snow, looking back from time to time to be sure they were following. With limited visibility because of the blinding snow that seemed to be falling more that ever, they trudged up the steep mountainside.

Although they were in good shape physically, the elements of God's creation began to take their toll on Josh and Charlene as they climbed upward toward the top of the initial mountain. The dog was having a hard time because the snow was getting deeper as they ascended the steep area now. Breathing heavily, Josh said while putting his arm around Charlene, "We didn't tell anyone where we were going."

"I just thought of that too, but the others are going to the warm orphan home, I'm sure, so they may not even miss us," Charlene said. "It's so very cold and treacherous trying to maneuver up the mountain, such that I have really had second thoughts about our following this dog. Why don't we sit over here near the fallen tree to rest some?"

"That's a good idea," Josh gladly responded. "I am really tired and we haven't even made it over the first mountain. It's so very cold so we should be careful not to get frostbitten."

Soon they were continuing blindly on their journey with the snow falling and their getting colder and colder as they headed toward the mountain top. They were not making good progress because climbing the rough terrain was difficult even at times when there was no snow. "We need to conserve our energy," Josh loudly told Charlene, as he assisted her over another fallen small tree.

Josh and Charlene had seen the dog earlier when it was almost frozen, but with renewed vigor he seemed to be moving along much stronger now that he had followers. It seemed like an eternity, but they finally reached the top of the mountain with the wind and snow making blizzard like conditions. "I believe we should find a place to get some rest and try to thaw out just a little, or else we may be overcome by the cold," Josh said to Charlene who was certainly in agreement with his suggestion. "The wind is blowing from the west so let's try to discover a comfortable place on the east side."

Shortly, they found a fir tree that had recently fallen so they moved some branches aside as Charlene and Josh climbed underneath to try to find shelter and warmth from the cold and snow. Even the beagle seemed to welcome the respite from a most difficult journey that had brought them to this point. Josh unrolled one of the sleeping bags, and after unzipping it wrapped it around their cold bodies. The dog snuggled up with them as though they were his master.

"Why don't you take a little nap?" Josh said, as he pulled the sleeping bag more snugly around Charlene's shoulders.

Leaning on his shoulder and much warmer now, she replied, "I might rest my eyes just a little."

Leaving their roosting place after a well needed period of rest, the team of three continued their journey around the crest of the high, rugged mountain. The dog always seemed to exude confidence as he made his way atop his range of high southwest Virginia mountains. Walking had become more difficult for Charlene as the snow and ice were swiftly taking their toll on her stamina, and Josh, too, for all that mattered. Stopping periodically to rest, progress was slowed tremendously as the morning darkness was subsiding.

It was important to be sure that the dog was physically able to continue because without him they would not know where to go. They were traveling on faith that the dog was on the missing plane, and that he was leading them to the crash site. There were two points that kept them going on this journey. First, there were no dogs in the Hollow and suddenly a brown and white dog comes to their house, the same kind and color of the dog that Bob Waters had told them was on the airplane that was missing. Secondly, a dog would not venture out in weather where he had almost frozen earlier unless there was some ultimate goal.

"Charlene, how are you making it?" Josh asked, as he looked at her with ice having formed on parts of her hair sticking from her hat that was bound to her head with a long tattered scarf. Examining her more closely, he could see that her eyebrows were frozen as her being looked very much like a walking snowman. Walking, such as it was now, was very slow and plodding as the energy for both of them was swiftly dissipating with each step. The weather was gradually winning the battle as their will to continue was being sapped by the cold temperature on the mountain top. The dog too was showing signs of given in to the elements.

"We need to find a place to rest," Josh said to Charlene, as he pulled her close to him, wrapping both arms around her.

"I don't feel like I have much energy left," she responded weakly.

Although Josh knew the craggy side of the mountain was the most dangerous, his earlier travels in the hill country revealed that ledges had been formed, and some provided shelter where animals would go for warmth. Walking near the edge, soon Josh spotted a rocky shelf from above that could be reached safely, if they went down the slope gradually. Breathing heavily as they traversed the embankment one small step at a time, holding onto young trees all the while, they soon arrived safely to an area free of snow but obviously not from the bitter cold.

When they were somewhat settled, Josh rounded up some dry leaves and twigs and larger dry branches to start a fire. Just looking at the red flames was a psychological boost to their morale that had plummeted somewhat because they were so cold. The dog seemed to be enjoying the fire as much as they were.

Seeing a brief smile on Charlene's face brought an even bigger smile to the face of Josh. "The warmth of the fire really feels good, doesn't it?" Josh said.

"I am glad we are taking a rest," Charlene indicated. "I don't believe I could have gone much farther because my hands and feet were so numb."

"The dog seems to know where he is going because he never appears to be unsure about his direction," Josh pointed out.

"We are certainly putting a lot of trust in the young animal," Charlene noted. "How far have we come so far?"

"It's very difficult to judge, but I would guess that we have walked about four to five miles so far," Josh replied.

"How far do you think we will have to go to find the missing plane?" Charlene quickly added to the questioning.

"Several weeks ago the Hollow council made an informal survey of the entire area, and we discovered five mountain ranges to the east, the direction we are going now," Josh pointed out. "The most isolated is yet to come as we move farther east, so I believe that the plane could have been lost in that area. When we came before, we all marveled over the sharp and tall mountain peaks with trees that seemed to defy the cold of the higher elevations."

"How far then would you guess that location is from here?" Charlene asked.

"It is my thinking that it would be between two to three more miles," he said, "but I hasten to add that the ruggedness of the terrain increases tremendously in this area."

MISSING PAIR

In the commons area of the orphan home the Hollow folks were gathered during this cold and snowy period along with the several orphans, and Madu who had returned with the rescue team that went to Abedistan. He really enjoyed living in the Hollow and was learning well in school. Approaching noon, their concern for Josh and Charlene who always led the group was being elevated to much worry.

"Tom, let's you and me go up the Hollow to get them to come to be with us until the weather is better," Robert said.

"That's a good idea," Tom retorted.

Covering themselves with coats, gloves and caps, they headed out into the deep snow. Soon they arrived at the back door, having already observed that there was no smoke coming from the chimney.

"You know they would have a fire," Robert stated.

"Without one they would freeze to death," Tom reacted.

An eerie feeling came over both of them as Robert rapped on the door, and there was no sound coming from the inside. As always, the door was unlocked so the two of them went inside to discover a cold, empty house.

"Obviously, no one is here," Robert said, as they turned to leave.

"Look at this," Tom said, as he kneeled down near the door.

"It looks like a paw print of a dog, doesn't it?" Robert stated, as he too stooped beside his friend.

"To my knowledge, there are no dogs in the Hollow," Tom responded.

"Do you think that this dog print has anything to do with their disappearance," Robert asked, as they peeked inside the church.

"I really think that they have probably gone with Bob Waters," Tom said, realizing that the dilapidated old van and the bus were parked by the church.

"When we return to the orphan home we can inquire of our group some more," Robert said. "Maybe Josh and Charlene went somewhere, and one of our group failed to remember it."

Back at the orphan house there was a very worried group after Tom and Robert told them that Josh and Charlene seemed to have disappeared from the Hollow. Many believed though that they had gone with Bob Waters and forgot to tell anyone about it.

Accepting this notion, the group dealt with life in their normal behavior until Bob Waters pulled up in the Hum-V alone.

"Where are Josh and Charlene?" Robert asked immediately before Bob hardly got out of the vehicle.

"Aren't they with you?" Bob shot back with his own question.

"We went to their house and they were not there," Robert quickly responded.

After going inside Bob asked, "Does anyone here know where they are?"

"We have checked with everybody here and no one

knows anything about them," Robert responded.

"Are the vehicles here?" Bob asked, getting more worried with each question.

"They both are parked near the church," Tom interjected.

"I have some food and other items in the Hum-V so let's unload it, and then several of us can ride up the hill to their house to look around again," Bob stated, as he was now directing the group.

First the group looked in the church before they moved to the house where in both places they found nothing that appeared in anyway awry. Completing their thorough examination of the buildings, they found themselves at a loss for further searches.

As they were piling into Bob's large military vehicle owned by a friend, Robert said, "Let's go back to the porch area where I want to show you all something."

Arriving at the porch, Tom leaned down to point to a paw print of a dog. "What do you make of this?" he asked.

"As you may not know, there are no dogs in the Hollow," Robert said to Bob.

"This is obviously a print of a dog that probably wandered into this area," Bob noted.

Upon their return to the orphan house many questions were asked at once to the search group, but soon their questioning was over, and the Hollow folks sat quietly harboring their private thoughts about the situation.

Suddenly, Bob jumped up and said loudly, "I think I know where they are. Do you all remember a few days ago an airplane disappeared somewhere between Ohio and here? On the plane with the family of four was a dog. My theory is that the plane has come down into one of our mountains here, and the dog made its way to their house. I believe they are now somewhere in the mountains looking for the missing plane."

"Do you really think they are?" June anxiously asked.

"If that's the case Bob, why didn't they come and get us to help them search?" Clem compassionately inquired.

"I don't really have an answer to that question," Bob stated, except that last evening we were seeing the worst of the storm as snow quickly blanketed the entire area. As you recall, the wind began to blow which caused it to be very cold, so I believe that they knew that to come to get you all would take too much time so they headed out alone."

"Where does the dog fit into your theory?" Seth asked.

"I don't really know, but I believe the dog prompted their search in the first place," Bob replied with more assurance in his audible thoughts being expressed to his friends. "Three days ago I told Josh about the missing plane, and just as I left him, I told him about a brown and white beagle that was on the plane that was missing."

"Bob, it's so very cold, don't you think it's dangerous to be outside doing anything?" Corbin asked.

"It certainly is dangerous," Bob replied. "They have probably been out in this bad weather since late afternoon yesterday so they have been exposed for nearly twenty-four hours or more. That's a long time. You all know how they are as they fully give of themselves for others, and I'm sure they are doing the same thing this time."

Tom asked the group to hold hands as he uttered a beautiful prayer asking God to have his Holy Spirit to hover over Josh and Charlene during this period of danger. "Please remain standing as I read Psalm 91 from our treasured scripture."

1 He who dwells in the shelter of the Most High will rest in the shadow of the Almighty.
2 I will say of the LORD, "He is my refuge and my fortress, my God, in whom I trust."
3 Surely he will save you from the fowler's snare and from the deadly pestilence.

4 He will cover you with his feathers, and under his wings you will find refuge; his faithfulness will be your shield and rampart.

5 You will not fear the terror of night, nor the arrow that flies by day,

6 nor the pestilence that stalks in the darkness, nor the plague that destroys at midday.

7 A thousand may fall at your side, ten thousand at your right hand, but it will not come near you.

8 You will only observe with your eyes and see the punishment of the wicked.

9 If you make the Most High your dwelling-- even the LORD, who is my refuge--

10 then no harm will befall you, no disaster will come near your tent.

11 For he will command his angels concerning you to guard you in all your ways;

12 they will lift you up in their hands, so that you will not strike your foot against a stone.

13 You will tread upon the lion and the cobra; you will trample the great lion and the serpent.

14 "Because he loves me," says the LORD, "I will rescue him; I will protect him, for he acknowledges my name.

15 He will call upon me, and I will answer him; I will be with him in trouble, I will deliver him and honor him.

16 With long life will I satisfy him and show him my salvation."

Many questions swirled through Bob's mind as he drove carefully out of the Hollow on the snow covered road. Stopping at the intersection, Bob dialed his good friend Devin, the newspaper owner, to advise him of his theory regarding the disappearance of his two special friends.

Paul H. Jones

SEARCHERS CONTINUE

Meanwhile, Josh and Charlene trudged after the brown and white beagle dog that they too realized was stretching the limits of his endurance. Always cognizant that they were following, the young dog moved forward as though on a mission about which he only knew. Suddenly turning to head down the steep mountainside, Josh and Charlene knew that much danger lurked ahead because the footing would now be less sure. "Charlene, it's really time for another rest, but maybe we can make it to the bottom of the mountain and then stop for a while," Josh said, trying to urge both of them onward.

"I can't make it much farther," Charlene uttered in a very weak voice.

Josh finally retrieved a rope from his frozen backpack for them to use to move more securely down the steep slope. Placing the rope around a tree and throwing the two ends down the hill, he told Charlene, "Hold the two ropes in your hands and repel backward until you get to the end. I'll follow you, and we'll repeat the same process over and over again until we get to the bottom."

Repeating this procedure numerous times, they finally made it to the bottom. The two of them and the dog were now ready for a well deserved rest made possible by

Josh who cleaned snow out of a large area. With some dry leaves and small, dry twigs, soon a fire began to blaze up. What a welcome sight!

After a while the fire was much larger, thanks to Josh's finding several large pieces of dry wood. Soon the young dog was asleep near the fire as Josh and Charlene too were feeling the effect of this quality time around the fire. Some of the enjoyment of this time was lost because both of them could see this very steep mountainside that they knew they would have to climb.

At the end of their respite they packed up and slowly began to plod up the steep slope, taking one small step at a time. They had thawed somewhat, but their energy had not been totally replenished such that each step now was a major undertaking. Even the beagle was having much difficulty moving up the mountainside. Using the rope from time to time to give them something to hold onto, they were making it ever so slowly, as they stopped often to regain their strength to continue. Far into the mountains by this time, they had no choice except to keep going toward their destination, that of discovering the missing plane.

Sitting near the top of the steep, snowy and cold mountain, Josh hugged Charlene and said, "We'll build a fire and rest a long time on the top."

"I hope so," she faintly responded. "I don't believe I can travel much more."

Making it to the top just barely, they held each other as though they had achieved a huge victory, which they had, but both of them knew the game was not nearly over. Josh had really done a good job in making fires for them so before too long, he had a roaring fire accompanied by much smoke filling the beautiful evening sky. Charlene leaned on Josh as he held her tightly around her shoulders. They were totally exhausted.

Suddenly, the beagle jumped up and his ears pointed toward the sky, such that it startled them. With his tail now wagging as though he was trying to convey a happy message to them, he moved near them but always looking in an eastward direction.

"I believe he hears something," Josh said. "His ears are so much more sensitive than ours so he must be hearing something that we can't hear."

It was obvious that the dog was really excited at this time, displaying characteristics that had been absent before. Even as Josh continued to pile the limbs and sticks on the fire, the young dog focused on the east. Just as Josh sat back down, the dog barked loudly several times as though indicating where he was in relationship to the sound he was hearing.

Just as Josh said, "I believe something is out there," it happened. A shrill weak sound was heard coming from the base of the mountain.

Josh followed with a high-pitched whistle of his own, and he received a reciprocal response.

"Do you think we have discovered the missing plane?" Charlene very excitedly asked.

"Who would be out in this weather?" Josh replied.

Extinguishing the fire immediately, the team moved down the mountainside with much energy to attempt to meet up with the people in the downed aircraft. Although it seemed like an eternity, they were getting closer and closer to their goal.

At the bottom the dog couldn't contain himself any more as he yelped with greater enthusiasm because he knew he was near the airplane now. Standing together in a ravine, Josh and Charlene looked in the direction the dog was barking. Just then they heard the shrill sound again coming from a thicket where they now realized the plane was located. The dog broke away and ran under the brush to reunite with his family. Moving closer themselves, Josh yelled, "Are you all okay?"

"We are alive," a weak voice was heard.

"We'll be there in a minute," Josh said, as he and Charlene headed to the far side to get a better view of the demolished small airplane now covered totally with snow. Pushing branches as they crawled under the thick growth of small trees, honeysuckle, briars, and small pines, they emerged right against a large part of the aircraft that had separated from the main section. There was still no sign of life except for the audible joyful greeting of their young dog that had gone on ahead.

Just as Josh helped Charlene over a wing section, they discovered the lost family all hovering together inside what was left of the cockpit of their small plane. Blood stains on their faces and much more on their clothes clearly indicated that they had injuries. "How they survived this crash we'll never know," Josh thought, as he moved in beside them.

With a closer observation now Josh realized that the man and his wife both were pinned inside the wreckage such that their makeshift structure for warmth had to be constructed around them. "How long have you all been here?" Josh asked, not knowing really what questions to ask first.

"This is our fourth day," the young son stated rather clearly.

"Have you all assessed your injuries?" Josh asked.

"My wife and I have broken legs, we think," the man stated who appeared to be in his mid thirties. "My wife believes she has at least one broken rib. I think we have stopped all the bleeding with makeshift tourniquets. Our daughter has multiple cuts and bruises, and we think a dislocated shoulder that we put back in place. Although our son seems to be the healthiest of the bunch, he has suffered a huge gash on his leg that I'm sure will take several sutures later on."

Continuing with their assessment for several minutes, then the questioning took on a different twist. "Where are we?" the man asked.

"You are in the mountains of southwest Virginia," Charlene answered.

"We just lost our way the other night, and we couldn't make contact with anyone," he pointed out. "How did you two find us?"

"Your beagle dog wound up at our house so we have been following him the last two days, and as you can see, he found you all," Josh said. "Obviously, we all have witnessed a miracle on this day. Let's all hold hands while I pray?"

It was a sight to behold as the six of them nearly frozen to death, joined hands as Josh said a beautiful prayer thanking God for sparing the lives of this special family. In addition he asked God for deliverance from the cold and safe passage to secure medical help for the young family that had experienced this tragedy.

"We have been so excited about finding you that we failed to introduce ourselves to you," Josh noted. "This is Charlene Morrow and I am Josh Morrow, a pastor."

"I am Bill Avery and this is my wife Betty and our two children, Tommy and Mollie," Bill stated. "You all have certainly risked your lives in this snow and severe cold to find us."

"We have been guided by our gracious God all the while," Josh responded.

The job to free Bill and Betty from part of the wreckage that had bent their legs backward was going to be difficult, but Josh and Charlene knew it was time to begin. With renewed energy and enthusiasm Josh used all of his strength to pull away a support bar from the wing to use as a pry rod to separate the metal lodged against their legs.

"This is not going to be easy," Josh thought, as he slid beside Bill to get a better look at a large piece of metal crunched against both legs such that Josh just knew they must be broken.

The local newspaper carried the story about the attempt to rescue those who were involved in the missing aircraft. Following the headline, "Brave Attempt to Rescue," was a compassionate article telling about what the Hollow folks believed was a daring rescue attempt. "The Hollow folks discovered their leader and his wife missing shortly after the snow storm began. There was no message of any kind left for their friends and neighbors of the Hollow except one small indication that they were headed to rescue those in the aircraft that had been missing several days. You see, there are no dogs in the Hollow, but on the porch of Josh and Charlene Morrow were paw prints of a dog.

"Do you all remember the story of the missing plane? There was a brown and white beagle dog on it. The Hollow folks believe their pastor and his wife are in the mountains covered with snow and ice searching for this lost family. Too, most believe that they are being guided by a brown and white beagle dog. As you all know who have followed the quiet exploits of the Morrow couple, they never see obstacles in the way of a successful mission. Nothing ever stands in their way."

The article was lengthy and well done, and soon was followed by another newspaper's inclusion of the same in its paper, thus causing two pilots with small planes in the area to resume their search for the missing aircraft. With the help of many volunteers, including the Department of Transportation, the runway was soon cleared such that the pilots with their spotters could take off.

Laboring feverishly while struggling to get in the best position, Josh finally removed all debris from Bill's legs so that now they could pull them free with the help of

Charlene. It was obvious now that they both had broken limbs that required very gentle maneuvering to get them totally removed from the downed craft. Josh built a fire away from the aircraft because of the fear of the gasoline on the ground from the ruptured tanks being ignited. The snow now was melted more freely in a shallow container to provide water for the group.

Josh soon had a large fire providing warmth for the family that they had assisted mightily to their new home away from the crashed aircraft. Hope of a rescue was elevated now that Josh and Charlene were present such that they all joined in singing several popular hymns. "We do thank you all so very much," Betty said, as she hugged Charlene.

"Your little dog is the real hero here," Charlene pointed out. "Without him we would not have known where to look."

"I used to do a lot of rabbit hunting on our Ohio farm," Bill said. "The children wanted a dog so we all decided that it should be a beagle that Tommy and Mollie picked from a kennel nearby. He has been a wonderful pet and has shown us many times just how intelligent he really is."

"He was really nearly frozen to death when he arrived at our house," Charlene stated. "It didn't take long though until he was ready to go."

As Josh and Charlene tried to make the young family as comfortable as possible, Bill looked up at Josh and said somewhat excitedly, "Your names seem very familiar to me, but I can't quite pull it up in my memory. I have always been a huge basketball fan, having played four years at our state university. Have you all ever had anything to do with sports?"

"Our daughter plays basketball in college," Charlene said.

"Where does she go to college?" Bill asked, now generating interest of the entire family.

"She is a sophomore at Bacon College not too far from here," Charlene indicated.

"Oh my goodness!" Bill emotionally stated. "Bacon is our favorite team and we watch them all the time on television. Isn't your daughter's name Maggie?"

"That's correct," Charlene quickly answered. "She just loves Bacon College and all the people there. You really have a good memory."

"I hope that one day I can go there to college," Mollie said. "I am really working hard to get better. I am presently starting on my Five A high school team."

"Coach Anna will probably want to talk to you," Josh said. "What is the name of your high school?"

"It's Walker Senior High and is located in Lenolda in Ohio," Mollie responded.

"Would you tell me about Esther?" Mollie excitedly asked.

Just as Josh was preparing to respond to her inquiry, they heard an aircraft overhead.

"I hear a plane," Tommy yelled out.

Surely enough, a small red and white aircraft was observed directly over their head, but soon was out of sight, hidden by the tall mountain.

"Do you think they are searching for us?" Bill asked.

"Probably so," Josh responded, as he gathered his sleeping bag. "Charlene, I'm going to burn our sleeping bag to generate much more smoke to be seen by the passing aircraft."

Huge billows of smoke were emitted from the fire such that one of the planes above saw the signal. Making his turn, the pilot contacted his base now filled with reporters. The pilot stated over his radio, "We have made contact; we have made contact; we have made contact," he blurted out because he was so very excited.

"This is base," a young man answered, while numerous reporters hovered around him. "Where are they located?"

"They are east of the Canton Range but to the north near the junction of McCoy and Eastridge Mountains," the pilot related.

"Are there survivors of the crash?" the base operator asked.

"At this point I'm not sure of their condition," the pilot replied. "I'm going to fly over several times to see what I can discover. Call the emergency helicopter unit at the hospital to advise them. There is no way out except by helicopter."

Josh knew that he needed to get a message to the pilot about the family's condition so he rapidly moved to a small opening where he could be seen. With the plane circling overhead leaning so they could see him, he made an "O" with his arms, and as best he could he made a "K" with his arms against his body. Understanding the message the pilot waggled the wings of the plane.

"Pilot to base," the pilot more calmly stated.

"This is base, come in pilot," the base operator quickly replied.

"Our signal received from a person on the ground indicated they are okay. Have you contacted the hospital helicopter?" he inquired.

"They are preparing to leave as we speak with sufficient equipment to pull them up to their craft to be delivered to the hospital," he stated. "With the repeller and medic included on the trip they will only be able to get but two at a time."

Soon the rescue helicopter was overhead to permit the brave young man to repel to the crash scene. On the ground he was greeted as he assessed the situation to determine who should go first. It was decided that Bill and Betty needed the most attention, so with Josh and Charlene's help they strapped Betty securely in the body basket to be lifted to the aircraft that was showing the effects of the wind that had whipped up during the last hour. Soon both Bill and Betty were securely strapped inside the chopper for a trip over the mountains to a nearby hospital.

As they delivered the popular patients through the emergency doors of the hospital, several doctors converged on the scene to render their assistance. As the repeller returned to head for the chopper to get the children, a man stopped him and asked, "Would you mind giving these items to Josh on the ground where the wreckage is located?"

"I would be glad to give these things to him," he said. "He is quite a worker. I don't know what I would have done without him and his wife on the ground. Who are these people anyway?"

"They are Josh and Charlene Morrow from the Hollow a few miles from here," Bob Waters stated.

The helicopter was being bounced around rather strongly while they were lifting Tommy and Mollie to the craft. "We'll be back to get you all and the dog in a little while after we get these young people to the hospital."

"Don't worry about us," Josh said, as he hugged Charlene.

With the wind picking up tremendously, Josh put more wood on the fire, pulled Charlene up to him and began to open the surprise package. Inside was food and a bright orange cell phone with several numbers written on a piece of paper. "This package is from Bob Waters," Josh excitedly noted. "He has sent a telephone and several numbers. He has listed his number and that of the athletic dormitory. In the letter he indicates that the Hollow folks and the basketball team are really worried about us, and especially Maggie who desperately wants to hear that we are safe before they go on the trip to play their final two games before the Christmas holidays."

Maudie was really excited to hear Charlene's voice on the telephone, and she quickly called Maggie who broke down and cried with tears of joy to hear that her mom and dad were okay. "The helicopter is coming back soon to take get us out of the mountains," Charlene told their only child. "We'll be at Bacon to watch you all on television."

Bidding farewell to a happy group of basketball players, Josh dialed Bob who was headed to the Hollow. "Thank you so very much for the food and telephone," Josh immediately told his good friend. "Please tell everyone in the Hollow that the lost family is doing well, and as we speak, recovering in the hospital." Both telephone calls helped to ease the concern of many of their friends.

"Let us know when you are lifting off for home," Bob said, as they closed their conversation.

Strong winds caused the rescue to be halted that night, but by the next morning the winds had subsided tremendously, so the helicopter air lifted Josh and Charlene with the dog to the Hollow to be reunited with their warm and loving family of Hollow folks. For a few days the brown and white beagle dog was a genuine pet for the orphan children now living so very comfortably in the Hollow.

With the return of Josh and Charlene to safety back to the Hollow, peace and tranquility was restored in this quiet community. But much was going on in the lives of others of their extended family. Maudie had received a letter from Mit's parents indicating that they were being asked to transfer to an African country to revitalize the evangelical mission in an eastern country. There was serious reluctance for them because they were so very happy living with their many friends in the jungle area of Costa Rica. Maudie could sense that God was calling them to become a force in this new country to spread the Good News of Jesus Christ just as they had done so masterfully in the Corbri village.

Robert's situation was different. His sister's teenage daughter was pregnant and was determined to have an abortion so the whole family in South Carolina was trying to convince her to do otherwise, but to this point they were losing the battle. Robert and Hattie had written to encourage her not to abort the child that they said would be a scourge on her life that could never be removed. They anxiously waited.

Glenn Colson, the superintendent who had resigned his position, came to the Hollow to talk to Josh from time to time. In fact, he and his wife were becoming regular guests each Friday evening when the Hollow folks came together to eat their weekly meal. Joining them often were Mrs. Joy Brown, the school division supervisor, and the elementary principal, Mrs. Sally Dunden.

As the girls were packing to leave for their trip to play two more basketball games before Christmas, Maudie slipped into Esther's room and whispered, "I want to talk to you about other special benevolent acts when you return from your trip."